HOLLOW

A Novel

by
Matthew Cole Levine

For information contact:
Unsolicited Press
Portland, Oregon
www.unsolicitedpress.com
orders@unsolicitedpress.com
619-354-8005

Cover Design: Kathryn Gerhardt
Editor: Kristen Marckmann

ISBN: 978-1-956692-20-4

To Mom and Dad, who have indulged every whim and story;
and to Kelly, who constantly shows me how
sacred and explosive a good book can be.

HOLLOW

A Novel

Chapter 1 — Smoke Like the Devil's Tail

It was a still afternoon in late October and the woods had begun to growl.

This being northern Wisconsin, the gray chill of winter had arrived long before the solstice marked the onset of the season. Already, red-orange leaves had fallen flailing from the trees in desperate flurries. The days were becoming shorter, the long nights smothered by the eerie dim glow of the moon. And the forests, once so lush and inviting, now turned barren and dark.

It was in one such forest on this late October day that a noise could be heard, a metal beast awakening with a roar. Its rumblings spread through the muddy hills, the skeletal trees, trying to find somewhere hospitable to alight. Futile.

The sound came from the heart of the forest, and any passerby might have guessed that the earth itself was emitting this howl. But its source was, in fact, manmade, as sources of unthinkable evil often are; and at the heart of the forest you could stumble upon the machine that roared so woefully—an electric generator, the size of a wheelbarrow and corroded with a sick blood-colored rust, convulsing as it supplied what little power it contained.

The generator stood next to a tiny, withering cabin, the size of a single cramped room. It was patched together with rotting wood, putrid mud, and what looked, upon closer analysis, to be matted animal pelts. A crooked pipe of jagged steel extended from the roof; a thick, fetid smog billowed from it, spreading an awful odor through an acre of land, the smell of carrion and bubbling sulfur.

Inside the cabin, the bellow of the generator became, at once, muffled and pervasive, as though the sound came from inside your own head. Four electric lanterns hung from the ceiling. There was a locked freezer standing in the corner, its contents unknown. Directly below a gaping wound in the ceiling, a trail of noxious fumes could be traced to a stone cauldron suspended by hooks over a spitting fire. In the cauldron, a thick, black ooze sputtered and reeked, a horrid mixture of herbs and dismembered animal parts better left unnamed. The rim of the cauldron was dotted with blood. The smoke curled upwards, writhing like the devil's tail.

A narrow cot stood against the western wall, covered with a frayed blanket. A bare pillow (yellow, pungent) was balled up at the head. Some unfortunate soul had been staying here; the blanket was tousled, indicating at least one sleepless night.

There was no wood to line the floor—only the dirt and grass of the forest, turned muddy by the dankness of the cabin. It was into this ground that a circular pit had been dug. It was lined with polished stones and contained a fine, mysterious ash, gray and almost silky to the touch. A chicken clucked at the perimeter, circling the floor, unsure of how it got here in the first place.

Next to the pit stood an ugly, staunch table, sagging and splintered yet seemingly immovable. There were a few objects here: a strange sculpture made of hardened clay, with naked, squirming figures bowing to an immense lizard whose tongue ascended upwards, coming to a razor-sharp point; and a small, empty bowl with a wooden spoon next to it.

There was a hand next to the spoon. A young hand; the skin had become clammy and pale over the last few days.

It belonged to a boy, nine years old, who sat on a rough wooden chair between the table and the cauldron. The hand was outstretched, palm faced down, fingertips embedded with painful splinters. The boy, somehow, could do nothing to remove them, couldn't squeeze at the flesh until the shrapnel was expunged. He could, in fact, do nothing at all but stare in abject terror. His wide eyes darted around the cabin, frantic beneath a swath of hair matted to his forehead, sweat and brackish mud glistening.

Something was there in the cabin. Some sinister presence, seizing the boy in a paralytic trance—and he knew it, even if the phantom hid itself away in the shadows.

Until, at last: peering into the corners of the room, he saw something move. Only slightly, a twitch and a stumble. Then a single step forward. At first, the figure was merely a black shape, hunched over at a pathetic angle. Then, as it shuffled into the spotlight of a lantern, its features became clear. It appeared to be an old woman, not just aged but ancient, her cloudy eyes glinting beneath a wild shock of white hair. Her gaunt, narrow face was engraved with wrinkles. She wore a black, mud-stained dress covered with a ragged cloak and shawl. Now and then, at random intervals, her mouth opened in a fishlike oval; a revolting *clack* escaped from somewhere deep inside her throat. As she emitted vile sounds and dragged herself across the floor, she never looked away from the boy's uncomprehending eyes.

The witch (for that seems the best way to describe her) slithered across the cabin, her left foot dragging through the mud, leaving a sloppy trail in its wake. The boy watched her as she came to his side. He whimpered twice—long, desperate squeals—but only stared ahead. With great difficulty, she bent her spine at a ninety-degree angle; the vertebrae scraped against each other, she merely winced through the pain.

At last, her eyes, speckled and milky like a distant galaxy, were directly in front of the boy's, a brittle eyelash away, and he could feel the sticky heat of her breath cling to his skin. She felt his fear, breathed it in, and thanked God for such innocent creatures and their frail corruptibility.

With greater speed than the boy thought possible, she reached out a clawed hand and clutched his jaw. Her skin was leathery gauze over sharp and icy bone. Her grip tightened; his mouth contorted. She stared into the back of his throat, eyes squinting; then she let out three hoarse cackles and released her grip.

Shuffling behind him with the empty stone bowl in her hand, she made her way to the cauldron suspended over the fire, her musty shawl billowing against the boy's shoulder. Unable to crane his neck (much less dart for safety through the cabin's door), he could only listen and wince as her limping feet cut through the dirt.

The liquid in the cauldron had become a bubbling soup, thickened to a black tar; the odor, somehow, had grown more awful. Satisfied by its revolting state, she grabbed a ladle made of knotty wood and dipped it in the brew. She heaped two spoonfuls into the bowl, barely noticing when it splashed against her skin, scalding. With onerous sighs, she returned the ladle to a hook on the wall and set the stone bowl on the table with a thud.

Something inside the boy loosened its grip—like an elastic band stretched nearly to its breaking point, snapping back to a relaxed state. His legs remained immense stone pillars fixing his body in place, but his arms twitched to life. As the liquid sat before him, the creature's expectation was obvious. But now that he had the slightest control over his own body, he chose to defy her through inaction, stubbornly (unconvincingly) demonstrating his resolve.

In response, the witch's hand again shot toward the boy. She clutched his matted blond hair and jerked his head back; a blaze of pain shot through him. She grabbed the spoon with her other hand and shoved it into the boy's fist. She leaned closer, lips hovering next to his ear, and intoned, in an otherworldly sigh, the only word he had yet heard her utter:

"Eat. Eat."

He did. The potion boiled and steamed but felt cold entering his body, spreading a chill through his barren stomach. A violent tremor shook him. A river of blood halted in his veins.

Nearby, the chicken witnessed this bizarre torture, its head cocked, only to resume its imbecilic clucking momentarily.

4

Outside, the generator roared, violent and incessant. Leaves continued to fall.

*****

Four miles away, school bells were ringing. The town of Grange had less than four hundred residents, but its elementary school, small as it was, displayed a pomposity befitting the finest academy in some nearby metropolis. A handsome two-story building on a lonely stretch of land, it was made of limestone and brick and resembled a modest cathedral more than a typical school building. A bell tower even protruded into the sky, forcing the groundskeeper to climb three flights of stairs after every class period and send the bell's resounding knell past the village limits.

As it was half past three, the school was preparing for the onslaught that greeted the end of classes each day. Dilapidated yellow school buses lined the curbs, rumbling expectantly. Watchful parents idled in rusty sedans. A pair of crossing guards oversaw a crawl of traffic that never surpassed ten miles an hour. Even the obligatory American flag in the courtyard waved with particular majesty, unable to contain its jittery excitement.

Grange was a sleepy, peculiar place, its area encompassing barely more than a dozen square blocks, and it was usually defined by a languid calm that suited its dreary beauty. Each day when school let out, Grange typically saw its greatest bustle of activity—though as soon as the school's halls were vacated, the town would yawn and stretch and resume its quiet lethargy.

The bells rang a second time (the groundskeeper, an ailing Vietnam vet named Wallace, wheezed as he pulled the immense rope toward him). A tiny flock of birds, disturbed by the pealing din, flew elsewhere. Twittering voices could be heard inside.

There was a man standing in the schoolyard. Twenty feet from the front doors, near the base of the flagpole. Beside him, the lawn was empty, awaiting several hundred trampling footsteps. Nearly forty and balding, with the coarse shadow of an unshaved beard, Nathan Amherst looked at least a decade older than he was. He stood rigidly, his fists clenched and sweaty in the pockets of his unwashed jeans. He rocked slightly on the balls of his feet. He squinted at the large oak doors, refusing to blink or breathe until *someone* exited through them.

At last, with the release of a thunderclap, the front doors burst open. Two young girls, both blond, fall jackets slung over their arms, skipped through the entryway, leaping down the short flight of stairs that led to the schoolyard.

Nathan took a half step forward, eyes widening at the sudden burst of activity—then stopped where he was. He ran his right hand through his wispy hair, then returned it to his pocket.

The girls walked past him, barely casting him a glance (they were too busy deciding which bridge to bike to). He should have been an anomalous sight, standing restively in a schoolyard as students marched past. But the parents and bus drivers nearby assumed (if they even noticed him) that Nathan was merely another attentive father in a community that prided itself on its familial Old World values.

A few seconds later, another group of schoolchildren exploded from Grange Elementary, one of whom—a ruddy ten-year-old with a piggish snout—flew down the staircase in an irrepressible burst. He was followed by a massing stream of kids, their avid conversation and chirping laughter piercing the air. They dispersed themselves in every direction, enlivened by their newfound freedom. Had Mr. Amherst paid them any more attention, he likely would have been shattered by their display of carefree youth—a bliss he had not known for several decades, which slipped through his grasp when he least noticed it and which seemed so alien to him now. But he was not concerned with this. He was still waiting, watching, eyes peeled. He stepped against the children scurrying his way, lifting his feet as though they were enmeshed in tar.

Soon a handful of teachers began exiting the doors alongside their students, though they exhibited considerably less zeal. They had their own pleasures to entice them away: quiet nights reading by the fire, long jogs through frost-coated trails, too many pints downed at a dimly lit dive bar, the warmth of the ones they love. Grange had its share of beauty, to be sure. Or maybe they were thinking, instead, of its horrors.

At last, a man by the name of John Linden stepped through the doors—a diminutive yet elegant figure, draped in a tweed jacket and heavy black scarf, with long gray hair and darting eyes that could burn a hole in their target. You could guess from looking at him that he was a schoolteacher; you could probably even guess that he taught fifth-grade English with an ardor that disconcerted his students. In his right hand he gripped a leather satchel, which was currently filled with a stack of three-page papers on *Something Wicked This Way Comes*.

A convulsive jolt went through Nathan upon seeing John Linden; this, clearly, was the man he had been waiting for. And the moment's pause given by Linden on the front steps, as he readjusted his scarf and returned Nathan's gaze, made it clear that he recognized him too.

But the display of recognition was fleeting. Unwilling to entrap himself in conversation, Linden jerked his head away, skipped down the last four steps, and scurried along the building toward the parking lot. Nervously brushing off Linden's indifference, Nathan lurched into pursuit, jogging against the wave of students coming his way. He had cut the distance in half by the time John rounded the corner of the building and was a mere ten feet away when he reached the same point.

"Mr. Linden!" shouted Nathan at the man whose piercing stare encouraged even his peers to address him as *Mister*. "John! Please, wait a second."

By this point, Linden was nearly at his car, a red hatchback missing three hubcaps. Seeing that evasion was impossible, Linden halted on the sidewalk, drooped his shoulders, and offered a beleaguered sigh. Then he turned to await his pursuer.

"Thanks," Nathan said as he offered his hand to Linden. He shook it curtly and nodded once. When it suited him, Linden could deliver the small talk of a master salesman, but tactful conversation was currently the last thing on his mind. "Good to see you, John."

"What can I do for you, Nathan? I'm kind of in a hurry…"

"I was hoping we could talk for a minute, just a minute. I don't want to take up your time." He spoke the way he acted, in sharp, spasmodic bursts, as though he was never sure of the correct behavior and wanted to get it over with as quickly as possible.

Linden held out his hand suggestively, inviting Nathan to broach the conversation.

"Somewhere…a little more private?" Nathan suggested.

Again, Linden let out a sigh but finally relented. "My car's just over here," he said over his shoulder, sauntering to the nearby hatchback.

The front seat was cramped and stuffy; there seemed to be much less space inside the car than appeared from the outside. Nathan's knees were crooked up painfully as he searched for somewhere to rest his fidgeting arms. A trio of schoolchildren bounded past, giggling. Linden eyed them coolly, now immune to the joys of childhood. Nathan failed to notice, consumed by one overriding concern.

"Well, John…you know, it's about business, I guess."

"What do you want to know, exactly?"

"Is everything still…working out? You know, coming along smoothly?"

"There have been no problems."

"Okay. Okay." Nathan nodded, trying to appease himself. "John, I'm starting to have…not *regrets*, exactly, but certain doubts. Worries. Things are taking longer than expected."

Linden shrugged. "These things take time, Nathan. It's not something you can rush."

Nathan laughed without mirth, his eyes flitting. "Yes, I know, but John…well look, we had a deal, and I kept up my end of the bargain.

But still, I've received—I don't want to sound, you know, out of line or anything, but I've received nothing on my end. For my troubles."

Linden's response had the dry decorum of a business transaction, as though his words were carefully mandated by corporate policy: "We will not renege on our obligations, Mr. Amherst. We have a contract, and we will satisfy that contract."

"When?"

At this reasonable question, Linden's façade of cool professionalism morphed into something wickeder. "*When?*" he repeated.

"Yeah, you know, I'm sorry John, but...if I had a timeframe, an estimate of when I might be—what's the word?—*compensated*, it might come as less of a shock."

"Again, these things don't follow a schedule, Nathan. There are difficulties to consider. Certain third parties are...unpredictable, and their demands must be satisfied before the operation can proceed. But things are, in your words, coming along. You may expect compensation as early as tonight, maybe. Is that satisfactory?"

Nathan said nothing. His leg jittered. He glanced in alarm at a corpulent fourth-grader who stormed past the car, guffawing.

"You know, this is a business transaction, and we want to make sure you're happy. Customer satisfaction is our foremost concern, Mr. Amherst."

Linden waited for a response, but all Nathan could do was gaze vacantly at the packs of schoolchildren. He had seemed to age another year over the last five minutes. Impervious to Nathan's agony, Linden sighed and turned the key in the ignition, satisfied with his halfhearted attempt at reassurance. He saw himself as nothing more than a facilitator, an expedient middleman whose job responsibilities did not include compassion. A sugary pop song blared on the radio, accompanied by the throb of the car's engine.

"I just wanted to ask if he's okay. For the time being, I mean."

There was a long pause as Linden buckled his seatbelt, adjusted the collar of his jacket, and turned to stare down Nathan. "No. He's not. That's what you agreed to."

Up to this point, Nathan had done an admirable job concealing his grief, his torment and self-loathing, despite the nervous discontent that was his permanent characteristic. Now, though, after swallowing hard with a throat made of sandpaper, Nathan could not hold back two violent sobs. He bit his lip and stared into eyes devoid of empathy.

"Any other questions?"

Silently, slowly, Nathan clutched the door handle to his right, pulled it towards him, stepped out of the hatchback, and dragged his feet along the pavement, directionless. Linden peeled away almost immediately, though he had to stop after only thirty feet in order to yield to the last remaining school bus.

Chapter 2 — Men of Like Mind

Three hundred miles southeast of Grange, in a city with a population two thousand times larger, things were less quiet. The station house for the Milwaukee Police Department's Second District was nestled between a public park, a fenced-in schoolyard, and the Kinnickinnic River, now churning loudly. Police sedans and SUVs, both marked and unmarked, abounded in the parking lot and against the curb. There was the usual soundtrack of a city afternoon, the hum of vehicles and distant horns and sirens.

Squad car 220 veered into the parking lot at half past three, nearly the same time Nathan Amherst stepped onto the front lawn of Grange Elementary. At the wheel was a sixteen-year MPD veteran named Alex Washington, with a shaved head and a uniform shirt one size too small (ironed every morning) to show off his impressive physique, maintained as a way to fend off middle age.

The man in the passenger seat was his partner of four years, Ben Dmitrovich, and the two of them sitting in close proximity served as a study in polar opposites. Where Alex appeared polished and professional, Ben sat as though the air slowly leaked out of him, deflated in every sense of the word. His dark blond hair was greasy and unkempt, framing a face that had grown lifeless. His eyes were bloodshot, glassy; his skin was pale and drooped as though it had lost the energy to hold itself together. He slumped in the seat, wallowing in a wrinkled uniform, gazing out the window at a brick-and-limestone building that had once meant everything to him, his future and his calling. He looked as though he hadn't slept in days, which, incidentally, he hadn't.

Officer Washington had witnessed this sordid progression. His partner and friend was once so different—calm, composed, blithe and confident. Years ago, he might even have been considered a voice of reason. But then so much had happened. Ben Dmitrovich had been transformed by life and misery, turning him into something unrecognizable.

As they pulled into the parking garage beneath the precinct, Washington looked at his partner sideways and opened his mouth uncertainly. At that moment, however, the police radio crackled to life—a flat voice intoning a drunk-and-disorderly on Milwaukee's East Side—and Washington allowed this sound to fill the void. The sedan pulled into a parking spot a few seconds later, front bumper grazing the concrete wall.

"You got the car?" Ben mumbled, barely glancing in his partner's direction.

"Yeah." So much sadness in one brief word.

As Washington returned the keys and gas receipts to the garage attendant, Officer Dmitrovich trudged up the stairs, gaping at everything in a haze of self-loathing. A few officers passed him by, offering cursory nods, knowing well enough by now not to broach conversation.

He stood beneath a tepid shower spray minutes later, focusing his empty eyes on a crack in the plain white tile. His fingers trailed through his hair and over his body, hardly recognizing them as his own.

At four o'clock, as he threw on a white T-shirt and rubbed toothpaste in his mouth with the tip of his finger, a Sergeant Nichols found him in a corner of the precinct locker room.

"Dmitrovich," he said, his tone emotionless. "Captain wants to see you."

He jerked away before Ben could respond. The locker door clanged shut with a hollow sound.

Miranda Prost had been captain of the second district for a little more than two years. She carried herself as female officials are often forced to: amicable on the surface, but with a steely temper that could be sparked at the least provocation. At the moment, as Dmitrovich neared her office on the third floor, she was seated at the edge of her laminate desk, dark hair pulled into a taut ponytail, streaks of gray barely visible. She spoke to a man seated in front of her, back facing the door, and though Ben couldn't make out who it was, his rigid posture and close-cropped hair suggested the caustic air of authority.

Ben nodded once at the assistant outside Prost's office, then stepped onto the thick carpet at her doorway. His knuckles rapped against flimsy wood. The conversation taking place inside ceased abruptly, as Prost and the man in front of her raised their eyes in Ben's direction.

"Ben," offered Captain Prost with unconvincing levity. "Thanks for coming in." She raised herself from the edge of the desk and walked, in three knifing steps, to Dmitrovich. The large window behind her framed a dreary view of the Kinnickinnic, gray industrial buildings wheezing in the distance. Her gaze was sharp and mercurial, always reading and deliberating, allowing her to decipher anyone, it seemed, in an instant.

The man, meanwhile, rose to his feet, pivoted and faced Ben directly. He was a full ten inches taller than Captain Prost, but less skilled in diplomacy—there was no concealing the look of disdain he cast at Ben Dmitrovich.

Prost shook Ben's hand, then motioned to the man hovering behind her. "This is Lieutenant Burnham of IAD." She paused, allowing the men to greet each other, but aside from two curt and obligatory nods, there was nothing to be said. "We, uh…wanted to talk to you. Have a seat."

He obeyed, moving slowly in a stiff black jacket, and Prost resumed her position on the other side of the desk, sitting and placing her elbows on the polished surface. Burnham sat in a chair near the corner of the office, glaring from the shadows. Ben collapsed in the chair, then tried to right himself, squirming into a posture that might be deemed respectable.

"So," the captain said finally. "Officer Dmitrovich. How you feeling?"

"Fine."

"Hm. Getting enough sleep?"

"Sure."

There was a brief, conspiratorial look between Prost and Burnham.

"Well. Ben, I'm sure you have some idea why you're here. Why Internal Affairs might want to talk to you."

"Some idea, yes."

For the first time, Burnham's cold, abrasive voice emerged from the corner of the room.

"What idea is that, Officer?"

Ben simply returned his look, searching for the whiteness of his eyes. He was either too tired or debased to conjure an answer.

"What he means," Prost interjected, "is we'd like to hear your explanation of the events. Specifically, what transpired on the afternoon of August twenty-fifth."

"August twenty-fifth." Ben pondered the date, repeating it in his mind, as though considering that point in time might produce an explanation. "Sure. Me and Officer Washington were on patrol. A call came in for a ten-fifteen—domestic disturbance near, I think it was, 38th and National. We arrived at the scene—"

"Who was driving?" Burnham asked.

"I was. We arrived and parked in an alley behind the location. It was a townhouse, split-level. When we came closer, we heard noises—people shouting, crying. There were a lot of loud crashing sounds, like dishes being thrown."

He paused here, swallowing hard. The river, brown and teeming through the window, suddenly drew his attention. Captain Prost brought him back to the matter at hand.

"Then what happened?"

"Officer Washington and I approached."

"You initiated?" Burnham asked.

"I proceeded first, yes. We went up the back stairwell. The backdoor was open, but the screen was shut. I knocked and identified myself."

"By name?" pressed Burnham.

"No. I said we were MPD, got a call about a disturbance."

"And he exited the apartment? Mr. Twozinski?"

Twozinski. Was that his name? Ben's mind raced, performing somersaults. Had he known that before?

Finally, he answered. "No, not initially. He yelled at us from inside. First he said everything was okay, it was all a misunderstanding. Then he said it was his wife's fault, or his girlfriend's, I forget. She tried to stab him, he said."

"Was your weapon drawn?" Prost asked.

"No, ma'am. I could see through the backdoor somewhat, into the kitchen. There were broken glasses, plates. I saw a young boy, maybe four or five, curled up in the corner of the room, fetal position. He was crying, shaking. Appeared to be in shock." An unmistakable trace of sympathy crept onto Captain Prost's face. "After about five to seven minutes, the man came out. Mister…Twozinski. We retreated to the alley, tried to placate the suspect. He was clearly drunk and agitated. We had reason to believe he assaulted his wife, his child."

"Although you didn't observe this directly and hadn't spoken to the rest of the family," Burnham said.

"No. He had a few cuts on his knuckles, blood on his hands. He became unruly. I tried to calm him—put a hand on his shoulder."

"In what manner?" Prost asked.

Ben shook his head. "Not threatening. But he took it that way. He lunged at me, tried to swat at me. Hit me a few times. In defending myself, I drew my hand from my holster, leaving it unprotected. The man went for my gun."

Burnham shifted in his seat across the room, spurred by a new agitation. Prost merely looked at Ben, her eyes unwavering.

"I felt him draw my weapon. Officer Washington tried to restrain him, but the man was stronger than we anticipated. Maybe under the influence of a narcotic."

Another hovering silence in the room.

"Seeing that the man got a hold of my firearm, I drew my baton and used it on him. Struck him in the face, two or three times."

"Three times. You broke his nose, Officer," Prost said, her tone becoming admonitory. "You must have known that."

"I saw he had a facial wound, yes. There was blood. But he wasn't taken down. As I remember, I hit him in the side, twice. He collapsed, but tried to get up. I incapacitated the suspect. Kicked him several times in the chest and torso. Eventually he stopped moving. I could see his wife, or his girlfriend, and his son, standing at the screen door." He opened his mouth to say something else, then stopped.

"This is the version you'll swear to on the stand," Burnham seethed.

"At his hearing? Mister…Twozinski's? Yeah, of course."

"That's not what we're talking about." Prost shifted in her seat, elbows sliding as she leaned toward him. "What he means is, a civil suit has been brought against the MPD. By Mr. Twozinski. Alleging police brutality on your part, Officer Dmitrovich."

Ben laughed and coughed at once, a crude and sputtering sound, far from genuine. He'd been expecting this for weeks now, he sensed how this story was going to end, but still he felt indignation at the fate he'd brought against himself.

"You can't be serious."

"We are, and he is," Burnham said. "What's more, he has a convincing case. You don't read the news do you?"

Ben shrugged. Burnham spread out his hands in a rectangle, as though outlining a boldfaced headline.

"*Police beating caught on camera.* From several angles, too, if you look at the videos online. Middle of a residential neighborhood in broad daylight. The man has a lot of neighbors, and every one of them has a camera in their pocket. But that didn't occur to you."

Ben said nothing.

"You know what, though?" Burnham continued. "Not a single one shows Richard Twozinski with his hand on your service weapon. Or even reaching for it, as far as I can tell. It shows the moment you break his nose, you can actually *hear* it happen. And it shows you kicking him on the ground 'til you fracture his ribs. But not much else."

Ben squinted at him. Even in his current delirium, he wondered if Lieutenant Burnham was truly, sanctimoniously outraged or simply dreading the PR nightmare that loomed before him.

"And, of course, you neglected to turn on your body cam," Burnham finished with a scowl. "But maybe that's for the best."

"Ben," Prost said in a slightly warmer tone. "I understand…your recent history has been difficult. You've been through a lot. It's not surprising that it's taken a toll on your work."

"It *hasn't*," Ben said abruptly, with more fervor than he'd managed up to that point. "Captain, I'm more than capable. I'm not affected."

"All due respect, Ben, it's clear that you are. You're not the same."

Ben swallowed hard. There was no denying that.

"Your meetings with Dr. Kildare," Prost said suggestively. "Have they been helpful?"

He shifted in his seat, feeling sweat suddenly pool from every pore in his body. "I told you what happened," he replied at length, glaring at Burnham. "What is this?"

"A preliminary meeting," he said.

"A witch hunt," Ben sneered back.

Prost stood then, straightening her black shirt and looking at Ben solemnly. In her eyes was something dark and sad, shifting every moment.

17

"Let them do their job, Ben. If you cooperate, you have no reason to worry." Ben stared at her more intensely, trying to interpret her words. "In the meantime, during the course of the investigation…you'll be taking a leave of absence."

"You're suspending me."

"Technically, no," Burnham said, standing. His voice took on a drawn-out, officious tone. "A state agency may not suspend a law enforcement officer solely because of a civil complaint. You can thank your union for that."

"*But*," Prost added, "you are to consider this a mandatory hiatus. You will not be involved with any police activity. I would advise you to leave the city. The media will try to contact you, you'll feel the need to explain yourself. You'll be harassed."

"Best you disappear while this all…works itself out," Burnham said.

Ben shriveled in his chair, looking between the two of them, bloated with fatigue. What could he say? That day, August 25th, it really had started to fade and distort itself, becoming half-remembered, clouded by shame. Maybe it did happen how they said; after all, there were the videos, clear and damning. Maybe an escape from everything would allow him to piece reality back together. A thought came to him then, burrowing its way through his battered mind: his family's cabin, on a solitary lake somewhere in northern Wisconsin.

Prost demanded his service weapon, breaking the heavy silence, and watched as the SIG Sauer P320 slid across the desk. Burnham continued to hover in the corner, eyes piercing. Ben was silent through all of this, unable to plead his innocence and unsure if he even wanted to. Sirens echoed on the street outside, pounding in Ben Dmitrovich's brain.

Chapter 3 — Fathers and Sons

Exiting Grange to the south—as most people do, returning to more hospitable locales after vacationing at northern cabins and lake homes—you take Highway 63 south toward a body of water known as Sarona Lake. You take a soft left through rolling hills and, out of nowhere, the lake appears to you: an impossibly deep blue, reflecting a vast and cloudless sky, flanked by a forest whose trees are dotted with burnt orange and red leaves. The air jostles you awake. It reminds you of the majesty of the natural world, so often hidden in plain sight.

Only three miles south of Grange, however, things have changed. The skies have become gray and menacing, an army of clouds has congregated here. The trees, no longer radiant, have become gaunt and skeletal, scraping into the sky. The chill in the air is different now; it has been removed of life, it smothers you. There is something here as devilish as the nearby environs are godly.

There is an opening, too, only half a mile further, in a thicket of trees that rests on the eastern side of the highway. Not a driveway or even a path—just an aperture where the trees have been shoved aside and the forest taunts you to enter. Most people who drive through here shudder unexpectedly, unable to shake the feeling that something vile has touched them.

Straight ahead through this opening only four hundred feet, over sloping, muddy ground, there was a cabin. Inside the cabin, there were three figures. An aged creature, something between human and devil; a young boy, whose presence in the cabin could not be explained; and a chicken, whose head was currently being severed by a butcher's knife.

The witch held the blade in her right hand—it seemed almost too immense for her feeble grip—and pinned the animal against the wet ground with her left. The chicken clucked in terror. She hurried the rusty blade to its neck and snipped through leathery flesh. There was a snapping like a rubber band. Hideous noises came from it.

She rose with surprising dexterity and brought the dying animal to the firepit. Withering flames danced there on a pile of embers and smoldering ash. The witch's chanting, obscure and incessant, rose now in volume and pitch. The flames sputtered as a stream of blood spat over them. Four dim lanterns cast eerie spotlights on the scene.

The boy was its audience, its paralyzed participant. The fear he felt could only rage inside of him, clawing at the inside of his eyeballs.

The witch, muttering endlessly, flung the chicken's head into the firepit. Then she turned and stumbled toward the boy, carrying the carcass with her. On the table before him lay the sculpture: that of a monstrous lizard surrounded by crawling supplicants, its sharpened tongue extending upward. She impaled the animal's corpse on the icon, heaving it down the length of the blade. Somehow this communion of blood and clay, soundtracked by the witch's growls, was too grim for the boy to handle. Something inside of him crumbled, his last flickering shred of hope withered into nothing, and a gust of evil spread through the humid air.

The old creature beckoned for the boy to rise with nothing more than an upraised hand and her intonations. His heart sprinted, his breath became shallow and desperate. Still he could do nothing. His only movements were those she ordained. His young bones cracked as he stood; he had not moved for nearly two days, and the blue denim he wore (with a hole torn in the left knee from a playground football game three days prior) had almost adhered itself to the scarred wood. She curled two gaunt fingers toward her—the yellowed nails and sickly skin looked cadaverous in the light—and gestured for him to come closer. His arms remained still and his legs wavered as he trudged across the room. His gray T-shirt had become damp and blackened from the grimy air of the cabin. It hung loosely from his body, a sign of the weight he had lost over the course of two days.

The moon that night was full and gleaming, lending the forest a ghostly glow. The pale light cut through buckling trees and cast an array of shadows on the ground, where they danced a morbid waltz. For the last few days, the boy's only wish had been to escape into the outside world; but as soon as he was guided from the cabin by his captor, he knew this forest, in its hovering gloom, provided only a bleaker nightmare.

His legs moved mechanically, propelled by some unseen force, weary pistons slopping through the mud. He shuffled over loping hills. The witch followed behind him, matching his movements from a ten-foot distance. Her lips contorted; her voice slashed at the night air, though its fervor had diminished in the cold.

What kind of fear shuddered through the boy now? With each involuntary step his eyes darted, convinced that a watchful spirit waited in the dark.

After a quarter-mile, their solemn procession came to an end: rising over a barren hill, they approached a glade bordered by emaciated foliage. A brackish puddle squirmed in the middle of the clearing, flanked by a circle of smooth rocks that were marked with unknown etchings. A rotten odor of decay and sulfur drifted through the forest. There was no momentary chill here—this place instilled a pervasive evil that burrowed deep and stayed within.

At the edge of the clearing the boy stopped, his right foot hovering over some unseen border. He squealed against his will, a desperate, pleading shriek, teetering on one leg. The figure behind him, nothing more than a silhouette, stopped chanting mid-sentence, only to repeat her words more viciously. Finally the boy stumbled into the clearing, as though shoved from behind. The shape behind him took three steps closer, then planted her feet firmly at the top of the hill. The boy had entered a realm too hideous even for her to follow.

*****

Nathan Amherst pulled into the parking lot of the Sarona Lake Motel, a dreary line of cramped rooms in the shape of a sideways L. Only the red lights of the buzzing sign (emblazoned, as always, with the word "Vacancy") illuminated the building; it seemed to wince under the sick fluorescence. There were several motels on nearby shores with similar names, but this might have been the most uninviting. The red lights and pea-green paint on the walls combined to form a sickening palette.

Room 4 had been Nathan's shelter for the last three days, a refuge from a quaint home that had recently begun to frighten him. Only a year ago, he could convince himself that he was strong and estimable. Though the definitions remained elusive and the proof withholding, he believed himself a "good man." And why shouldn't he? Life for all of us is a series of attempts to prove that we're worthy of belonging. But Nathan was forced to confront evidence to the contrary. His natural yet reckless assumption that he was strong enough to endure tragedy was proven wrong.

First, there was Maria. She was ripped away so suddenly. Nathan had first found peace with her, an image of domestic tranquility he had resisted most of his life. But just when a blissful future with her seemed both a wonder and a certainty, a cold destiny found them. On a frigid night in March, Maria was returning home from her sister's baby shower, turning left onto County J shortly before midnight. A late-winter snowfall had fended off spring for several weeks, and patches of invisible ice lingered on the road. There was no drunk driver, no one to blame; she skidded over a patch of ice, soared through the intersection, slammed headfirst into a telephone pole. At first they thought she'd make it through. But no. There was a cerebral hemorrhage, they said, that proved inoperable. Nathan said almost nothing at her funeral, eyes sere and hollow, sleepwalking through a legion of mourners whose consolatory words only drained him further. He kept reaching blindly for Maria, expecting her to make contact and gently squeeze his hand as she always used to—but of course he touched only empty air. He couldn't fathom the cruelty. How could God, as a gesture of power,

22

prove how easily He could take her away from him? It was the beginning of Nathan's atheism, his bitter realization that there was no benevolent deity to usher him through life.

At least, Nathan told himself, their son Ryan hadn't been with her. To lose grasp of his family entirely, after he had finally eased into the role of loving patriarch that had always mortified him—it would have been a merciless, demented joke. For the first four months after Maria died, Ryan was an accomplice to Nathan's misery. The boy's confusion at his mother's absence, his unwillingness to adapt to a life without her (even as he was forced to), was a morbid comfort for a father who didn't know how to cope. Nathan knew he should have wanted happiness for his son, and this is what he told him. But what Nathan would never admit is that the shattered, empty look on Ryan's face provided consolation, a reminder that he was not alone.

After a few months, though, Nathan realized that the sight of his son no longer comforted him. The face that had once promised a blissful future now served only as a reminder of what he had lost. Ryan had always resembled his father more closely, a fact that once elated Nathan, though now it simply repulsed him. He would stare at his son when he thought he wasn't looking, seeking out a semblance of Maria's curly raven hair and glimmering brown eyes, but he couldn't find them. Somewhere beneath his misery, from the humane and rational corner of his soul, Nathan hurled furious insults at himself, ashamed of the weakness that had been exposed. But this only prolonged the cycle of withdrawal and self-loathing, casting Nathan further into the abyss.

The human will is a curious thing—or so Nathan told himself when his depression assumed a more pensive tone. We really can't fathom its strengths and flaws until it's tested under extreme conditions. Nathan had always taken pride in his resilience, but where was it when he needed it most? How easily, he thought sometimes, our perceptions can be shattered, especially when our fragile natures are given a slight tug in the wrong direction.

These dark thoughts flashed through Nathan's lifeless eyes. His mind wandered unpredictably this evening, thanks to the five or six shots of Jim Beam plowing their way through his bloodstream. Even so, another unopened bottle was nestled in his arms as he threw open the door of the motel room. A dreary vision greeted him: the minuscule confines of the boxy room, hazily illuminated by crimson lighting; a gray-and-white flecked carpet clashing with the pale green walls; a small cathode television on a low, narrow dresser; a queen-sized bed with floral-pattern sheets, recently remade; two hideous paintings of a lighthouse on a foggy cove and a bland forest path covered with snow.

Nathan kicked the door closed behind him and tossed the bottle of whiskey on the bed. He stumbled to the dresser in the darkness and flipped on the television. The TV blinked awake, casting its glow upon the walls; an insipid cop show commenced, the one in which a sassy, clairvoyant bus driver teams up with a detective on the verge of retirement. Nathan turned up the volume. The device provided only noise and images for him.

Taking two lopsided steps to the bathroom, Nathan unzipped his puffy green jacket and flicked on the lights. Keeping his eyes cast firmly downward to avoid his reflection in the mirror, he fumbled for the cold-water faucet and pulled it toward him. With a groan, he leaned his head to the sink, splashing frigid water on his sweaty skin. The sensation was electrifying but didn't last long. Nathan wanted the water to be colder, more painful.

Finally, out of morbid curiosity perhaps, he lifted his eyes to the mirror. They had become bloodshot, though the irises were still placid blue. His hair had taken on a smear of white at the temples. *How ridiculous to be concerned with your appearance,* growled an unwelcome voice in Nathan's head. *Imagine if you could see what's inside.*

He heard the voice often; it was a part of him and always had been, though he had come to know it more fully within the last year. As always, he tried to drown it out. He shut off the faucet and returned to the bedroom, where *Seeing Redd* was just returning from a commercial break. Unaccountably fatigued, his legs buckled; luckily, the thin mattress was there to catch his fall. The brown paper bag and its bottle of liquor brushed against his thigh.

For a full minute Nathan lay there, his mind ravaged by unfathomable thoughts. Until, in a voice barely above a whisper: "Ryan." But it was too weak; he couldn't hear himself over the babbling TV. His eyes swam over the room, wet and glassy, and for a moment he thought he glimpsed his son standing in the shadows.

Chapter 4 — A Menagerie

He had no earthly idea what was happening.

For days he had suffered from a complete dismantling, an inability to trust his mad, entangled senses. But the boy was certain of one thing: he had come to know an utter fear he had long ago dismissed as fantasy. The ghost stories uttered furtively by his parents, the pranks staged by his friends on playgrounds and in cornfields—they had always failed to frighten him. His only phobia, earlier in life, had been a senseless fear of rats. Now, such mild terrors were a relic of a more innocent time. For the first time in his life, he knew fear.

To exert an active mind within a petrified body—the feeling that your skin has trapped your soul. The young boy kneeling at a black puddle in the forest could feel his limbs, his bones, the sickening sensation of mud seeping through his jeans, but his body's movements were controlled by something else, jerking to life with a sudden spasm.

The generator at the cabin had been shut off, muting the metallic echo that had bounded through the woods. Yet this hum was replaced by an equally foreboding howl, its source unknown. The wind gave a low whistle, but there was something else on top of it—a rumble from some awakening demon, jostling the leaves and shuddering the evergreens.

The boy's knees sunk slowly in the mud. His body resembled a macabre stone statue, some ancient Roman depiction of damnation. His lungs ached with every breath. He could hear the witch chanting behind him, the sound of nails scraping through the throat. Ahead of him, there was a modest hill bordered by a line of half-barren birch trees, their branches forming spidery silhouettes in the moonlight.

There was a noise. A shuffling of leaves, scraping against the dry soil. A feral grunt. The sounds came nearer.

Over the sloping hill, two red eyes appeared, blazing in the darkness and targeting the boy's still body. At first, the eyes were all that he saw; he wondered if the crimson dots were simply illusions of the frosty woods. Then an image began to take shape. He noticed the horns emerging from the shadows: two cartilaginous growths spiraling upwards, coming to a sharpened point. And the snout—a massive thing, smeared with viscous spit and cold dew, emitting a cloud of steam with each breath. It had the head of a bull, massive, four times the size of a man's; and its torso, gradually appearing over the top of the hill, was as staunch as the oldest trees in the forest. As the creature came into light, its shape became clearer yet still more troubling. Its entire body was covered with thick, matted fur, encrusted with the oozing spit of the forest and what looked to be dried blood. Its arms and legs tapered into cleft, blockish hooves, though it still walked as a biped. Awful possibilities ricocheted through the boy's mind. He was almost relieved to see the beast stop at the crest of the hill, apparently unable to penetrate the clearing, its red-eyed gaze unwavering.

Where did it come from? Did it always make these woods its home? Mysteries and riddles with bleak and depraved answers.

As soon as the bull planted its hooves in the ground, another noise could be heard approaching. There would be more spectators for tonight's entertainment. This noise, too, could curdle blood, a sound that could not exist: a high-pitched slithering marked with dry, periodic thumps, accompanied by a piercing hiss that drifted through the sky. The witch's chanting ceased; her work, it seemed, was done. But this new ambience carried a greater horror.

At last, the source of the noises crept to the top of the hill. A monstrosity—a thick-bodied snake, seemingly midway through human transformation. The creature's hide was covered in glutinous scales, though a tuft of wispy hair still sprouted from its scalp. The mouth had widened into something close to human form, though it struggled to

27

contain an immense, pitchforked tongue. There was no snout above it, simply two crooked holes etched into the misshapen face. Its skull was indented and bruised, caving in at various points. The creature had begun to grow limbs: on its right side, a fleshy arm and leg, bent horribly beneath its body in an effort to propel itself forward. The limbs here ended in a mangled abhorrence, as though hands and feet had begun to grow in a dismal attempt at evolution. On the left side of the body, the disfigured limbs were not nearly so advanced—flaccid stumps resembling the fins of a fish. With laborious difficulty and a symphony of shrieks, the revolting thing slithered to the top of the hill, its narrow eyes returning the boy's pleading stare.

There was a third and final participant in that night's ceremony. A fluttering of feathers and the sickening slosh of displaced mud announced its arrival. The boy's wide eyes were trained on the summit of the hill. His knees sunk slowly into the earth, palms planted in the liquid ground.

It walked on sticklike appendages, taut and emaciated; daggered talons stabbed into the soil. Its movements were grueling. A piercing scream tore into the sky. The boy could see it now. Its chest puffed out as though performing a mating call, feathers bent in every direction, wet with blood and the mist of the forest. A silhouette against the moonlight, its head looked nearly human, though an immense beak had begun to tear through the flesh. At the top of the hill, it stumbled once and anchored itself to the ground. In a fury, it fluttered its malformed wings, which tore through the creature's back at awful angles. In the darkness, the boy thought he glimpsed two rows of glittering teeth— human teeth—smirking in his direction.

A nightmare vision: the kneeling boy, a trio of monstrosities, the panting witch in the shadows, arranged in perfect symmetry. No one moved. Even the wind halted.

There was a sound, a low, reverberating rumble, the kind you feel before you hear. Its source was distant, untraceable. The boy, sinking deeper into the ground, sensed it most. Against the skin of his open palms, something throbbed and pulsed below, the echo of a monstrous heartbeat.

The boy was jerked into roiling mud by a forceful hand that came from nowhere. His lips were immobile but he still made sounds, frenzied whimpers, high-pitched, helpless. His shrieks resounded as he planted his hands, trying to keep himself aboveground; but the earth had become pregnable, inescapable, swallowing him with a growing hunger. He could see now that the water had many colors. It was flecked with red and electric blue, like a trail of oil dancing across the surface. Its smell was hideous, festering, and sour, hiding something unthinkable within.

His whimpers intensified; his prayers went unanswered. Four pairs of eyes watched as his face broke the surface. His fists clenched in the mud. He opened his eyes underwater.

How could this be? He was somewhere else. He was drifting over a barren terrain, an endless canyon with towering cliffs of red sand, its basin littered with jagged rocks and a narrow, bubbling river. The light here was different, specked with clouds of dust and ash, and the sun did not emit warmth. He was soaring, somehow granted a godlike perspective, though the vision was not divine. It made him miss home.

By now, the clearing had become a muddy swamp. From his kneeling position, the boy was sucked underground, first his face, then shoulders, then torso and legs sinking deeper. The wind rose again. The light of the moon became sharper. Finally, his shoes gurgled into the black void, the last visible trace of him before he disappeared from sight.

The dirt and mud began to settle slowly; the earth righted itself. A quartet of strange creatures gazed in awe at this display of power. They waited a few moments to savor the horror, then parted ways. The night's performance had finished.

*****

When her eyes open for the second time she feels slapped awake. But what reality has she woken into?

The flux of sight and sound was dreary, unfamiliar. A TV news program blared in the next room, something about the likelihood of civil war. A steely pulse of blue light drifted into the bathroom. There was an opaque mass hovering in front of her; she reached out and felt a plastic shower curtain. She glanced in alarm at her body, though she already knew she was naked. She touched her flesh, doubting its reality, and the feel of her skin was a strange sensation. Her eyes darted in every direction, demanding an answer. The paint was drab and gray, the room narrow, the walls thin—a motel? How the hell did she end up here? Her brain scrambled for an explanation, but the more she considered it the more impossible it seemed.

The simple acts of moving and breathing came back to her quickly, though it took a moment to reacclimate to their necessity. Each movement was an effort in reawakening, a calculated process of thought and action, the routine of human life forgotten, by its absence, in less than a year.

Slowly, she gripped the shower curtain and pulled herself upward. There was a sharp but pleasurable pain as she tucked her legs and rose to her knees. The corporeal method of thought and response, the passage of brain activity along synapses, it was all coming back to her now. She was surprised to realize that her body, when she found it again, had a pleasing familiarity: a pattern of scars on her right knee from an old biking accident, arms that were naturally toned and muscular like her mother's, which helped compensate for her general disinterest in exercise.

She parted the shower curtain and raised her leg over the tub, trying not to make a sound. A few drops of water fell to the floor, splattering. She grabbed a pair of towels from a rack on the wall and wrapped one around her shivering body; with the other, she wrung out her sopping hair, unable to remember how it had become wet.

She heard a sudden, disgruntled noise from the next room—a gruff sigh and the groaning of bedsprings—but after standing immobile for more than a minute, she convinced herself that the man in the next room was asleep. She could guess who it was lying there, snoring vehemently, though she prayed that she was wrong.

On the wall across from the open doorway, a narrow mirror stood above the sink. Her curiosity grew, mingled with uncertainty: she hadn't glimpsed her reflection for almost eight months. With her fear subsiding, she tiptoed to the mirror and glanced behind her into the next room. She could faintly detect the shape of a man passed out in the dancing light of the television. A half-empty bottle lay next to him on the bed. She couldn't make out his features, though she was reassured by his apparent state of dormancy.

She returned her attention to the mirror, inching toward it. She watched with longing, puzzlement, fury as her reflection came into view. It was like seeing an old friend, their features familiar but hazy and almost forgotten. She prodded her cheeks, batted her eyelashes, clutched her jaw; there were flecks of gray in the deep brown of her iris that had always pleased her, and dimples that had nearly vanished over time. She almost smiled at seeing herself again—then pondered how she had arrived here, tried to fathom its absurdity.

With a surge of anger, she whipped her head around and peered once again at the man in the bed. She stepped onto the thin carpet of the bedroom. She no longer felt terror, only a quiet, dislocated rage. To wake at all from such an otherworldly peace was a brutal torment, sadistic and callous; to find a derelict motel room awaiting her only heightened its cruelty.

She paused in front of the television, her bare toes scratching against the floor. She thought about silencing the TV, but the canned imitation of human voices provided a gentle reintroduction to life on earth.

She took two more steps. By now, she was at the foot of the bed. Through half-closed curtains, moonlight met a familiar face. Her

31

assumptions proved to be true—it was her husband, her widower Nathan. She squinted at the bags beneath his eyes, the severe wrinkles, the ghostly pallor of his skin. He had changed so much since spring. But still she could feel no pity.

Already her legs felt weak, her pulse frenzied. Of course, she was not used to exerting them. There was a tiny, circular table adjacent to the window, flanked by two chairs made of gaudy fake wood. She collapsed in one of them, ran her slender fingers through a mane of black hair, and glowered at the man lying a few feet away. She once knew him so well; she once loved him. Her post-high school dreams of reverent globetrotting had been put on hold when they met. As a child, she had craved seeing another world beyond this one, discovering cultures a planet away from small-town Wisconsin. She had ached with curiosity. But in the summer of limbo after graduation, she and Nathan were paired off by mutual friends who couldn't believe Maria's protests that she was happy in solitude, among her own thoughts. Their first blind date was at a local softball game; there must have been something about the tangerine sky and late May weather that weakened her self-made armor, making her heart buzz with a new sense of wonder. Back then, so many years ago, Nathan could make her laugh with ease, could listen for hours while she prophesied her future, which turned out to be more sedentary than she'd pictured in her fantasies.

Now Nathan had betrayed her unforgivably. She wanted to scream, pummel him, flay him. She gripped her narrow jaw with her left hand and, feeling the soft flesh between her thumb and forefinger, bit down hard. The pain electrified her; the taste of blood trickling onto her tongue provided a momentary release.

On the floor in front of her sat Nathan's open suitcase, its contents thrown into a haphazard heap. A plain gray sweatshirt was visible on top, with a frayed leg of black flannel pajamas underneath. The thought of slipping into his clothing sickened her, but the red light grazing her naked, shivering shoulders compelled her to get dressed. She sniffed the sweatshirt before throwing it over her. It reeked of cigarettes and old beer, but she knew she had few options.

Outside, she heard the whir of tires over lonely pavement. She spread the curtains aside, gazing through them. The dusty motel parking lot was dotted with four vehicles, bathed in crimson light. She shifted in her chair, which had already grown uncomfortable. She resolved to wait until morning, when their impossible conversation might take place.

The TV news program had shifted abruptly to an inane sitcom—the buoyant idiocy of the characters onscreen seemed out of place. A twisted sense of humor snickered from somewhere in her soul: *of course I would spend my first night alive subjected to a late-night sitcom marathon.* A pre-recorded audience laughed as she turned her attention to the man snoring next to her. If she didn't know so acutely the difference between sleep and wakefulness, there would be no dissuading her that this was a dream.

Chapter 5 — A New Day

Dawn came early, at almost six; the fleeting chirp of birds could be heard over the din of the television. Nathan Amherst blinked his eyes open, trying to impede the encroaching sunlight. The bed sighed as he raised himself, tenderly swung his legs over the side, and planted his sweat-dampened socks on the carpet with a tremulous moan. He brought his hand to his temple, massaging it gingerly. A nuclear blast detonated inside his head. He could feel a cold, bitter chill break down the door; winter officially had arrived, a few months early. The jovial voices of the morning talk-show hosts on TV, tittering over the revered Oscar nominee they would soon welcome to the stage, were too much for his pulverized brain. He reached toward the end table, felt the remote control, pointed it at the TV and found the power button. The newfound silence lessened his catastrophic headache, but only slightly. Nathan's ongoing torment was bad enough, but as if in retribution, his body had jolted him awake at dawn every day for the last week, somehow even denying him the transient pleasure of sleep.

A bright shard of sunlight pierced through his tightly shut eyelids. The world was hazy, a shadow-play of unknown shapes. Even in his delirium he found this odd—he hadn't opened the curtains once since his arrival. He squinted toward the light.

There was someone there, a human shape sitting next to the bed. Its knee hovered only inches away from him. He choked as his eyes darted upward, into the light. He saw only a silhouette with black, shoulder-length hair. He inhaled deeply. A scent greeted him that he thought familiar, if strange. As quickly as he could maneuver his pounding body, Nathan jerked to life. His eyes struggled to focus.

Maria. It was her. Nathan knew this with certainty not because it looked like her but because it *felt* like her—the black-hole pull of her disorientation, the out-of-placeness of her. How terribly ironic that she would appear to him in his own tattered clothes.

With another movement, apparently involuntary, Nathan knelt before her—he collapsed to the ground, his weakened body flung from the bed. He peered into the light, into her shadowy expression, trying to decode her silence. He shook his head and covered his mouth with the back of his hand, choking back a response that couldn't form itself anyway. A pathetic groan escaped.

"It's you. It is."

His left hand crept toward her leg, clad in his withered pajamas. He gasped in shock as it made contact, *physical* contact, and Maria jerked her leg away a second later. She kicked against the floor and pushed herself away from him, scratching against the carpet. He gazed at her, eyes glassy and agape.

"I can't believe it. It really is. Is it?"

She stared at him, taking momentary pleasure in his bewilderment. Her eyes were dark and murky, unreadable. Finally, she answered. "I need coffee."

Nathan, stunned by her voice uttering such meaningless words, couldn't comprehend. He turned to the tiny plastic coffeemaker on the end table. A pouch of instant coffee, mauled but unopened, sat next to an empty pot.

"I can't work the coffeemaker." *How to explain?* she thought. She could remember the hiss and pungent smell of coffee brewing each morning, its sharp and bitter taste was vivid in her memory, but the tedious step-by-step tasks were somehow completely alien to her. Nathan looked back at Maria, narrowed his eyes in confusion, but acquiesced. He stood with a groan and stepped to the coffeemaker. There was a soft rip as he tore the packet of coffee open, the plodding of his footsteps and trickle of the faucet as he filled the minuscule coffeepot with tap water. Throughout this mundane process, he glanced at her repeatedly. She sat there, anchored in sunlight, both angelic and disturbingly real, anomalous in a derelict motel room, there and not there. He knew this ugly miracle was his doing but couldn't begin to fathom the logistics of it. Where had she been? What had she been through? The questions were cold but unavoidable.

After two silent minutes, the water began to bubble and the odor of cheap coffee infested the room. Nathan debated sitting with her at the table, but her anger, obvious if restrained, made him sit meekly at the headboard of the bed, his spine arched, head drooping.

"It'll be ready soon," he rasped. Another silent interlude, thick with fury and shame. "Do you remember what happened?"

"I remember enough." Her words sounded lonely and lost.

"Do you know where you are?" he asked.

"No."

"I guess it doesn't really matter."

His response infuriated her, but she held her anger at bay. It would demean and debase her; it was too human.

"A motel room. *This* is the first thing I see."

She laughed a sharp, derisive laugh and looked out the window once more. She was paler now than she had been before. He was astounded by her beauty—more so, perhaps, because it was unattainable and mocked him plainly.

"Can you explain it to me?"

"Nathan, I'm not going to indulge your curiosity."

He swung his legs over the bed and rested his elbows on his knees, leaning toward the floor. With the first violent sob, he dismissed all sense of decorum and buried his head in his hands. The sound of his convulsive cries only deepened her disgust; sympathy was nowhere in sight.

"I can't pretend to know what you went through," he sighed as he lifted his head. "For me, I can tell you, it was...emptiness. A hatred of everything I used to love. Going through life in some kind of void. I see and hear everything but none of it makes sense. I can't explain it…"

"Then don't try."

He was stung by the words and silenced himself. His body was in pain, torn to shreds from the inside out. He thought she had committed them to silence, but then she leaned toward him across the table.

"Nathan, you can't explain what you did. You just can't. There's no human explanation for it. Wherever I was—and believe me when I say I can't possibly put it into words, even if I wanted to—I had such *awareness* of everything. I knew everything there was to know, from the tiniest atom to the furthest corner of the universe. And you and Ryan. That was the hardest. At first I felt such painful love for you. It hurt me that you could never know that, but it's true."

He swallowed hard. Outside, it was silent. The birds, it seemed, had vanished.

"But then…I saw everything. Everything you did. I watched you change. I watched Ryan. How scared he was." Her ironclad armor cracked for a moment; she looked away and cried silently. "I don't know who you are, Nathan. You're not the man I married."

He shifted on the bed, running his hand through his hair. So she knew about his "arrangement." This was one of the finer points that he hadn't expected. It sickened him with guilt.

"I know," he finally admitted. "I know that."

Like Maria, he let his eyes wander to the window, tracing the morning fog as it drifted through the world. The coffeemaker belched and gurgled three times. A vapor of steam chugged from it as the last of the black liquid fell into the pot. Nathan rose and filled two Styrofoam cups. He handed one to Maria, who took it silently. He returned to the bed. Maria brought the cup to her lips, blew on it, sipped it. The plastic taste of cheap coffee and tap water was strangely gratifying—the forgotten flavor of morning routines. Nathan sipped his loudly. There was no comfort in it for him.

She laughed suddenly and shook her head, her movements tense. "What am I supposed to do now? How am I supposed to feel?"

A long pause, an infinite distance between them. Finally, Nathan replied.

"You said I can't explain it, Maria, and you're right. There's no way. I was angry at everything, furious. At God. I told myself I would do *anything* to have you back. And I believed it. And, Maria, now that I have you back—"

"You *don't*, Nathan. You don't have me back. Let's get that one goddamn thing straight. I'm sitting here because I don't have a choice."

"Okay…right, I know. Anyway, now that you're *here*, I realize how pointless it all was."

"*Now* you do. And now our son is gone, Nathan. He's gone!" The conversation had, until now, volleyed back and forth in hushed tones. But at this point Maria screamed, her voice rupturing, rage tearing itself from her body through her vocal chords.

She leaned back in her chair and sipped her coffee.

"Take me home."

Nathan perked up, wondering if he heard her correctly. She noted his upraised spirits and clarified her words.

"I need to stop there. I need some things. Can you drive me?"

"Of course." He stood abruptly, smoothing out his wrinkled pant legs. "Yeah, just let me clean up."

He stumbled to the bathroom, swished toothpaste in his mouth and splashed icy water on his face. When he returned to the bedroom, Maria was already standing by the door. She twisted the knob and pulled it toward her. An explosion of light poured into the tiny room.

She stepped outside, her bare feet gliding over concrete and onto a jagged bed of gravel. She felt its sharp corners dig into her skin, welcoming the painful jolt. The minor miracles of sensation, thin specks of natural beauty—they had been granted to her once again, but their

luster had been drained entirely. After what she had seen, thi
of existence had become mundane.

*****

For Ben Dmitrovich, too, life on Earth had lost its beauty. The
minute pleasures that appear to us every day, consoling in their
plainness—the first chill breeze as seasons change, the way sunlight falls
upon the mold of the world, a scent in the air that takes you back
instantly to your childhood—had become mocking and worthless to
Ben. It all seemed simply like a veil, layered over the surface of reality to
conceal its dark underside.

The scene in front of him now appeared pristine: a quaint white
home in a well-off suburb of Milwaukee, bordered by a picket fence and
a lush, green garden. The street was wide and quiet and calm, the air
was sharp and clear. This was a world that knew little of worry, or at
least that's what it wanted to believe. Ben lived in a suburb much like
this one, albeit one in a lower tax bracket; sheltered away outside of the
city, he could keep believing in his myths of justice and supremacy,
indifferent to the suffering felt by those he so often targeted and
oppressed.

He sat at the wheel of his rusty black Jeep, which looked out of
place among the Lexuses and SUVs gleaming in the October sun. His
visor was down, the mirror pulled open, revealing a close-up of Ben's
enervated face. The skin was pale and baggy and his eyes now swam
with a dull, empty sheen. He had tamed his alcoholism, hadn't had a
drink in forty-eight days, but there were still the lack of sleep and
unhealthy diet to contend with. Even so, he told himself (desperately)
that he was still blessed with good looks—icy blue eyes and a mess of
blond hair and high cheekbones, even more pronounced by his recent
drastic weight loss. He put a few stray locks of hair back in place, rubbed

his eyes aggressively, and flashed a grin at his reflection. It would have to do for now.

This is where she lived, for the moment. The little white house belonged to a tax accountant named Brad Smoley, an ex-boyfriend of hers who had provided friendship and eventually more after the calamitous breakup of her marriage. Sarah Dmitrovich reverted to her maiden name, Ellison, before the divorce was finalized. Then, after nearly a month of living with her parents, reliable old Brad had made an offer that she couldn't refuse: his home and his companionship, the specter of happiness once again. It had all returned to her with remarkable ease, or so Ben thought. Sarah, of course, would disagree.

She hadn't told him any of this; Ben and Sarah hadn't spoken in more than a month. He had only learned this information from Sarah's father, a retired contractor named Mark Ellison who pitied his former son-in-law and the tragedy he had been through. How could he not? To lose your son at only five years old, fallen prey to a devil called acute lymphoblastic leukemia—can anyone know what that does to a soul? With a little more pressing from Ben, Mark had even told him the address that Sarah was staying at—Brad Smoley's little white house.

Ben opened his car door in one jerking movement, before he had the time or common sense to reconsider. It appeared desperate, he knew, showing up unannounced as though he simply happened to be in the area. But if this were an opportunity for a clean break, a chance to hit the reset button on all his life's recent failures, then of course it would have to start with Sarah.

There was an abundance of cars parked on the street, and Ben soon realized that they all seemed to converge on Smoley's house. Just before Ben stepped onto a walkway that cut through the house's immaculate front yard, a well-dressed couple appeared before him, smiling and nodding while trying to hide a trace of distrust. A young girl skipped in front of them carrying a large box wrapped in glossy pink paper. She was oblivious to Ben.

He followed them with faltering steps, watching them enter the front door of the little white house (behind an irrepressible burst from the young girl at the fore). The steady, buzzing sound of conversation could be heard mounting from the backyard, accompanied by the laughter of children.

Ben waited on the front step, teetering. His hand hovered over the doorknob, nearly ready to take the plunge inside. But something kept him from entering. After another uneasy moment, he wandered to the side of the house, peering down a row of spider lily bushes and over a low, wooden fence. There was a tent erected in the backyard, a banner reading "Happy Birthday, Sam!," a long table covered with gifts and a heavily frosted cake, half-devoured, with eight extinguished candles lying next to it on a paper plate.

Of course—Sarah was a stepmother now, or soon to be. Brad had a daughter from a previous marriage, as Sarah's father had told Ben, though the full implication of that fact didn't sink in until now. This was still a part of her life, precocious birthday parties and afterschool events, expectancy for the future. He wondered how often Sarah thought of Aaron today—their son, who had no more birthdays awaiting him—and he wished he could ask her how she coped when he appeared to her, whenever his ghost arose from nothing.

Then he saw her, lurking near the rear of the party, wearing a long white sweater and old, beat-up jeans that he recognized instantly. An unbroken piñata loomed behind her, awaiting its massacre. She stood apart from the rest of the guests, watching silently, but Ben remembered she had always been like that at parties, preferring to observe from a distance. There was a smile on her face as she watched Sam play Twister, contorting her body with glee, but the smile on Sarah's face was hard to read and seemed to be tinged with regret. Or maybe that was simply Ben's imagination.

He lurked at the front of the house, peering into the distance with unsettling focus. A shred of hope remained a second longer, but then Ben pictured the scene to himself: traipsing into the backyard, an

41

unwanted memory reappearing on this day of joy; then inevitable pain and anger, tears and words of violence, a clean slate broken from the start. Brad Smoley putting a friendly hand on his back and steering him off his property. Young Sam looking scared and confused on a day meant for her, wondering what these adults were shouting over. It wasn't until all of this played out in his mind that Ben realized what he should have known to begin with: this was a mistake, showing up here, nothing but a desperate bid to heal himself.

He cleared his throat with a violent sound and wiped his eyes, finding wetness there. Before he turned and plodded back to his Jeep, he took another burning look at Sarah, at the face and body he had known so intimately and taken for granted, as though they belonged to him. He wondered before leaving if this was as close as he'd ever come to her again.

Chapter 6— Skeletons

1211 Arcadia Street in Grange, Wisconsin—formerly known as the residence of the Amherst family, replete with a ravishing garden lining the front yard and a pair of magisterial oaks casting shade on a cozy front porch—had gone to seed lately. A backlog of mail protruded from the mailbox, agitating the postman with each new visit. The lawn, though coated with a dusting of frost, had begun to sprout a cancer of weeds. This was hardly surprising; Nathan's interest in maintaining social appearances had dwindled long ago. Even so, the fading home provided a bittersweet sight for Nathan and Maria. The soft-blue siding, sloping roof, and picket fence lining a smoothly paved driveway—they had once provided a semblance of untouchable peace, a guarantee that this family would forge into an unclouded future.

Rolling past the driveway, Nathan elected to park against the curb—better to maintain the illusion of transience. The car sputtered and spat as it slowed, drawing the attention of a few prying neighbors who peered through half-closed blinds. Their voyeurism stemmed mostly from an innate love of gossip rather than the shocking reappearance of Maria Amherst, whose funeral many of them had attended earlier that year. In fact, this morbid miracle somehow failed to astound them.

Before Nathan could ask her to enter the house covertly, Maria had already swung the door open and planted her feet on the cold, hard soil. She walked quickly, drawn to the house by an irresistible force. Nathan emerged behind her, offering a meek "Maria…".

On the porch she closed her eyes; her hand reached for the doorknob, feeling the chilly brass in her palm. She jostled the doorknob, pushing it brusquely. Locked, of course. Her anger resurfaced. How could something as crude as a locked door keep her from her home? She slapped the wood paneling with her left hand, feeling a sudden sting. She pivoted and started trudging down a walkway that bordered the garden, hoping the back door would provide easier access. Nathan jogged to her side.

"Maria, wait."

"It's locked," she said, walking ahead.

"I know. Just wait."

She stopped, refused to look at him. "Open it," she growled.

For the first time in four days, Nathan inserted a key in the front door. Pushing on it gently, the door swung open. A small, dim foyer opened into a deep-red hallway. Maria approached the front door again, looking past Nathan into the lonely house. He nodded his head and held his arm out invitingly. She walked past him, spurred on by a strange alacrity.

And so she returned to a beloved home whose memories had been obscured by cosmic travels. She experienced again long-lost sensations, sights and textures both new and familiar. She traced her fingers along a dusty wood tabletop, once the receptacle for discarded keys and Ryan's beat-up hat and gloves. A mirror hung on the wall next to her. A pair of Ryan's tennis shoes were kicked to the side of the door. She noticed them, winced, and moved ahead.

Nathan, taciturn, lingered by the door, eyeing Maria as she drifted down the hallway. There was a dazed expression on his face.

The topography of the Amherst home came back to Maria swiftly. A closet in the central hallway, overstuffed with musty winter coats no longer to be worn by her or her son; a dining room lined with quaint family photographs, each smile now a wicked sneer; a kitchen conspicuously devoid of food, the curtains drawn to block the sunlight. She ambled down hallways, through rooms, savoring the worn carpet beneath her feet, the smooth texture of the walls. Six months after their marriage they'd bought this home, and for a time it provided Maria with an all-consuming purpose, a way to persuade her that this is what she wanted from life. This exact floral wallpaper, just the right grain of wood on this sideboard, a rug chosen among hundreds to mesh with the color of the walls just so. At the time, these had seemed to Maria like the most imperative decisions one could make, symbols for a happy home where everything is neatly and perfectly in order. But now Maria became convinced of what she had already suspected: this house, condemned to live in the past, could never welcome her again.

She circled back to the living room, where Nathan sat on an antique couch. "Where are my things?" she asked.

"What things?"

"Anything. Clothes, shoes."

He looked away from her, toward the empty fireplace. "Basement."

How fitting, she thought—*dead and buried*. She nudged open the rickety basement door, tiptoed down the staircase, and made her way into the dank cellar. The unfinished décor, marked with wooden beams and half-exposed walls, suggested an unknown future; the boxes of outworn things denoted a fading past. Time stood still here, and Maria took comfort in its stagnation.

Ryan's old baseball mitt attracted her attention first, standing proud atop an assortment of old sports equipment; a Brewers pennant was curled beneath it, paired with two tennis racquets that Nathan and Maria had overused in the first years of their relationship. Pleased by the distraction, she sifted through the box, retreating further into her family's history—a turquoise prom dress she had worn her senior year only because her mother told her to, Nathan's old letterman's jacket, Ryan's mistreated action figures. At one point, a small card drifted from a stack of papers in her arms. She knelt down and turned it over, revealing Ryan's third grade soccer picture, taken on the first day of practice; he was draped in a bright orange T-shirt and massive shin guards that looked like walking boots. Choking back laughter and tears, she pressed the card against her heart, then slid it gently into her pocket. However long her detour on Earth would last, this reminder of her son would remain always at her side.

Finally, she found two plastic bins that housed her own possessions. They were open and unkempt, as though they'd been recently perused. She rifled through them and discovered a favorite sweater—red, natty, enormous—and loose-fitting jeans. With greater effort, she found a pair of worn sneakers at the bottom of the pile. Glancing nervously over her shoulder, she slipped off Nathan's clothing and donned her own. She was surprised how much it comforted her, like stepping into her own skin.

As she pulled the sweater over her head, sweeping aside her black hair with a lazy wave, something caught her eye. In the corner of the basement, looking unreal in a sharp ray of sunshine that made the dust glitter. It appeared to be an old workbench, cobbled together from rough blocks of wood; its angles were sharp and uneven, as though it were constructed in a frenzy. This had never been here before, Maria knew that. Nathan must have brought it here sometime after her death.

She stepped toward it, sneakers grazing over concrete. Its splintered surface came into view, looking ugly in the bright glare of the sun. The entire workbench was gashed with angry scars, a blade stabbed and slashed through the wood. The knife marks created a face more hideous than anything Maria had seen before. A misshapen skull without hair or skin. Two deep-set eyes, gouged into the pane of wood. A grinning mouth, lined with vicious fangs. There were strange words, too, in a language Nathan couldn't possibly have known, and cryptic seals and pictograms that made Maria shiver; *pactum foederis*, read one message etched in the corner, next to a pentagram turned on its head. The wood was warped and rotted with knots, and in the corner Maria saw a red-brown splotch, the size of a fist, where blood had been shed and had seeped into the surface.

Was this horrible creation Nathan's doing? Maria shook her head, recoiling in fear. No matter how low her opinion of Nathan had become, she couldn't imagine him capable of something like this— something so savage and evil, as though a malevolent spirit had guided his hand.

She heard laughter nearby, so close she was certain it came from inside the basement. She stumbled back, letting out a strange and violent gasp, and might have fallen to the ground if a wooden beam hadn't caught her. She saw it then, staring down at her from the basement window, crouching on the grass outside. It was the size of a child no more than five and wore a light pink dress, its blond hair cropped just below the ears. But Maria, squinting into the brilliant sun, could see this was no child. Its eyes were entirely black, sparkling and reptilian, resolute as they stared at her. It laughed again, a shrieking sound, and Maria thought for a moment the glass in the window might shatter. As it grinned with sadistic glee, its mouth widened beyond the edges of its face, lips curling backwards, revealing a crimson void. Maria opened her mouth in a silent scream.

There was another noise then, a monstrous rumbling that shook the foundations of the house. Through the window in the distance, Maria could see the tops of the trees waver. The little creature outside quieted itself, returning its disfigured face to something resembling a human form. Then it rose and spun on its heels, sprinting into the distance and returning from wherever it came—as though the thunder nearby was nothing more than a parent's watchful call to a misbehaving child.

Silence reigned. Maria sagged against the beam; her fingernails dug into the wood. She shouldn't have been surprised. She knew all too well what this town was capable of, the twisted ways in which it toyed with death and impossibility. She herself was evidence of that. But such close contact with otherworldly evil can never be dismissed so easily.

At last she forced herself to climb the stairs. She thought about roaming the house, soaking up memories in every room, but what was the point? These walls and floors were dead to her now. And in any case, she was no longer in the mood for wistful remembrance.

She returned to the living room, where Nathan had fallen asleep with his head resting against an open palm. His snoring rattled the chair—it was a flaw that Maria had once found endearing. Weakened by her body's unexpected exertions, she collapsed onto a sofa and gazed at him. His pitiful appearance—mouth agape, thin rivulet of drool, the odor of whiskey emanating in a lazy cloud—begged for sympathy. But she could only regard him as the man who slapped her awake, simply as a hopeless bid for companionship.

Maria rose, walked to his side and jostled him.

"Nathan."

He shook his head. For a disorienting moment, he tried to grasp where he was. At last, the off-white walls of the living room became recognizable, and he squinted darkly at Maria as she loomed over him.

"What time is it?" he asked.

"About nine."

He leaned forward, adopting his favorite pose—shoulders hunched, elbows rested on his knees—and rubbed his eyes.

Maria stepped to the broad front window and pulled the curtains aside with a screech. "I want to leave. I want to go for a drive."

"Okay. Where?"

"I don't know. Anywhere. I don't want to be here."

This may have been the first subject of agreement between the two of them. With a belabored sigh, Nathan forced himself to stand.

"Just give me a minute," he said.

She heard him step to the bathroom; the water faucet spurted to life. For the second time that morning, Maria waited as Nathan tried to make himself appear presentable. In the living room, Maria's eyes were trained on the well-manicured calm of Arcadia Street, the stately oaks, tidy front lawns, the sedans and pickup trucks whirring over pavement. The normalcy of it all was ravishing, Maria thought—so convincing it could distract anyone from the nightmares it concealed.

*****

It was a bright, sunny day, galvanized by the sharp October air, but Maria and Nathan took little pleasure in the beauty it offered. They were driving south on Highway 63, wallowing in silence. About three miles south of Grange—shortly after both of them felt an inexplicable chill that curdled their blood—Nathan decided to exit the highway, creeping down a dusty offramp and onto a placid rural road, lined with vacant cornfields and thinning forests.

His thoughts were adrift. He had the cowardly feeling that he was not entirely responsible for Ryan's disappearance. Now, when it no longer mattered, Nathan was baffled by the absurdity of his actions, the sheer stupidity of his desperation, and could not fathom where these thoughts and decisions had come from.

Despite the forty-degree weather, Maria rolled down the window impulsively. A blast of freezing wind tore through the car, digging its fangs into her skin.

"What are you doing?" Nathan asked, giving her a sideways glance.

"I want it open," she replied.

Her eyes took in the blurred landscape, a smear of colors dancing on the horizon. Where could she go? Could she find something sublime in life when she had already experienced its aftermath? Her brain ached; a thick, throbbing knot had formed between her temples.

Another possibility occurred to her: a reckless violence, the abandonment of reason. Something like a death wish, as her death had proved so fleeting. She blinked twice. Something beckoned to her beyond the vast fields and the brilliant sun fleeing through the sky.

"Can you stop here, please?" Maria asked then, her voice softer. Nathan peered around them—there was only a barren cornfield and a forest of fiery leaves.

"Here?"

"I think I'm going to be sick." Nathan gawked in concern. What if there were side effects to her (how do you say) resurrection?

The Buick inched toward the shoulder and Nathan activated the hazard lights, absurdly. "Are you okay?" he asked, reaching out a hand— it hovered inches away from her trembling shoulder.

Before she could answer, her hand was on the door handle. She almost leapt from the car, trotting into the desiccated field. Her hand clutched her stomach. She had been looking for a way to escape, but this sudden wave of nausea was not a ploy. After walking twenty feet, she fell to her knees and retched. From somewhere inside, a voice of reason reminded her that she hadn't eaten, essentially, in eight months.

Nathan jolted from the car and stood next to it, watching her.

"What's wrong? Do you need help?"

As an answer, she held up her hand in his direction, gesturing for him to stay away. Despite the pain knotting in her abdomen, she smiled. It was as though her body, in communion with her battered mind, had provided an avenue for liberation.

As her nausea lessened and she wiped a smear of vomit from her lips, Maria raised her eyes and took in her surroundings: only about fifty feet of brittle, cultivated soil, then a thick forest sloping into the distance. What lay beyond she couldn't guess, but the prospect of the unknown instilled a glimmer of hope.

Rising to her feet, she peered over her shoulder. A lucky break: Nathan was staring in the opposite direction, leaning against his dinosaur of a car. He wanted to give her privacy, she assumed, and that feeble attempt at sensitivity would grant her freedom.

She planted her feet in the ground and forced herself to stand. Her first steps were woozy and uneven; her stomach reeled in pain. With each movement, though, her resolve strengthened, her body grew steelier. She escalated into a jog and finally a sprint, as the tree-lined border of the forest was nearly within reach.

It was at this moment, though, that Nathan turned back to her, eager to call out meek reassurances. He saw, instead, his dearly departed wife sprinting through a wintry field with greater speed than he'd thought possible even while she was alive.

"Maria!" he shouted, the name echoing. He sidestepped the Buick and kickstarted his sluggish body, forcing himself into a sprint. As Maria had hoped, the stagnant whiskey festering in his gut did not make movement easy.

He was only ten feet through the cornfield when Maria broke into the forest. More than anything, Nathan was desperate: he had sacrificed so much to bring her back to him, he couldn't possibly let her go no matter how grueling their reunion. And so he ran, a pathetic image of a man chasing after his last shred of happiness. From the perspective of a god, they were merely two specks darting over the landscape, rocketing through a brief life they struggled frantically to comprehend.

Chapter 7 — Destinations

For those who lived in Grange, the horror show playing out in their town was an unmentionable fact—a shared secret too wicked to put into words. Some residents knew all the gruesome details, believing themselves noble for appeasing the thing in the woods. Others had only a grim awareness of the mysterious vanishings and reappearances. It was all too easy for them to sustain this performance on their insular stage, without the intrusion of outside spectators.

Try as they might, though, there was no hermetic border to separate Grange from the rest of the world. From time to time, intruders stumbled onstage, unwitting extras in an already convoluted drama. What was it that brought them to this tiny locale, nestled between glittering lakes and gently sloping hills—the senseless contortions of chance or a more sinister fate? Maybe the strangers who found themselves in Grange were guided there for a reason: to be tested, to be judged.

As the wheels of his Jeep sped ever closer to town, hurtling northward on Highway 63, Ben Dmitrovich had very different thoughts clamoring in his head. Off and on over the last five hours, he had imagined Sarah sitting next to him in the passenger seat. She said nothing in these fantasies of his—simply gazed out the window, her lips curled in a carefree smile.

Through the windshield, sun-speckled scenery flew by. Ben pressed on the gas, approaching seventy. He let his eyes glaze over.

He felt Aaron there, too, sensed his presence in the backseat, and as Ben's eyes drifted to the rearview mirror, he saw his son's face in the tiny rectangular frame: light-colored curls, cheeks flushed with red, a look of wonder. These could only be memories now, visions from a fading past.

The vehicle hurtled over a hill. Ben snapped awake, focusing his eyes barely in time. There was a woman sprinting onto the highway, her stride uneven, skin white and pallid. She didn't even glance in his direction. She seemed, in fact, to slow and stop as she reached the center of the lane.

Ben slammed on the brakes, clutching the steering wheel with a painful grip. He closed his eyes and winced, awaiting the inevitable— there was no way he could stop in time. The selfish but reasonable thought came to him: *This is just what I need*. The tires screamed bloody murder, scarring the street with a gash of rubber. The Jeep screeched to a halt. His eyelids fluttered; he hadn't heard the grisly thud of a hunk of metal slamming into flesh. He squinted outside, his eyes adjusting. There she stood, a few feet away, gazing at him with what appeared to be an inquisitive smirk. He shook his head in disbelief, eased his grip on the wheel and exhaled. The Jeep hummed, idling in the middle of the lane.

In the distance, a car appeared over a rise in the road. His nerves rattled, hands shaking, Ben pulled over to the shoulder and shut off the ignition. By the time he stepped out of the Jeep she had jogged away again. He scanned the woods and spotted her about twenty feet ahead on the western side of the highway. He zipped his jacket, breathed a puff of steam, and ran after her.

"Wait!" The ground was uneven, littered with gnarled roots and sloping hills. "Are you all right?"

Maria heard him calling, but what could she do? She had never seen him before, she realized with relief—if the man had been from Grange he'd be alerting half the town already. There was a soft anxiety in the stranger's voice that conveyed genuine concern, but Maria knew that it was futile to enlist his help. When she finally stopped and doubled over, panting and placing her hands on her knees, it was due only to an exhaustion she could no longer bear. Ben ran to her side, his footsteps growing louder on the fallen leaves, and bent down to peer at her, reaching a hand toward her trembling shoulder.

"You okay?"

Maria straightened herself, breath escaping her. Her eyes asked as many questions as his. She said nothing.

"What the hell were you thinking back there?"

She smiled in spite of herself. "I'm sorry."

"Is everything all right? What are you running from?"

She shook her head. "Just running."

"Yeah," Ben said, disbelieving. "I understand you don't trust me. Uh…" Ben pulled a wallet from his back pocket and flung it open, revealing his badge and ID card, drab and bureaucratic, with a small photo and blockish letters. Maria squinted at it. "I'm a police officer. I can help you."

"Milwaukee?"

"Yeah."

"Long way from home."

"Yeah. Vacation," he admitted with a shrug. "Really, miss, whatever the problem is, I can help you. Don't be afraid."

Maria didn't answer. Her brain was pounding, ablaze with questions. If she tried to explain it all to him—and if, somehow, he was persuaded despite its cosmic absurdity—what then? A troop of officers, guns drawn, descending on a tiny village and its horde of monstrosities? No; more likely, a stay in a psychiatric hospital, where troublesome outcasts are often tucked away. Then there was a question of retribution, not divine but demonic, from some inescapable force.

So she said nothing. Ben gazed into her eyes, imploring, searching for the glimmer of an answer.

"Can I take you somewhere?" he finally asked. "Wherever you need. I can protect you."

She laughed at this, with more venom than she intended. She shook her head and looked up at the sun. "There's nowhere you can take me."

Suddenly, they heard a noise behind them: soft at first, but rising steadily. Once more, the sharp sound of footsteps on dead leaves, stumbling through the forest. Someone was jogging toward them with tremendous difficulty, the shape of a middle-aged man whose health had long since waned. Leaning against trees and heaving in an effort to catch his breath, he approached them as quickly as he could. Ben cast a questioning look at Maria, but all she could do was watch as Nathan feebly tracked her down.

With embarrassing distress he teetered up to them, glaring sideways at Ben. Leaning his arm against a buckling birch, Nathan opened his mouth to say something—only to feel a torrent of day-old whiskey and microwave dinner hurling through his body. He doubled over and kept himself from vomiting, though he couldn't suppress a repugnant gag. Ben and Maria watched him with an inevitable tinge of pity. At last, Nathan was able to right himself, wiping sweat from his forehead with the back of his sleeve.

"I—I'm sorry…that's embarrassing." He squinted at Ben, shaking as he panted. "Who are you?"

Ben retrieved his wallet and flipped it open again. "My name's Ben Dmitrovich. I'm a police officer," he drawled, the words sounding forced even as they left his lips. He noticed a queasy tremor pass over Nathan's features. "And you are?"

"You're…investigating something here?" Nathan asked.

"No, actually, just passing through." He glanced at Maria, trying to interpret her silence. "I came very close to hitting this woman as she ran across the highway. She's lucky—one second later and I wouldn't have been able to stop in time."

"Lucky me," she said.

Ben grimaced at her, then turned to Nathan. "You two know each other?"

"Uh, yes Officer," Nathan answered, overly obedient. He extended his arm for an impertinent handshake. Ben shook it as tersely as he could. "Nathan Amherst. My wife here has a tendency to run off every now and then." Despite the easygoing tone he forced into his words, there was no concealing the vicious glare he flung at Maria. "She's a nature lover, you know. Gets a little carried away sometimes."

Ben turned to her. "That true?"

She glanced at him. "I guess so. I love to escape."

Nathan took a few steps toward Maria, who winced at his approach. He placed a hand around her arm. When she tried to draw it away, Ben noticed Nathan's grip tighten. "Sorry to bother you, Officer. We were just on our way to go hiking when Maria wanted to pull over and go for a stroll."

"More like a sprint, wasn't it?" Ben asked.

"Like I said, she gets carried away. So, you're just passing through?"

"That was the plan, yeah. Maybe I'll stay and check out the sights, though. Beautiful scenery."

Nathan shrugged, scanning the forest with demonstrative indifference. "Well, Grange is an alright town, but there's not much to see. You know, four bars on Main Street and that's about it."

"Hm," Ben grunted in response. "Grange, you said? Might as well check it out while I'm here. I've driven past this way so many times, but I never explored the area. That's what vacation is for, right? Got all the time in the world."

"Suit yourself." Nathan turned to Maria and gave her a nudge. "Well, honey, should we head out? It's getting colder."

"Yes it is."

As Nathan took a step, Ben spoke again, his words drained of any sort of civility: "You sure everything's okay? I can't help but worry when I see someone running across a busy highway."

"Oh, sure," Nathan said overzealously.

"You're staying in town?" Maria asked, ensuring Ben couldn't mistake the weight of her words. "There's a nice motel just off the next exit. Sarona Lake. You can't miss it."

Ben smiled and nodded. "Sarona Lake Motel. Good to know."

Nathan pushed Maria forward, this time with unmistakable force. He grinned over his shoulder at Ben as they left. "Nice to meet you, Officer. Sorry for the trouble."

"Enjoy your hike."

Ben stared after them as Nathan and Maria stepped over icy ground. He shivered; the air had become damp and the light cutting through the trees now pulsed with a sinister glare. He considered his next move, hardly grasping the weight of its consequence. Should he intrude in something that was probably nothing more than a domestic spat, banal in its regularity—not to mention far outside his jurisdiction? A calm, pragmatic voice in Ben's head told him to continue northward to his mandatory exile. But the unasked questions in Maria's eyes prevented him from leaving so easily.

*****

In a massive cream-colored Buick shuddering along Highway 63, Nathan and Maria drowned in a sea of animosity. No words were spoken. They stared ahead, seething in anger and confusion. Maria had opened her window again, permitting a blast of icy air. Nathan's fingers picked at the steering wheel. His shame had morphed by now into a smug hostility. After all, hadn't he sacrificed everything to bring her back to him?

"I hope you're not planning on talking to him."

"Who?"

"Who do you think? That cop."

"About what?"

57

"Don't play dumb, Maria." As he expected, she responded with silence. He jerked a pack of cigarettes from the dashboard, flipped open a lighter, ignited and inhaled sumptuously. "What do you think would happen if you told him? I mean, even if he *did* believe you, which no sane, rational person ever would. You think the *law* would come in and clean up for us? You think we'd be saved?"

Maria shook her head, gazing out the window.

"You know what would happen. It would come for you before you said a single word. Just...be smart."

"Be smart and do what, Nathan? Play your obedient wife? Learn to fit in? Are you kidding?"

"Do it for me then. We have another chance. In time, maybe—"

"No," she hissed. "Never. I'm going to say this one last time, Nathan, there is *nothing* I can do. You've taken everything from me. I can't run, I can't speak. And I sure as hell can't play the happy housewife for you. So *if*—and this is a gigantic fucking if—*if* I were to find that cop and tell him what I know, and I'm, what, dragged to Hell or something, would that be any different than the life I have waiting for me here?"

Nathan swallowed. "And the death of that cop after you tell him what's happening? You're willing to have that on your hands?"

Maria considered this before answering. "You assume this...*thing* we have here is unstoppable. You're probably right. So what do we do? We give in to it, we embrace it. It's sickening."

Accompanied by the soft hum of wheels on pavement, they turned onto Arcadia Street, nearing home. The slanted roof and protruding chimney resembled, for Maria, the turrets of a prison. Nathan opened his door with a creak and flung his legs onto concrete, bounding toward the home they used to share. Maria brought the back of her hand to her mouth, suppressing a scream, and stared as her widower stepped through the front door.

Chapter 8 — Something Underground

Ben Dmitrovich was at that moment taking in his first vision of Grange, Wisconsin. Like many rural towns nestled by well-traveled highways, gas stations acted as symbolic gateways, luminescent meccas for weary travelers. Only a mile north of exit 276, the town limits of Grange were demarcated by a now-barren cornfield and a crumbling farmhouse owned by the Santo family, whose ancestors were some of the town's earliest settlers. Just past the Santo plot was a long, narrow car-repair shop—recently renovated, judging from the sleek gray siding and spotless windows of the office—surrounded by a dusty lot of vehicles in various stages of disrepair. Next door stood one of Grange's five bars—Good Sports, it was called—with a parking lot currently inhabited by four pickup trucks and two sedans. It was at this point that the road split off: a scenic avenue extended northeast, toward the trickling current of Sarona Lake; and a wider road, lined with streetlights, approached Main Street in the heart of town.

Ben continued onward, seeing signs of life in the near distance: an immense baseball field to the left followed by a well-maintained church, its modest steeple the tallest structure as far as the eye could see. It was a quiet city with, Ben thought, a humble charm. As he rolled down his window, the whistle of wind and distant laughter provided a serene invitation. He had grown up in a small town much like this one, but years of living near Milwaukee had made him forget the lucidity of silence.

As Ben rolled past a sign touting Grange's "150-Year-Old Downtown District," a mild commotion up the road drew his attention. Two police vehicles were parked in the right-hand lane, their sirens quietly blinking; three wooden blockades were erected in the street, blocking off a twenty-foot stretch near the shoulder. Two uniformed police officers stood at the side of the road, one of them scribbling notes on a clipboard.

Ben squinted into the setting sun but couldn't make out the obstruction that lay ahead. He pulled to the side of the road, his car nearly sideswiped by two boys riding bicycles. He stepped into a chilly October afternoon. It was almost five o'clock and nightfall wasn't far away.

He strolled down the pavement, quickening his pace as he approached the mysterious gathering. He glanced at a group of onlookers in the distance, most of whom loitered with a peculiar blend of curiosity and indifference. There were two men—one in a rumpled business suit, thin-rimmed glasses clinging to his nose; the other wearing a frayed flannel shirt, his cheeks red and battered from the wind—joking with each other, easygoing smiles on their faces. A few yards ahead of them stood an elderly woman, her silver ponytail vibrant against a long black peacoat, and an avid young girl, presumably her granddaughter, wriggling out of her grasp, struggling to lean over the blockade for a better view. As Ben walked toward them, the young girl happened to glance in his direction, her dark, playful eyes magnetizing his. She mouthed something to her grandmother, the words inaudible, though she never looked away from Ben. He smiled warmly, unsure how else to respond; but she only continued staring at him as her grandmother interrupted her.

The wind picked up; a bell pealed in the church nearby as five o'clock was struck. Ben looked away, strangely shaken.

He hurried toward the cordoned stretch of road, pulling his jacket closer to his body. The spectacle came into view: from the shoulder to the dividing line, a massive pit had collapsed into the earth, nearly the size of a semi-trailer. Obliterated concrete and soupy mud commingled in the abyss. Ben smiled in amusement. Something had primed him to expect an otherworldly terror, not a mere consequence of physics and geology.

There was a uniformed officer standing at the sinkhole's perimeter, a trio of stripes stitched onto his jacket. He glanced behind him as Ben's feet slid over gravel, then returned his attention to the clipboard in his hands. Ben stepped around a blockade and approached the officer's side, where he noticed a Chief of Police insignia sewn onto the sleeve. Clean-cut with a well-polished mustache, the man was an imposing figure even from Ben's oblique perspective—tall, broad-shouldered, dark-skinned, standing with dignified severity.

"Please stay behind the blockades, sir," he muttered without looking up. "That's why they're there."

"No, I know. I don't want to bother you." For the third time today, he pulled his wallet from his pocket and flipped it open with sad pomp and circumstance. "I'm an officer, actually. Milwaukee PD, second district." For a split second, Ben thought he noticed a distrustful sneer as the chief eyed his badge. But before he could respond, the man's expression softened and permitted a sideways smirk. He extended his right hand (still holding a cheap plastic pen) for an earnest handshake.

"Didn't know we called anyone up here," he muttered.

"Well, no, you didn't," Ben responded, returning his handshake. "I was heading up north, just passing through. Saw you had some kind of disturbance and figured, I don't know, maybe I could help."

"Sure it wasn't just morbid curiosity?" the man asked with a grin.

Ben offered an agreeable laugh. "Anyway…it looks like you have things under control."

"You ever seen one of these before, Officer…what was it?"

"Dmitrovich. Ben."

"Dmitrovich?" Ben nodded. "Russian?"

"How could you tell?" Ben answered with a smile.

"Good name, strong. Mine's Arnold, Terence Arnold. I was named after my grandmother." He abandoned his clipboard and eyed Ben expectantly, but such subtle wit went unnoticed. "That's a joke. It's okay."

Ben nodded in strained appreciation. "Oh. Yeah."

"So you ever seen one of these before?"

"You mean a...what are they called?"

"A sinkhole." For the first time, Chief Arnold turned to face Ben, his mounting excitement obvious. "But they're also known as swallets, shakeholes, and dolines. I've done my research—see, we get these pretty often here, so it's sort of a local subject of interest. Apparently our bedrock is made of this limestone—very porous stuff, you know—and it mixes with the water table from the lake. It just *dissolves* over time and then gets swallowed up. Did you know that?"

Ben shook his head. Arnold's words, by this point, acted as little more than indiscriminate noise. He had been staring into the sinkhole, its bubbling ooze of decaying rock, and found it impossible to look away. Such morbid fascination was absurd, he realized; but even so, there was something unsettling in that exposed earth, something that caused his heart to skip an extra frenzied beat.

"A few, uh, geologists even came to visit from the university, on account of how often this kind of thing happens up here. It's not unheard of, just...a little weird."

"Uh-huh." Ben forced his vacant eyes to drift away from the sinkhole. They landed on the document affixed to the chief's clipboard, a mundane incident report jotted with information. It was tedious enough to snap Ben back to reality. "Speaking of weird," he said, "there was something that happened just now, before I got here. It shook me up a little bit."

"Oh?" Arnold raised his eyes toward Ben, suspicion creeping back into his expression.

"Yeah, there was a woman—I was driving north on 63, and she just ran onto the highway. I still don't know how I stopped in time; I was sure I would hit her. But the strangest thing is how she looked at me. She was standing in the middle of the road, staring me down—there was no panic, no confusion. Like she was waiting for me, somehow."

"Did you talk to her?"

Ben nodded. "Yeah. Actually, her husband showed up. Nathan Amherst—you know him?"

Arnold shook with a sudden spasm, which he tried to conceal. "Sure, I know him. Know just about everyone here."

"And?" Ben realized that his questions were becoming importunate. "Can you vouch for him? Is there anything, you know, disreputable about him?"

"Nathan Amherst? No. Nice guy, real quiet. Nothing *disreputable*."

"How do they get along—he and his wife, I mean. Any signs of distress?"

"What makes you ask that, Officer?" Ben shifted, fumbling for an answer. "What I mean is, did you observe anything suspicious?"

"Well, all of it was suspicious," Ben replied. "Why did she run in the first place?"

Arnold shrugged. "What did they say?"

"Not much. Their afternoon hike was interrupted by a sudden race through the woods, supposedly."

"But Maria went with him willingly? There were no signs of a struggle?"

"There was no outwardly suspicious behavior, no," Ben nearly interrupted. "I couldn't detain them. But I knew something was wrong. The woman, Maria—she wanted to tell me more, but she couldn't. Just tell me, there hasn't been a violent history between them? Nothing I should know about?"

With an exclamatory gesture, Arnold jotted a final period on his incident report and brought the clipboard to his side. He pivoted on his right foot, spun in the opposite direction, and began trudging toward the police cruiser parked nearby. "Nothing at all," he said over his shoulder, "considering you have no jurisdiction here."

"I know," Ben replied, following after him.

"I don't really give a shit about that, though. If I knew anything, I'd tell you. Just to give you a little peace of mind. You do seem…shook up."

"But there's nothing to tell?"

Arnold flung open the passenger door of his squad car, tossed the clipboard on the seat, and turned back to Ben, his eyes grave and piercing. "Nope. It's a small town, Dmitrovich. Gossip spreads fast. You come to know who's unhappy, who to watch out for. The situations that might…*escalate*, you know. And I can tell you that Nathan and Maria Amherst—they're not the ones you worry about. You see 'em at church, you see 'em around town. They're happy."

"They have any kids?"

Arnold looked away briefly. A crow cawed; the chief's eyes became cold. "No. No kids."

"Hm." Ben looked around them. The crowd of onlookers had mostly dispersed. In the distance, the elegant older woman was dragging her granddaughter down the sidewalk, her diminishing patience obvious from fifty feet away.

"You married, Officer?"

Ben hesitated before shaking his head. "No."

"People fight. That's what happens. You spend your life with someone and you argue, you clash. You work hard. It's worth it, but it's not all good. There's unhappiness. It's not a crime."

Ben nodded. "I know. I'm sure you're right. Just asking you to keep an eye out, if you can." Arnold peered at him silently. Ben hesitated, shuffled two steps backward. "Sorry I bothered you." He turned and walked away, staring at the ground.

Arnold called after him: "So you're heading up north, you said?" He took four strides in his direction, cutting their distance in half. Ben stopped and faced him.

"Yes sir."

"Well, safe travels." He leaned forward and extended his hand—compensating, it seemed to Ben, for any perceivable lack of tact. Ben retraced two steps and shook his hand once more. "Hope you enjoy your little detour here," the chief said with an avid grin.

Ben smiled meekly. Over Arnold's right shoulder, the gaping wound in the violated earth called for his attention. Ben even thought he detected noxious fumes emanating from its depths. Shaking his head, he turned and hurried up the road. "Thanks again," he called behind him.

It was nearly black outside when Ben returned to his Jeep, drowning in the shadows cast by a humming streetlight. Two boys continued to ride bikes down the road, barely visible in the darkness, their brash laughter drifting through town. The sky blinked with dreamy white illumination, cast by the warning lights on the blockades. Ben paused by his open door, breathing in the air. He couldn't quite understand the electricity he felt. There was something alive and volatile in the black-blue horizon and quiet streets. Maybe, he thought, it was simply the hazy memories of his own upbringing in a tiny town similar to this one.

*****

Later that night, an A-major chord floated through the halls of Grange Elementary, filling the empty rooms with a splendor to which the building was not accustomed. It was part of a piano sonata—No. 11 by Mozart, said the program—performed by a young woman named Amy Dorian, twelve years old, whose eyes flitted behind thick-framed eyeglasses, tracing a line of musical notes as her fingers danced over ivory.

The grade school auditorium was hardly impressive. Seating was comprised of only five rows of folding chairs, and the walls of the building had not been selected with acoustics in mind. A row of

65

fluorescent lights was kept on near the exit, casting a harsh yellow glow against faux-wooden walls. Only a few dozen people occupied the seats in the hall, and nearly all of them were parents or relatives of the students performing that evening. The school's music instructor, a red-haired woman by the name of Fackelberg, was perched on the edge of her seat in the front row, mimicking her pupils' hand movements even as she tried to restrain herself.

There were no musical experts in attendance that evening, but all of them knew Amy Dorian had special talent. Perhaps the pace was slower than usual, and a fair share of flat notes and faulty chords snuck into the melody; but she was, after all, a fifth-grader who had only been studying the piano for three years. More noticeable were the variations in volume and tempo, the feeling of passion in the way she plucked the keys, a subtlety and drama that could not be taught.

It was a surprise to Amy, too. She had only taken lessons because her grandmother pressed her, and because she had sought a way to occupy her copious free time. Her mother had died when she was only a newborn, and her father had left not long after that. These facts only became known to her over time; all she knew when she was young was that her parents were gone and none of the other kids wanted to talk to her, for some inexplicable reason. She hated piano at first, its never-ending lessons and impossible hand contortions, but soon she became awed at the sounds she could create. When she played a piece well, giving voice to something fleeting and beautiful, she had the rare sensation of feeling in control.

In the audience, a woman held a cellphone in front of her, capturing it all in pixelated shapes and colors. Hannah Dorian was in her early sixties; she'd had the fortune of aging gracefully, her silver hair bordering a narrow face with porcelain skin and amber eyes. On the little plastic screen in front of her, she saw her granddaughter poised at the piano bench, exhibiting a talent that was prodigious for her age. Yet even as Hannah took in this sight, she asked herself why it failed to affect her.

As if young Amy could perceive these thoughts, her eyes turned suddenly to Hannah, making out her dim shape in the shadows of the auditorium. Mozart's sonata came to an end. Hannah continued to hold her cellphone in front of her, recording an image of Amy's direct stare. The whites of her eyes became shapeless, floating dots, looking unreal on the tiny screen.

There were three more performers in that night's recital, another pianist and two violinists whose music sounded like free-jazz shrieks. Nothing compared to Amy's solo, which had moaned with a sadness that should not be familiar to a twelve-year-old.

At nearly nine o'clock, after the last of the performers had finished, Hannah ventured down one of the school's hallways, searching for Amy in the music classroom. She'd had a long day: her eight-hour shift at Frommer's Grocery had turned into ten hours, leaving her no time to change out of her white blouse and blue apron. Her feet screamed in pain, her eyes struggled to stay open. Her one desire was to go home and get enough sleep before doing it all over again tomorrow.

She found her, finally, leaning against a brick wall between the music classroom and an exit hallway, backpack slung over her shoulder, legs crossed in front of her. Amy was laughing, a coy but sincere laugh, with a boy who returned her sparkling smile. He'd performed a guitar solo earlier that evening, or at least half of one, which succeeded only in proving that music had no role in his future. He carried himself as preteen boys often do, cocky and insecure at once. Amy, too, felt a strange exhilaration. Her breath quickened and her heartbeat skipped, causing her to question why her body was behaving so oddly recently in the company of the opposite sex.

It pained Hannah to see this—made her cringe on the inside and cast a spiteful look at Amy, which went unnoticed. She was only twelve, after all—much too early for Hannah to have to worry about these things. But Hannah knew better. She'd already gone through this with her daughter Rebecca, the same bad decisions and delusions of love. Time was moving quickly and led to the same destination.

Hannah and Amy burst through the exit doors a minute later, clomping through the parking lot toward a Pontiac that took up one-and-a-half parking spots. Hannah was distracted, though she forced out effusive praise.

"You've really come so far, Amy." Their footsteps flitted over pavement, sending rapid click-clacks through the chilly night. "I can't even imagine how good you'll sound a year from now."

"Thanks," Amy muttered.

"See, look at what happens after all those lessons. All that practicing."

Amy couldn't think of any response and offered a quiet chuckle. They had reached the Pontiac by now; two doors swung open and they ducked inside.

"Who were you talking to?" Hannah asked after she started the ignition.

Amy shrugged. "Jake, I think? I don't know his name."

"A friend?"

"Just somebody in class."

This is how their conversations went: hurried attempts at generational bonding, curt replies that fizzled with disinterest. Amy in the passenger seat, illuminated by the glow of her cellphone. Always a conspicuous absence between them—the space not filled by Rebecca, who died at the moment of Amy's birth.

Morbid thoughts were no stranger to Hannah. But even as she pondered all of this, staring out the windshield as she drove Amy home, a new and unexpected image came to her. A narrow rodent face she had seen at church this past weekend, trying to smile at her but only managing a sneer. He had told her they should meet and talk—he had a business proposition to discuss. On that Sunday, she had told John Linden no, they had nothing to talk about, and she found Amy and whisked her from the church with their hands intertwined, cutting through the congregation as they raced away. But now here he was again, the grinning face of John Linden colonizing her thoughts; and even as she tried to shut him out of mind, he kept returning to her, vile and persistent, a malevolent being that takes possession when the soul is at its weakest.

Chapter 9 — Like a Bad Dream

A leisurely drive through downtown Grange revealed a hidden marvel; if it was not in fact a hundred fifty years old, it was immaculately made to look like it. Half-paved bricks still protruded through the streets. The narrow, classical architecture resembled a late-nineteenth century German village. There was an ice cream parlor, a library, a bank, even a small neighborhood theatre that typically functioned as a political forum, its diatribes growing more divisive as of late.

Ben rambled through the six blocks of downtown Grange, his thoughts more tumultuous than usual. He thought about Maria and Nathan—what were they doing now? Rushing home after their late afternoon hike? Had they already made up, returning to a haven of domestic bliss? Were they laughing at the chivalrous policeman who had readily offered his services? Ben suddenly resented them, even the crackling hostility they had tried to conceal—a tension that, at the very least, requires intimacy.

This made him think, inevitably, of Sarah. Her strength, her tenderness. Her patience, which had only *seemed* infinite—Ben should have known it had its limit. His loneliness had recently become less extreme, less pervasive, but still it surged from time to time. The darkest irony: his adamant need to prove his strength by shutting down became his greatest weakness. *How could she have done anything else?* he asked himself. *I would have done the same.*

It was in the midst of these reveries that he drove past the Sarona Lake Motel. He continued south down a narrow, gravelly road, the murmur of a rolling lake nearby.

Something at the side of the road snapped him back to reality. Barely visible in the passing headlights, Ben saw someone walking through a thick patch of bushes near the shoulder. Someone or *something*, Ben thought to himself as he spotted the figure in the corner of his eye: it moved at a glacial pace, shuffling over frigid ground, and stared resolutely ahead. In the split second that Ben saw it, he could feel his heart stop beating. It looked like a man, almost seven feet tall, pale and emaciated, with sunken cheeks that appeared to be rotting away. Its head was hairless, gray scalp gleaming in the moonlight. Its eyes were wide and gazed in shock at some phantom thing scuttling on the ground in front of it. Stranger still were the clothes it wore: an old white shirt made of ragged cloth and a leather vest beneath a long, black frock coat, with leather boots fastened by enormous brass buckles. The figure had seemed to wander in from another century.

Ben veered to the side of the road, tires squealing. The Jeep lurched to a halt. He gripped the steering wheel and collected his breath. Then he reached over and pulled a flashlight from the glove compartment, bounding from the Jeep and circling the front of it with urgent strides. He passed through the glare of the headlights, creating monstrous shadows. The keys were still in the ignition, Jeep idling.

The man had vanished, slipping into the thick, black shadows of the woods. Maybe he'd simply imagined it, Ben tried to convince himself. But something felt wrong here, something innate and primeval. The invigorating chill Ben had felt in Grange, setting his mind at rest, had now become a feverish shiver, turning the scenery stark and ugly.

His flashlight passed through bushes and trees, revealing sudden movements that Ben told himself were only illusions. Finding the stranger nowhere in sight, he trampled to the edge of the forest. A wall of trees made it seem impenetrable, though Ben thought he heard something deep within—a low, pulsing echo mixed with the high-pitched calls of animals that didn't sound natural, snickering in the night.

At last he worked up the courage to sidestep the base of a maple tree and enter the forest, massive boots moving slowly. He gripped thin branches of wavering trees. The beam of his flashlight roamed, looking ghostly. Here and there, peering at him from hills and treetops, Ben thought he detected grinning faces, looking almost human in the shadows and fog. But as soon as he would squint and try to make out these figures, they would vanish abruptly, making Ben feel foolish and causing him to question his sanity.

He ventured about a hundred feet into the woods, treading over icy grass and dying leaves. He roamed there in endless circles, puffing steam from his mouth as he exhaled. There was only one thing he found, however—one tangible thing that was unquestionably there. At the bottom of a small hill, tucked beneath a looming hemlock, was a tiny structure made of brittle twigs and black, frozen mud. It looked like a tent with a small opening near the front, lined with thin branches. Swallowing hard, Ben shined his flashlight and peered inside. It was empty, he noted with relief. But the stench was unbearable, exuding filth and decay, and on the cold ground he could make out something else: a small blanket with a light-blue floral pattern, now smeared with dirt and grime and ripped nearly to shreds. Ben grimaced at the fragile blanket, wondering how it had ended up here—in what hands it had been carried to such an ungodly place.

But there was nothing else in the surrounding woods, no other signs of life. Ben had only searched for about ten minutes, but he found himself depleted when he returned to the road. Wild thoughts and gruesome fantasies raged in his brain. For some reason he thought back to the sinkhole in Grange, the weird, bubbling liquids that rose from within.

At last he was able to focus somewhat, forcing his body to climb into the Jeep and turn in the other direction, toward the Sarona Lake Motel. He found it half a mile down the road. The cursive name blazed on a burnt-red neon sign. The low, flat building hardly struck an impressive chord, but its location was idyllic. There were only two other cars in the parking lot. The building was almost entirely dark, aside from a single room in which a television flickered.

He pulled into the parking lot, tires crunching over gravel. He parked, rubbed his eyes, and strolled to the front office. The room was cramped but comfortable, with a thick reddish carpet and knotty-wood paneling. The sounds of a football radio broadcast hollered from a back room; aside from Ben, the place was empty.

He walked up to the counter and paused to take in his surroundings. About two-dozen photographs, lopsided in thin black frames, showed fishermen displaying their catches with self-satisfied grins—massive fish, some four feet long or more, sturgeon and walleye and largemouth bass enticed from Sarona Lake. A rack of magazines on regional tourism, now mostly depleted, beckoned from the corner. Behind a drawn curtain made of faded gray cloth, someone was humming to themselves.

Finally, Ben flicked a bell on the counter. Moments after the high-pitched *ding*, a short, gaunt hotelman emerged from the back room, beaming a phony smile at Ben.

"Hi! Hope you weren't waiting long."

"Nope. Just need a room please." He felt sleep encroaching, struggling to keep his eyes open. Dusk always took more out of him than the dead of night.

"Sure. Plenty of options." The deskman turned behind him and grabbed a key from a hook on the wall. "Room five it is. Would you mind signing in?" He smirked again as he pointed at the guest registry. Ben scrawled his information with a nearly inkless pen, struggling to print his name clearly in case Maria came searching for him.

"Just the one night?"

The question startled Ben, and he didn't know how to answer. The man cocked his head.

"Just staying one night?"

"Oh." Ben thought it best to avoid attention and fashioned the least interesting cover story imaginable. "Probably a few, actually. Two or three. I'm meeting a friend for a fishing weekend—old times, you know."

"Oh yeah, we get plenty of those." He slid the key across the desk, along with a shrewdly included pamphlet on the most highly populated stretches of the lake during autumn months. "Not much biting this time of year, but if you go early enough you should find something."

"Thanks. I can use all the help I can get."

Room number five was (like all the other rooms at the Sarona Lake Motel) a drab, boxy layover for desperate nomads, drowning in beige wallpaper and the harsh illumination of ten-dollar lamps. When Ben nudged open the door, though, he smiled at the generic landscape paintings and faux-wood furniture. He inched open a nearby window and was struck by the quiet surrounding him. Only the song of crickets and an occasional *plunk* in the nearby lake could be heard.

On this night (and many others), Ben was afflicted with a nervy restlessness. The thought constantly plagued him that there was *something* to do—some way to help Maria, the woman he barely knew and who may not need helping at all; some way to reconnect with Sarah, to bandage the wounded, self-loathing part of him.

He clicked the television awake without thinking. He was happy to see an old movie flicker to life in black and white, something with Humphrey Bogart and Lauren Bacall—she's swooning in the front seat of a car as he presses his lips against hers. But Ben's interest soon diminished (on solitary nights like this one, his attention span was almost nil), and the memory of Maria sprinting across the highway came back to him.

He pulled a laptop from his bag, flopped onto the thin mattress (shoes still on), and raised the screen toward him. He feared the Sarona Lake Motel hadn't yet made the leap to Wi-Fi but was surprised to see a few bars light up onscreen—in the digital age, he reminded himself, only the most barren frontiers remain unlinked.

The internet was slow but obliging, and gradually a search bar appeared onscreen. He entered a few words: "Grange, Wisconsin." There were few results: a map that revealed only the vaguest geographical information; a travel writer who had spent a capricious weekend in town, much to her chagrin; and a few fishing websites bemoaning Sarona Lake's paltry offerings. But there were no scandalous news stories, nothing about one Police Chief Terence Arnold, and no mention of Nathan or Maria Amherst. Had he expected otherwise? He slammed the laptop shut, suddenly ashamed of his zeal.

Maria was the one who mentioned this place, he told himself. *If she needs help—even someone to talk to—she knows where I am.*

Unless, whispered a devious voice in his head. *Unless it's too late.*

He stood, casting the laptop aside; paced a few times in front of the window. He hadn't always been so moody, so galvanic. There was a time when he was surprisingly mellow, considering his line of work. But then he had lost so much. The rotten underbelly of life made itself visible and turned him bitter.

For a time, he hoped. *That time is behind me.*

He thought about going for a nighttime run—that always expended some energy—but as if on cue the skies opened up. With alarming quickness, a brisk fall day had turned into a freezing, rain-soaked night. Before long, a flash of lighting blazed through the sky, casting an electric glow on the towering trees outside. He shrugged, forgiving himself a lazy, mindless evening. He reached over, flipped off the light, and turned up the volume as Bogey growled an innuendo onscreen.

*****

Soon a different movie was playing in Ben Dmitrovich's head—one ripped from his memories, though clouded by film-noir shadows. The lighting here was sharp and extreme, black meeting brightness in jagged lines, but even so he immediately recognized the scene that bobbed up from the depths of his subconscious: a twenty-four hour diner in south Milwaukee, owned by third-generation Serbians and boasting plates of sarma and kaymak to prove it. Ben stood on the

75

corner across the street, in the shadow of a grand old basilica, and breathed on the back of his hand, inhaling deeply to detect the scent of alcohol. The diner was two blocks away from his precinct, but he'd allowed himself, after his patrol, to down two bottles of beer at a bowling alley around the corner. He knew Sarah was waiting for him, but expecting him to go ahead with this rendezvous sober was simply too much to ask.

The odor was there, of course, the musty smell of cheap beer, so he popped a piece of gum into his mouth and chewed in desperation. The diner was housed between walls of white dolostone, cyan awnings bright beneath the streetlights. He could see her through one of the windows: Sarah. It was mid-August—the fourteenth, he would never forget the date—and she wore a sleeveless red blouse, her blond hair pulled into a tightly coiled bun. She sucked lemonade through a straw, nibbling on the end impatiently. They didn't serve alcohol here, and Sarah must have been well aware of that when she proposed this location for their difficult but imperative "talk."

No point delaying the inevitable, he thought, whatever that might be. He bounded off the curb and into the empty street. It was past eleven thirty by now—Sarah had *wanted* to meet around eleven—and the city had resumed its simmering late-night quiet, a siren wailing somewhere in the distance. While jogging across the street, Ben licked his hands, slicked back his light hair, and straightened the Oxford shirt he'd thrown on in the precinct locker room. Surface appearances didn't matter anymore, Ben knew, but he needed to be presentable tonight, if only to salvage his last shred of confidence.

Ben heaved open the front door. A bell jingled. To his left, in a booth in the far corner, two elderly men were embroiled in conversation, sputtered quickly in a foreign tongue, accents thickened by speed and intensity. Music came through speakers in the walls, played low despite its heavy nature—it sounded vaguely Balkan, accordions dueling with lush guitars. A woman in a white and blue apron stood behind the counter, looking tired.

Ben hardly noticed these things; they passed in and out of his mind like half-formed thoughts. There was only one thing commanding his attention: the back of the beautiful woman straight ahead, the slope of her shoulders as they arched uneasily, tense and severe. How much resolve it must have taken her to meet him here tonight. She was setting herself up for more misery, even he knew this—more rage and disappointment.

He walked past her, suddenly appearing in her periphery, and slid into the booth across from her, bouncing on the seat. Her lemonade was nearly empty, an inch of liquid commingling with ice. There was a plate in front of her, covered only with a discarded fork and the remnants of what looked like a slice of cherry pie.

"Hi," he said, his voice too eager.

She smiled meekly and raised her eyebrows.

"You're late."

"Sorry. You know work. Never over 'til it's over."

She nodded, trying to grant him an ounce of sympathy. "Rough night?"

Ben shrugged. It had, in fact, been a relatively easy day, made strenuous only by his lack of sleep and characteristic hangover. The most eventful stretch came when he and his partner responded to a robbery call from an upscale clothing store in the Third Ward. The man suspected of stealing shirts and ties—unshaved, unwashed, partially unstable—was simply looking for a job and seemed not to know where he was. They took the man to a shelter and ensured he had a bed for the night, though when they left, Ben and his partner thought they saw him trying to slip through the door, screaming that he didn't belong here and lunging toward the streets.

So Ben simply said: "Same as usual."

There was a long pause. Sarah fidgeted, eyes wandering.

"Well, thanks for coming," she finally said. "We need to talk, you know."

"I know."

It was at this point that the waitress limped over, fighting with tiny white shoes that strangled her feet.

"Hello, welcome," she said in a lilting accent.

"Hi. Just coffee, please," Ben said.

She walked away without a response, leaving Ben and Sarah to stew in their displeasure.

"Ben...you know what we need to talk about."

He returned her stare for a moment longer, then looked away—at a crumpled napkin on the floor, at a framed photograph of Belgrade in the seventies, at anything else. Yes, he knew. She had moved out five days ago, after the "spaghetti plate incident." Nearly every night, he'd come home drunk, somewhere along a scale from buzzed to fucking hammered. With their son Aaron no longer there, all civility was gone, each utterance barbed and toxic. He had blamed her for giving up on him. He'd blamed her for mocking him when she should (he said) be supportive. He'd blamed her for not loving their son. What did he think was going to happen?

She had moved in with her parents, temporarily. She'd found comfort there over the last few days, being reminded she was someone's daughter, she was needed and loved. Her body and mind couldn't stand the abuse from her husband, the man she still loved, though he'd grown sick and feeble from an illness called grief.

"I think so," Ben muttered at last.

"How are you? Really?"

His mug of coffee arrived, cradled by the woman whose nametag read Mirjana, pungent steam drifting through the lights. Mirjana left, retreating behind the counter, thinking about her family and how she wouldn't see her son awake tonight.

Ben sipped. The coffee was rejuvenating.

"How do you think I am, Sarah? I...think about him every day. When I least expect it, he comes to me. In the middle of patrol, I see him next to me, trying to hold my hand. I do everything I can to shut him out, keep him away."

"You shouldn't do that, Ben. Keep him close to you."

"Is that what you do?"

It was her turn to look away and shrug. "I try."

"You're getting along okay?"

She looked back at him. "What do you want me to say? I'm trying to move on."

He said nothing for a while, simply tossing sugar and cream into his coffee, loud and emphatic. "It's not that easy for me. I can't just...*will* him out of my mind, Sarah—"

"And you think it's easy for me?"

"—and say, 'well, time to move on' and keep living my life. What fucking life? I can't do it."

"Calm down. No one's asking you to do that."

He did calm down, or he tried. He took a deep breath and gripped his coffee mug with vicelike fingers. A new song was whispering through the speakers, with a falsetto male voice that sounded mournful and lost.

Uncertainly, as though afraid to make contact, Sarah leaned a hand across the table and squeezed Ben's skinny forearm.

"No one said it would be easy."

Ben gulped his coffee, shrugging off her touch. "How do you do it?" he asked after swallowing. "Really, I...need to know."

She sighed and leaned back in the booth. Finally she looked him in the eyes. "Ben, do you remember last Friday? I went out with friends for the first time in months. Just a few of us from work, we needed to...unwind." Ben said nothing but knew where this was going. Sarah worked for a nonprofit that helped immigrants and refugees accustom themselves to life in the States, placing them in English classes, full-time work, community events, and multilingual schools for children and adults. A social worker, some people called her, but she saw herself as more than that. An ambassador, a listening ear. She and Ben had bonded over their jobs early on, occupations which, at least in theory, were devoted to helping people. They saw goodness in each other because of this, even if, as time went on, that goodness became harder to find. "*I* needed to unwind," Sarah continued. "I wasn't sure if I could at first. They looked at me with such pity, like I was this fragile thing, and I knew Aaron was all they could think about. Or maybe it was just all I could think about.

"But then something happened. We just *talked*. About work, obviously, and the people we try to help, who picked up their lives and moved across the world and are just lost…hopeful, but lost and scared. About politics, you know, even though it pisses me off to talk about that. But the most important thing we talked about that night was just stupid, meaningless bullshit. Some TV show, you know? Weekend plans. Bad dates." She laughed sadly. "Just the countless things that remind you of a life outside your own. And it was the happiest I've been in…I don't know how long, Ben. Honestly, I can't even remember the last time I was happy for just, like, two minutes.

"Then I came home. It was around midnight. You were watching some movie. As soon as I walked in, you got up and you started screaming at me. Didn't even turn off the movie, just started yelling at me over all the noise."

"I said I was sorry."

"And you accused me of *forgetting* about you. Said you needed me. You said if we didn't work together, there's no way we'd get through this."

"I know I was wrong, Sarah…"

"But it happened again on Saturday. You drank too much—God, a whole twelve-pack, right?—and kept saying his name, and I knew it was only a matter of time until you blamed *me* for what happened."

"Is this why you asked me here tonight…?"

"You blamed me for our son's death." Tears came now, stalled in Sarah's eyes, but she blinked them away and cast a vicious look at the man sitting across from her. "Not leukemia, not some angry god, but *me.* Do you even know what that's like? Can you imagine, at all, how that made me feel?"

"Sarah…"

"We didn't see each other on Sunday, thank God. And by Monday I started to forgive you. Because of everything we've been through together, I thought maybe this could still work. Maybe we're strong enough. And then Monday happened."

No words from Ben this time. Just an empty look at a scuffed patch of Formica on the table.

"And you know what happened then. Maybe you don't actually *remember* throwing a plate of spaghetti at me," she said, venomously stressing each word, "and you obviously don't remember passing out right there at the table. But I know you remember waking up and seeing a hole in the wall across from you, and me being gone."

"I'm asking you for advice, Sarah. I need to know how you—"

"Do you think there's a fucking instruction manual, Ben? I don't pretend like nothing's changed, I didn't just move on. I am in *pain* every day because of Aaron. I'll never be the same. And if I ever have kids again, do you think I won't be remembering him all the time, every second, until I see my child safe and in my arms?"

Ben, of course, had nothing to say to this. He gazed out the window at Lincoln Avenue, its wide and barren lanes. Sarah quieted herself and looked around, trading momentary glances with Mirjana, whose expression asked her silently if she needed help, if she was in trouble.

Sarah looked back at Ben, her eyes a little softer. She reached down to her right side, pulling a black file folder from a suede bag. She slid the folder across the table and placed a heavy silver pen on top of it. Ben looked from the folder to Sarah and back. She had tried not to pity him, but his imploring look now made that difficult.

"What's this?"

"It's all we can do."

Slowly, his limbs struggling through a wet, black void, Ben removed the pen and peeled back the cover. The paper was heavy and embellished with watermarks; a regal letterhead at the top displayed an attorney's name, one Nicholas Ambrowiak. It was written in the dry babble known as legalese, but parts of it were easy enough to understand. *The parties agree this Divorce Settlement contains a fair, just, and equitable division of property and debts and is satisfactory to both parties…*

"What is this?" Ben asked again.

"Please, Ben."

They both cried now. He rubbed his closed eyes with the heels of his hands, so forceful it sent sparks of light scrambling in his retinas.

"You can't. You can't do this."

"Ben, we have no choice. You have to know that. You think we can stay together and not be haunted by him?"

"That's *why* we need to stay together. Give each other strength, that's the only way."

"I thought so too, at first." She nodded quickly. "That made sense to me. But what I've realized these past few days, when I've been away from you, is that I've *been* stronger. Without you. I'm sorry, Ben, I'm not trying to hurt you, I am not blaming you for anything. But being with you does not make any of this easier. It makes it…*so* much harder. Please understand that."

"I don't."

"I think you will, soon."

She could have spouted off statistics. She had done her research. Marriages in the wake of the death of a child don't always end in divorce. But everything is heightened, every emotion amplified. Togetherness does not equal strength—each suffering is unique, each pain individual. That's even truer when you're married to a police officer, someone taught to mask any weakness with the fury of a caged animal. So even though Sarah knew that men typically dealt with grief internally, and for less extended periods of time than women (or so the preachy self-help books told her), this is where the research lost its value for her. She only knew how she felt, and she felt this most of all: Ben's first recourse in the midst of grief was to drag other people into his void. This was somewhere she couldn't be, for her own survival.

"When did you see a divorce lawyer?"

"Yesterday."

"Yesterday," he repeated.

"I'm sorry, Ben. I tried to understand, and honestly I do. I do understand. This is your own path."

"My own *path*," Ben echoed spitefully.

"I can't help you. You can't help me. That's just how it is."

He balanced the pen in his hand, feeling it was too heavy for his grip. The lines on the paper began to blur together, words losing meaning, forming a wicked, sneering face. Sarah gathered her bag, slinging it over her shoulder. She tossed a few dollar bills on the table, covering her lemonade and pie.

"I do love you, Ben. I hope you know that."

She stood abruptly, spun on her heels, and bounded across the tiled floor. She was out of the restaurant in a flash, bells jingling again, sounding nasty this time, Ben thought. He could see her silhouette float across the intersection, then disappear in the shadow of St. Josaphat's basilica.

Ben looked around the restaurant, feeling trapped in a dream. The amber lights flickered. The walls trembled and moaned. Mirjana glared at him, black eyes narrowed.

The divorce agreement lay before him, an awful and innocuous piece of paper. It was already marked with one set of ballpoint lines, tracing the signature of Sarah Dmitrovich (soon to revert to her maiden name, Ellison). A blank line sat beneath it, underscored with the name Ben Dmitrovich. He hated the way the name looked and sounded, hated it now because it had come to signify a man who'd lost everything he loved.

Chapter 10 — Three Dead Crows

At 11:17 there was a knock at the door.

A hurried, violent knock that struck like a cannon. Ben's eyes fluttered as he raised himself—he had dozed off. There was a different movie on TV, he noticed, this one in garish color. Ben shook his head, half-remembering a dream, an unpleasant scene conjured from his past.

He reached for the remote, turned off the TV. There was another knock, faster and sharper. Ben shook off his disorientation and stood, flipping the lights on and loping toward the door. A blitzkrieg of rain pounded against the roof, and Ben realized it was storming more ferociously than before. A rumble erupted from the woods.

Ben squinted through the peephole, though the storm made it hard to see anything at all. He could make out a figure standing there, dwarfed in a thick black parka, though the hood was down for some inexplicable reason. It was a woman, Ben realized, her sopping black hair plastered to her face. He unlocked the door and pulled it toward him.

Maria was standing there. She had the same intense look as earlier, but otherwise her demeanor had totally changed: she was trembling, gasping, her eyes careening in every direction. *Was it only the weather?* Ben wondered.

She stomped twice at the doorway and shuffled inside, unzipping her coat. Ben leaned outside and surveyed the motel, ensuring that no one had seen them. Reassured, he pushed the door shut and spun to Maria, who was wrapping her arms around herself. Ben locked the deadbolt and fixed the chain, then touched Maria's shoulder softly.

"Maria."

Her mouth opened, but a violent shiver interrupted whatever she was going to say. There was, Ben thought, both fear and gratitude in her eyes.

"Here, let me take your coat."

She glanced at him again; he responded with a nearly imperceptible nod. She loosened her shoulders and wiggled out of the jacket, which was heavy with water and dripping a vast puddle on the carpet. In one fluid motion (though it was clumsy from Ben's perspective), he cradled Maria's coat, swooped into the bathroom, and hung her parka over the shower curtain. He tried to squeeze it out, unleashing a torrent of chilly rainwater into the bathtub. He grabbed an armful of towels and returned to the bedroom, offering them to Maria.

"Why didn't you have your hood up? You're soaking."

She shrugged, cleared her throat. "Felt good."

Even so, she plucked a towel from the pile and began drying her hair, relishing the warmth and blackness as she pulled the cloth around her head. Ben placed the rest of the towels on the small tabletop, then stepped toward the wall and leaned against it, giving Maria some distance.

"Do you need anything? I can make some tea."

She moved the towel long enough to smile at him. "Sure. Thanks."

Her billowing red sweater looked dry enough, but Ben noticed that her jeans, from the thighs all the way down, were completely drenched, made heavy and rigid from the raging downpour.

"Or a change of clothes? I have some sweatpants you could wear."

She shook her head, damp hair flinging in every direction, then grabbed another towel from the table and went to work on her sopping pant legs. "I'm okay."

Ben busied himself with the tea, filling the coffeemaker with brackish tap water from the bathroom. Before long, tepid water began dripping into a small Styrofoam cup, sizzling quietly. He grabbed a cheap teabag from the table—it would probably taste bitter and lukewarm, but he hoped it would soothe her slightly.

"You should sit. Are you all right?"

She finished wringing out her pant legs, then looked up at Ben from her hunched position. She wasn't yet prepared to answer this question, so she simply responded, "Thanks." She tried to fold the towel before placing it back on the table, but Ben forced a laugh.

"Don't worry about that. Sit down."

She did so without a word. A deafening clap of thunder roared outside. Both of them could feel the motel's foundation rattle, cowering beneath the storm. They glanced out the window, then met each other's eyes. So many questions, such confessions—how to begin?

It was she, finally, who smirked and broke the silence. "I'm sorry to show up like this."

"No! I'm glad you did."

"I know it seems...dramatic. I didn't know where else to go."

Ben took a seat in the flimsy chair across from her.

"I was worried. I'm glad you came."

"I guess I should also apologize for scaring the hell out of you earlier. I would have felt terrible if you'd hit me."

Ben let out a single, perplexed laugh at this admission. Maria snickered in response. Its absurdity lingered with him, sad and nonsensical, igniting a wave of laughter. His body shook with uncontrollable guffaws and it felt cathartic even as he tried to stop himself.

At last, the cackling subsided and Ben exhaled. "Why are we laughing?"

"You mean why are *you* laughing?"

That shut him up; he cleared his throat and the levity drained away. "I'm sorry. Sorry."

"It's okay." She forced a smile.

"Does your husband—does Nathan know you're here?"

With a loud, sudden spatter, the last of the water drained into the Styrofoam cup. Ben reached over and grabbed it, the teabag drooping into it, and placed the steaming cup before Maria. She brought it to her lips and sipped vacantly.

"No."

"He seems like the protective type."

She frowned. "You could say that."

"How did you get away?"

The room exploded in whiteness as lightning pelted the earth. A shriek of thunder echoed simultaneously.

"I got him drunk."

Ben leaned forward. There was such remorse in her voice.

"It was easy. Sad how easy it was. There was no beer at home—nothing really, only rotting food—but there was a half-full bottle of whiskey stashed away. It's empty now. He didn't want a drink at first. I think he knew what I was doing. But I started playing the good wife—perking up, you know, fixing a drink, telling him he just needed to unwind, forget about things. I could actually *see* him weakening, the willpower draining out of him. I made him one drink. Then a second, and a third, until that bottle was empty. I was worried he would get violent—"

"Does that happen a lot?" Ben interrupted.

"No," she said, shaking her head. "Never when we were married."

"Are you separated?" Ben couldn't contain the surprise—maybe even the excitement—in his voice.

Maria glanced at him, then looked away, her eyes focusing on a drab corner of the ceiling. "He's a different person than he was. I didn't know what he would be like, now. But the more he drank, he just…shriveled away from me. Crawled inside of his shell, I guess. He fell asleep in the den. His keys were on him, in his pocket. But it didn't matter. He was so goddamn drunk I could have taken a kidney and he wouldn't have woken up."

She grew quiet, unsure what to tell him—how much to reveal. Ben waited for her, refusing to pressure her, trying to fend off the too-familiar memories that pounded at the ramparts of his mind. She sighed.

"I drove here. It was difficult."

"Yeah, this storm…came out of nowhere."

She met his gaze directly, her eyes clouding over.

"Yes, but…other things too. I haven't driven in a while. Almost a year, actually. The last time I drove, I…it didn't end well. I got in an accident," she explained with a trembling voice.

"I'm sorry," Ben said. "I'm glad you're okay."

"I guess. To tell the honest truth, getting in a car terrifies me. I can't tell you how much. I can't breathe as soon as I get in. And, you know—I've had difficulty remembering things recently. I just forget how to do them. Then I get angry and confused and it makes it worse. I got in Nathan's car and didn't know what to do. Took me forever to find the headlights, and I forgot how to change gears. Can you believe that?"

"Why do you think that is?"

Maria shook her head. For her, this conversation was a torturous exercise: how to say everything while saying nothing at all.

"Brain trauma from the accident, maybe? I don't know. Anyway, I got here. I left almost an hour ago, but I got here."

"And you found my name in the guestbook?" She nodded. "Was there anyone at the desk? What did you tell him?"

"I was lucky—he wasn't there." There was a long silence. Maria looked in every direction, then finally raised her eyes to Ben's. Her voice trembled when she spoke again. "There was another name in the register. Marcus Brown. Did you see it?" Ben nodded—he had taken a mental snapshot when he signed in. "That's Nathan, my husband. Former husband. Marcus Brown was his best friend growing up. Drowned when he was eighteen."

"Nathan was staying here?"

Maria nodded. "Almost a week. Just went back home today."

Why? That was the obvious question, struggling to erupt from Ben's lips. But it was easy to see her fear, a terror not only for herself but also, somehow, for Ben. With each bolt of lightning he noticed her shiver, squinting through the blinds as though she expected the storm to carry with it some horrible intruder. It was Ben who finally broke the silence.

"You know, I'm happy you're here, Maria. I've been worried about you."

"I know. I'm sorry."

"Don't be. You don't have to apologize. But I knew something was wrong. You did the right thing, coming here. You can trust me."

He hoped this would provoke some kind of revelation from her, but the words remained withheld.

"Maria, is Nathan abusive? Has he hurt you?"

Her mouth hung open. She breathed quickly. The wind pelted the window.

"I don't just mean physically. If he's hurt you verbally, psychologically, we can protect you. You don't have to be afraid."

Ben was surprised to see a pair of desperate tears trickle from her eyes. The fear was still there, but Maria was straining to conquer it.

"Yes I do. So do you. This is not a case of domestic abuse, Officer."

Under normal circumstances, he would have encouraged her to call him Ben—but this time, the words didn't come.

"That accident, seven months ago," Maria continued. "It was so meaningless. A patch of ice on the road. I slammed into a telephone pole. They tried to resuscitate me. They couldn't."

The thunder was louder this time, angry—a shroud of sheet metal enveloping the room.

"What are you saying?" Ben asked.

"Nathan had an arrangement. A sort of business deal. There's a man here in Grange—just a middleman, but he sets everything up. John

89

Linden. He teaches English at the elementary school. He taught our son."

Ben felt a cancerous fear expand in the pit of his stomach, remembering what Terence Arnold had said about the Amhersts: *No. No kids.*

"Your son? Where is he?"

"Nathan and John—like I said, they had this agreement. It was all set up. An exchange. Our son for…for me."

Another peal of thunder stabbed at the motel; a tremor passed over the building, rattling the windows. The lamplights flickered. Maria's hands clawed at each other on the table, scraping into flesh. Ben reached over and covered them with his palm, in what he hoped was a consoling gesture.

"Where is your son?"

On Maria's face, a look of utter misery. "Gone."

There was another noise—but this one was different. A vicious thud against the nearby door as brittle wood shuddered in pain. Then a second and third as something large slammed against it. Lightning struck again, casting shadows on the window. Then the lights went out for good. They were plunged into darkness. The rain cascaded. Ben stood, closing the blinds.

"Could Nathan have followed you?"

Maria shook her head in resignation. "Someone could have driven him. I don't think it's him."

He squinted at her. She was sitting in the chair, spine straight and rigid, and Ben thought her eyes were closed. He strode to his bag, where a Kel-Tec 9mm was stowed in a holster. Not his service pistol—this was for personal use.

Ben unholstered the gun and checked the magazine. He walked to the door, glaring through the peephole. He saw nothing. He slid the chain from its lock and rested his fingers on the deadbolt. He looked at

Maria sitting to his right; she sat unmoving, the back of her head facing him.

"Whatever happens," he muttered, "lock the door. Stay inside. Wait 'til morning if you have to."

Before he unlocked the door, she turned to face him.

"Ben, I'm sorry I got you involved. I wish you hadn't come here."

Her tone was distant, sorrowful. He felt a chill run through him. "We'll figure this out together." He unlocked the deadbolt.

A violent stream of rainwater slanted inside as the door opened, drenching the carpet. Ben closed it behind him. On the concrete beneath him, he discovered what had been assaulting the door: three dead crows, their black feathers matted and glittering in the darkness. He shuddered, mystified. Hadn't he heard somewhere that crows were a symbol of death?

Behind him, he heard the chain and deadbolt lock and breathed a sigh of relief. He squinted into the roaring night as another flash of lightning exploded; he thought he could hear it touch down in the nearby woods. In the brief illumination, he scanned the parking lot. There were four vehicles parked there: his Jeep and the Amhersts' immense white Buick; a tiny blue sedan parked three rooms away, belonging to the motel's only other guest; and a red hatchback parked at the southernmost end of the building, barely visible. The wind gusted and blew Ben backwards. As another strike of lightning flashed, he thought he saw a large tree limb—about one-fourth the size of a fully-grown oak—hurtling down the highway in the storm.

He braced himself against the wind, reaching out to the cheap vinyl siding of the motel for support. The rain was a scrim of needles, pelting the earth with senseless rage. There was a noise beneath the rainfall and howl of thunder—an angry, rumbling echo from the woods, plowing through the storm to make itself heard.

Ben took four uneven steps toward the southern end of the building, where the hatchback was parked. Someone must have left the crows at his door as a kind of sick warning, a prelude to violence. With great difficulty, he brought his hands to his mouth and cupped them together. "Who's there?!" he bellowed through the storm.

He could hardly hear his own voice. His skin, by now, was drenched and freezing. The water pooled in the small of his back and trickled down his legs, forming heavy pools in his shoes. Lightning cracked again, splitting the sky in two. This time, Ben saw something in the momentary spark of light: there was someone in the hatchback, a misshapen shadow slouching in the driver's seat. It sat there, still, a nearly invisible mass. Ben tried to quicken his pace, leaning into the wind. The silhouette in the car never moved; it seemed to be returning Ben's unwavering stare.

One more step and he was at the second last motel room, number nine—dim and abandoned, like most of the others. He was close enough now to make out vague features on the silhouette in the car: tufts of wild hair poking out from beneath a baseball cap, a narrow, squinting face. Another explosion, splinters of light in a trembling sky. Maybe it was Ben's imagination, but he thought he saw a crooked smile.

Then he saw something else: two black shapes, human but enormous, hobbling through the parking lot toward Ben. They moved quickly, carried by the wind. They both held something in their hands. One clutched an upraised baseball bat. It was hard to tell what the second shape carried, but Ben thought he saw the metallic glimmer of a rifle barrel.

He saw them too late. He raised his gun toward the first figure, screaming uselessly, but the blunt force of the baseball bat was already upon him, slamming into his temple. A tremendous gust of wind quickened the bat's trajectory—its impact was catastrophic. The world shook as Ben felt it strike. Something electric clanged about his skull; the din of the storm was muffled by a gnawing hum spiked with a high-pitched shriek. He stumbled on the slippery concrete, held his arm out for support but didn't find it. He raised his gun meekly at where he thought the assailants were, but his eyeballs swam from the shot his brain had taken. He couldn't have fired if he'd tried.

The second devastating swing of the bat came a moment later, plummeting into the pit of Ben's stomach as he collapsed. His gut lunged upward into his throat. A flood of water washed over him, turning everything into a liquid blur. His last thought before he blacked out was, predictably, one of self-loathing.

How worthless of me. I should have been more alert. I've failed her.

Consciousness was fading, retreating into the murky distance. But the shadows in the parking lot weren't satisfied. The second one—the one wielding a high-powered rifle like a club—took two rapid steps, raised the gun into the air, and brought the end of it down hard, grunting. A gust of wind pushed the rifle off course; it glanced off of Ben's cheek and slammed into his left shoulder. Even so, the impact sent him reeling to the ground. As though someone blew out a candle powering the light of existence, Ben plunged into blackness, limp and prostrate. His hand weakened and his pistol clattered to the pavement. His head teetered and he finally collapsed.

The two men towered over him, bathed in the red light of the motel sign. They gripped their weapons and stared at their victim. Their bloodlust had been awakened, though hardly satiated. Rain pelted their thick black jackets, rolling off of them. In tandem, they looked to the mysterious shadow gazing at them from the hatchback, awaiting his approval. It was not forthcoming—there was no mistaking the emphatic shake of his head. They loosened their grip on the weapons in their hands. They wanted to wield the power, the arrogance and finality of murder—but it would have to wait for another night.

Chapter 11 — Retribution

Forty feet away, Maria peered through the blinds. The lights were off, the room silent except for the monsoon outside. She separated two frail blinds with her fingers and leaned her head for a clearer view, but saw nothing. Ben had wandered out of sight, into the empty blackness. She tried to control her nerves, which had been in a nonstop pitch of hysteria; tried to tell herself that a trained officer was the best companion to have in this situation. But a sinister voice cropped up inside her head: *And what situation is that? When does this come up in the training exercises?*

She pulled her fingers back from the blinds and let the thin plastic snap together. Once upon a time, she had loved storms. Two years ago, she would have felt coddled and enlivened by this weather. She remembered holding Nathan's hand while lying on the bed the first night they spent together in their newly bought home, watching the shadows of raindrops on the ceiling, her doubts and reservations cast out of mind by the simple, quiet pleasure of the moment. But she had never experienced anything like this. As she tried to convince herself that Ben would soon reappear unfazed, she was forced to ignore a bleaker certainty—that they were being targeted and terrorized. The storm had seemed to rise from dark, untraceable depths. There was something in its ferocity, she thought, that belied Mother Nature; it carried instead a human anger, or some demonic spite.

Minutes passed. With each one, Maria's guilt deepened. She hated herself for leading Ben here. She hadn't told him much, but even those vague admissions might have stamped their death sentence.

She thought about her maiden name, Elekan. She had been thinking about it a lot that day—partly out of her desire to rid herself of Nathan, to become the person she was before they married, but also because there was something deeper in a name. A self-perception, a change. She had always liked the sophistication of *Elekan*, its flavor of well-heeled Greek royalty. If she ever had the chance to introduce herself to someone new—a stranger in a bar on her first night in a new city like Cleveland, she had always wanted to go there—that's the name she would use. This was someone she wanted to meet: a distant version of herself that glimmered from the future, like a postcard that had yet to be sent.

Another seismic peal of thunder and lightning. Maria realized then that she had drifted into fantasy. She shook herself awake and her eyes darted to the window, where the white blinds blazed with a fulminatory glow.

There was a shadow on the other side of the window. Its silhouette morphed as it crept its way toward the room.

Ben? she hoped. But she knew that was impossible from the shape that sauntered towards her—lunging, emaciated, growing inhumanly tall as it approached the window, its body elongating.

Maria gasped but air escaped her. Her fingers rested, shaking, on the blinds. She closed her eyes and prayed to nothing in particular. The undying spirit of hope, impervious to even the clearest evidence of its futility.

The shadow's head ballooned in every direction. Its circumference, somehow, took up the entire window. Maria pulled two blinds apart with her fingertips. The first thing she saw was its charred, viscous flesh.

Something exploded from the bathroom—a sharp crash, a clatter of glass. Her head whipped around. Her pulse raced, a tired heart struggling to keep up. The bathroom window had erupted, turning the floor into a minefield of jagged glass shards. She saw a rectangular void in the bathroom wall, a few pieces of glass hanging from it, admitting a calamitous wind and a deluge that flooded the room.

She turned back to the window before her. There was nothing—no monstrous shadow, nothing with red, singed flesh. Somehow, she didn't feel relieved. She spun away and crept to the bathroom. A pair of plump towels hanging from a rack swung in the wind. The shower curtain wavered. But the bathroom was empty.

She stepped halfway through it, straining to peer outside. All she could see through the bathroom window were black, roiling clouds and the nightmarish dance of trees in a windstorm. She walked on tiptoes, craning her neck for a better view. When that didn't work, she planted both hands on the rim of the bathroom sink and raised herself upward. It was then that she saw him: a boy in the clearing between the motel and the forest, standing wide-eyed and fragile. Not just a boy. Maria could make him out in a murderous bolt of lightning, the oversized gray t-shirt and sopping blond hair: Ryan. There was no mistaking him. He waved in the wind, shaking from the wet and the cold. An oozing sea of mud expanded beneath him, threatening to swallow him whole.

Somewhere in the rational part of her brain, a calm and steady voice told Maria that this was not possible. Ryan was gone. This she had seen with her own disembodied eyes, imprisoned in this world to witness his torture. He was a trick, an illusion, exactly the kind of wicked game she should have expected. But it didn't just look like him; it *felt* like him, too. She had seen this pleading, terrified look before—only four days ago, in fact, as Nathan handed their son over to a throng of coldblooded men, half-concealed in cavernous black hoods. But then she could do nothing. Her body was mere air, intangible and helpless. Not so anymore. This time she could save him.

She whispered it first, hardly trusting her voice: "Ryan." Then she screamed his name so sharply that it scraped her throat on the way out. The boy didn't react. He barely moved, swaying there like a buoy on storm-swept waves. His pale eyes were still and vacant; they looked translucent as another blade of lightning struck the earth. Maria reached out to the windowsill, her nails digging into pliant wood. The hole where the window had been was small but wide, and she thought she could pull herself through it. She never thought of retreating to the front door and circling around the building; there was no way she would let her son out of her sight, not this time.

She called his name again, her voice overwhelmed by thunder. Without waiting for a response, she raised her knee onto the lip of the sink, then clutched each side of the vacant window, pulling herself up. Too late, she realized that the window was still lined with broken glass. The blood streamed, staining the wood. She cast the pain aside, clutching the windowpane as she raised herself up to it, resting both knees on the sink.

Her head arched through the small hole, a newborn writhing into a hellish world. She was drenched once again, her clothes thick and heavy. Her shoulders came next, wriggling carefully, though she felt the tiny blades of glass tear through her sweatshirt, finding skin. Before moving her abdomen through the window, she knocked away the remaining glass, sending it clattering to the bathroom floor. No use accidentally disemboweling herself on the way out.

Her path cleared, Maria edged the upper half of her body through the window, her waist balanced painfully on the sill. With one final shrieking movement, she pushed her feet against the bathroom sink and emerged into the calamitous night. Her head fell toward the muddy ground; barely in time, she angled her body and thudded onto her side. A layer of mud splashed onto her sopping clothes, her wincing face.

From her pitiful position, she looked up at Ryan. He was still there, motionless, staring at her. Even on the ground Maria felt smothered by the wind and wondered how her son stayed standing. Another bellow of thunder and lightning. There was, again, that sinister rumble beneath it, a wicked growl. This time, it called Ryan toward it; at once, he spun on his feet and stumbled through the foliage, sliding through the mud as a gale of wind drove him onward.

She planted her hands in the sea of mud, feeling dirt and grime penetrate the cuts on her hands; but she forced herself to push down, raising herself to her knees and finally, with great effort, to her feet. She rocked there briefly, weaker than the evil forces that raged. She looked up in time to see Ryan disappear into the woods. His right shoe slipped through a shuddering bush, then disappeared. There was a pain in her stomach, a sickening ball of dread that she hadn't felt since the moment of her death.

She stepped after Ryan, tripping on the slimy soil. Soon her legs grew accustomed to the mud and she was able to work up a nervous jog. She slipped through the crack in the forest wall, spearing her way through two thorny plants.

The dank forest welcomed her. It felt like another world—dreamier, with a graceful terror. The rain and wind mauled at the vegetation, proving they could conquer it. She could see Ryan about twenty feet ahead, a blur of gray and white against the charcoal landscape. Her jog turned into a sprint, though the liquid ground slowed her pace. The pursuit was endless, over slight hills and through black valleys. The forest seemed infinite—had the nearby lake simply vanished?

Maria focused only on the fleeting sight of her son, racing from her, refusing her his touch. She thought suddenly of the last time she held him in her arms. Not the day she died; the night before, when she had compelled him to brush his teeth by bear-hugging him and kissing the top of his head—a surefire way to force a nine-year-old boy to do *anything*. He had shrunk from her touch, cringing. She had laughed and tucked him in and turned off the light and smiled radiantly. *That was another life*, she thought, acknowledging the literality of it. A sob tore through her as she remembered his touch, the soft cloth of his pajamas, his jutting shoulder blades, the smell of his hair. She ran faster.

She reached the top of a small hill, scrambling on her hands and knees. The forest floor slanted gently downward. She could see Ryan sliding over it, still out of reach. He stopped, turned, and opened his mouth in a wide and desperate scream, silent to Maria.

There was a noise to her left, a shriek followed by a patter of clicks, like a murderous cricket in a frenzy. She stopped and looked in its direction. Something massive emerged from behind a dying oak tree, a towering creature with its spine curved at an impossible angle. It wore a gray cloak, wet and blackened in the storm. An enormous hood enveloped it, but with another crack of lightning its face was dimly visible: impossibly white, the color of ivory, with a fat red tongue forking its way through two chipped fangs. It bellowed again, raising its unseen head to the sky. A webbed hand protruded from a gaping sleeve, fumbling toward her. She tried to scream but couldn't. Her heart congealed in her throat and blocked any sound from escaping. She stepped to her right. Her foot sank into the slimy earth and she fell onto her side. She was, by now, caked with dripping mud, resembling some pathetic bog creature. But the whites of her eyes shone in the blackness, desperate, pleading.

Ryan disappeared over a slight rise. The sounds clamoring around Maria began to transform. The deafening howl of the wind and thunder softened. Instead, a din of feral noises—birds of prey screeching, a low and throbbing growl, the raspy hiss of scales slithering—erupted in the woods, mocking her.

She slopped over the forest floor, eyes scanning the trees for whatever creatures spawned such awful sounds. Suddenly she felt a viscous mass plummet from somewhere above, glancing off her shoulder and onto the ground. It was silky but thickened with a milk-white slime. Maria stopped for a second to observe it, repulsed; then ran ahead, too terrified to slow her pace. As her legs churned, her eyes peered into the whirling sky above her. She thought she could discern a mass of eight spidery legs, outstretched across the canopies of four buckling trees.

A final titanic bolt of lightning flashed. Not just close but precisely aimed, a sharpshooter sending a warning. It touched down with a ferocious blaze only fifteen feet ahead, splitting a massive evergreen at its base and scattering embers over the ground. The fire drew an army of creatures closer, hideous moths to a hellbound flame.

She planted her feet in the black mud, trying to gain traction. Her wet, numb hands scraped at the ground, clutching at twigs and gurgling ooze. Finally she scraped her way to the crest of a small hill. Crawling, she lifted her head over the rise. It appeared to her again, in full view: the red, charred flesh, an almost plastic sheen; the wide hooves, keeping the bottomless mud at bay; thin legs bent backward at the knees, which jutted out like pinpoint arrowheads; outstretched wings behind a tree-trunk torso, slatted with ribs that, here and there, curved through rubbery skin; a mangled mess of blood and skin and bone. And worst, the eyes. An opaque white ablaze with burning fire. The left eye drooped, fat and swollen, though a blood-red pupil glowed within. The thing stood erect with pride, nearly ten feet tall and staring her down.

Maria felt her soul exposed. Ryan was nowhere in sight.

*****

His eyelids fluttered. An involuntary twitch of the head, still reeling from pain. A torrent of wet ice smothering him. Ben blinked again, slowly this time, and let out a heavy groan. Where was he? The ground beneath him was rough and hard, and it took him a moment, hands fumbling about, to realize he was lying on concrete. It started to come back to him: the Sarona Lake Motel, three dead crows, the man with the baseball bat. Maria.

Maria. The thought of her catalyzed him. He raised his upper body from the ground in one jerking movement, sending another spasm of pain through his body. He winced and touched his face, feeling tender pockets of flesh at his temple and beneath his eye. He squinted into the storm; it seemed a bit weaker now, the wind no longer a deathly force, but the sky still raged. The world spun. Ben knew he had a concussion. But what choice did he have? Moving more slowly than he would have liked, he planted his hands against the concrete and brought his legs beneath him, standing.

The red hatchback was gone, and he noticed with anger that his pistol was too. He shivered and convulsed, his body soaked with frigid water, and he wondered how long he'd been lying there in the freezing night.

He searched for his room, number five; it was only forty feet away, though it seemed like an infinity. The door was closed and the lights were off, which lent him a glimmer of hope. He stumbled toward it, the world somersaulting.

He arrived at the door many seconds later and leaned his hand against it for support. There, at his feet, three ebony birds shimmered on wet concrete. He balled his fist and pounded on the door. Screamed her name as loud as his voice would allow: "Maria!"

He pounded again, feeling the door rattle. Waited five seconds, though it seemed much longer. No answer.

Ben pulled the door key from his pocket, thankful he hadn't removed it. It was a lone silver key, fixed to a plastic placard with a short chain. He unlocked the deadbolt and heaved the door open. Of course—the chain was still attached. He brought his mouth to the gap in the open door and bellowed her name again. It was then that he saw something in the bathroom: towels and curtains dancing madly, shards of glass glittering on the floor. Fleeting hope was washed away. Dreading the agony it would send through his body, Ben took a step back, raised his right leg, and slammed it into the door, as close to the chain as his body would allow. The door buckled and shook and the chain tore itself from the wall.

He lunged inside and scanned the room, shocked to find Maria gone. Her Styrofoam cup of tea, half-empty, sat on the table; her raincoat still hung from the back of a chair. So how was the chain still attached?

His eyes shot to the bathroom, to the now-empty window permitting the indomitable wind. He brought his hand to his soaking hair, mystified. What the hell had made her climb out the window? What had lured her away?

He stumbled into the bathroom and squinted outside, his boots wading through a two-inch puddle. He saw nothing between the motel and the forest beside a primordial ooze of mud and rain. He pulled away and noticed with a shudder bloody handprints smeared on the windowsill. The blood had begun to run in the rain, sending pale-red trickles down the bathroom wall.

Ben gripped the sides of the window with fumbling hands and pulled himself toward the void in the wall. It was a doomed decision to begin with: his head teetered, his grip loosened, both feet lost traction and slipped out from under him. He reached out for support but, before he knew what was happening, his shoulder slammed into the sink and he fell to the floor. His brain and body screamed at him for this endless abuse; reeling, moaning, paralyzed, he reached a level of pain that he hadn't felt in years, since he was shot in the shoulder with an M16. In that case, it was military duty—ground combat in the Anbar Province of Iraq. Monstrous in its own way, but conceivable, explicable—nothing more or less hideous than human violence.

It took him a full minute to bring himself to his feet, and even then he wavered, his entire body throbbing. With slow, cautious steps, he retreated to the motel room door. It hung open, the wind and rain roaring in.

Ben stepped into the parking lot and stopped by his Jeep; he reached inside and, for the second time that night, retrieved a high-powered flashlight. The motel grew distorted as Ben circumvented it, stretching further into the distance with each step he took. Pessimism was his natural state of being, but he refused to give in. Driven by a refusal to fail Maria, to fail himself, he walked on, his body succumbing to the ferocity of his will.

At last he brought himself to the rear of the building, and finally to the muddy clearing behind room five. It was easy to spot: a gaping hole in the wall where once a window had been. He flicked on his flashlight. Needles of half-frozen rain took on a pale glow in its beam. He passed his light over the muddy ground, struggling to maintain his balance. At least Maria's footprints were easy to detect, though they would soon disappear—the torrent of rain struggled to conceal her flight. He cast the flashlight along a path of footprints that led to a thicket of bushes at the edge of the forest. His confusion grew. What could have forced her to wander blindly into the woods?

He followed after her, brushing aside two skeletal bushes spiked with thorns, and stepped into the forest. Somehow, he felt cocooned here. The shriek of thunder and wind silenced itself; taking its place was a low, ominous rumble that carried a mocking scorn. The beam of his flashlight penetrated the darkness, illuminating ghostly visions that vanished as soon as he saw them.

As Ben stumbled after Maria's vanishing trail, his stomach repeatedly throttled by waves of nausea, he thought he could detect a second trail of footprints whose dimensions morphed as they went on— small, narrow, and uncertain here, then long and outstretched, planted firmly in the mud. The footprints plodded on through the woods. Ben thought, after what seemed like miles, that he should be neck-deep in the lake by now.

Finally he came upon a firm impression in the soil, as though a body had scraped and scrambled here. An odd silence had replaced the scream of the storm and the prolonged growl of the forest; he could hear only a trickle of raindrops and the distant calls of insects. Ben slipped down an uneven hill, coming to a clearing where he noticed a mass of pearly slime glittering in the light.

Rising to the crest of a tiny knoll, he noticed something else: a throng of trees had apparently been struck by lightning, their skin singed, bodies split in half and drooping in every direction. A layer of ash covered the ground, turning the mud into a squalid gray mixture.

Another noise could be heard—or, more precisely, a new layer of sounds, forming an eerie ambience. There was, most noticeably, the soft gurgle of lake water, of leisurely waves lapping against a rocky shore; a natural sound, at least, which reminded Ben of a more comprehensible world outside of this one. But there was something else, too. It sounded like a birdcall but echoed endlessly, drifting to the clouds and back to a helpless earth. Something was close by.

Beyond the burned trees there was a narrow stream bordering a much larger hill. Over its crest, the night sky could be seen, gray and deathly velvet. Ben cast his light onto the muddy hill, where the traces of bodies changed shape: one set of massive footprints, with four hooked claws digging into the earth, followed by a wide smudge, as though a body were being dragged.

Ben planted his right foot into the hill and clawed at the mud with his hands, struggling for traction. He was dangerously concussed, he knew by now—the sky and earth switched positions frequently and sharp explosions of light scraped at his eyes. Even so, he forced himself ahead. The high-pitched birdcall became more rapid, excitable.

At last, Ben dug his fingers into the firm soil at the top of the hill. Panting, dizzied, he brought his head over the rise. In any other circumstance, he would have been struck by the beautiful vista: he was at the top of a high cliff overlooking Sarona Lake, the gauzy moonlight skipping off the crystal water, towering evergreens swaying in the breeze. But all he cared about was Maria, and she was nowhere in sight.

Ben pulled himself up the rest of the way and stood a few feet from the sheer precipice. Cautiously, his head swooning, he leaned over the edge and looked down, arcing the flashlight. There was a border of jagged rocks lining the lake at the base of the cliff, but Ben was relieved to find nothing else. Impervious hope, still clinging to life.

But then that shrieking birdcall, so close this time it crawled inside Ben's ears. There was no mistaking where it came from—straight ahead, direct and piercing, daring Ben to seek it out. His head snapped upward. The beam of his flashlight followed.

At first he saw only masses of color: a tiny white speck standing atop a cliff about forty yards away, on the other side of a small peninsula. Behind it, a towering smudge of red. Ben squinted into the distance, tracing his beam of light.

The image became sharper. Unthinkable horror in razor detail. The white speck was her—Maria. She stood erect, unmoving, staring ahead—staring at Ben. There was something unnatural about her stance. Petrified, stonelike, a body removed of humanity.

The red shape looming behind her was…what? Ben couldn't know. He couldn't think, couldn't breathe. He had never seen anything like it. The creature's knees were bent sickeningly backwards, as though they'd been broken. The skin was not only crimson, it was sheer like stripped carrion; it glistened like an exoskeleton, matted with bone and flesh.

A wave of panic stopped his heart. It was staring at him. The red face was crooked, monstrous, wearing a gleeful savagery. It was grinning. A black void behind five crooked fangs, dangling by a thread.

It had waited for this moment. It wanted Ben to see this.

One final birdcall, spreading through the sky like a mushroom cloud. The demon spread a pair of enormous, scaled wings, stretching five feet in either direction. Its chest rattled as the creature roared. Ben thought he could see its bones shake.

Maria's eyes never left Ben as she toppled over the side of the cliff.

Ben sank to his knees and crawled forward, nearly plummeting over the edge himself. He wanted to scream. All he could do was cover his mouth with his forearm, emitting a frenzied yelp. He couldn't look away. He saw her crash onto the rocks below; forced himself to shut his eyes, then looked again. Her body was contorted, mangled. It was a horror that would never leave him.

The lake whispered. The devil continued to grin, basking in its torture.

Chapter 12 — Evidence of the Impossible

Flashing blue-red lights, spinning in the night sky. A smattering of voices, hushed and dreary, hoping not to raise the dead. The storm had ceased, seemingly satisfied, but a new one had taken its place: a bustle of yellow caution tape and commands over two-way radio and the dogged stillness of tragedy.

Ben sat, hunched and gaping, in the back of an ambulance. A thick gray blanket hung around him, drooping off his shoulders.

He had wanted to leap over the cliff in one sheer bound, had wanted to hold Maria's body in his arms and prove to her, through painful soundless sobs, his sorrow and self-condemnation. But all he could do was kneel in the mud and observe her body lying in the sick moonlight. The red creature must have withdrawn at some point, its task completed. It must have reveled in Ben's horror as it skulked away.

After ten agonizing minutes, Ben's body had conquered his lifeless mind and he had stumbled back to the motel. A pragmatic part of his brain had dreaded the call he would make to Chief Arnold, the conversation in which he would admit that the subject of his inquiry had fallen to her death before his eyes.

He had walked back to the motel, eyes glazed. The storm had settled into a light rainfall and a cool breeze drifted from the lake. He had rounded the northern corner of the building and was about to shuffle into the office when he noticed someone standing in front of a door seven rooms down. Squinting into the electric light, he had thought he recognized the motel's owner standing by an open doorway. As he inched closer he could see someone else, a portly middle-aged man in a white T-shirt and boxers, leaning his head out of the half-closed door. As he was talking, the deskman had glanced to his left and noticed

Ben stumbling toward them, then turned back to the man in room number seven.

"Well, I'm glad you're all right. Let me know if you need anything."

He had waved his hand in a friendly gesture as the man closed his door, unnerved. Ben had shuffled a few more steps, his face a grim topography of throbbing bumps and black-purple bruises. The deskman had looked at him, repulsed.

"Jesus. You okay?"

"Yeah. I need to use your phone."

He had called the Grange Police Department, ultimately reaching a Deputy Will Moss, whose voice sounded young and sympathetic. Ben had advised Deputy Moss to send an ambulance and a body bag along with Chief Arnold and his officers. He had felt the queasy sensation of his brain unscrambling as the night went on.

Now, as he sat in the back of the ambulance, one horrible image played in Ben's head on an endless loop. The more he forced himself to shut it out of mind, the grislier the details became. Maria's freefall, her body drifting through the air with morbid grace, descending in dreamy slow-motion. Then—impact.

His eyes were trained on a nondescript patch of concrete. He noticed two morgue attendants slip down a forest trail with a body bag and a stretcher, and he couldn't help envisioning the ghostly dance of Maria's corpse as she was ushered back up the cliff.

A paramedic approached from Ben's left side. She held a small penlight and lifted it to his eyes.

"Look at me please."

Ben stared ahead as light erupted in his vision, sending a sharp twitch of pain through his addled head. He struggled to follow the light as it jittered in front of him. As she finished her test, another paramedic approached and velcroed a blood-pressure gauge around his arm.

Straight ahead of them in the distance, Chief Arnold spoke to the rattled deskman, who paled in horror as he began to learn the morbid details of the night's events. The man shook his head and wrapped his arms around himself in shocked disbelief. After a minute more of harried conversation, Arnold patted him on the shoulder, then spun on his heel and loped toward the ambulance. Ben shifted, dreading what would happen next. He thought he could see the look on Arnold's face, a rigid mask of outrage and exasperation, soften into a paternal expression of disappointment.

Arnold slopped through a patch of mud and stopped in front of Ben.

"Officer Dmitrovich."

"Chief Arnold."

"Some fucking mess."

Ben nodded woozily.

"Sorry to hear about Maria. I knew her well."

Ben could only look back at him, eyes adrift.

"Which is why I'd like to know what the hell happened here," Chief Arnold said finally. "How she ends up dead near the Sarona Lake Motel, thrown from a cliff. A motel you happen to be staying at."

Ben opened his mouth to answer, but before he could one of the paramedics came to Chief Arnold's side and whispered in his ear. He could only pick up a few words, but they confirmed what he already knew: he had a severe concussion. Maybe it was for the best, he thought. His brain was too obliterated to think about anything too long. It would get even worse when he could.

The paramedic stepped aside as Arnold turned to Ben. Before the police chief could say anything, Ben muttered with a fragile jaw: "I have a concussion. I'm going to the hospital."

Arnold grimaced and nodded.

"They really did a number on you. Did you see 'em?"

Ben shut his eyes. "Two assailants. Came at me in the storm. A third man waited in a car, a red hatchback. That's all."

The paramedic appeared again and offered an arm of support, raising Ben gently into the ambulance. She climbed in after him, strapping him in.

"Okay. We'll talk about it at the hospital," Arnold said pointedly. Ben nodded before the door clicked shut. Moments later, the vehicle slid away down the reeling highway.

Chief Arnold pivoted and walked to the northern end of the motel—noticing, as he did, a uniformed officer with white latex gloves picking up three dead crows with a large pair of tweezers, placing them uncertainly in an evidence bag.

A few more officers, slow and plodding, pored over the muddy ground near the motel and deep into the forest. Their flashlights cut eerie arcing paths through the night. Small orange plastic flags with black numbers were placed sporadically—a clear footprint here, a mauled patch of tree bark there.

Terence Arnold often felt insecure about the small size of his police force, thinking it might be construed as a lack of proficiency. So he trained his officers rigorously in crime-scene investigation, even if his squad rarely had the chance to practice such prowess in the field. At this time, though, Arnold thought he noticed a sluggishness among them, and not only because it was nearly two in the morning and the smog of death still lingered in the air.

Their feeling of futility was made clear a moment later. As Arnold stepped through the squirming mud, a 49-year-old officer named Richard Neff—whose family had joined the Arnolds for a home-cooked meal only four days beforehand—approached him, nearly out of breath but hiding it admirably.

"Chief."

"Hi, Richard," Arnold said.

"Terry, do you mind if I ask you an honest question? I'm not the only one wondering, a lot of us are."

Two other officers within earshot—a twenty-four year old woman with blazing eyes and a lean, severe man who rarely said anything—quieted themselves, awaiting Arnold's answer.

"I think I know what you're gonna ask," he said with a huff.

"Well…you know, I mean, why are we here? We know what did this."

Arnold stepped away, gazing into the sky with an almost comical air of gravity. "You're forgetting the oath you took, Officer, as a member of law enforcement. Protect the community. Honor the badge that you wear. There's a crisis—we investigate, we answer questions. In this case like any other. That's how it's supposed to be, anyway."

"Okay…but why the dog and pony show? Any evidence will just prove what we already know. I don't mean any disrespect, Chief, but we're all thinking it."

Arnold nodded and looked around him, through a forest that seemed oddly abandoned despite the presence of his team. He turned to Neff. His voice took on a strange and ethereal tone.

"Any evidence we find could prove the supernatural. The impossible. It could tell us something about *existence*, nothing less than that. Where these things come from, what they mean. We're here for our own…edification."

"Yes, sir," Neff said after a pause, nodding gravely. He turned back to his work, mystified by Arnold's words, joining two other officers as they traced a line of muddied prints.

Arnold walked on, following the path of orange flags. Coming over a rise, he saw a mass of glutinous white slime shimmering in the dark, then radioed one of his men to bring a thermos from his squad car. Squinting at the milky slime on the forest floor, he thought he could see something throbbing inside: hundreds of tiny eggs, perfectly spherical, pulsing with some kind of hideous life.

At last Arnold arrived at a steep hill in the ground, which he was able to climb only by heaving himself forward on his knees. He arose at the top, his jacket and trim black pants now smeared with mud. He groaned and looked around him, feeling miserably alone. It was a gorgeous small peninsula, the radiant glow of moonlight skidding across the water. Arnold squinted at the patch of rocks that had become Maria Amherst's resting place (her second and surely final resting place, he couldn't help but think). He could barely make out a black-crimson smear stained across one of the boulders.

Most of the time he was proud of his vocation, believing in the honor of his work—to protect his land and his people. But here, just outside of Grange, such a task became perverted, making a mockery of his faith in justice. What he was asked to do for the sake of the townspeople was a corruption of his soul. On nights like this, when the traces of devilish creatures could be sensed without question, he was frightened to feel a certain decay eating away inside of him.

Chapter 13 — Ghosts

There was a small medical clinic just north of Grange, a two-story brick compound with an air of hushed solemnity. An electric sign marked only with the word "Clinic" shone in a front courtyard that abutted a small, nearly vacant parking lot. At this time of day—half past two in the morning on Thursday, the twenty-ninth of October—the hallways were nearly deserted. It assumed the ghostly air of an abandoned hospital, the kind that shrieked with the moans of dead patients. But signs of life glimmered here and there: the soft patter of white tennis shoes on linoleum, the muffled pop music of a bored receptionist listening to headphones.

Ben Dmitrovich was perched on the edge of a hospital bed in Room 104, his fingers scratching the coarse paper bedcover. The lights were sharp and nauseating. The oppressive air grew heavier as the walls and ceiling came unmoored and, as far as Ben could tell, decided flippantly to switch positions.

His mind was in a state of delirium, softened into a frail, bewildered mass. Memories emerged, interweaving with the present. He realized with faltering certainty that he was in the tiny town of Grange, but one eyeblink later and he found himself in the Milwaukee operating room where his tonsils were removed when he was ten years old. He forced his eyes shut, trying to will himself into coherency. But when they opened again he was standing, or maybe floating, in a delivery room five years ago, seeing the woman he loved give birth.

The entrance of a nurse a few moments later brought Ben back to Room 104. She wore white-framed eyeglasses, red highlights in her hair, and a nametag reading Kari. She was willfully upbeat—out of place, Ben thought, but he welcomed her aggressive buoyancy. She performed a series of tests—a temperature reading, patterns of light shined into pupils, a brief and woozy walk around the claustrophobic room—and asked him questions that should have been easily answerable.

"Any health concerns we should know about?

"On any medication?

"Ben, can you tell me why you're here in Grange? How did you get here?

"Have you experienced any traumatic brain injuries in the past? Please, bear with me…we're almost done."

Through staggering headaches he offered muddled answers, though he found himself perplexed by the last one. Brain injuries? He narrowed his eyes and struggled to recollect the past in one swift montage. As soon as a particular memory started to emerge, it blurred again, assuming the haze of fantasy. He had played basketball in high school, he remembered, and thought he recalled a catastrophic fall onto hardwood many years ago; and then, of course, there was his tour of duty in Anbar Province, though that name stubbornly refused to arise from the depths of his brain. His responses were uncertain and chaotic, tumbling from his mouth like brackish syrup.

Ben was depleted by the time her examination finished, so it was with relief that he heard her state the obvious. His concussion required at least one night of medical observation; he wouldn't be leaving the hospital until the following morning. Most other times, Ben's need to appear invincible would have caused him to protest and lurch out the door. Tonight, though, he obeyed her orders to change into a turquoise hospital gown, an arduous effort in itself.

Sometime after three, once Kari had vacated the room and extinguished the lights, Ben thought he heard quiet voices clamoring outside his door. One of them belonged to Kari, who reasserted Ben's weakened physical and mental state. The other voice, though more obscure, belonged to Chief Arnold—or so Ben surmised, fending off the possibility that someone with deadlier designs might have reappeared to finish the job.

This, however, was the last worry that scattered through his brain before it shut itself off, granting Ben the rest he desperately needed.

The brain is a mystical thing, subject to the laws of neurology yet pulsing with its own invisible life. Ben would never remember the thoughts that swam along his synapses that night, but it would surprise him to learn that his mind was focused not on Maria Amherst but on the tapestry of his own past.

In a deeper sleep than he had ever known, he saw her on the night they first met—Sarah. Her sunny blond hair curling over her face. An intensity in her eyes, even during her happiest moments. She was a friend of a friend, recently single, emerging with a halo from a flickering bonfire. The attraction undeniable, irresistible. His last week in the States before his first tour of duty, every moment enlivened by its immediacy. She was in college, interning for the city government, and that night she had proudly (and drunkenly) prophesied her imminent career in social justice.

He had driven her home to an apartment complex with a vast and quiet parking lot; they'd fooled around in his beat-up Honda, relishing the heat of the moment. He would see her again in sixteen months, after an endless flight home that was both euphoric and deflating, days before she had defended her thesis on the positive and negative effects of building revitalization in American inner cities. He had been tense and restless when he returned, propelled by a volatile energy that had been bottled inside of him during his year and a half in western Iraq. This reunion didn't appear to him, though, while he lay in a tiny hospital bed in Grange. He remembered only the electricity of their first night together, when the future was limitless and time hadn't yet played its merciless tricks.

Then he saw something else. A boy, five years old, was seated at a kitchen table. Ben somehow knew, in his dormant state of mind, that he was looking through the boy's unclouded eyes. A bowl sat in front of him on the table; a plastic spoon to the right. Cereal in the bowl, somewhat sugary, becoming liquescent from the milk.

Was it him? Aaron? One of those dark ironies of dreams: Ben knew that it was, but his mind fought against this certainty. Someone stepped into the boy's line of sight, a man in a black uniform with a gold badge, wearing a smile. A thick black belt hung tight around his waist, marked with the conspicuous handles of weapons. Ben was seeing himself, a relic from an untainted past. The boy spooned his cereal and evaporated.

Another image came to him, this time inexplicable, ordained by a twisted logic. Ben saw a barren landscape from a horrid God's-eye view, a web of scarred canyons and jutting mountaintops etched into a reddish land. A river cut through it, thick and translucent, and a multitude of organisms breathed within, monstrosities and humanoid things gasping for breath they could never attain. The image shook Ben in his sleep, rattling the hospital bed.

When Ben finally fluttered his eyelids awake, it was half past noon. Golden sunlight cut into the room at a sharp angle, illuminating the tiled floor almost to the bed. After wincing through the pain that lingered on his battered face, he took in the amber sheen of the sun dousing an outdoor garden.

Rolling onto his left side, Ben saw something to dampen his mood: a man with the beige uniform and railroad insignia of a police chief, seated in a small padded chair, a wide-brimmed hat resting in his lap. It was Terence Arnold, glowering at Ben's dormant body, a grim and plaintive expression on his otherwise amiable face. Ben winced as he raised himself, his head still woozy. No words were spoken for what seemed like a minute, only anxious glances traded back and forth.

Finally Arnold's voice, stern but kindly, broke the silence.

"How ya feelin'?"

Ben emitted a dour grunt in response. Arnold glanced at his hat, then glared at Ben with upturned eyes.

"Stupid question, I know. I just hope you don't feel as bad as you look."

Ben struggled to come up with a suitably pithy response, but his mind buckled from the strain. A birdcall poured in through the window.

A moment later, a nurse's voice could be heard on the loudspeakers, requesting Dr. Fauger to assist in OR 2. Ben blinked, coming to his senses.

"What time is it?"

"Almost one."

With a fluid movement, as though he had been anticipating this very scene, Arnold rose to his feet and hovered over Ben, his gaze suddenly harsh and unwavering.

"Got somewhere to be?"

Ben shot a vicious, impatient look at Arnold. "Why are you here?" Ben finally asked.

"Well, why do you think, Ben? Got some questions to ask you. Oh, by the way, they brought your breakfast earlier." Turning to his right, Arnold gripped a rectangular tray on a wheeled cart and brought it closer to the bed. A heap of plastic yellow eggs and rubbery fruit came into view, a Styrofoam cup of water in the corner. A wave of famine washed over Ben as he realized he hadn't eaten in sixteen hours. He pulled the cart toward him, lifted a plastic fork and stabbed the waxy food, devouring it.

After three wolfish bites he looked up at Arnold, swallowed and said: "So what do you want to ask me?"

Arnold returned his stare, trying to read a man who was proving very difficult to decipher. "Let's start with how Maria Amherst was killed a hundred yards from the motel you were staying at," he drawled. "Was she there to see you?"

"She knew I was staying there. Yeah, she came and she wanted to talk to me."

"About what?"

Ben stared at Arnold, his head drifting, an untethered balloon threatening to float into space. Why, Ben asked himself, had Arnold claimed that the Amhersts had no kids? Because he knew about their "exchange," as Maria had called it? Him for her, she had said.

116

Ben reached for the cup of water on the corner of the tray.

"Well, I don't know. She didn't really have time to say anything."

"What do you mean?"

"She told me that her husband was drunk and she drove out to meet me. She started to tell me about this…exchange she had been involved with."

Arnold shuffled his hat in his hands. "What kind of exchange?"

"Well, that's when there was a knock at the door. In the middle of the storm, which was…violent, you know?" An incredulous tremor worked its way into Ben's carefully plotted answer. "Angry. The dead crows outside the door, I know you saw them."

Arnold nodded. "Where do you think they came from?"

"I think they were a warning. Left for me by the men who attacked me. A demonstration of power."

"Two men, you said."

"They came around the corner, moving with the wind. I didn't have time to react."

"And they went after Maria?" Arnold asked this eagerly, a false note in his voice.

Ben shook his head; a sharp stab of pain in his temples forced him to stop. "No. Maybe they were involved. But they didn't kill her."

"How do you know that?"

"Because I *saw* what killed her." He shuddered as the memory struck him, bobbing to the surface. But he said nothing—his eyes only widened, lost on a tile of linoleum.

"What did you see?"

Ben looked at Arnold, defiant through a glimmer of fear. "Is there something you're not telling me? Do you know what's out there?"

"No," Arnold answered. "Why don't you tell me?"

It was at this moment that a nurse arrived, bearing medical charts and a curt, unadorned energy. He read Ben's temperature and checked his pupils, finally permitting Ben to check himself out if he felt "mentally and physically sound." The nurse, in his low and halting voice, prescribed as much rest as possible, along with a mild painkiller in case the headaches worsen.

"You were lucky, though," the nurse said with a smirk. "X-rays were negative, no brain damage. You might just want to avoid men wielding baseball bats for a while." He smiled to himself, clearly impressed with his own wit.

"Come on," barked Arnold. "I'll give you a ride to the motel." Ben inhaled the rest of his eggs in three ravenous forkfuls, too weak to offer protest.

*****

It was one of those autumn days, cold but bright and dazzling, that flecked the leaves with color and looked forward to a flushed spring five months later. Ben was reentering a state of cogency, but as he sat in the passenger seat of Chief Arnold's police cruiser—the window rolled down, crisp air whistling in—he looked at the lush scenery roaring past with a new foreboding. In one night, his knowledge of the world had been upended. A row of towering balsam fir trees waved in the wind; as they danced, Ben wondered what terrors were hidden on the other side.

Arnold's mellow voice brought him back to reality.

"Is there anything else you want to tell me, Officer Dmitrovich?"

"No."

"Okay, well, just for the sake of clarity then. Maria Amherst arrived at your motel room just to talk. About this 'exchange.' Then you're attacked by two assailants and Maria decides to frolic off into the woods, where she's thrown from a cliff. So the question, then, is by whom?"

"Not *who*," Ben said, shaking his head.

"Then *what?*" Arnold's venomous tone struggled to hide his diminishing patience.

For the first time during the car ride, Ben looked at him, hoping to decode Arnold's reaction. "I don't know. It was red, a sort of deep red. Crimson. Tall, maybe ten feet. Burnt flesh—looked like snakeskin, you know? Not human."

Ben thought he noticed a shudder of resignation, rather than surprise, pass over Arnold's features.

"What are you saying?"

"I don't know, Chief, they're your woods. You must know what's out there."

A long silence followed, buzzing with tension. The car rolled into the town of Grange, past the small sporting goods store that marked its northernmost boundary. Finally, Arnold broke the silence.

"Remind me again how you ended up here."

"I was on my way north, driving through," Ben said. "Maria ran onto the highway. I almost hit her. Pure coincidence."

"Really? I don't know if anything is pure coincidence. I guess that's a different conversation, though. Where were you driving?"

Ben glanced at Arnold, finding the question irrelevant, but answered. "My family has a cabin up north, on Chippanazie Lake. Nice little place, it's been in the family for years."

"So just a vacation, then?"

"Yeah."

"Well, that's good, I'm happy to hear it. Everyone needs a vacation, you know? We work too damn hard, most of us, you gotta do something to maintain your sanity. Get away from everything, at least once in a while. I actually *require* my officers to take regular vacations; keeps the mind sharp, the body ready. That's good you're on vacation."

"Seems like it may have been cut short."

Arnold shook his head. "No, I don't think so. A little detour, maybe. But nothing's stopping you now."

"I'm not leaving, I can't. I have more questions now than when I got here."

Arnold sighed, calm but simmering, and stared out the windshield. "I, uh, called your precinct this morning. Second district, I remembered you said that. Spoke to your captain there, Prost—seemed like a nice woman, a little blunt maybe, but helpful."

"You're checking up on me?"

Arnold nodded. "Yes, I am," he said, disarming Ben's air of indignation. "I am indeed. She had good things to say about you. Smart officer, good man. But she told me something else, too, about this vacation of yours. How it's not exactly voluntary." He paused, allowing Ben to respond—an opportunity he decided to ignore. "More of a mandatory nature, she said."

"What else did she tell you?"

"That you're under investigation by the MPD. Supposed to get three months' probation, but she's convinced you'll get off with a temporary leave of absence. Two weeks, paid vacation. Not a bad deal, really."

Ben squinted. The first of many debilitating headaches had begun to alight.

"She also told me," Arnold continued in a cool, even tone, "*why* you were supposed to receive three months' probation. Beat the hell out of a suspect in a domestic violence case. Broke two of his ribs and his nose. There's a lawsuit against Milwaukee PD because of you, did you know that?"

"Yes." The word slithered out, leaving an angry hiss in its wake.

"I mean, she defended you, went on about how you were a good, careful officer. Extenuating circumstances and all that. I would just as soon say that you're defiling the badge that you wear, but what do I know? 'Judge not,' and so on."

Ben shifted in his seat, gazing somewhere just beyond the windshield. The hardened clothes he had been wearing the night before crackled on his body, still caked with mud. "It was a mistake. I was under a lot of stress, I wasn't myself. So, yeah, here I am, two weeks' vacation *strongly encouraged*. I'm not proud of it."

"I'd hope not." Ben was growing tired of his sanctimonious tone. "But you understand why this sheds a rather suspicious light on your character, Officer Dmitrovich? Not to mention your account of Nathan and Maria's behavior."

"Yes, I understand," he muttered. "But that's not who I am. Everything I told you about Maria is true. Something bad is happening here. And maybe you really don't know what it is, that might be. But I think you do. I think you can feel it, even if you can't explain it. Am I right?"

Arnold looked sideways at Ben, then trained his eyes forward, burning a hole through the windshield. He was relieved to see the Sarona Lake Motel emerge in the distance to the left, looking especially desolate in the brilliant sun, traces of last night's storm still apparent in the landscape.

"My officers are a well-trained team, Ben. You assume, because of the size of my force, that we're incapable of investigating Maria's death properly. But we take her death and the investigation surrounding it very seriously, you can be sure of that." There was a whisper of tires crunching over gravel as the car rolled into the parking lot, toward the recently re-hinged door of room number five. "Take your vacation," Arnold said in a caustic tone that sounded like an order.

"I can't leave. You gotta understand—"

"You will impede this investigation by staying in Grange." The car lurched to a halt but the engine kept running. "There's nothing you can do here. Do you understand what I'm saying?"

Ben reached out his right hand. It hovered over the door handle.

"There's nothing I can do."

After a long pause brimming with hostility, Ben swung the door open, springing from the car with a violence that made his head reel all over again. He swung the door shut behind him. Arnold stared after him until Ben clicked his key into place and opened the motel room door. A sliver of sunlight bounced off the rear-view mirror, causing Arnold to squint, brows furrowed.

Terence Arnold had never had a crisis of faith, exactly. Even when his principles weakened in order to conceal whatever happened in Grange, he could always tell himself that he was doing it for the greater good. Secrecy was, in their case, paramount. Better to understand it and, if possible, live alongside it. Make compromises. But as much as he tried to silence his own doubts, believing in the virtue of his obfuscation, there were times when he hated the world he was born into and the lies he was forced to spread in the name of so-called justice.

Chapter 14 — A Bright Future

That Thursday evening at Grange Elementary, a peculiar custom was taking place—a ritual by no means confined to this Wisconsin town. Its occurrence was even boldly displayed in plastic letters on the marquee in the front schoolyard: PARENT-TEACHER CONFERENCES, 7:00PM. School boards everywhere hold the reasonable assumption that parents are unaware of what actually takes place in their children's lives for much of the year. And so, harried adults stumble from one classroom to the next, either basking in the adulation of their well-mannered children or grimacing at teachers' assertions that their kids' futures are fated for delinquency.

The hallways of the school were drowning in beige: cream-colored lockers, brownish tiling on the walls and floor, a pale orange light that oozed from the fluorescents overhead. Hannah Dorian drifted through them, her tall figure cutting a regal image as she took in her surroundings. She thought about avoiding these conversations entirely, instead wandering the school for an hour in bitter awe of a youthful experience so far removed from her own. But then there would be the inevitable note from Amy's teachers, inquiring about her absence.

No, it was unavoidable. She glanced at a printout of Amy's schedule, searching for her nearest classroom.

It wasn't that Hannah was uncaring toward her granddaughter; she felt a solemn wave of affection every time she looked at her. But Hannah shuddered to think that she was responsible for Amy's future. She had invested so much already—so much care and expectancy, a complete self-sacrifice—and at some point it had started to deplete her, exhaust and corrode her, to Hannah's own horror. What if (she wondered with a quiet shiver) she could only find spite where there used to be love?

Someone laughed shrilly to her right, a high and bounding laugh that made Hannah jump as she walked past an open doorway. Glancing at the room number outside, she realized that the room belonged to Mr. Martin, a long-haired math teacher who fruitlessly tried to instill in his fifth graders an ardor for quotients and dividends. He was one of Amy's teachers, Hannah verified as she rechecked the schedule, and looked around the room with mild interest as she stepped inside. There was a jovial woman with a frenzied perm sitting across from Mr. Martin at his desk. Toward the back of the room, next to a candy-colored multiplication table, stood a bored middle-aged couple waiting for their turn.

Luckily, Mr. Martin made short work of the diminutive woman at his desk. Shortly after Hannah entered and retreated to the back of the room, Mr. Martin stood, nearly sending the chair toppling over behind him. Extending two hands to the woman in an awkward handshake, Mr. Martin nodded wildly, like a marionette with a snapped string. "Greta, I mean it when I say it's a *pleasure* having your son in class. He's a pleasure, really. Great kid."

Greta beamed as she stood to shake his hand, nervously pulling at her stiff dress to smooth out the wrinkles. "Thank you. Oh, it means so much to hear that! I worry about him—"

Mr. Martin cut her off with a deft balance of curtness and tact, well aware that he had a long night of placating ahead of him. "Oh, it's a parent's nature to worry. But believe me when I say you don't need to. No need! Okay?!"

Greta let loose a sputtering laugh, and Hannah wondered if Mr. Martin performed the same mollifying spiel for everyone who walked into this room.

Not exactly, as it turned out: he had less effusive things to say about the next couple's boy, who spent more time flicking the earlobes of the girl in front of him than solving math problems. Tiptoeing closer to eavesdrop, Hannah thought she noticed the boy's father flash the trace of a smile, apparently proud of his son's lack of mathematical vigor.

Less than ten minutes after she walked in, Mr. Martin ushered out the previous couple and grinned at Hannah, gesturing to the open seat at his desk. "Who's next?" he bellowed, which was something of a joke as they were the only two people left in the room.

"Hi," Hannah muttered as she approached.

"Hello, sorry to keep you waiting. Miss Dorian, I presume?" he asked in a vaguely comical faux-British accent.

Hannah nodded, her eyes flitting in every direction except at Mr. Martin. She had seen him before, of course—in a town the size of Grange, no one really stood outside the public congregation—but she didn't think she had ever spoken to him until now. Mr. Martin, though, addressed Hannah with that careful blend of reverence and pity to which she had grown overly accustomed. Everyone spoke to Hannah as though she were an old and intimate friend. *We've been through so much but triumphed*, their tone always seemed to say.

Her first three interlocutors that evening—Mr. Martin, followed by a young and boisterous science teacher named Mr. Ulmer and Amy's kindly, red-haired music instructor, Mrs. Fackelberg—played the same role. They may as well have been given the same script to follow. Hannah knew she was being snide and cynical, but after hearing for the third time that Amy was "a gift to be cherished" and "a fountain of unlimited potential," she would have found even the most heartfelt commendation half-assed. Of course Hannah smiled and shook hands warmly and could hardly protest when they told her how angelic her granddaughter was, but it was a good thing she didn't have to hold up her own end of the conversation. Words were failing her tonight, thoughts suffocating her.

By the time she left Mrs. Fackelberg's classroom (to yet another pronouncement that Amy was a prodigy on the piano bench), it was ten after eight. Glancing at the now-weathered schedule of Amy's classes in the hallway, she saw only two more instructors she was supposed to visit. One of them, she decided instantly, could be skipped; she had always hated gym class as a child and didn't need to hear about how active bodies support active minds.

The other name, though, loomed on that fading printout, inescapable. She told herself he wasn't really the reason she came tonight. She told herself in hushed yet vicious tones, "Go. Now. Time to go." She even folded the paper, put it in her jacket pocket, and spun on her heels to retreat in the direction of the exit.

After five steps, she halted. The quiet sound of jovial conversation floated down the hallway, close but far away. She had memorized his room number, 161. It was back in the other direction, at the end of the hallway. She remembered what he had said at church last weekend, reminding her of parent-teacher conferences: *It'll be good for you to go. We can talk and catch up.*

She spun on her feet again, running her hand through her hair. She walked quickly now, her pace escalating, as though driven by a force outside herself. She saw the open doorway near the end of the hallway, a sliver of light spilling out. And as she got closer, she saw the plastic letters screaming at her next to the doorway, *one-six-one.*

She stepped inside John Linden's English classroom, his name written in grand and authoritative cursive on the board, and discovered four other parents semi-patiently waiting to speak with him. Mr. Linden, though, now saw only Hannah: he noted her entrance from the corner of his eye, glanced at her with a spasm of excitement, swallowed, looked back at the husband and wife across from him, and grinned his best devilish smile. Hannah immediately regretted entering the room— there was now an unspoken thickness in the air, a gray unease between them—but she was also unable to leave. Unwilling, maybe, though Hannah suspected there wasn't much difference between the two.

Perhaps John Linden plowed through each of that night's conversations with the recklessness of a speed-dater, but Hannah doubted it. She inferred, with mounting anxiety, that he now wanted only to speak to her and treated every other parent in the room with an indifference bordering on hostility. Whatever the case, his next three

126

conversations lasted no more than a few minutes each. A herd of unfortunate parents and guardians were ushered from the room in dazed confusion, unsure whether Mr. Linden had lauded or lambasted their kids. John didn't care.

When the last husband and wife stepped numbly out the door, leaving John and Hannah alone together, Linden paused at the doorway, straightened his tie, exhaled and shut the door with an ear-splitting *click*.

He twisted his body to look at her and smiled. Hannah stood across the classroom, cowering where a pair of bookcases intersected, her hands folded in front of her. Realizing how demure she must have appeared, she arched her shoulders and planted her hands in her pockets. Linden finally pivoted, took three slow steps to the desk, and pulled out a chair for her, its legs screeching.

"Hannah. Have a seat, please."

She stayed where she was for now. "I'm just here to talk about Amy."

"I know." His voice was smooth and unctuous.

She reconsidered her words—what they meant to Linden. "How she's doing in school."

He greeted her leery gaze with a gentle smirk. "Sit down. We'll talk about it."

Unsure what else to do, Hannah walked to the green plastic chair in front of Linden's desk. She lowered herself onto the seat with as much grace as possible, her black coat billowing around her. After she had settled in and pulled her chair closer, Linden straightened his jacket and took his seat across from her. For a moment, there were no words—only a volley of glances, his sly and beseeching, hers narrowed and quizzical. He finally broke the silence, beginning with the headstrong fervor of a sales pitch.

"So, I'm glad you're here, Hannah. I really am. How have you been? Tell me."

"I've been okay, John, thank you," she said with a sigh. He nodded graciously, allowing her to continue. "How have you been?"

"Good. I've been good. It was great seeing you in church this weekend."

"Yes." She nodded, her skin crawling from the pretense of polite civility on display. "Yes it was."

"So!" Linden barked after another moment of torturous silence. He clasped his hands. "I bet you want to hear about Amy, don't you?"

Hannah swallowed and nodded.

"Well, what can I say?" Linden's reptilian smirk reappeared. "Such a bright girl. So *thoughtful*, as I know you can verify. Sure, I can see that English isn't her passion. I know she's a gifted musician, or so I've heard. And sometimes, you know, I wish she would devote a *tiny* ounce of the enthusiasm she has for the piano to—well, not just to my class, but to reading in general and writing about the way it makes her feel." Linden took a breather, using the moment of respite to inch closer to the desk. Hannah narrowed her eyes, caught somewhat off guard. She hadn't expected a word from Linden about Amy's classroom performance, much less an exhaustive analysis.

Linden continued: "That's the bad news. And it's not so bad. The good news, as you know, is that Amy never stops thinking about the world around her. She asks questions, she thinks critically. She participates in class discussions even when it's obvious she hasn't read the assignment. That curious, perceptive nature is *so* valuable, especially at her age. And that's something you can't teach." For a second it seemed he had finished his rundown, but when Hannah failed to respond, Linden said with arch sincerity: "It really is a pleasure having her in my class."

All Hannah could offer was a hesitant smile. "Well, that's good to hear."

"It is!" Linden bellowed. "It's good news. Were you expecting otherwise?"

"No!" Hannah shifted on her seat. "No, of course not."

"How is she at home, Hannah?"

She scoffed in response, unprepared for the question. "Well, she's great, of course. She's a good girl. As you've so glowingly proclaimed yourself."

Linden laughed and leaned back in his chair. He still wore the sugary smile, but Hannah thought she saw something different in his eyes. Something flintier, challenging her silently.

"She *is* a good girl. You're one-hundred percent right. You're lucky, Ms. Dorian."

Hannah nodded again—the gesture was becoming redundant—but there was worry in her eyes as a tear started to form. She blinked it back into submission. She gripped the sides of the chair and wanted to propel herself upwards, then instantaneously out the classroom door and back out the building, but something kept her from doing so. Something dark and brittle inside of her that was waging a war and quietly winning.

Linden spoke again before Hannah could rise to her feet. "But you don't see it that way, do you, Hannah? You wouldn't call yourself lucky by any stretch of the imagination. Would you?"

There was no holding back the stubborn tears this time. The war waged on.

"I think I'm lucky to be alive," she said at last.

Linden nodded thoughtfully. "That's true. Life is the greatest gift anyone can offer."

Suddenly the door lurched open to Linden's left, accompanied by the soft knocking of a portly young man and his wife. "Excuse us—John Linden, right? You're our last—"

"One minute!" Linden shouted with unmistakable ferocity. But he followed it with a sniveling laugh, got to his feet, and walked to the door, where he patted the young man lightly on the shoulder. "Private conversation, sorry, personal matters. Give me five minutes." He began closing the door on them before they had fully exited the room. "Please. Thanks. Thank you."

129

He slammed the door shut and returned to his desk, sitting with pronounced gravity. He closed his eyes and took a moment to gather his thoughts. "We *are* fortunate to be alive, Hannah, you're right. Think of everyone who's had life so cruelly taken away from them before it was their time. All the people we love that we're forced to say goodbye to. I mean, I can't even say I understand, Hannah, losing your child and then your husband. No one knows what that's like, no matter what they say to you. It's a terrible weight to bear. I can't even imagine the strength it takes."

Hannah was furious at herself for losing her composure in front of Linden, but her feelings of guilt were becoming smothered by hatred for this man. No matter how vulnerable she felt, she could detect Linden's masterful sales pitch—a routine, she suspected, he had long since honed for those on the brink of desperation. But could she honestly tell herself that his words had no truth to them? That ruthless voice inside of her agreed with Linden heartily, relishing his words and reminding Hannah how much she had lost. Lucky? More like she was the victim of a thousand hateful cosmic jokes. She had angered the gods and incited their wrath, their wicked sense of humor. That's how lucky she felt.

"I *am* strong, John." She steeled herself, her voice becoming barbed and defensive. "I don't care how much I've lost and how much it hurts, I'm not going to betray my family."

"Who said anything about betraying your family?" Linden replied with a spurned laugh. "I'm just saying, all this suffering for one human soul, it's not fair. It's too much." He glanced at the clock on the far side of the room; it read 8:45pm. In fifteen minutes, they'd be hurried out of the building whether or not they had completed any kind of transaction.

"The universe owes you something *good*, Hannah," he proclaimed. "Call it karma if you want. Some kind of infinite balance, the good and the bad—you take away, you give back. Whatever it is, you have an opportunity to grab hold of the happiness that you deserve. It was taken from you years ago, but now you can have it again. *You* have that chance."

Hannah shook her head no, hair whipping back and forth. "I know how it works," she said. "I can't. I owe it to Amy. I can't."

Linden leaned closer. His words were pleading. "*You* owe it to Amy? Why have you appointed yourself a saint, why do you deserve that? Answer me this, Hannah: what are *you* owed? Why can't you have the life you want?"

She had dammed her flow of tears but now a grim and vacant stare, trained on the dark-gray windows, had taken their place. "Not Amy, then. I owe it to my daughter. I owe it to Rebecca." She nodded her head decisively. "It gives her death meaning."

Linden tried for a lugubrious smile, an attempt at consolation. "You can give Rebecca something else, something infinitely more valuable. You can give her *life* again. She'll be there, by your side. The way it was supposed to be, before everything was taken from you. A miracle, Hannah."

She glared at John. "Playing God."

"Well, maybe you'd be better at the job, no?" In spite of herself, Hannah snickered and widened her eyes at Linden, who held up his hands in defense. "I know, I know—utter sacrilege. Especially for a God-fearing man like myself. But think of what he's done for you, Hannah. Has he been merciful? Benevolent, understanding? Or has he ripped away from you the people you love the most? Well, I know he has his reasons, but I sure as hell can't figure 'em out and I'm just about done trying. I think I'd be more comfortable with you playing God, honestly."

Hannah stared back at him, her eyes dim and glazed with wetness. She clutched her coat tightly around herself, but said nothing.

With ten minutes left until nine o'clock, Linden leaned back in his chair, reached toward the floor, and rifled around in a red leather attaché case by his feet. It appeared well-organized, a neat assortment of file folders and color-coded plastic tabs. His fingers brushed past a student's essay to retrieve a single manila folder from the bowels of the briefcase.

Turning back to the desk with a groan, Linden placed the folder on its surface and nudged it toward Hannah with a cool, fluid movement. Her eyelids fluttered, eliciting another grin from Linden's lips. "I'm offering this to you, Hannah, for your perusal. It's not an agreement, it's not binding. It's for your own curiosity. Read it over, see what the process actually entails. You might be surprised, it's very painless. If you decide not to go through with it, great—no hard feelings. You and Amy keep on living the way you have been. But if you read through it and find the arrangement agreeable—well, you know where to find me. I'm always available."

Hannah sat there, made of stone, her eyes shifting between Linden's supplicant smile and the plain manila folder. A clock echoed somewhere in the room. She saw shadows on the other side of the door. Her right hand shot out almost of its own volition, clutched the folder and brought it to her side. She felt shame immediately, though not enough to loosen her grasp.

She rose to her feet just as abruptly, shot a piercing look at Linden, and tried to muster the energy to provide the usual niceties and salutations—but it seemed vulgar at this point. She spun on her heels and thundered toward the door, heaving it open and bursting from the room. She almost ran over the two twenty-something parents waiting in the hallway, both of them clad in dull, ill-fitting sweaters. Hannah was several steps from the classroom before Linden even made it to the open doorway, calling gently after her.

"She really is wonderful, Ms. Dorian. An absolute angel."

As soon as he said so, he noticed the two young parents standing by his doorway, looking at him expectantly. "Well!" huffed the young father irritably. "Some conversation the two of you had there."

"Oh. Yes, well," Linden stuttered, clearly having forgotten the two of them were waiting for him. "Your son is great. Real hard worker."

"Oh, actually it's our daughter in your cla—," said the mother, though that's as far as she got.

"Bright kid, promising future. Keep it up."

Before either of them could say another word, the door to Linden's classroom slammed shut.

Hannah heard it close behind her, the thud resounding in her ears, deafening. She felt a black smog hovering over her as she walked, a cloud of self-loathing that she thought was obvious to everyone around her. She felt tears lingering on her cheeks. A girls' restroom appeared to Hannah's right; she ducked into it, analyzing herself in the mirror for traces of mascara or bags puffed out beneath her eyes. She straightened her hair and splashed icy water on her face, committing one final close-up inspection. Until recently, she had considered herself lucky that she'd aged so gracefully, the silver specks in her hair and dotted freckles complementing her sharp cheekbones and marble skin. By now, though, there was nothing pleasurable in the face that stared back at her from the mirror. Unable to scrutinize herself any longer, she turned and left the room, turning off the lights on the way out.

*****

Hannah returned home at half past nine, each movement slow and robotic. There was a firestorm raging in her head; she tried and failed to tame the thoughts that formed in a black hole somewhere inside her.

Amy was in her bedroom, a single lamp glowing on a nightstand. She lay on a red-and-white checkered bedspread, large headphones dwarfing her tiny head, drowning out the world. Aside from the stack of sheet music scattered on her bookshelf, no one would guess this was the bedroom of a musical savant; by all appearances it was the room of a preteen girl, the airbrushed faces of pop starlets beaming from posters, fantasy paperbacks and pastel-colored clothes thrown into heaps on the floor.

Hannah opened her door as she knocked lightly, knowing Amy wouldn't hear her anyway—she liked her music loud. At once, Amy pulled off her headphones, an up-tempo rhythm barely audible. She tossed her cellphone aside; a time-wasting puzzle game glowed on the screen, interspersed with text messages from her best friend, Katie.

Hannah smiled sadly from the doorway.

"Hi."

"Hey, Grandma," Amy said, unable to hide the fact that she was not in the mood for conversation.

Hannah took this as permission to enter. She tiptoed over the carpet, sidestepping a stray Lego.

"How you doin'?" Amy shrugged. "Mind if we talk?"

Amy didn't have an answer for this, simply returning Hannah's pleading stare. It had been a while—months, at least—since her grandmother had attempted one of these profound heart-to-hearts. But Hannah found it difficult to find the words tonight, so Amy broke the silence: "How were conferences? What did Mr. Martin say? I told you it would go bad, I *hate* math…"

"No," Hannah interrupted her, "no, they were great. Your teachers love you, everyone loves you." Amy smiled, allowing Hannah to continue. "No, I…it got me thinking about your mom. We haven't talked about her in a while."

"I don't like talking about her," Amy said. She had a habit of speaking harshly all of a sudden, in that brusque, adult way that implies that conversation just makes everything worse.

"Don't you want to know about her?"

Amy looked away. Her voice sounded lonely when she spoke, but of course it often did.

"Grandma, I never knew Mom. You can tell me all about her, but…it doesn't mean anything to me."

Hannah swallowed roughly, remembering now why she'd given up on these earnest recollections.

"You and Grandpa didn't really take pictures of her. I don't know what she was like, I never met her. She's just...a stranger." Still, Hannah said nothing. "I feel like you want me to love her, but I can't."

There was a long pause after this, filled only with the sound of muted pop music, which Amy quickly silenced. Finally, Hannah gave it another effort.

"Amy, I just want to know what you're feeling. I can't read your mind, you know. And I can imagine how hard it is for you, only having me around. I know that's not what you would have wanted."

Amy shrugged again, a gesture that summed up her entire worldview. "It doesn't matter. You can't always have what you want."

"It matters to me." The tears came now, a show of emotion that Hannah tried to disguise, and she leaned toward Amy on the bed. "I need to know what you want out of life, Amy. I don't want you to be unhappy."

"I'm *not* unhappy," Amy replied with more conviction than Hannah expected. "I'm fine, Grandma. I don't care if everything isn't perfect. That kind of life is just...make-believe. But I don't like talking about it. I've told you that *thousands* of times," she said with a dramatic eye-roll, for the first time sounding like the twelve-year-old that she was.

Hannah nodded slowly. Amy was right, of course—she couldn't argue with anything she said. This realization, though, always made it more difficult. It became obvious that these conversations were for Hannah's benefit only, a desperate attempt to feel that she wasn't alone, stranded with her memories. She cried harder. There were no tears from Amy—only a sad sympathy for her grandmother and a pain she couldn't quite know. She contorted on the bed, shifting her legs beneath her, and wrapped her arms around Hannah, trying to offer a tiny shred of solace. She behaved like someone three times her age, as she had been forced to do for much of her life.

At that moment, feeling Amy's arms around her, a tremor of fear passed through Hannah's body, a chill that she couldn't suppress. For it was then that she realized Amy's embrace meant nothing to her. There was no joy or comfort in it—only a bitter desire that it was her own daughter's arms enveloping her instead.

Chapter 15 — The Road of Dreams

There is a trail, wide and unpaved, stretching uphill and to the left, to the west. He ambles along it, slow and tranquil; time is not an issue, it stretches on, endless. The hill slopes upward and the trail disappears behind a thin veil of trees. It looks like the path continues to rise from here, taking leave of the earth, stretching toward the sun.

Where am I?

He trudges on, heavy boots scraping against the gravel and grass. There are other footsteps, softer, pattering behind him. He wants to turn around but his body disobeys his mind. In the twisted logic of dreams, though, he is able to slow his pace, waiting for his companions to join him.

Ben realizes now this isn't a dream, or not entirely. It's something closer to a memory, a fragment from an infinite timeline whose shapes and forms have been disfigured. They've been coming to him frequently of late, whenever he drifts to sleep. Even so, this particular memory coalesces, becomes concrete: a hiking trail just north of Milwaukee, a little more than a year ago, one of the first weeks of September.

The footsteps come closer until he is joined by two people. Not just people—those he loves, his kindred, he can feel their souls buzzing. Sarah and Aaron appear to his right, laughing at a joke he doesn't know. It's sunny but cold enough for a winter coat; Sarah's is deep red and trails beneath a gray scarf and hat, her light hair tumbling out, blowing in the wind. Aaron is four years old, his cheeks still padded with baby fat. Sarah's hand hovers next to Aaron's, palm open, but Aaron has now mastered the art of walking and takes pride in his staggering shuffle.

I remember this, every second. A bee, angry at the changing seasons, darts around Aaron and lands on his shoulder. His eyes grow wide and he swats at the air while shrieking. Sarah and I laugh. Thankfully, it flies away without stinging him. A cold tear stalls on his face, and almost as soon as it dries Aaron is happy again, smiling as Sarah kneels next to him, pinching his arm.

"Don't worry, it's just a bee," I tell him, still working on my fatherly voice. "He's not gonna hurt you unless you scare him. They're here just like you are, enjoying the scenery." He doesn't understand, gazing at me with a question on his face, and his smile wavers.

It happens exactly as Ben remembers, even now, replayed on the inside of closed eyelids. The three of them continue walking, Aaron shuffling ahead, Ben and Sarah reveling in the sight of their son, hands entwined.

They reach the top of the hill, and this is where something seems different. *What's wrong?* Ben shudders, suddenly watchful and alert in his sleep. The top of the hill has grown colder and the sound of birds has died. Aaron walks ahead but he seems to be sprinting, or maybe Ben and Sarah have slowed to an imperceptible pace. The clouds have amassed, gathering strength. Ben looks down at a sprawling valley, carpeted with waist-high grass and bordered by green hills.

There is something in the valley. A distant black shape slithering through the grass. Ben squints. It wears something, a cloak, a massive looming hood. It is walking south but changes direction, turns as though levitating, inching toward them. Aaron walks ahead oblivious, but Ben and Sarah have spotted it.

He glances at her—she is both vivid and hazy, her features sharp one moment and fading the next—and sees terror on her face. They step closer to one another, trembling.

He looks back and the thing is gone. It has cut a narrow path through the grass, the leaves smothered and bent, but the creature has vanished.

He takes a step away from Sarah, then a second and third, his feet lurching into action, and the ground changes beneath him. There's now a rough bed of grass pillowing his every step. It's colder here. Sarah is nowhere to be found. The sun cuts through the canopy, thinning in the cold.

They're in the heart of the woods, retracing their favorite path, Aaron stumbling thirty feet ahead. Ben tries to sprint, hoping to join his son, but all he can muster is a lazy jog. The distance between them never lessens.

He sees Aaron round a bend in the hiking trail. They have covered this ground ten, twenty, thirty times, but it now seems alien, dark and treacherous. Over a weedy swamp a rickety boardwalk curves, four feet wide and dotted with fragile knots in the ancient wood. The jagged boards have been coated with an icy sheen.

Aaron steps onto it. His blue coat disappears behind a dying bush. Ben plods over the frigid ground, each step slower, slower.

When he rounds the bend he sees him, Aaron, planting his tiny foot onto the wood. There is a thin puddle there, invisible. His leg swings out from under him. His arms flail, a flightless bird plummeting. His body falls over the bridge and into the pond, icy water swallowing Aaron as though starved.

Ben tries to scream. He drops to his knees. He is able to crawl, plowing through the dirt, to the bridge, to the place where his son has vanished. His hands grip the edge of the wood. He looks over the side. Aaron sinks slowly, his pale face stretched toward the dimming sky.

Ben squints into the water.

What is this? What is this?

He sees an army of gray-white hands reaching from the depths, disembodied, grasping at the boy as he plummets toward them. Aaron hits the sandy floor of the pond, a cloud of dust floating, spreading, rising, obscuring the arms and hands reaching up from nothing and dragging him below.

A rhythmic beeping, slow and sickening. Aaron is somewhere else now. His body lies still, a hospital bed beneath him. Aaron's clothes, his blue-and-yellow coat with the large hood and tiny, frozen jeans, have been replaced by a short white hospital gown, covered with light blue dots. The most terrifying image, a scene to stop your heart and squeeze your lungs: the sight of your child intubated, arms attached to spindly IVs, prone on a hospital bed. Pulse and respiration denoted on small flat screens, a life conveyed in lines and shapes.

Someone speaks behind Ben, a voice that's kind and grave, but all he can see is Aaron's closed eyes, his pale skin damp with sweat.

The disembodied voice becomes muffled and distorted.

"...Aaron is afflicted with something called acute lymphoblastic leukemia. It's not uncommon in children his age. I'm sorry to say it can be a very painful experience, as you've already seen. This current bout of pneumonia is a direct result of the leukemia. Essentially, Aaron's bone marrow simply can't produce the blood cells he needs..."

God damn your voice. Just stop talking. Stop talking.

Even now, all over again, he tries to stay calm, he tries to be strong, and even in dreams he cannot, it's too much.

The voice rises again, though it's becoming garbled, incomprehensible.

"The good news—and there is good news—is that it's very possible to cure. About eighty per"—this is where the words cut out, becoming impossible noises and sharp, pulsing drones—"ing to be difficult, but it can be done. Unfortunately, we're going to need to start Aaron on a rather intense regimen of chemotherapy to see how his body han—"

And now the world is dark. Now it's Ben who lies on the hospital bed, his eyes closed under fiery lights in a black anaesthetized void. It's a calm place, not of dreams but of medically induced stupor, free of pain. But he stands outside of himself and he knows what he's going to see, he's had this dream many times. He inches toward the hospital bed, a ghost in the shadows. He sees his inner thigh cut open and spread apart; sees the immense needle plunging through muscle and into his pelvic bone, a tiny camera affixed to the end relaying a grisly image to a small screen in the operating room. In his sleep, Ben feels a tremendous pain radiate through his body, but it's not enough to wake him. The needle finds the innermost part of his bone, into his marrow, it steals his cells away, and six months later Ben will find that it makes no difference anyway.

His eyes blink open. It's late June, oppressively hot. He finds himself in a tiny kitchen, its walls white and sweating and lined with floral wallpaper. The kitchen is small but blissful, or at least it was once. The shadows dancing on the walls are eerie—night looms outside the window but a strange light like sunshine pours through.

Sarah. Don't tell me this again. I can't bear to hear it.

But of course she does, and he does. He hears her words even though the lips don't match—a split-second delay, as if from a television broadcast. The sound comes from elsewhere.

"I need you *here*," she says. "I need you with me, Ben. We both need help."

The lights dim, then flash again, angry. The face is not Sarah's, it belongs to someone else. Maria. This is a nightmare he has not yet had.

"I know you're in pain," she says. "I am too. But you can't do this to me, I need you. Be strong."

She leans forward, speaking in quiet tones, realizing the weight of the words she utters. Sarah, Maria. They melt into each other as the lights flicker.

"If you can't...you know this, Ben, it'll be easier without you. Just...you need to let me in."

The lights go out. There is a canyon lined with red rocks. A lake of liquid fire, teeming with horrible life. Ben soars over it, falling closer, closer.

You need to let me in.

*****

141

When he woke from his dream there was no sitting bolt upright in bed, no violent gasp of wakefulness. His eyes simply fluttered open as he gripped the corners of the pillow. It was still dim outside but a sharp light peeked over the roof of the motel, the sun cutting into the parking lot. It was early, almost seven, on Friday morning.

With a long sigh, Ben swung his legs over the side of the bed and rubbed his eyes. His head was swimming, body shaking, though more from the cold than any lingering memory of his nightmare—which, in fact, had already begun to fade. Ben felt healthy, actually, despite the memory of Maria haunting him—clear-minded for the first time in days, though a mild headache still crept to the surface. To be expected, he thought, as he gingerly prodded the black-purple bruise above his eye.

A morning run had long been his preferred method for mental detox, the colder and more bracing the better. Still half-asleep, he rummaged through his bag and found two beat-up sneakers and a ragged pair of sweatpants.

The air that morning was clear and stark, and its sharpness cut through Ben as he forced himself into a quick jog. He realized all over again the beauty of the land—its rolling hills lined with autumn leaves, the gentle song of the lake water lapping nearby—and was almost able to silence his thoughts entirely. His usual five-mile jog lasted only half the distance this time; after a mile, the world started to spin and he slowed his pace, his feet following one after the other robotically. He returned to the motel twenty minutes later, hobbling but invigorated.

As he stood under a scalding spray of shower water soon after—reminding him of those high-powered heat guns designed to strip away layers of paint—something like a plan of action cohered. Aside from Nathan Amherst and John Linden, there was a third elusive suspect that might be able to provide answers: the town of Grange itself, whose secrets had only begun to crawl into light.

The motel's water pressure was more than adequate, but its rumbling heating system and sparse insulation permitted the icy morning air to enter the room unimpeded. Ben dressed quickly, rifling through his suitcase until he found a pair of light jeans and a loose black sweater—it made him look dashing and nondescript at once, or so he hoped. He threw on a bulky gray jacket and stepped out the door.

Part of him feared there would be no funeral for Maria, especially if they had already held a ceremony after her car accident seven months ago (his head ached at the mental gymnastics this particular strain of logic required). But he also sensed that Grange was a tight-knit community weaned on centuries of tradition. If the whole town did know of whatever chaos reigned in the woods, something like a funeral ceremony would provide exactly the moral absolution they needed—a way to believe that they were still pious in the shadow of the darkness nearby. If only for the sake of appearances, Ben guessed, there would be an arbitrary service.

There was only one church in town—he had seen it two days ago when he first drove in, its steeple keeping watch over the rest of the buildings. But it would be foolish, he knew, to simply stroll in and ask about Maria's funeral. As Arnold had said, everyone knew everyone here in Grange. The clergy would not readily spout information to a nosy stranger wearing a bulbous purple mass over his left eye.

Before heading into town, Ben walked to the motel's front desk four doors away. When he swung open the office door, the blinds shuddered and a gust of wind trickled inside. The room was vacant but the sizzle of frying eggs could be heard behind a doorway, accompanied by the scent of bacon and the sounds of a classic-rock radio station turned down low. Ben tapped the bell on the front desk, sending a vibrato ring through the office. At once, he heard the radio diminish and a few plodding footsteps approached the front room.

"Hello?" the man asked from around the corner. When he entered the room, dressed in a grease-stained apron covering a ratty white sweater, there was no mistaking the look of dismay as he spotted Ben at the desk. "Oh, it's you. Anything wrong?"

"No, no. Nothing's wrong. Smells great." Ben nodded his head toward the kitchen around back.

"Yup." There was an awkward silence, which the deskman reticently broke. "You know, it's not really a continental breakfast kind of place, but I can whip something up for you. If you want."

Ben grinned. "No, thanks. I just have a question. I'm wondering if you know the church in town, I forget the name of it."

The man eyed him crookedly but answered. "Sure. Holy Angels. It's at the southeast edge downtown."

"You, uh—you don't happen to know the phone number, do you?"

"Why do you ask?"

Ben shrugged. "Maybe you wouldn't think so, but I've always been religious. Used to go to church three, four times a week. It's less now—life gets in the way, you know—but I was hoping they'd have a service sometime today. Or I could just spend some time with the Lord, one on one. Considering everything that's happened here recently..."

"You're a police officer, right? From Milwaukee?"

Ben's smile faltered. "Yeah. Why?"

"That's what Chief Arnold told me. You know, I thought you were in town for a fishing trip, but I guess that's not the case. Is it?"

Ben nodded and shuffled his feet. "It is, yeah. That was the plan. Everything else that happened is just...coincidence. Believe me, I could have done without it."

They stood on opposite sides of the desk, appraising each other. The spatter of eggs and bacon escalated. Finally, Ben tapped the desk with his fingertips and stepped away.

"Look, you don't trust me. I get it, it's okay. I know where the church is, I'll go check it out. I was just hoping to save myself a trip."

"So you're staying a while longer?"

"Just a day or two. I'm already here, figure I might as well. Don't worry, I'll be out of your hair by Monday." Taking a risk, Ben pivoted and pushed on the door with the heel of his hand—but, as he hoped,

144

he heard the deskman's voice call to him as he stepped onto the sidewalk.

"Hey, wait."

Ben froze, pulled his leg back inside, and let the door shut behind him. He looked at the man.

"Sorry…you know, I'm just a little shook up still."

"I hear you."

As he stepped back into the room, Ben saw him flip through an antiquated Rolodex, hands shaking. At last, two fingers came to rest on a single scrap of paper, which he jerked from the Rolodex in one curt movement.

"Can't say no to a praying man. Here you go." He handed Ben the hole-punched index card, which was scrawled with the name Reverend Simon Scariot and a septet of numbers, followed by the words Holy Angels—the last of which taunted Ben in their incongruity. Ben already had his phone in his hand and spoke while he focused on the screen. "Thanks, I'm really sor—"

When he looked up, the man was gone. He had likely regained his post at the stove in the cramped kitchen, spatula in hand, overcooked eggs stuck to a weathered frying pan.

Ben stepped outside a moment later. His sorry-looking Jeep stood less than twenty feet away, beckoning, but Ben zipped up his jacket and walked away to the north, eager to acclimate himself to the town of Grange on foot. By the time he made it to the sloping, gravel-covered shoulder, he had already dialed Reverend Scariot's number. The phone was glued to the side of his head, a dial tone screaming back at him. It rang twelve times before Ben's thumb drifted to the disconnect button, but finally someone answered—a low, impatient voice, uttering an emphatic "Yes?"

Ben sought a frank, familiar tone, calling Reverend Scariot by name and asking when Maria's funeral might be. He thought he heard a din of movement and preparation in the background—the sound, perhaps, of funeral arrangements being made. Reverend Scariot, apparently flustered, provided the answer with more readiness than Ben anticipated: the funeral was to take place the next morning at eleven. Then there was a shuffling noise and what sounded like a long, painful swallow on the other end, after which Scariot promptly hung up.

Ben returned his phone to his pocket and raised his eyes to the forest scenery. He squinted into the open air—the wrinkle of his eyes made him wince in pain, reminding him that his injuries were nowhere close to healed—and felt like he was venturing into unknown territory. He vaguely remembered the route he had taken to the motel two nights ago and set off north along the shoulder of the narrow road. To his right, he could hear the gentle throb of Sarona Lake, though it lurked barely out of sight beyond the forest. Across the road to his left there was a long, flat plateau, its yellow-brown grass waving in the wind, a few young trees rising from the ground. Seeing saplings like these always comforted Ben. How had they gotten here? Seeds dropped by birds or tossed about by unruly winds, burrowing beneath the soil and sprouting, against all logic, alone among the cowering grass. He had to admire the unlikelihood.

The air warmed as Ben walked on, sending a pleasant chill up his spine. The sunlight turned from stunning early-morning gold to burnt-yellow. The lakeside road only stretched for another half-mile, at which point it intersected with a wide boulevard. He turned left and walked away from the sun, spotting Grange's quiet downtown district a few blocks ahead. Houses lined the road here, tall and narrow, newer than the farmhouses that dotted the outskirts of town but still dating back almost a century. Big Wheels lay on their side in front yards, American flags fluttered obligatorily, mailboxes stood guard at the end of pockmarked driveways, emblazoned with address numbers and family surnames. "The Neustadts," read one, betraying the area's pervasive German heritage.

There were two antique stores, a dentist's office, a small appliance store touting its specials on flat-screen TVs in the front window. Ben passed a few people on his jaunt into town, one of them walking an immense St. Bernard that slobbered affably upon seeing him. The humans, on the other hand, regarded him with a wary smile and a twisted glance, inspecting the stranger they had never seen wandering Grange's sidewalks.

It was around eight by the time he arrived downtown, and the temperature had escalated to a steady forty degrees. It would be in the low thirties by the time night descended. There was something electric, Ben thought, about his aimlessness—it was as though he could feel the town, its heavy air and unspoken secrets, seeping into his skin as he walked.

It didn't take long for Ben to find Grange's public library, a one-story brick building in a drab square shape, sandwiched between a coffeeshop that epitomized quaint (Cuppa Joe was its unfortunate name) and Grange's one and only supermarket. There was a small signboard placed in front of the library's entrance, which currently spelled in black plastic letters, "Trick or Treating. Saturday 3pm. Be Safe!" Ben had completely forgotten about Halloween, which had once, long ago, been his favorite holiday, an occasion that invited people to experience terror—a displaced and cathartic fear well-loved by those unaccustomed to trauma.

Ben pulled open the library's front door and stepped inside. The heat was working overtime, blasting the entryway with a torrent of musty air. Immediately, Ben unzipped his jacket, licked his fingers, and smoothed his close-cut hair along its edges. On the way in, he passed a glass case populated with pamphlets and local advertisements, double-checking his blurry reflection as he did so. Aside from the bruised mass protruding from the upper-left portion of his face, he was satisfied.

The library was small but inviting; it wasn't just the 74-degree setting on the thermostat that made you want to spend the entire day here. The main room was nearly vacant save for an elderly woman perched on a chair near the windows, holding a book on her lap with a trashy-romance cover, the kind illustrated with a half-naked man who boasted impossibly broad pectorals. Ben scanned the room further, spying a thin man with black hair, a gigantic Adam's apple, and an impassive expression at the front desk. He was dutifully stamping checkout cards with the meticulous rhythm of an assembly-line minion. It wasn't his appearance that Ben distrusted but his air of stolid professionalism, a sense that he had been working here for decades and resented any kind of intrusion.

There seemed to be no one else in the library, however, and Ben guessed that he might have to try his luck with the librarian at the front desk. Then he heard a noise behind a shelf of non-fiction books, nothing more than a soft thud as a hard-covered text plummeted to the carpet. Ben slid to his left and saw someone, a young woman, standing by a cart, placing a book in the lowermost row with time-biding exactitude. She wore a white turtleneck and long black skirt. Her light brown hair was laced into a disheveled ponytail, her gray eyes magnified by rimless eyeglasses. She looked young, Ben noted, in her early twenties, and it was her possibly reckless youth that appealed to him; he hoped she was craving a newness, a hint of danger, that the community's more entrenched members had long ago dismissed as folly.

Ben tiptoed over the gray-white carpet (nevertheless attracting the disdain of the woman by the windows) and cleared his throat. He donned his most shameless matinee-idol smirk as he approached, noting the lack of a wedding ring on her finger. *How do you innocently flirt with a stranger?* he wondered as he roused his confidence from its ruinous state. He hadn't faced such a challenge since Sarah.

"Excuse me." He took a final step and knelt down next to her, resting his elbow on his outstretched knee. "I, uh, I'm sorry to bother you."

She spoke to him without looking up, training her attention on the spine of a book called *The Road of Dreams*. "What are you looking for?"

"Well…it might be an odd request, I guess. That's why I'm…sorry for the bother."

She glanced up at him, prepared to offer a terse reply, but her expression softened when she saw him. Whether it was the forced twinkle in his eye or the oily smile that he smeared across his face, she seemed suddenly more interested in the stranger kneeling before her.

"What can I help you find?" Her tone was different this time—easier, more suggestive.

"Well, some books—you probably could've guessed that." He smiled and she laughed a bubbly response. The cynic in him was bristling. "Some rare books, I think. Historical books."

Breathless, he waited for her response, fearing she would assume an armor of suspicion. Instead she scanned him with her eyes, smirking, uncertain but intrigued. "I've never seen you before."

"Nope," he said with a laugh.

"What are you doing in Grange?"

"Research."

"Quite a shiner you got there." She nodded at the misshapen black eye.

"Yeah. You know, just defending a woman's honor, saving a school bus full of children, the usual."

This elicited a bright laugh from the librarian, who placed a book on the circulation cart and offered Ben a burning look. She raised herself upright, towering above him. As he rose, Ben realized with self-reproach that he was already feverish in the young woman's company. A painful malady that had afflicted him since his teens: he fell in love (or call it lust) within minutes of meeting someone, feeling beholden to them somehow, shackled by his desire.

"So, research?" she asked.

Ben stood next to her, placing his hands in his pockets. "Yeah, I—well, first I want to know your name."

Another laugh. "Why do you want to know my name?"

"Don't you want to know mine?"

She shrugged, enjoying the gamesmanship. "I feel mostly indifferent at the thought."

"I'll tell you anyway. I'm Ben." He extended his hand, hoping there was no trace of sweat, and was thrilled to feel her skin as it embraced his.

"I guess I have to return the favor now, is that right?"

"Yeah, exactly."

"Lara." She said it with a smile. The name unsettled Ben, though he didn't know why. "Research, huh?" she asked again.

"Yeah. Yeah, I'm studying at Madison."

"Uh-huh. So, that black eye, that's not from a barfight or anything, right?" She asked him with a trace of jealousy, a raucous life she would probably never experience.

Ben smiled. "You got me."

"What are you studying?"

Ben remembered what Arnold had told him two days ago while a gaping sinkhole strangled his attention: it was a geological minefield, a marvel of the earth's diversity.

"Geology."

"Ah. Yeah, we've had some geologists up here."

"You have?"

"Sarona Lake is a….well, it's a unique environment."

"Yes. Yeah, it is. Actually, though, I'm kind of a double major. History and geology. You know, it's not just the science that interests me. It's the history of a place, the story it tells. How the past shapes the present in ways that many scientists don't care to analyze. You know what I mean?"

She nodded, her eyebrows raised. "Sure. The life of a place."

"Exactly."

"What kind of historical books are you looking for?"

"Well, Lara, the reason my research brought me to Grange is because the bedrock is so unusual here." He was getting into the role, enjoying the part he'd assigned himself to play. He took a step closer as he spoke. "Most of this part of the state has a—"

"*Shhhhh!*" Their conversation was interrupted by a grating noise. They looked behind Ben to find the other librarian, tight-lipped and casting a severe glare, standing at the end of the aisle like one of Kafka's doorkeepers. Lara grabbed Ben by the elbow and dragged him in the opposite direction.

"Sorry," she said in a raspy whisper as they walked away.

The two of them skulked down the aisle and rounded it to the right, where a heavy door was embedded in the wall, a blinking exit sign above it. Before Ben could say anything, Lara heaved open the door and brought him into the stairwell, which wallowed in a creamed-corn color.

"I think I should apologize—," Ben began.

"No, you shouldn't. Lyle's sweet but he takes his job a little too seriously, you know?"

Ben laughed. As Lara skidded down the stairs in front of him, Ben followed and watched her ponytailed hair bob and bounce as she moved.

"You were saying?"

"What?"

"You were telling me about Grange's rich geological history," she said with a trace of sarcasm.

"Oh," Ben chuckled. "Well I was just saying, much of the area has a strong bedrock, thanks to the glaciers that passed through during the Ice Age. But around here, the ground is very weak, sort of porous. Why is that? What happened here to transform the earth? That's what I want to find out." He was making it all up as he went on, of course, but hoped her knowledge of geology was middling at best.

They reached the bottom of the stairwell. Lara pushed open another door and held it for Ben as he followed. The lights here were dim, almost nonexistent, casting grayness over everything in the basement. The cavernous feel seemed appropriate: there were stacks of books, maps, microfilm, newspapers, the infinite signifiers of a history told in scraps and fragments.

"I don't know exactly what you're looking for, but it's probably down here somewhere."

He looked around the room, wide-eyed. A fluorescent light flickered overhead; a sound like a bug-zapper sputtered from the ceiling. Lara continued.

"We haven't finished an electronic catalog for everything down here. I don't think we're ever going to," she admitted over her shoulder. "But we still have a Dewey system for all of it." She pointed at a chest of drawers shoved into the far corner of the basement, which, Ben would soon discover, was overwhelmed with cards of various information, haphazardly organized into something resembling a coherent system.

"What exactly am I looking at?" Ben asked.

Lara turned back to him. Her eyes glinted with an intrigue she clearly relished. "Diaries, journals from the town's founders. Early maps. News articles dating back to the 1890s. You're looking at the past."

Ben smiled at her; there was nothing artificial about the warmth he exuded this time. "Lara, thank you—thank you, thank you, this is more than I could have asked for."

She grinned and resituated her glasses, which had become crooked. "I'll be upstairs if you need anything." She stepped past him and, at the doorway, turned one last time. "Also…I know you need citations, that's fine, but don't tell anyone where you found them. I'm not really supposed to let anyone down here."

Before Ben could thank her again, she spun around and walked up the stairs, letting the door close behind her.

For a paralyzing moment Ben stood in the middle of the room, unsure how to proceed. He was surrounded by a million traces of an unspeakable history, one that he was sure held its own dark secrets. A file cabinet hidden in the corner first caught his eye. It was covered with a label (or, more accurately, a name scrawled in black Sharpie over masking tape) reading GRANGE HERALD, 1890–1899. This seemed as appropriate a starting point as any.

The cabinet drawers contained compact rolls of microfilm stuffed into tiny cardboard boxes. Many of the rolls of film were unspooled and severely damaged, bent and fragile and reeking with a vinegar smell—hardly surprising for microfilm housed in a file cabinet for decades. The microfiche itself had a rickety motor and a dwindling lightbulb, but Ben was pleasantly surprised to find that it functioned at all.

The only problem was the tedium of the newspapers' contents, from county fairs boasting the state's largest pumpkin to the dairy-farming practices that might compensate for the erratic fertility of the region's soil. One name kept reappearing: the town's founder, Matthias Grange, a German immigrant who had settled on the southern shores of Sarona Lake in 1851. He had stayed there even after his wife and two daughters died from undisclosed causes.

Having mostly exhausted the mundane history of the *Grange Herald*, Ben stumbled over to the card catalog that Lara had pointed out, sidestepping stacks of file folders and yellowing papers. He began rifling through its contents. After at least ten minutes of frenetic searching, he began to decode the catalog's system of subject, author, and title. He hunted down as much information as he could regarding the esteemed Matthias Grange. It was ten-thirty by the time he uncovered a small stack of papers relating to the town's founder, including—most promisingly—a series of journals that Matthias himself had penned from 1851 to his death in 1862.

Ben placed Matthias Grange's earliest journal in front of him, the rigid brown leather crackling with each movement. As he drew open the front cover, sending a fine cloud of dust and a sharp, sour odor into the air, Ben squinted at the fading ink on withered pages. Of course, Ben thought with a shiver—these pages were marked more than one hundred fifty years ago. They were legible nonetheless, and Ben was thankful that Matthias had chosen his adopted language of English to record his sordid history.

Chapter 16 — The Story of Matthias Grange

9 MAY, 1851. I fear, after travelling through much of this State during 'mild' Spring Months, that my Family has been forced to settle in hostile Terrain. The Land is certainly beautiful and diverse; long Plateaus suitable for sowing abridge dense Forests and Bodies of Water, providing ample Irrigation. However, our Journey has taken us to every farflung corner of this Place. Much of the ideal Farmland is already occupied or much too costly, and as such, we have finally settled after the fertilest planting dates for Corn have passed us by. The coarse Soil to be found here makes me doubt whether our Fall Harvest will prepare us for the brutal Winter Months I know await. Therese is patient and abiding; she has a Faith I have long since lost.

I have purchased fifty Kilograms of Corn Seed from a man in a nearby Town called Springbrook; a fellow German by the Name of Hans Weller, I do trust him to be an honest Salesman (I hope for Reasons beyond national Brotherhood). Despite my Misgivings, it is a lush and pliant Land, Therese and I are happy and busy ourselves often, and the thrill of being in a new World compensates for my ceaseless worry.

Ben's fingers skipped over brittle pages, his eyes searching for something vile and out-of-place—something to explain what kind of evil had taken root here. There followed a series of mundane journal entries, pertaining mostly to the founding of the Granges' farm and the planting of the summer corn crop. At last he came to rest on a passage two months later.

31 JULY, 1851. Therese and I are with Child. I have discovered this today. Of course I feel Joy and Wonder at this news, and yet I cannot help but feel that God has tormented me. We have tried for Years and Years to bear Child, we have taken medicinal Roots and charted Fertility Periods, yet in our native Land we proved forever barren. Now, less than a year in the new World, we find ourselves suddenly bearing Life—just as I am tortured by the Possibility that we will be unable to support it if our Crop does not bear Harvest. Therese and I have built a beautyful Home for ourselves—it is a large Farmhouse with one hundred twenty Acres of Land adjacent, and a dense Forest separating us from a Lake of surprising Size and Depth—and I know I should thank Fate for providing us with temporary Solace. Yet now I know that I will soon be responsible for the Human Life that I've borne, a feeling of Dread overwhelms me.

2 OCTOBER, 1851. God has smiled upon us—our Crop is bountyful. Nearly all of our springtime Harvest has matured, and we've almost recouped our Investment already. I have journeyed to Spooner last week and sold a Bulk of our Corn at their Autumn Market; another will take place in four Weeks' Time. I must say I am surprised by the Land's Fertility. The Conditions of the Area, its Climate and its Soil, did not seem conducive to such Growth. Of course, I hope my incredulity does not suggest a lack of Gratitude.

With Therese expecting Child, I have hired two Farmhands from the Town of Hayward, a Pair of young Brothers who work efficiently and rarely converse with us outside of the Fields. We have planted our Winter Wheat and hope it to be as fertile as the Corn we have grown. If, God willing, our Harvest of Wheat is similarly rich, I do not tremble at the thought of bringing new Life into the Home we have made for ourselves.

In the library basement, Ben continued to flip through the pages of the journal, which spanned a timeframe of nearly two years. Matthias' entries became more infrequent as the demands of corn and wheat farming, paired with the arrival of new life, proved overwhelming. Even so, there were depictions of quiet Christmases spent in a small farmhouse next to a fire, the introduction of faraway neighbors who would join the Granges for massive feasts, the yearly thrill of the spring's first carriage-ride into Spooner to sell wheat and buy corn for the planting season. Matthias' journal described the slow birth of a community, as a smattering of desperate farmers from the east and immigrants from Europe settled around Sarona Lake, gradually developing a trading post and even a small hospital only a few miles away. The first years of Grange's existence were surprisingly calm and bountiful, so much so that Ben began to doubt a genealogy of evil might appear in the unofficial town archives. It wasn't until he cracked open Matthias' second journal, dated from the fall of 1853 to the winter of 1857, that his forebodings were confirmed.

25 OCTOBER, 1853. Young Mathilde has died. She has been on this Earth for less than two years, yet God has found it necessary to take her from us. Why? For what Reason would He punish Therese and myself? I know it is said the Creator has His reasons, and perhaps our Daughter was not meant long for this World. But it is also true that our Reason for travelling to America, for uprooting our Lives, was to grow our Family, extend our Namesake, and provide a hopeful Future for them. That Future, now, has been impeded, cut short and mocked.

Here, Ben was struck with a biting pain in his temple and a spasm that seemed to spread from his gut. He closed his eyes, sighed, pushed away the journal on the table. He was surprised to find himself relating closely to Matthias, this unlikeliest of avatars, explorer of a strange new land. Here, suddenly, was a tragedy that Ben understood with brutal intimacy: "A future cut short and mocked." Ben felt the truth of these words, which he had often thought without being able to express them.

The fluorescent lights flickered and zapped. A dank, sour smell permeated the room, growing heavier. At last, Ben swallowed and pulled the journal toward him.

While God has found it necessary to take our Daughter from us, He has also turned this Land cold and unforgiving. For the last two Years our

Harvest had been bountyful; the Soil has given Life and we have treated it well, tended it carefully, bathed it with Sunlight, showered it with Water. As Mathilde dies, however, so does our Land. Almost none of our Corn has grown, and we will have little to sell at Market this Fall and Winter. Perhaps it is good that our Mathilde is gone (though it tortures me to write such Words); for without Food and Money, she would not have lasted the Season any way.

I have Therese, of course, and as of yesterday we have planted our Wheat to harvest in the Spring. I am hopeful, as I must be, that our Springtime Crop will bring different Results. Yet my Hope for the Future has been beaten into Nothing, and I know these Winter Months will be painful for my Wife and myself. I hope our Neighbors will take Pity on us and lend us what they can.

Tomorrow, I will bury my Daughter in the Soil. We could not afford a Coffin, small though it would be, so I have begun crafting one with the Timber to be found in the Forest across our Plot of Land. It is there I will bury her. For a Tombstone I plant only a wooden Cross engraved with her Name, MATHILDE GRANGE, FEBRUARY 1852 – OCTOBER 1853, a reminder of how brief the Flame of Life may flicker on this Planet.

13 JUNE, 1854. As quickly as Life was snatched away from us, it has been restored—it is not yet July and already our Wheat and Rye have begun to flourish, reaching their Stalks into the warm Summer Air. Indeed, the Harvest occupies more of our time than we can spend. We've struggled to plant the Spring Wheat and Oats to supply our Livestock with Grain. Already we have hired three Hands from Spooner, who may stay on with us throughout the Season. This Land seems fickle, as though it responds to human Touch with a Mood and Temper all its own, but it is hard for me to take Issue when this year's Crop has been so fertile.

Ben skipped ahead in Grange's journal, flipping past winters and summers and years. Life trudged on with little fanfare. Neighbors had children or moved away. The town, still unnamed, bore a train station and a meat-packing plant. The next two years saw equally prosperous harvests for the Granges, though there was no life where they wanted it most: Matthias and Therese could not conceive a child, a fact that was expressed with obvious despair in the pages Matthias wrote. With unusual clarity, the Granges' lives took shape before Ben's eyes as he read; it was as though, by merely tracing these words, the memories passed firsthand into his consciousness.

So it was with growing alarm that Ben reached the end of the journal, witnessing a life that descended into chaos. The end of everything began with a happy occasion: the birth of the Granges' second daughter, Martha, in May of 1856. Ben discovered this event in the third and last of Matthias' journals. The handwriting here had grown sloppy and erratic, as though scrawled by someone who no longer felt his life needed commemorating. Even so, there was hope in Matthias' words, at least on this day.

27 MAY, 1856. Has God finally answered the Prayers that my Wife and I have uttered into a Void these last few years? Or is He no longer paying Attention? Whatever the case, it thrills me to say that we have created Life once more. Our young Martha was born last Night. The Birth was difficult for Therese; her Screams will ring in my Head on many restless Nights, and I will never forget the Look on my wife's Face one hour into Labor, a Look I can only describe as Resignation. But now she is calm and content, as is my day-old Daughter. The memory of Mathilde's first night on Earth, wide-eyed and aglow, comes back to me at once, and I live this fearful Miracle all over again.

Another flutter of pages; Ben skipped ahead, frantic. Without explanation, his eyes came to rest on an entry two months later.

24 JULY, 1856. We have been busy. The Summer excites and unsettles me. Harvesting Rye and Potatoes, tearing it from the Soil, the Land is agreeable but seems to have terrible Moods. Should have enough for the Winter, should have enough for the Winter.

I have not slept. Therese has not slept. We lie in Bed from ten til four A.M. Silent but restless. It is Martha, partially, a troubled Child, she screams and screams til her Voice is hoarse, we find her in her Crib, her Body red and damp with Sweat. We are worried, but the Doctor says it is not uncommon for Infants. She is still acclimating to the World. Some Nights, after lying still for Hours, I sit in a Chair by her Crib and watch her silently. I think of who she will be in five, ten, twenty Years; then, unavoidably, think of Mathilde, and I want to skip through Time and see my Daughter safe and grown.

It is partly Martha that keeps us from sleeping. But other Things, too. The Air is thick and often smells of something burning when no Fire is in sight. Many times when working the Fields, I peer into the nearby Forest, thick and shadowy, with an inexplicable Fear. I know two Eyes are on me. Burning Eyes. I shiver in the Warmth.

A strange Story. I was walking this Sunday. Therese was with Martha, resting. I was walking through the Forest. I have not explored this Land much, though it belongs to us. It is beautyful but desolate.

I walked for half an Hour and came to a clearing, a small Piece of Land free of Trees. All was Dead. The Grass was Brown and Black, dry under my Feet. It was carpeted with many Birds, two dozen or more, all Dead, black and pityful on the Ground. The Smell was ugly, the heavy Odor of an Abattoir. A strange red Liquid seeped from one Tree, oozing from the Trunk, spilling onto the Soil. I touched it, stupidly perhaps, and trembled at the cold. I have not been able to wash its Stain from my Fingers.

I will wake early tomorrow to finish planting Rye. I hope I can sleep. But I fear this Night will be no different than any Other.

The entries became sporadic now, and even these were written with an angry pen, stabbed into the paper. They unsettled Ben as he pored over them. The next one, three weeks later, was in fact an illustration, blanketing the page with thick, black swaths of ink.

The image showed a bull rising over a hill. Its rear hooves were planted in the dirt, pushing upwards. Its front legs were long and hung

159

awkwardly at its sides like a human, though immense and muscular. Its shape was distorted, elongated, so its massive head was in grotesque close-up. The eyes were narrowed, scraped into the page, with jagged abrasions for its pupils. A stream of saliva hung from its open mouth, trickling through matted fur. There were no words to accompany the picture, no explanation. Ben shivered. The air in the basement grew colder.

He flipped ahead, scanning the journal entries, though many of them now were deranged and hopeless. Once every few months there was a mundane description of the Granges' harvest, as though Matthias intermittently remembered his vocation. Yet even these assumed the dark chaos of a nightmare.

Our Wheat Crop was plentyful, read an entry two years later. *We will survive on it this Year. It was a fearsome Experience, however. Each Stalk I pulled from the Ground, I closed my Eyes and opened them and saw something soft and fleshy in my Hands, an Organ ripped from a Body. Sometimes the Organ pulsed, its Veins coursing with Blood. I pulled another and another, and saw another and another. Piled into Baskets and Crates, Masses of Flesh. Did not tell Therese, of course, she cannot know, and I think there are Things she cannot tell me. I am frightened.*

Now near the end of the journal, Ben's fingers skimmed, with a life all their own, to the entry he had been dreading. He knew it was coming. The newspapers had told him so: Matthias Grange survived his wife and two daughters. But that didn't prepare him.

There was a year of dwindling harvests, another summer of famish in which the Granges relied upon the charity of neighbors. A land, once again, turned suddenly ruthless. Then a scrawl of prose that stopped Ben's heart.

3 NOVEMBER, 1858. I know now not to speak of Prayers to God or His Omniscience. That is a Fantasy. There is something else here.

Martha is Dead. Martha is Dead. Martha is Dead. I write it and write it and the Words mean nothing, but I know it is true, Martha is Dead.

I held her in my Arms. I walked her over our Land. I showed her the World. She cried, as she does every Day, she cried. It was simply Fever that took her from us. She was three Years and Five and a half Months old. She is already buried.

She died a Day later than Mathilde. Of course, six Years later than Mathilde. But a Day later. I will never again trust the Month of October. This is the Time when Things are taken from us. It was a Fever, they say, but it was something else, too. Something I can feel. It is not God here, but it is something, and it wakes and is hungry, and it has taken Martha.

I know our Crop will flourish, I know. It is a pattern, this is what I have learned, Death for Life, and that is not only here.

I have buried my Daughter. She has died. I will build her a Gravestone.

The last entry of the journal had no date. It also had no words. It was another illustration, grim and naked, slathered with ink.

It was of a woman wearing a long black dress, hanging from the beams of a lonely barn, a noose tightened around her neck. The black shadows of the image were deep and enormous, threatening to swallow the entire page. But the ghostly white of the woman's face stood out most of all.

Ben closed the journal, its cover falling softly, and placed it on the stack of Matthias' other books. He pushed them away, eyes wide and sere. Then, trembling as if they carried a communicable disease, he placed the journals in the corner of the basement where he found them.

He tried to find further mention of Therese Grange—specifically of her death, apparently by suicide, in 1858—but there was nothing to be found. Nothing in the milquetoast newspapers, to be sure, and nothing in the scattered diaries of the other town founders, who by the late 1850s were mentioning the Granges with tactful remove. The journal of the town's first mayor, Frederick Lang, did mention the naming ceremony of the town in the summer of 1861, a regal occasion that paid tribute to Grange's original inhabitant—who, by that time driven mute by madness, sat on a red-bedecked stage in silence. When a banner was strung up on the town's Main Street proclaiming the name of Grange, all Matthias could offer was a skeletal smile and, Frederick wrote, "a tense and insular state of dread." Matthias returned to his lonely farmhouse an hour later, according to Mr. Lang, and died only five months after that.

It was midday by this point, and Ben could no longer ignore the growing emptiness in his stomach. But it was impossible to tear himself away from this room, its scattered remnants of a haunted past. He scoured the shelves for further information, no longer using the card catalog for guidance. Many "official" town histories were vague and secretive, touting Grange's Independence Day parades and vaunted agricultural history while little of the town's governance or populace were mentioned.

In another corner of the basement, buried beneath several shoeboxes containing poorly preserved photographs, were two immense volumes bound in thick, frayed leather. Ben lifted the first of these, feeling the heft of its contents in his hands. He tossed it onto the tiny desk that had become his refuge for the day. He cracked open the cover, uneasy, breathless, and read a title on the front page: *Thomas Von Hubbel, Cartographer*. Thin sheets of tracing paper covered with checkered diagrams protruded from the book. As Ben flipped through its contents, he discovered that these were maps charting the terrain of northern Wisconsin, folded in half, the charcoal pencil markings faded but discernible. It was a welcome departure from the dry, officious anecdotes he had been reading, though he doubted there would be much of interest inside.

He was wrong. Though Ben knew nothing of cartography, Mr. Von Hubbel had also inscribed brief journal entries that proved unexpectedly helpful. He had arrived in the upper Midwest, he wrote, in the early 1840s, mostly for the purpose of charting the regional waterways, though the classification of Native American tribes also served a purpose. At this point, Ben came to an inserted map of what he assumed to be Grange and its outlying areas. The crudely drawn diagram on brittle paper was hard to decode, but there was no mistaking the mass of water that represented Sarona Lake. The next map was an impressive topography of the region, with a pocket of forest lying to the south and east of the verdant stretch of land that Grange would later occupy. Sarona Lake bordered both of them to the east.

Von Hubbel's written entries were mostly lavish descriptions of the area's beauty; at one point he went so far as to say, "The northwest portion of the Wisconsin territory gives credence to the claim that the New World is the most divine of God's creations." Ben was about to discard the vast collection of Von Hubbel's maps to its habitat in the basement, but an entry on the second-last page made him stop. It was accompanied by a magnified map of one of the forested areas that bordered Grange to the south. Ben was more focused, however, on a brief written entry, which explained in pensive tones what took place when Von Hubbel ventured deep into the forest.

"There was a strange area of the woods," he wrote, "in which all life, flora and fauna, was suddenly absent. The ground was covered in putrid dirt; seemingly, no grass could grow. I swear I could detect a noxious odor in the air, perhaps a rotting carcass or nearby sulfur deposit. Strangest of all, however, was a message left in the area by a previous civilization—nomadic, probably, one that left quickly after it arrived."

It was in a dialect that Von Hubbel couldn't understand, though he reproduced it in his journal:

Baapiniziwaagan maji-manidoo.

Von Hubbel conjectured in the margin of his journal that the dialect belonged to a native tribe. Ben racked his brain, trying to remember the American History class he had taken the single year he attended college. Which Native American tribes occupied the northwest part of the state? The Sioux? Ojibwe, Menominee? He suddenly felt ashamed.

Only a few pages later, a title reading "Language and Culture of the Ojibwe Clans" seemed to answer his question. One lengthy recounting of Ojibwe lore drew his rapt attention: early in their existence, it was told, in the Land of the Dawn that lay in the eastern part of the country that would become America, a prophet had a vision. One of the great *miigis*, or "radiant beings," appeared to foretell of the "pale-skinned people" that would arrive from another land, endangering the Ojibwe way of life. If their culture was to survive, the *miigi* warned, they must move west—and so they did, with some clans settling near the Great Lakes of the American Midwest. Ben raised his eyes from the page, adrift in thought. He had never sensed so strongly the feeling of being someplace that did not belong to him.

When his eyes returned to Von Hubbel's journal, they drifted to a series of words on the next page, most of them practical and mundane: *wiisiniwin* (food), *iikaan* (friend), *nibi* (water). But, covering the bottom half of the page, those two words stabbed into the tree stump reappeared, *Baapiniziwaagan maji-manidoo*.

Underneath them, in woozy lines as though traced by a trembling hand, stood their translation: *Beware Devils*. Von Hubbel had added a footnote to this translation: that second word, *maji-manidoo*, described not a myth or a parable but an actual thing, something observable. It was a zoological term, classifying beings that were known to exist.

There was a muffled knock in the far corner of the basement, a low echo that came from within the walls. Ben's eyes shot up in alarm and he realized how painful they were, how dry and over-accustomed to the dark. He waited another moment but there was nothing else to be heard, and he worried that his sanity was dismantling itself.

Feeling weak and withered, Ben lugged the immense volume to a workbench in the far corner of the basement, where a pair of fluorescent bulbs hovered. He flipped open the cartographer's journal to a final set of maps marked with latitude and longitude lines. A small square was set off near the lower right corner of the map, with a series of numbers— 45° 31' N, 91° 58' W—noted with particular emphasis. Ben wondered where exactly this barren stretch of land might be found—in proximity, maybe, to the woods outside the Sarona Lake Motel.

Ben clutched at his phone, nearly dropping it to the floor. He moved quickly, snapping pictures that were crude and gray and uneven but (most importantly) legible. With each press of the button, a flare of gaudy digital light erupted through the cramped room, soaking into the ceiling tiles and causing the lonely sheaths of paper to shrink away, blinded, in the limelight.

The feeling that Matthias Grange had of two eyes watching him, two burning eyes trained on him from the shadowy woods in 1853— Ben could relate. Not a vague feeling of paranoia and dread, but the sensation of the air and ambient sound shuffling slightly in another's presence. He had this feeling now. He blinked and shot his head to the left, narrowing his eyes toward the shadows of the basement. There was nothing but the contours of disorganized boxes and the milky light of anemic lightbulbs. What else did he expect?

He raised his phone, refocused, flipped between pages, jettisoned Von Hubbel's notes and maps into the digital ether. He didn't know what he would do with the evidence, didn't know if this grim and fanciful knowledge made the situation more or less comprehensible.

Another flash of light, a blinding pulse stretching to the walls.

There was something there this time. Ben was sure of it. A black bulbous shape crouched in the corner, behind a stack of file boxes, raising itself.

He whipped in its direction. His eyes were frantic, somehow sweating. The hours he had been down here turned suddenly to days.

"Hello?" His voice leaked out.

He remembered the device that he held in his hands. He glanced at his cellphone screen and illuminated a flashlight. He lifted the phone and shined it in the corners of the room. Simply the liminal grayness of light turning into shadow.

Unless.

Unless the black silhouette behind a plastic bookshelf, crammed into a space so narrow it could hardly hold a human body, was really there.

Ridiculous. Now he was sure his sanity was in peril, assailed by legends of devils and ghosts. But on the other hand, didn't it also make sense that this archive would be protected by something that refused to loose such knowledge into the world?

Ben stretched his phone in the direction of the bookshelf, squinting his eyes toward the empty space where he thought, he was *sure*, a long and narrow shape stared back at him. But the space behind the bookshelf vanished in a pale wash of light and Ben turned off his phone, realizing his mistake.

The gray, looming shape in the corner of the basement emerged again in the darkness. He had convinced himself, almost, that he was simply seeing things, he was starved and fatigued and his eyes would right themselves and there would be nothing there. But the figure floated in the corner, its contours shimmering, one darker shade of gray than the rest of the shadows. Ben crept closer, one step, another. If it was a living thing, crouching there concealed, it stared directly at him, never moving.

He finally reached the bookshelf, the sort of thing purchased for twenty dollars at K-Mart, buckling under the weight of a few lopsided boxes. He was relieved no one else was there. He didn't have to pretend he wasn't terrified.

Then its eyes opened, glinting yellow eyes sunk into a gaunt and sallow face, opened and erupted, blazing with rage. Whatever it was, for some unknown reason, it shrank into the corner, hunched over, wedged between a wall and a file cabinet, a head connected to a scoliotic spine by only a wispy thread of tissue.

It continued to rise, ascending from its hunched position, and Ben knew now why it crouched in the corner—it was the only way it could fit into the room. Its gray legs straightened, muscle and sinew straining. Its curved spine bent upright, chipped bones scraping against each other. The head, shining two orange flames of fury, stretched to the ceiling, covered with a slimy sheen. And its arms spread in a horrible show of power, the color of gray and rotted meat, spanning the length of the bookshelf.

People don't scream when they're truly terrified—fear grabs the throat and makes sound impossible. A scratchy whimper fell from Ben's mouth as he gawked at the creature, stepping back once, twice to take in its towering size.

There was a swift roar behind Ben to his right. His head whipped around. The cartographer's book of maps was engulfed in flames on the workbench. The fire licked at the hovering lights, shattering them, glass scattering into the inferno.

This was all the warning Ben needed. He stumbled backwards, feet slipping on the floor. His eyes turned back to the thing in the corner, the creature that had formed out of nothing as archaic tomes cracked open. Doubting his eyes, he needed to see it again, to cower beneath it and see that such things are possible.

The yellow eyes blazed in response to Ben's disbelief. Its mouth opened in a hideous, gaping void and a wavering moan crawled over the walls and ceiling.

Ben reached behind himself, felt the metallic doorknob with a right hand coated with sweat. He slipped out the door, crawling backwards. The roar of fire and an acrid smell licked at Ben as he entered the stairway. There, a fire extinguisher blazed red, attached to the wall. He was driven wild by fear, legs weak, breath frenzied, but a pretense of heroism bubbled up from somewhere inside, preventing him from leaping up the stairs in self-preservation.

He jerked the extinguisher from the wall, shouldered the basement door open, and sprinted across the narrow room in six stumbling steps. To his left, a high-pitched shriek erupted and Ben felt a trail of blood trickle from his eardrum. But he refused to look, refused to think, until he pulled the pin and squeezed the handle on the extinguisher and felt a whitish spray of carbon dioxide spew from the nozzle. The flames on the workbench sputtered in response; Thomas Von Hubbel's maps were now a heap of char and ash, but at least the fire hadn't swallowed up the rest of the archive, leaving Grange's history in its state of dormancy.

The row of bookshelves to his left suddenly crashed to the floor, creating a violent clatter as the creature screamed again, hovering in Ben's peripheral vision. Cardboard boxes, reams of paper, leather-bound albums spilled onto tile, nearly knocking Ben to his knees. A heavy blast of hot air swallowed the basement, singing Ben's hair and turning his exposed skin a raw and throbbing pink. He threw the extinguisher to the floor, forcing himself to believe the fire had been suffocated, then spun and slid across the room and heaved the door open, each nerve and sensation screaming.

The burning odor faded away as Ben leapt up the stairs, three at a time. A piercing scream lingered in his left ear, turning him nearly deaf. He felt for the cellphone in his pocket, reassured when he felt it crookedly through the denim, then shoved open the library door on the main level, slipping back into reality.

As soon as the heavy door slammed shut behind him (next to a sign comprised only of a draconian "*Quiet!*"), Ben realized his plan to leave covertly had failed. He stopped for a split-second, balancing on one foot, as though shocked by the reappearance of people and windows. Then he jolted into motion, darting at the front doors like a squirrel evading two-lane traffic.

Across the library, by a rack of magazines bordering the front windows, Lara heard a pair of heavy loping feet. She glanced in Ben's direction, aiming for a look of indifference. A stack of disheveled magazines was cradled in her arms. He flashed into sight, his eyes trained only on the floor, stomping toward the exit.

Lara smiled and stepped in his direction, expecting him to stop and smirk and continue their game of casual flirtation.

"So, Ben, what did you find—"

Before she could say another word, a low whoosh rang out from the door as Ben shoved his way through it, hellbent on escape. Lara glared after him, mystified, her fleeting hopes dashed in Ben's wake.

"So that's that," she muttered, turning back to the windows, where she could see Ben skittering into the distance. From behind the front desk, tight-lipped Lyle merely watched, his eyebrows raised a centimeter in an expression that could only be described as muted outrage.

Chapter 17 — How to Live a Life

Hannah Dorian's day was no better or worse than most. There was the alarm at six o'clock, when it was still dark at this time of year, though she often woke before the alarm sounded; her daily reading of the newspaper over a cup of black tea, the *New York Times*, even though it had gotten so expensive she could hardly rationalize the subscription. (Most sensible people got their news online now anyway—or they simply ignored it.)

Amy woke up thirty minutes later, ate a bowl of cereal in silence while trying to finish her homework. She rode to school in the passenger seat of Hannah's car, saying nothing, cellphone glued to hand. Hannah made sure to have her second cup of tea ready for the car ride. She would drop off Amy at seven fifteen precisely, and Amy would smile and glance at her grandmother and breathe out a hurried, "Thanks, see you later." Hannah couldn't fault Amy for this. What preteen girl wants to devote every waking moment to bonding with her grandmother?

Hannah reminded herself of this every morning as she watched Amy enter the school's front doors. She hated herself for having to rationalize caring for her granddaughter, to come up with a context for loving her. Then came the guilt and, in a convenient case of dime-store psychology, more resentment toward angelic Amy, an avalanching cycle.

Her shift at the supermarket, Frommer's Grocery, started at seven thirty, leaving Hannah only ten minutes to drive across town and throw on her uniform, a white shirt with a red collar and nametag. The cashier position at Frommer's wasn't a bad stint. She used to enjoy the fleeting interactions with regulars and neighbors, and her boss, Jerry Frommer, was an agreeable guy. Over the last two years, though, everything about it had become unbearable, a relentless torment. It was more than familiarity—it was inescapability.

Hannah's day continued. Half an hour for lunch at one, a magazine read in the downstairs break room and turkey sandwich cut neatly in two, reveling in the silence. And remembering. Remembering the trips she and her husband would take early in their marriage to hiking trails up north and state fairs in Milwaukee; then later, the weekend trips with her daughter to the Twin Cities, to art museums and restaurants, just the ratio of cultured activity to quiet seclusion that she liked in her life.

Two and a half more hours at Frommer's, stocking shelves and ringing up produce, her mood brightened occasionally by the few residents of Grange with whom she remained in contact.

Hannah's blue Pontiac parked like clockwork at Grange Elementary's western curb by four-thirty. Three days a week, Amy had piano lessons with a music instructor who gushed, to anyone who would listen, that Amy would be the most famous person to come out of Grange, just wait and see. Amy would wander out promptly at four-thirty, some piano etude looping in her head, and find her grandmother's car parked there without thinking twice, rarely wondering how Hannah had spent the last eight hours of her day.

Dinner together with the television on, obligatory attempts at conversation—*how was school, how was work, what'd you learn, who'd you see*—only moderately successful. Hannah used to invest so much planning and energy into these family meals, she had tried new pasta recipes and told Amy about her own childhood, or what Amy's mother Rebecca was like as a young girl. But that was years ago.

Tonight, by seven o'clock, there was a small scattering of dirty dishes in the sink and the sound of Amy practicing Brahms, plunking her fingers along the black-and-white keys, hitting the same flat note at the same measure every time. Most nights, Hannah pushed her granddaughter to carry out an hour or so of practice; what point were the lessons, Hannah would say, the expenditure and the expectations, if Amy didn't demand perfection from herself? It was Hannah who had encouraged her to take up lessons, it was Hannah who decided to keep her parents' piano when selling it would have loosened her finances, and it was Hannah who now told her granddaughter how heavenly the music sounded at her fingertips. And it did; Hannah wasn't deaf, she knew Amy was talented. So why did every compliment, every gushing testament to Amy's genius, sound so forced and meaningless?

Maybe Hannah's indifference to Amy's prowess came, like so many things, from Rebecca. Hannah's daughter, Amy's mother, the generational link that had vanished at the very moment of Amy's birth. A *hemorrhage*, the doctors told Hannah almost thirteen years ago, a word that sounded as violent as the event it classified, like massive blood loss and a body too weak and besieged to go on.

Rebecca was a dabbler. She had dabbled in guitar, in saxophone, in choir, in cheerleading, trying to cover all of her bases while she was still in high school with the premature knowledge, it seemed, of how briefly it would last. She hadn't found success in any musical field, but she was a fast runner—she could run for miles, it let her escape, and if she had run track or tried to pursue a scholarship, who knows where she could have gone.

But she wasn't a musical savant, and her daughter Amy was. This is not a travesty, though every piano chord sounded by Amy could only remind Hannah of her daughter, the deceased chameleon.

Tonight, Hannah scrubbed cheap marinara off a brown thrift-store plate, the solemn sound of Brahms' chords floating around her like smoke from the oven. It was dark by now, the in-between zone that separates dusk and pure night, and in the waning sunlight Hannah could see a bird's nest in one of the hawthorn trees in her backyard. Without thinking, the hand holding a sponge stopped scrubbing and she peered out the window. There was a fat bird puffed-up in the nest, a sparrow Hannah guessed, offering some minuscule grub to the three chirping newborns that surrounded her. Hannah watched them as if in close-up, the maternal bird and its offspring, and she resented the bird's self-apparent life: to live, to fly, to propagate, to care for young and die.

172

There was no ambiguity in the bird's life. It did not have the tragic ability to reflect upon its existence and think it might be spent otherwise.

Hannah had once looked forward to her sixties—she thought they would be the years when self-imposed responsibility no longer mattered, when she could explore the world that had always fascinated her from a distance. But then tragedy came, visiting her again and again, the snickering houseguest that won't go away. When Rebecca died, Hannah lost her best friend. Rebecca's husband Tyler left a year later, uninterested in raising a daughter by himself and no longer willing to pretend otherwise; and though Hannah was angry, she was surprised it hadn't happened sooner. Tyler had his good moments, Hannah would say, and there was no question in her mind that he had loved her daughter painfully. But his gender politics hadn't advanced past the 1950s—child-raising, he felt, was a woman's domain. Maybe it would have been different if they'd had a boy, someone Tyler could mold into an ideal version of himself. In any case, he soon boarded a bus for Minneapolis followed by an Amtrak to wherever, as long as it kept heading west.

Now down to Hannah and her husband, kind old Henry, who had not planned on raising another child in his fifties but was too amenable to complain. There were even moments of bliss, both of them had to admit, in playing the parenthood role over the next eight years. But tragedy stuck around, waiting cloaked in the wings, enjoying its torment too much to stop now. Nine years into Amy's life she lost Henry, her sixty-year-old grandfather, whose heart finally buckled under the strain of cheap cigarettes and copious whiskey. Hannah could only be grateful (though she'd hardly describe it as such) that Henry died in his sleep and that she had found him, eyes open, in bed at dawn, his mouth crooked and ghostly, unreadable. Better than Amy finding him collapsed on the kitchen floor. She had already experienced so much loss.

The past flooded Hannah's mind tonight as she thrust the last of the plates into the dishwasher and collapsed on a chair at the table,

173

pouring herself a glass of Syrah. Her thoughts kept her company as she savored its bitter taste, both relishing and resenting Amy's music from the living room.

At seven thirty-three, Hannah pushed away her empty glass, dragged her chair along the floor with a shriek, stood and walked to the wireless phone sitting at the end of the kitchen counter. She pulled a business card from her pocket; John Linden's name was inscribed on it, over the words MONOGRAPH SPECIALIST. She flipped the card over. Linden's personal cellphone number was written here, scrawled with a blue ballpoint pen.

Seven digits, entered as quickly as possible to avoid second-guessing; a simple movement, bleak and awful. After two rings, a low, exasperated voice answered. "Hello?"

"Hello?" Hannah didn't know what to say, how to proceed.

"Hello? This is John Linden, who is this?"

From the next room, Amy's music faltered as she trained one ear on the nearby hallway, struggling to hear Hannah's words.

"Hannah Dorian." She cleared her throat, her name sounding crude as she uttered it into the phone. "Can we talk somewhere?"

"Hannah!" Linden's fervor on the other end of the line grew vulgar. "Hi, I'm very happy you called." There was a slight fumbling noise from Linden's end. "Of course we can talk."

By this point, Amy's music had slowed to a few piano keys flicked arbitrarily.

"Where would you like to meet?"

Hannah's eyes shot to the dimly lit hallway, then back to a scuffed mark on the counter. "Your place is fine. It won't take long."

"Great. I'll be waiting."

Hannah said nothing, disarmed by Linden's avid demeanor. She hung up, the phone anvil-heavy in her hand. In the living room, Amy's fingers stopped moving. She leaned her head in the direction of her grandmother's voice, a D-minor chord lingering in the air.

Chapter 18 — Mourning

At eight-thirty on the morning of October 31st, Ben Dmitrovich wandered through the bright buzzing light of a ShopKo aisle, searching for cheap black pants, a white dress shirt, and a plain, dark necktie. He hadn't come prepared with funeral attire and couldn't allow himself to show up in a patched-together outfit, raggedy and disrespectful. He'd always held the ceremonial nature of funerals in reverent esteem. Most people do, of course. But Ben understood the significance and impossibility of saying goodbye in a way that feels definitive.

The air that Saturday was thick and solemn, weighted with storm clouds that threatened to unleash themselves. It was a mournful day, appropriately. *I will never again trust the Month of October*, Matthias Grange had written in his journal.

Ben paid for his clothes, mutely offering the cashier two twenty-dollar bills, and drove the fifteen minutes back to Grange, stopping along the way for his third cup of coffee. He had barely slept. Aaron visited him again, in flickering dreams and in the ghostly pre-dawn shadows of his motel room. Aaron's presence was never far from Ben, but it had been pervasive the last two days. And at the worst possible time, Ben realized with a tinge of self-reproach. He had finally fought his way to what his police psychiatrist, Dr. Kent Kildare, had labeled the fourth and penultimate stage of coping with grief: depression. It didn't sound promising, but he had already muscled his way through Self-Exile and Anger and The Need to Regain Control, as Dr. Kildare had instructed with lectures, diagrams, brochures.

But now Maria's death blindsided him, sent him slipping down Mount Dmitrovich (another Kildare device) at least as far back as "the bargaining stage." At this point, halfway up the mountain (Kildare had said), you find a root cause for your tragedy, you try to explain your loss away. You make a deal with God: I'd do anything to have another chance.

When he was two minutes south of Grange, driving north on Highway 63 with a patch of woods separating him from Sarona Lake, he pulled to the shoulder and stopped. At first, he didn't know why; merely an impulse. But as he rolled down the windows of his wheezing Jeep, taking in the noxious air, it came to him. Wasn't this where Thomas Von Hubbel, more than a century and a half ago, had stumbled upon a deathly clearing marked with unknown warnings? Ben gazed into the forest, weary eyes narrowing, trying to pierce their way fifty yards into the distance, where *something* lurked. He thought for a moment about cutting the engine, trampling into the woods, and exploring until some kind of presence made itself known.

But it would have to wait. He had a funeral to attend.

By the time he arrived at Holy Angels Evangelical Church, the parking lot was half-full. The service wouldn't start for another hour, but already a throng of black-clad mourners had drifted through the immense front doors, some of them conversing gloomily on the steps.

Ben veered into an empty spot and stepped out of his Jeep. A shrill and painful creak resounded as he closed the door. As soon as his feet touched pavement, he felt a few cagey pairs of eyes upon him. He glanced at the front entryway, where two middle-aged men, tall and austere-looking, focused their attention on him, continuing to mouth their silent conversation.

He was halfway through the parking lot when he saw it: a red hatchback, small but conspicuous, parked all the way at the end of the lot. He ambled over to it, striving to look casual. As he came closer, he peered through the windows. A flurry of papers and books were scattered in the back and a tweed jacket was draped over the driver's seat. He was certain this was the same car that had been parked at the Sarona Lake Motel a few nights ago, manned by someone with the power to give and take life. Ben pulled a small notebook from his pocket—an accessory he always carried and rarely used, though he liked how investigative it seemed, the genre-cliché nature of it—and jotted down the license plate number.

Two more cars arrived in the parking lot while he was doing this, the second of which, a rumbling black pickup, contained three passengers who leered at him as they passed. He would have to get used to this feeling of out-of-placeness.

As Ben returned to the entryway and threw open the doors, brushing off the narrow glances of the men conversing on the front steps, he felt a wave of piousness wash over him—that hushed-tone, organ-music aura that made his skin crawl on the rare occasions when he stepped inside a church on Sundays. Maybe, Ben thought as he drifted through the foyer, it was the horror of everything he'd seen that made the church's solemnity seem so unrighteous.

There was no one here he recognized, though he guessed that the gaunt, white-haired man in the priest's cassock was Reverend Scariot. The rules of modern civility led several of the congregants to offer a polite nod in Ben's direction, though even these attempts at tact carried an apprehensive squint. Ben merely nodded in response, half-smiling in the expression of unspoken sympathy so common to funerals.

He waded through them into the nave of the church, which was small but pleasantly subdued, lent a golden glow by the stained-glass windows. Maria's closed casket stood below the altar, next to a blown-up photo of her (from several years ago at least, Ben guessed) and a profuse yet tasteful array of floral bouquets. Their presence made Ben think back to late March, when Maria's car had skidded off the road into a telephone pole. *They tried to resuscitate me*, Maria had told him. *They couldn't.* Was there a funeral held for Maria then, too, with the same radiant photograph and the same ornate floral arrangement? Had the town attended dutifully then, paying their respects? Were they more effusive in their grief at that time, or had they only now become convinced that this was a time for mourning? Maybe this funeral, this *second* funeral (Ben shook his head at the grim and absurd thought)—

maybe it was something else entirely. A performance held on a holy stage, enacted for the benefit of a single stranger whose knowledge of death and finality was naïve in comparison to theirs.

Inside the church, there were people he recognized. Nathan Amherst, clean-shaven yet no less disheveled, stood near his former wife's casket, muttering to a few well-intentioned townspeople. And Terence Arnold, dressed in a lavish but ill-fitting suit, stood beneath a window representing St. Anne, his arm wrapped around the waist of a woman next to him, presumably his wife. The two of them were talking to a short, bespectacled man wearing a hideous dark-green shirt, though the uneasy look on all three of their faces suggested the dialogue was far from pleasant.

It took only a few seconds for Chief Arnold's gaze to drift to the entryway, where Ben stood skewed, surveying the scene. There was no use looking away: Ben simply returned Arnold's withering glare, aiming for a look between defiance and apology. Arnold said a few more words, though his eyes never left Ben's. The man in front of Arnold turned in Ben's direction, his straggly hair and rodent eyes inexplicably familiar. The stranger grinned with unsettling zeal in Ben's direction. Ben forced himself, finally, to look away.

After excusing himself, Arnold stepped down the carpeted aisle, readjusting his blazer as he walked. Ben rocked on his feet, dreading their impending conversation.

"Officer Dmitrovich." Terence Arnold came to rest only a few feet from Ben, arms crossed. "Why am I not surprised?"

"Because I told you I would be here."

"You know what I'm doing as soon as this funeral is over, Ben?"

"Sitting me down and confessing all of your darkest secrets?" It was a sour joke, uttered with no pretense of humor, and Arnold simply shrugged it off.

"I'm calling a friend of ours. Miranda Prost, Milwaukee PD. You know what I'm gonna tell her?"

Ben sighed in response.

178

"I'm telling her you happened to roll into our town with some kind of…deluded suspicion of wrongdoing. You looked into a possible domestic violence case, which is fine—any helpful officer would do the same. But it became clear you were wrong. Maria's death was just an unfortunate accident."

"What did you find out?"

"What do you mean?"

"Your investigation into Maria's death. You think it was an accident?"

Arnold glowered for a moment—taking the time, Ben thought, to prepare an empty answer.

"We've found no evidence of foul play. There was one set of footprints on the bluff where Maria fell, and they were hard enough to find—the whole place was soup by the time it stopped raining."

"And the motel room? The blood in the bathroom, you tested it?"

"I really don't think this is the place to discuss it."

"What did you find?" Ben interrupted.

Another long sigh. "It was Maria's blood. Why she decided to leave the motel by breaking out the bathroom window is another question."

"The glass was inside, on the bathroom floor," Ben said in a hushed voice. "She didn't break out—something broke in."

Arnold, exasperated, nodded. "Yes, my department is aware of that. Our investigation is underway, Ben, meaning we don't need your help. Your presence here, I might add—not just in Grange, but showing up *here*, at Maria's funeral—continues to unsettle this town, most of all the husband of the deceased." There was a slight click of the tongue from Arnold, overly demonstrative. "This town just wants to move on, Officer. You are not making that easy."

Ben said nothing in response. In fact, he was hypnotized by Nathan Amherst, who was performing a charade of neighborly decorum even as he could barely stay standing next to his wife's corpse. Ben could see it from fifty feet away, his sympathy mixing with revulsion, oil-and-water-like. Arnold noticed Ben's diverted attention and swung his head toward Nathan.

"He's been through so much," Arnold muttered. "No one can understand that."

Ben heard the words as if from another dimension. Finally he said, "I can." Then he walked away, plodding down the center aisle.

He was halfway to the altar before Nathan spotted him. He tried to hide his fear, but Nathan, utterly alone, just didn't have the energy. His eyes somehow widened and narrowed at once as he took an unwitting step back. The married couple he was speaking to—a short, ruddy-faced pair who might have been identical twins—looked behind them, caught off guard by Nathan's sudden change. The man they saw walking toward them was a stranger, unknown, and this more than any nameable suspicion caused them to stare at Ben, dumbfounded.

This, clearly, was a meeting that Nathan was not ready to have, so he touched the elbow of the woman in front of him and walked to his right, ushering the couple along. As Ben approached, he made out the last few words of their conversation, as Nathan uttered something about how hard it is to keep going, "but what else can you do?"

Ben didn't mind Nathan's departure; it allowed him to say goodbye to Maria in solitude. He might have known her for less than a day, but in her sudden disappearance she reminded him of all he had loved and lost. He remembered the last thing he had said to her: "We'll figure this out together." He was trying to console her then, of course, but now he wished that his words had proved to be true for his own sake.

He was now ten feet from the casket, its polished cedar reflecting the lights of the church. The flowers were aromatic, and Ben remembered the old myth that dead bodies sometimes emit the smell of hyacinth. Another step toward Maria, his feet sinking into carpet. He almost expected to feel her presence, but she was gone this time, irretrievably gone.

Then a strange thing happened as he took a final step. He blinked, then was somewhere else. The light was different, along with the ambient sound and the casket itself. This one was closed, too, but it was a darker shade of wood—poplar, if Ben remembered right. The nearby conversation was fuller, carried by familiar voices. This was in Milwaukee, only five months ago in May, at a Presbyterian church on the south side recommended by his parents.

Aaron Dmitrovich lay in the casket, five-year old Aaron, who died after fighting leukemia for eight months, fighting and losing. Sarah had wanted an open casket. She had wanted their friends and family to say goodbye to the boy they knew, to take comfort in the fact that he was no longer in pain. But Ben refused. How could he witness, at every moment, his son's lifeless body and not lose all hope? So a closed casket it was. This was the first piece of evidence to prove what Ben had known all along: that Sarah, in most ways, was stronger than him.

Back in May, Ben had dragged his fingers along the surface of the casket, picturing the body entombed inside—a gesture he repeated today, coming as close as he could to caressing Maria. His second funeral in five months. As though he was expected to have infinite reserves of strength. And in the fragile mind of someone wracked with grief, the bodies in the caskets became interchangeable, making Nathan responsible not only for his wife's death but the passing of Aaron, too. So here was Ben, slipping back down Mount Dmitrovich, in a stage he thought he'd already conquered.

It was still only ten-thirty, leaving Ben a half hour before the funeral began. He was shaken, no doubt, and had to fight to keep his hands from trembling, but he told himself there was work to be done. The church was filling quickly—Ben guessed there were almost a hundred people milling about—and wherever he went he could feel the weight of an angry, resentful glare. There were a few more people he recognized: an elegant, silver-haired woman tugging a young girl behind her, with large eyeglasses compounding her look of distress. Where had he seen them before? He couldn't remember, though he recalled their appearance with uncanny clarity.

He tried to elicit answers from the townspeople. He wandered from one pocket of guests to the next, intruding awkwardly, confronting an armor of hostility. If he detected a lull in conversation, he would simply nudge his way in: "How did you know Maria?" "Have you known her long?" "I'm so sorry for your loss." Most often he was greeted with silence; many of them took his intrusion as a cue simply to walk away, finding their seats on the pews. Some of them were angry, combative. One man asked, "What goddamn right do you have to be here?" while another told him that the arrival of a *foreigner* in Grange was the reason for Maria's death in the first place. He'd hoped that some of them might not know who he was—and he hoped they might be the ones to provide reticent answers—but it seemed Grange was even more tightknit than Chief Arnold had claimed. Word had spread about the policeman from Milwaukee poking around their town, the stranger looking for answers when he didn't even know what the question was.

He had nearly forced himself to give up these interrogations, convinced nothing would come from them, when he spotted a man across the foyer, limping in unmistakable pain. The man dragged himself across the floor, pulling at his pants leg with a shaking fist, until he approached the center of the room and stopped there suddenly. Even if death hadn't pervaded everything today, the word zombie would have instantly come to Ben's mind. There was no other way to describe him: gray skin the color of a corpse, jaundiced eyes that failed to discern reality, movements and expressions that seemed to function without the benefit of a brain. Worst of all was the moment when he returned Ben's stare: standing immobile in the middle of the foyer, those dead, yellow eyes caught Ben directly and refused to look away, widening incrementally. It was as though he had detected a new scent across the lobby, the scent of a stranger and its compromised soul.

Ben knifed his way between two gawking young women and stepped across the room. The man's suit was massive, at least two sizes too big for him, a ratty belt flopping from his waist and a brown jacket swallowing his frame like a starched black hole. His body had shrunk to almost nothing, sunken eyes above slanting cheekbones, and a blur of oily black hair sprang from his head in every direction. There was always the same look on the man's face, lip curled in a wicked sneer, eyes wide and glinting.

Ben came to rest a few feet away, shivering. He didn't know what to say—simply gaped at the thing in front of him.

"There was a fire at the mill," the man said in a high-pitched wheeze, as though his vocal chords no longer functioned correctly.

"I'm sorry?" Ben said, at a loss for words.

"Were you there? Did you see it? The bodies. No one made it out alive." He grinned at this, enjoying some private, morbid joke, revealing two rows of rotten teeth.

But this was as far as the conversation went. From the front doorway, a patter of footsteps could be heard. A dark-haired woman wearing pearls over her black dress and clutching a small blue handbag entered the room. She was followed by a teenage boy with floppy dark hair, hands thrust deep in the pockets of his loose dress pants. Ben stepped back instinctively, blending into the shadows.

"Where the hell is he this time?" the boy said, allowing his eyes to drift across the funeral-goers with general indifference. The woman had spotted the corpse-like figure in the foyer by now and raced toward him, nudging a few congregants out of the way. Her pointed shoes flitted over the carpet in a blur.

"Daniel, there you are. I told you to wait, dear. You know I don't like you going off by yourself." She came to his side and hooked her arm through his, clutching his elbow and holding him upright. "Let's go sit down."

"For the funeral," Daniel added uncertainly.

"That's right. Let's sit down for the funeral."

Daniel lurched into motion and slapped his leg three times, trying to kickstart it into motion. The woman—his wife, Ben presumed—whispered reassurances in his ear as they passed. The man's yellow eyes caught Ben's once again, twinkling with some vile, unknown thought.

It was nearly eleven o'clock by this point. Reverend Scariot began darting between funeral-goers, ushering them toward the doors as the service was about to commence. Like a flock of despondent sheep herded by an especially frantic shepherd, they filed through the double doors, slowly taking their seats, some of them finding solace by opening the Bibles in front of them. Ben followed after, tiptoeing to the rearmost pew and taking a seat; he tried not to draw attention to himself, though a few of the townspeople craned their necks to stare him down anyway.

The funeral began like almost any other. Reverend Scariot, looking flinty at the pulpit, invited the congregation to join in a hymn, "Guide Me O Thou Great Redeemer." The cacophonous voices singing "death of death and Hell's destruction, land me safe on Canaan's side" sent a shiver through Ben's body. Then Scariot provided his own words of comfort, accompanied, ever so often, by glances at the stranger in the back of the room.

"Friends, neighbors," Scariot began. "Well, I might as well say that you're my family. My brothers, sisters, sons, daughters. Because that's what life in Grange is like. In our town, on this beautiful patch of earth, we don't simply live next to each other and pass our neighbors on the street. No. Like good Christians, we consider each other family. We respect and love each other. The loss of Maria Amherst, felt so sharply by our brother Nathan, hurts us deeply. I know that all of us, every single one, now feels just a little emptier where Maria once had a place in our hearts. But I'd also like us to remember that it's here that she still lives," he intoned, touching his chest.

"Brothers, sisters, think back seven months to the end of March, when Maria"—and this was when Scariot, halting his speech, cast a quizzical look in Ben's direction—"had her accident. Nothing more than a patch of ice on the road. We almost lost her forever that night. But God, sometimes, is lenient and forgiving. It was not yet Maria's time to leave us behind. And so He returned her to us, allowing us to love and cherish her still. This is a sign of his benevolence—the Lord giveth, brothers and sisters, it is true. He gave Maria back to us, back to

Nathan, even when her death…" At this point, someone coughed in the audience, a harsh and scornful sound. "…appeared to be imminent.

"But the Lord also taketh away, as we all know," he continued in a pompous voice. "He may grant life, but He cannot grant *eternal* life. And so, Maria's return to this Earth turned out to be a layover—a detour. Life was given back to her, only to be snatched away again." There was a loud, sudden whimper followed by a series of choking sobs from the front row. Ben could barely make out Nathan Amherst drooping, shoulders hunched, as an elderly woman next to him—Maria's mother, Ben guessed—rubbed his back robotically.

"One of those cruel twists of fate, you might say," Scariot continued. "But I'd prefer to look at it another way. We were given a few more months with Maria, but she was always meant for…Heaven. She was always meant for Heaven. So despite the loss we feel—the pain that we share with Nathan, whom we all must support, now, and cherish and guide back to happiness—we should take comfort that Maria is where she's meant to be.

"Please join me in a prayer. Corinthians 15." Scariot looked at Ben again, but there was something different this time—a resolute look, burning and direct, and though the words were consolatory there was something dark beneath them. "So will it be with the resurrection of the dead. The body that is sown is perishable, it is raised imperishable; it is sown in dishonor, it is raised in glory; it is sown in weakness, it is raised in power; it is sown a natural body, it is raised a spiritual body…"

He placed his hands on the open pages of the Bible and looked up at the congregation. "My friends, family. Maria's natural body may be gone, but her spiritual body—Maria's soul—has been…raised."

Someone coughed again. Ben's eyes drifted to the clerestory of stained-glass windows. He pondered Reverend Scariot's words, searching for some kind of hidden meaning that the townspeople might decipher. Another hymn was sung, "Now the Green Blade Rises," and it struck Ben that this might have been the spark for religion in the first place—to convince the living that death is not permanent and absolute, that it can be conquered. It was hardly a coincidence, he thought, that Christianity's founding parable was based on resurrection. But if so, the town of Grange offered not a validation but a mockery of this belief. There was no solace in whatever "spiritual body" of Maria's still lingered. It was not led by angelic hands to some righteous Elysium. Whatever killed her made sure of that. Ben had seen it on its face.

The funeral rolled on in ignorance of this paradox, and as the hymn finished Ben snapped out of his morbid thoughts. There was a general rustling among the pews, a shifting of legs and involuntary sighs that suggested the crowd was growing restless, that this service might have been simply a necessary charade. Scariot spoke up again, a bit louder and more rapid, as he asked if anyone in attendance might like to share their memories of Maria. The silence was conspicuous now, dotted with half-suppressed noises of impatience.

At last, a tall woman with a dark blond ponytail raised herself, cradling a pregnant belly that couldn't have been more than a month from delivery. A man seated behind her grazed her back as she stood— Ben was struck by the quiet, loving gesture. She shuffled to the altar without a word, cutting through a beam of sunlight. "Ah!" Reverend Scariot exclaimed. "Good, Cheryl. Good."

Maria's sister labored up three steps to the pulpit. As she neared Reverend Scariot, he shook her hand and grazed the bottom of her elbow, in a gesture he had been informed was comforting. She said nothing, looking steadfast at the floor, and approached the altar with a tremulous feeling. Scariot stepped away, growing suspicious.

"Maria was..." Already she stifled a sob, looked away, covered her mouth—then regained her composure. "Well I don't have to tell you what Maria was. Just *good*. Decent. Which is more uncommon than you would think." Ben sensed a mounting tension in the room as Cheryl's words hardened.

"But you didn't grow up with her. I did. Here in Grange, like most of you. We had a perfect childhood, which, you know...I didn't realize until later how valuable that was." She swallowed hard, caressing her unborn baby. In the front pew next to Nathan, Maria and Cheryl's mother, a Miss Virginia Baker, whimpered and shook, her wall of resilience crumbling down. A man behind her leaned over and offered his handkerchief. Virginia took it coldly, crumpling it in her lap as she wrung her hands together.

On the altar, Cheryl continued. "But we had a good life, growing up. Maria had aspirations, like anyone. She made our parents buy a subscription to *National Geographic* when she was five, and my father never forgave her." She laughed—there was no levity in it. "She wanted to travel. She thought she had time."

At this, Scariot moved to Cheryl's side, grabbing her arm as he leaned forward and whispered something in her ear. When he stepped away, Ben noticed Cheryl glance in his direction, her attention faltering for a split-second. Then she sighed and continued. "I wish she had time. There was so much she wanted to see."

A pause so endless they could have sung another hymn. Then Cheryl stared at Nathan, her face unreadable, ever-changing.

"Maria deserved better. Most of us didn't understand her. And now she's gone." The tears came forward this time, breaking their levees, and Cheryl didn't seem to care. "I don't know how or why, but she was sacrificed for us. You all know it. It's not fair."

Ben sprang to the front of his seat at these words, but before Cheryl could continue, Scariot stepped to her side and placed his hand against her back—then gave her a not-so-gentle nudge, hardly attempting to disguise the gesture as compassionate. Ben even thought he heard a stifled gasp. He watched Cheryl trot rapidly to the furthest aisle and stomp to the back of the church, evading the hostile stares that Ben could *feel* more than he could see. Scariot cleared his throat, taking position at the pulpit once more.

"It's true. Cheryl's right—it's not fair. Maria had so much living left to do. It's never fair. But...all we can do is move on." A pair of sudden thuds from the back of the church as the doors slammed shut behind Cheryl. "Let us remember, though, that we are here to bid Maria farewell and celebrate her positive spirit. Won't someone else share their memories of Maria with us?"

A cough, the rustle of fabric—the very sound of unease. Ben thought he saw a young woman at the end of a pew raise herself into the aisle, only to collapse back onto her seat when the man next to her tugged at her shirt.

"I know we all remember her fondly," Scariot prodded. "Would anyone else like to pay their respects?"

Some of them started turning toward Nathan, who cowered turtle-like at the front of the church. Soon, Scariot's eyes followed them, joining the deluge of accusatory stares. What could Nathan do? He wrung his hands as he rose to his feet. The carpet was quicksand, each step an impossibility. The sun emerged from behind the storm clouds and intensified, plowing through the windows, casting a horrible spotlight on Nathan's movements. Eventually, he climbed the steps to the pulpit and took Scariot's position at the altar, looking out over an army of unmoved neighbors who demanded something of him he couldn't give.

His hands fumbled, muddy with sweat, and he coughed an unpleasant noise from his throat. "Maria…"

There it was, one word and then silence.

"Maria was my love. What can I say?"

Each word was a test of strength, a struggle of body over mind.

"I met her after high school. Never wanted anything but to be by her side, to marry her. We did, a few months later. Bought a house. We lived there, together, for sixteen years. I mis—"

Something reptilian, it seemed, was slithering up Nathan's throat, resulting in a sickening, guttural gag. Nathan shook his head. It was simply a spasm of misery, making speech impossible.

"I miss her. I don't know what to do without her."

In the haze created by tears forming in his eyes, it was difficult to tell that something was burning. He smelled it before he sensed the pain, the sour odor of singed flesh, then heard the gasps of shock that came from the congregation. Nathan blinked and looked around, his confusion growing more frantic. There was a trail of smoke coming from the palm of his left hand, where he felt the pain suddenly, his skin burning, bubbling away.

His palm was placed on the black-leather cover of the Holy Bible.

Chapter 19 — The Mark of the Beast

Nathan jerked his hand from the Bible, trembling in pain, a cloud of smoke lingering in the sunlight. His skin was red and plastic, marked with blisters. He collapsed to his knees, cradling his wrist, gazing in terror at his open palm.

Some people craned their necks to peer at the man kneeling above his wife's casket, paralyzed. In the front row a man stood, one of Nathan's only good friends, and scrambled onto the altar, kneeling next to Nathan with a hand on his shoulder. Reverend Scariot joined him on the other side, staring astonished at Nathan's burns. Ben scanned the crowd, finding some of the attendants oddly unimpressed.

Nathan winced, not knowing where the worst pain came from. In the middle of everything, from somewhere deep inside his gut, somehow *beneath* his gut, a wave of fury pulsed, expanding, rising to his brain. In one motion, Nathan stood, grabbed the Bible with his right hand, screamed, and heaved the book into the distance, sending it soaring through a stained-glass window—the one depicting the Last Judgment. Shards of glass fell onto concrete outside, a flood of sunlight leaked into the church. Scenes from the Last Judgment now sat on the sidewalk in fragments, human souls bound for Heaven or Hell interrupted midflight.

Nathan fell, depleted, on the carpet. The two men at the altar knelt at his side, protecting him from the view of the funeral-goers. Many of them milled about, whispering, some of them crying, terrified. Children hugged their parents. Reverend Scariot rose and turned to them, trying (and failing) to keep his own fear under control. "Please stay calm, everyone, Nathan's all right. We'll take care of him and then move on. Stay calm."

They obeyed in the way that unsettled masses of people often do; chaos was restrained but there was an electric tension, a bristling containment of rage. Scariot and the other man dragged Nathan from the altar, his arms draped around their shoulders. He was carried to a small row of chairs at the front of the church, separated from the nave by a narrow hallway. Inevitably, a small group of Samaritans wandered over, asking if they could help but mostly wanting to get a glimpse of the town's newest scandal. One of them jogged to a church office and retrieved a first-aid kit, returning to Nathan and applying ointment to his hand, finally covering it with gauze. Gradually Nathan came to, looking pale and weakened, shivering from exhaustion. There was only fear when he glanced at the gaping faces around him.

Fifteen minutes later, however, Nathan insisted he was ready to go on with the funeral—they still had to say goodbye to Maria "properly." Adjusting his overlarge sport coat and mustering more strength than can possibly be imagined, he walked back into the nave and raised his hand to the crowd in a rueful gesture. "Sorry, everyone. Sorry."

There was a general titter of relief among the crowd. Some of them even applauded, to Ben's disbelief. Nathan walked on, staring ahead, and came to rest by Maria's casket, readying himself for the line of mourners that would soon march past him, paying their respects. Reverend Scariot followed a moment later, proclaiming that the funeral could continue. At this, Cheryl and Virginia joined Nathan to his right, both of them walking with heavy, wavering steps. Maria's casket leered at them as they passed. Scariot moped at the end of their doleful little line-up, waiting to usher people down the aisles and out of the church.

At last, a line formed in the center aisle as the attendees prepared to view Maria's casket one last time. The young girl with large glasses and her enigmatic grandmother hurried to the front of the line, a thin trail of mascara barely visible, running down the woman's cheek.

Nathan handled himself during the procession about as well as could be expected: he said the same thing every time, a curt "Thank you, thanks," followed by a grave smile and a brusque nod of the head.

Robotic, desperate, disingenuous maybe, but not disgraceful. Maria's mother ensured that her tone was gracious and appreciative, but there remained nothing in her eyes, its reservoirs of grief momentarily drained. Cheryl made no attempt to conceal her bitterness while Scariot now functioned as little more than an usher, steering the line of people back to the foyer and out the door. As the townspeople passed by Maria's casket, their range of reactions varied widely, from a refusal to look at all to a choked-back flood of tears, from quiet indifference to quiet indignation.

Ben lingered at the rear of the church, pacing uncertainly as the line formed in front of him. When the last groups of people neared the pulpit, Ben shambled after them, joining the solemn posse. As he neared the casket—close enough to see his reflection in the polished wood—he offered a silent, wounded goodbye to Maria, apologizing for (in the words of his inner voice) failing her.

His son's coffin was darker and smaller. Both times, he forced himself to believe that the caskets in front of him were hollow.

Finally, Ben overheard Nathan mutter his thanks and goodbyes to the last of those in the procession. Ben stepped to his left, coming into Nathan's line of sight. His eyes, Nathan's, were puffy and enormous, old balloons whose air had been leaking out for days. Ben stepped close, wearing a steely, antagonistic look. Nathan shrunk back in momentary recognition, then simply stared ahead, waiting. Next to them, Cheryl glanced over, her curiosity piqued at this unexpected drama.

After a brimming pause, Ben nodded, somewhat dissatisfied. He held his hand forward. Nathan shook it, the movements rehearsed.

"Does everyone here know what you did?" Ben growled as they locked hands. "Or just me?"

Nathan barely responded. After shaking Ben's hand for three unwitting seconds, he suddenly jerked it away, returning it calmly to his side. Ben stared at Nathan; it was that old tug-of-war between hatred and compassion.

"I'm sorry for your loss."

Ben turned, walked away. He shook hands with Cheryl, then Virginia and Reverend Scariot. They regarded him coldly—even Cheryl, despite their shared displeasure with Nathan Amherst.

Halfway down the aisle, Ben looked back, the beam of sunlight from the broken window overexposing Maria's casket. Cheryl and Virginia hugged, one of the only signs of true consolation Ben had seen this morning. Nathan wandered back to Maria's casket, his bandaged hand tracing a gentle line along it. He offered silent apologies that would torture him always.

Loosening his necktie as he stormed through the crowds of people lingering near the entrance, Ben burst through the front doors, the bright, frigid air jostling him as he stepped outside. The rodent-faced man that Arnold had been talking to—the man with the ugly green shirt and pedantic air, a fifth-grade English teacher by the name of John Linden—watched Ben with some interest, a nasty smile edging onto his face.

Ben plodded across the parking lot, his nerves on high alert. He didn't know how badly the townspeople wanted him gone. There was an ear-splitting creak as Ben pulled his car door open, an involuntary wheeze as he collapsed onto the driver seat. He situated his rearview mirror, angling it toward the front of the church. Now Ben could only wait—wait until the battered, minuscule figure of Nathan Amherst stepped outside.

*****

As always happens, life resumed its tedium after the events of the funeral. A pair of attendants from Grange's only funeral home began wheeling the casket out a back hallway, where a refrigerated van awaited. Outside the church, an altar boy wearing a dusty white frock swept the shards of a stained-glass window into a dustpan.

In the basement of the church, something more sinister was taking place. Four people hung around a cramped meeting room cushioned with thin carpet and buzzing with opaque lights. Reverend Scariot stood by a coffeemaker on a small folding table, pouring dark and steaming liquid into a Styrofoam cup. There was a box of donuts next to it, where a corpulent white-haired man—the town's mayor, Zachary Tinsdale—plucked an apple fritter and devoured half of it in one bite. A short woman with a severe look—Felicia Buruli, a nurse at the Grange Medical Clinic—sat crookedly on a pea-green chair, her fingers dancing over a phone's keypad. And in a shadowy corner of the room, Chief Terence Arnold leaned against the wall, facing away from the rest of them—staring darkly through a window near the ceiling, a blur of yellow light filtered through the glass. He hated these meetings. He hated himself for attending them. But such things had to be done.

They waited, the room growing heavier with silence.

After several minutes, the door was thrust open. John Linden walked in, clutching a briefcase in one hand and a pair of folders in the other, leaving a frantic, unsettled wake behind him.

"Sorry," he blurted out before he even stepped into the room. He kicked the door shut with his left foot. Arnold thought he saw the flimsy walls waver, as though patched together on a community-theater stage. "Spent some time coddling Nathan Amherst upstairs. It was…awkward, let's say."

"I'm not surprised," Felicia said, putting away her phone.

"Thanks for sticking around," John continued. "Not the best timing, I know, but I figured since we're all here…"

"That cop really made things difficult today," Mayor Tinsdale interjected, licking his fingers and wiping off the sugary remnants with a napkin. He took a seat at the head of the table, glaring at Chief Arnold. "Had me worried."

"Especially after Cheryl and Nathan's *eulogies*," Scariot said, a crackle of scorn on the last word. "I thought we were…"

"Fucked?" Felicia offered.

"Compromised."

"And what was that bit with the prayer you offered?" Tinsdale asked the priest standing behind him. "Corinthians, really? 'The body that is raised'? You were practically taunting him."

Scariot shrugged. "It was appropriate. Don't forget, I was speaking to our people as well. The funeral wasn't only for the outsider's benefit. The town needed it, too. This kind of thing has happened before, and solidarity is always paramount. We need to believe we're doing the right thing. They're scared, Zachary, you can see it."

"Of course they are," Arnold said from the corner.

"Can't we just get rid of him?" Tinsdale asked, turning his attention to Arnold. "What if he finds something out?"

Arnold stepped toward the table, haloed under the fluorescent lights, and sat with a heavy sigh. "Sure. Because a missing police officer from Milwaukee is exactly what we need."

"He's not going to find anything out," John replied. "Nothing concrete."

"Well, who knows what Maria told him?" Felicia asked venomously.

"Nothing," John said. "She was there five minutes, tops, before we got there, and then…it took care of the rest."

"It's a good thing Nathan called you when he did," Tinsdale said. "I know you're not a fan of Mr. Amherst, but notifying us after Maria took his keys—letting us arrange everything—that was smart."

"Yeah, it was smart," Arnold said. "It also makes him think that he killed his wife. No wonder he's so torn up."

"He *did* kill his wife. And his son," Felicia replied. "No use pretending otherwise."

"Really?" Arnold asked. "Whatever we conjured that night, whatever's in those woods, *that* didn't kill her?"

Voices were raised; John and Felicia responded in unison, growing tired of Arnold's sanctimonious tone. The sharp, clear voice of Scariot cut through the din: "No one is blameless." John, Felicia, and Arnold quieted themselves, outdone by Scariot's composure. "Let us not forget we're working together on this. Doing what must be done."

There was a long pause, a silence filled with desperate exculpations. From somewhere upstairs, muffled footsteps could be heard as the church was cleaned and swept, resuming its idolatrous sheen. It was, finally, Scariot who spoke again: "So, what *are* we going to do with that policeman?"

Arnold shook his head. "I'm calling his superiors today. The kid's already in hot water, they'll bring him back home."

"And if they don't?" Tinsdale muttered.

"We'll take care of it," Felicia said, shrugging with grim finality.

Reverend Scariot shuffled to the coffeepot, refilling his cup. John Linden straightened his folders on the table in front of him, struggling to contain a smile.

"Anyway, we're getting off topic."

"And what topic is that?" Mayor Tinsdale snapped. "Why did you ask us here, John?"

"You know what day it is. All of us should realize the urgency of the situation. I'm sure Reverend Scariot does."

Scariot nodded bleakly, allowing Linden to continue.

"October 31st. The most liminal day of the year, spiritually speaking."

"Meaning what?" asked Buruli.

"Meaning the door between our world and another is left wide open," Scariot explained, gesturing ominously.

"It means that whatever we have here in Grange, it needs to be…propitiated," John added. "There has to be another offering by tomorrow night, at the latest."

"Or what?" Tinsdale asked.

"Or it's going to be a very unpleasant winter," Scariot said. "People will be lost."

"Confronting evil spirits when they're most powerful, that's what this day is all about," John offered. "Always has been, for centuries. If you'd done your homework on our little predicament, all of you, you would have known that."

"Sorry, John, I don't spend my nights reading up on devil worship," Buruli said with a sneer.

"Okay, so we need a sacrifice by tomorrow," Tinsdale said. "What about Hannah Dorian? Seemed like she was on the hook last time you talked to her, John."

Linden offered a grin as devilish as anything residing in the woods outside of Grange. "That, Mayor Tinsdale, is exactly why I asked you here." With ceremonial pomp, he pulled a thin stack of papers from a folder, neatly held together with a large black paperclip. He passed it to Chief Arnold, seated to his left. "Signed contract. Terry, take a look at Clause B, Paragraph 2. 'Hannah Dorian, the Client in Question, agrees to supply Amy Dorian, age twelve, as the Method of Payment in exchange for…'"

"Just tell us what it says, John," Buruli finally huffed.

"Amy for Rebecca. A natural, really."

Arnold rearranged the stack of papers and passed it to Felicia, trying to suppress a look of nausea as he did so.

"Nice work, John," Tinsdale said.

"When will it happen?" Scariot asked, peering over Buruli's shoulder as he stepped to her side.

"Tonight. Maybe tomorrow. Amy wanted to go trick-or-treating today, Hannah said."

All of them became silent at this, reminded for a moment of the human cost underlying their exchange. But, as often happens in business transactions of this sort, they soon shut such considerations out of mind, merely happy to meet their so-called quota. The contract was passed to Reverend Scariot, who flipped immediately to the last page. There was Hannah Dorian's scrawled signature, with three red splotches to the right. A contract signed in blood.

"Hey, how about that Bible trick with Nathan this morning?" Felicia added. "Wasn't expecting that."

Scariot nodded, his expression unreadable. Sometimes he could convince himself that he was trying to do God's work, making their community peaceful and inhabitable, taming the dark forces nearby. This was not one of those times.

"Nathan signed a contract," he replied. "Creates a link that can't be broken. He's marked."

"And so is Hannah," Arnold replied, scowling.

"Terry, I know you're a sensitive man," Linden said. "But try to be happy. Everything will work out."

Arnold simply glowered at him.

"So, if we need to…what, appease this thing," Buruli began, "and we have this outsider, this cop that already knows too much…wouldn't two sacrifices be better than one? I mean, you know—two birds, one stone, that sort of thing."

"I'm with Felicia," Mayor Tinsdale said. "People die in accidents all the time. Some cop on vacation up north—tragic drowning accident, maybe. Sad story, but it's not going to make much news."

"No," Arnold said, louder than he'd intended. "We do *not* want an outside police force poking around here. Let's not do anything stupid."

"Besides," Linden cut in, "we know it doesn't much care for…*mature* offerings. It prefers innocence."

Chief Arnold shot John a queasy look. The table grew quiet but the silence was calm and placated, reassured in its dominion. The contract made its way fully around the table, returning to the skeletal hands of John Linden. He replaced it in the folder and, moving with stern precision, returned the folder to its place in his briefcase—evidence of murder thus safely stowed away, concealed behind a stack of fifth-grade English papers that Linden had yet to grade.

Chapter 20 — The Last Judgment

It was almost twelve-thirty by the time Nathan walked out of the church, looking meek and ragged in a jacket that swallowed him whole. Cheryl and Virginia left at the same time, walking in the other direction. Nathan's mother-in-law turned and said something to him before they parted, but Cheryl only plowed ahead, unable to speak to the man she blamed for her sister's death.

The parking lot was almost deserted. Ben spied the front doors in his rearview mirror, no longer concerned about the watchful eyes of the townspeople. He shifted in his seat as he watched Nathan exit, turning to peer over his left shoulder. Nathan dragged himself to a gargantuan pale Buick. Then he lurched into the vehicle, turned the ignition, angled it out of the parking lot and onto the road, glass glittering in the sun. Ben waited until the Buick was a half block away until he started his Jeep and rolled out after him, praying that Nathan was too distraught to concern himself with anything as banal as self-preservation.

Through the town they crept, over the five blocks of the downtown district, right on Cedar Street, left on Fifth, past the grocery store and sports bars and the Grange Performance Hall. The outer radius of the town was mostly residential, wide tranquil avenues lined with two-story houses, a worthy attempt at normalcy.

What drifted through Ben's mind during this low-speed pursuit? What spurred him on as he inched along rural roads, tires crunching over gravel? If asked later about his intentions, he would respond by noting suspicion of murder and tactful surveillance; he would say that Nathan had not yet been exonerated. But as memories of two different funerals coalesced, forming one terrible slipstream of grief, he knew that he was driven by something darker, something that made him tremble with rage as he gripped the steering wheel.

Arcadia Street was a parody of suburban bliss, all neatly mowed lawns and multicolored leaves and dogs barking somewhere in the distance. As Ben approached a stop sign, he spotted Nathan's Buick curving into a driveway and coming to rest two blocks away, a cloud of gray ashen smoke chugging from the tailpipe. He waited there, observing from afar as Nathan craned himself from the Buick and walked to the front door, fumbling with his keys.

Ben turned onto Arcadia Street a moment later, sidling to the curb several houses away. The Jeep idled there, churning laboriously. Ben watched. He was confused, scared. He was shaking with some violent, unnamable emotion. Had he forced himself to remain calm and rational, he would have regrouped and approached Nathan peacefully. He would have remembered his duty as an officer of the law, the ideals that ostensibly defined him. He would have remembered late August, when a man accused of domestic violence lay unmoving on the pavement as Ben pummeled him, fist crunching into bone, and he would have vowed never to repeat that mistake. But rationale was not an option.

He cut the ignition.

He opened the door of his Jeep, stepped outside, moved to the sidewalk. A middle-schooler passed by on a bicycle. The Buick stood there, 1211 Arcadia. The blinds were closed. The house was proud but derelict, an image of domestic bliss gone to seed. As he approached, Ben considered walking up to the front door, bare and honest, but there were too many houses in the vicinity, too many eyes that could pry from behind veiled windows. So he walked to the back of the house, lined with dark-blue paneling. The sun was harsh and direct. There was a basketball hoop fixed to the garage, unused. He turned to his left, to the backdoor. There was a row of garbage bins here, and a bicycle turned on its side in the unkempt grass—a bike that Ben was certain belonged to Ryan Amherst, once.

He gritted his teeth, hunched his shoulders, clenched his fists as he tried to fend off the cold. He stepped onto a low landing at the backdoor. The screen was unlocked. He opened it and rapped twice on the wooden door inside, the sensation sharp on his knuckles.

A heavy boot kicking a man, twice. He was lying on the ground in a sweltering alley in August, drunk and sweaty and howling from pain. Blood flowed. A rib cracked, at least once, Ben could feel. He glanced up and saw some people, wide-eyed bystanders on back stoops and balconies, angry and aghast and capturing it all on cellphone video, hyperreal.

There was no answer. Ben stood there, rattled. The past overwhelmed the present today, unwelcome memories flooding back.

The call came in at 3:43pm. Kids were just getting home from school, dropped off by parents or careening out of yellow buses. Possible ten-fifteen, suspect may be armed, 38th and National. Ben was silent all day, wired, primed to detonate. His partner, Alex Washington, had asked him once on the hour if he was feeling all right, he looked pale and was sweating profusely, he looked like he hadn't slept in days…

A bird called somewhere in the distance. Ben looked around, trying to calm himself. He knocked again. Rapid, impatient.

There was music playing on a car radio in the distance and the sound of some kids, a hundred of them Ben thought, crying when they pulled up. The screen door was open, it was a hot afternoon, and they heard the volcanic sound of dishes being thrown as Ben stepped out of the vehicle, and his hand was already on his baton.

Ben looked at his watch. It was nearly one o'clock. Trick-or-treaters would begin roaming the sidewalks in two hours, families hoping to move on, barring murder from their thoughts. If any of them knocked on the door to 1211 Arcadia, the knocks would go unanswered. Nathan wanted no human contact, least of all with the children in his neighborhood. Probably, Ben guessed, he wouldn't leave his house until Maria was buried.

All of which meant Ben had to act quickly.

He knocked again, as hard as the calm afternoon would permit, and felt the door buckle against his hand.

"Mr. Amherst. Open up."

Three more staccato knocks, Ben's skin raw in the cold.

"Nathan, please. It won't take long."

He grimaced. Maybe it wouldn't matter. Maybe the meaninglessness of chance would steer Ben in a better direction.

His left foot pivoted. He moved to step off the landing when, at last, Ben heard a pair of locks unclasping inside, followed by the incremental opening of the door. Nathan stood there in the dim kitchen, barely visible through a crack in the door. Chance might be indifferent, but it can also be cruel, leading you to your lowest depths through nothing more than cause and effect.

Nathan blinked and swallowed as he spoke, giving his words a sad, guttural tremor. "It's you. What do you want?"

"I just want to talk, Mr. Amherst."

"About what?" The words slurred out of him, a slow leak.

"I just think you should talk to somebody. About everything. You've been through a lot, Nathan, I think it would be healthy for you."

Nathan stood there, looking gray in the shadows. Then, finally, "I don't want to talk."

He shoved the door with his left hand as he turned away from Ben. But instead of the soft click of the door shutting, he heard a muffled bang—the door encountered Ben's outstretched hand, hanging lazily open. Before Nathan could turn back to the door, Ben stepped inside, his boot sinking into a welcome mat made of straw.

Nathan stopped, narrowed his eyes, shook his head, unsure what to do. "Hey, I didn't say you could come in here," he said, gesturing meekly.

Ben closed the door behind him. This time, the click rang clearly through the kitchen. Above the door, a kitschy decoration of a hen wearing an apron looked down on them, amused.

Nathan stood more erect now, understanding the urgency of the moment.

"What is this?"

"Like I said, Nathan, I just want to talk."

Nathan waited, thin and trembling. He looked around his own kitchen and felt he had never been there before. "I'm calling the police."

He nodded emphatically, assuaging his own doubts. He turned and walked to the hallway, his shoes clacking against tile. He took four steps to the entryway, where his cellphone lay on a side table.

Ben stood there a moment, his eyes glittering in the dark. Then he stomped after Nathan, his footsteps quick and stealthy, springing across the kitchen floor. Through the shadows of the hallway, four long strides. Nathan heard him when it was too late—a quiet footstep behind him and a creak of the floorboards. The right side of his body twitched, trying to force itself into action. But before Nathan could turn Ben grabbed him by the shoulders, his hands shaking with adrenaline and a loss of self, and he shoved Nathan into the banister of the stairway, the bridge of his nose slamming into hard wood. Nathan felt it break, a rubber-band snap somewhere inside his head, and felt the blood flow. He was about to swear, exclaim the most foul thing he could come up with, but suddenly his mind reeled and words became impossible, he could barely move his jaw.

Then he felt hands on his shoulders again, pulling him from the banister while he cowered in pain. His body ragdoll limp, he was flung in the other direction, falling onto his side on the white carpet of the living room, the bloodstains bright and ugly. The sun struggled to pierce through closed windows, diffusing through the room in scattered light.

Ben stepped into the living room, silent. He could feel his pulse racing, clawing against his chest.

Shaking on the carpet, Nathan forced himself to utter a few meaningless words. "Jesus. Fuck."

Ben was a step away now. Nathan looked up at him, struggling to lift his eyes, and the face that he saw on the policeman's body terrified him—not because of the rage and the impending violence, which he expected, but because of the misery and desperation, which contorted his features into a scowl and made his eyes dance madly.

Ben planted his left leg, swung his right backwards, and landed it square in Nathan's chest, feeling his body rattle against the tip of his boot.

In a teeming alley on a hot August day, a man lay on his side on the pavement, children and neighbors gawking, when Ben Dmitrovich swung his right leg back and made contact with another man's ribs. Richard Twozinski, his name was, and he would soon be cleared of all charges as something of an apology from the Milwaukee judicial system.

Broke two of his ribs and his nose, didn't you? Well, you're developing a routine, Officer.

Ben shoved against Nathan's left shoulder with his boot, kicking him onto his back. Nathan's chest shuddered with pain, each nerve gasping.

Ben closed his eyes. He lifted his leg over Nathan's body and collapsed onto his chest, straddling him. He held Nathan's blood-splattered collar with unsteady hands. Then they moved upward, feeling the warm skin and throbbing veins of Nathan's throat, and squeezed around it. Nathan let out a sickening gasp, the air suddenly cut off, and his eyes widened, monstrous, pleading. It might have been a comical image, and maybe it still was: two pathetic men fighting about nothing, surreal against lush carpeting and overstuffed couches and wood-paneled walls that no longer belonged to anyone.

The worst part, at least in Ben's mind, was that Sarah could never know—he could never tell her. He wouldn't have been able to withstand the shame.

Ben's hands tightened around the neck of the man below him. He could feel the flesh and organs strain against the growing pressure.

But it had been all over the news and the internet, of course, the latest police scandal recorded on cellphones and reproduced for the world to see.

Inevitably she would find out, and it would all reaffirm her opinion of Ben Dmitrovich, the small, desperate man he is.

The memories came back to Ben as he straddled Nathan Amherst on the carpet. Ben's eyes were forced shut. He breathed in heavy, retching gasps, matching the sounds of his victim. Finally, slowly, he loosened his grip on Nathan's throat, no longer having the energy. Ben shook as Nathan peered at him, a twisted expression of shock and fear on Nathan's face. Once he realized that Ben had become a whimpering wreck, that death was no longer imminent, Nathan contorted his body, feeling a tremor of agony in his chest, and pulled himself away. With a vehement groan, Nathan came to rest on the floor against an oversized recliner.

Ben stayed there, kneeling on the carpet, for several seconds— though it seemed unbearably longer to Nathan, who could only observe this pitiful human statue. Then, finally, Ben opened his eyes, covering his mouth with a trembling forearm. He blinked, took in his surroundings, reacclimated himself to the Amhersts' home. He dried his tears with the sleeve of his jacket. He scurried away from Nathan until he found the white-gold sofa behind him, collapsing against it.

They stared at each other, Ben and Nathan—or at least Ben gazed in Nathan's direction at some void an infinite distance away. It was Nathan who spoke then, despite the pain.

"You gonna tell me what the fuck that was?"

Ben shifted and looked at him. It wasn't that Ben had forgotten about Nathan. It was rather, ludicrously, that he expected Nathan to be concerned about *his* injustice.

"I'm sorry," Ben said, the words thick with shame. Nathan would have laughed if he didn't expect it to feel like glass ricocheting in his chest. "I'm sorry, I am."

"I don't have to tell you shit."

"No. You don't."

Nathan wanted to rage, take vengeance for his humiliation, scream and pummel Ben, but the pain was too great. Instead, Nathan hissed: "What makes you think I won't call the police?"

"I know you will."

The seconds ticked by on a nearby clock, the room dusty and weighted with anger. It was, again, Nathan who spoke.

"Well…here we are. You want to talk, now's your chance."

Ben processed what he said and smiled sadly.

"I know what you've been through, Nathan. I lost my son, too, and my wife, all in the last couple months. My son, Aaron, he was five. Diagnosed last winter with leukemia," Ben said, voicing the last word with contempt. "Thought I could save him. He died in May. I never thought he was going to die, I never thought that was a real possibility. My wife was my own fault. I…wasn't strong enough. I did a lot of the same things you did."

"How the hell would you know what I've done?"

"Drinking," Ben went on. "Every night 'til I couldn't walk any more, couldn't think straight. Desperate, empty. Sarah moved out in August. She stayed as long as she could, I know. I was forcing her not to live her life, reminding her of Aaron every single second. It was… We're divorced. She's with someone else now."

Ben took a long time to regroup, breathing deeply.

"Somehow, I just realized how similar we are, you and me. The same story."

Nathan resituated against the chair, straining to move his back.

"Not the same at all. Don't compare yourself to me."

"I guess we're all the same, people like us. We realize how weak we are and take out our anger against the world."

Nathan shook his head remotely, ignoring Ben's last rumination.

"Come on, you break in here, beat the hell out of me, then expect me to feel for you?" Nathan shook his head. "No fucking way. We've all been through something."

Ben opened his mouth, on the verge of confessing everything. But he was already wracked with shame, trembling with regret, and he couldn't force himself to voice the words. So at length he said, simply:

"I have to believe it's possible. To move on. For both of us."

Nathan scoffed, caring little about Ben's sympathy. After another moment of silence broken by a pair of kids laughing outside, Ben continued.

"I want you to tell me about your son, Nathan."

There was a momentary twitch from Nathan, which he tried to conceal. He gaped at Ben, wearing a feigned look of witlessness.

"What do you mean?"

"I know you had a son. Ryan. Maria told me."

Anger, this time, flashed onto Nathan's face, again quickly subdued.

"I think it's time I call the police." Nathan planted his hand against the floor and started to rise to his feet, withstanding pain. "Can I assume you won't try to beat the hell out of me this time?"

"Let me say one thing." Nathan stayed sitting. "*My son for me.* An exchange. That was one of the last things your wife told me." Nathan flinched, struck by the thought of Maria in Ben's motel room moments before her death. "I think that woman, Cheryl, at the funeral was right—it was a sacrifice. Your son died to bring Maria back to life. And there's something in those woods that can make it happen. I've seen it. I saw whatever killed your wife, and it has been here for a very, very long time. Am I right?"

Nathan wore an empty expression but swallowed hard and stood. "I better make that phone call."

Ben, too, forced himself to stand, silhouetted against the windows.

"I'm not going to stop you," he said. "You do realize other kids are in danger. *All* of them are in danger."

Nathan, by now, had neared the front door. He held a phone in his hand but glared back at Ben before he dialed.

207

"Of course."

Chapter 21 — Evil Spirits Everywhere

In the full strobing sunlight of the early afternoon, a rusty blue pickup rumbled down I-63, shuddering as it muscled through the wind. The driver was not the smartest or kindest man in town and had a face like a lump of clay flattened in a vice, long and narrow. The windows were open despite the temperature, which hovered around the upper thirties today.

About a mile and a half up the road, he knew, on the eastern side of the highway, there would be a thin patch of bushes leaving barely enough room for a man to fit through. But this was the way, the route he had taken countless times since he started the job three years ago. By now, he knew the landmarks: a pair of V-shaped birch trees directly across the road, the red-leaved tamaracks that flanked the trail on either side about twenty feet in.

Like most jobs, this one had grown old before long. It consisted mostly of trips to and from Grange, errands for groceries and medicine and other things she needed, the woman in the cabin.

And, of course, sometimes there was the kidnapping. No, he didn't take part in that himself, his inner voice constantly reminded him; he didn't do the abducting at least. Just drive, quiet and safe, and keep the pickup waiting outside and, when they bring out the kid wriggling and screaming, start the ignition and drive away slowly but don't turn on the lights.

He was coming close now. He saw the tamaracks towering in the distance. In the back of the pickup truck were three bags of groceries, mostly canned soup; four mysterious plants, potted and stowed in a padded crate, grown from unrecognizable seeds that did not appear naturally in this land; and a live chicken, clucking in the wind, prancing about a layer of straw in a locked cage.

He put on his turn signal and came to a stop, then veered off the road where it seemed there was nowhere to go. The shoulder dipped down, turning to muddy gravel, then a bed of frosty grass and dead leaves beyond. The man inched the truck toward a patch of greenery that seemed impenetrable—but as the sky-blue fender pushed aside a juniper bush, a narrow road appeared. It was nothing more than a path, really, threatening to drop off into ditches on either side, but it cut a soft curve through the shaded forest.

The truck slithered down the path, the chicken suddenly silent. The driver knew the drill by now; he had rolled up his windows minutes ago and cranked the heat. The approach was bitingly cold and often carried with it a drifting, unbearable stench. The most disturbing thing about it now, the man always brags, is how little it affects him. The strange and deathly aura of the place has become, for him, the monotony of labor.

Less than two minutes later, he saw it approaching in the distance, a narrow patch of wood visible over the crest of a hill. A black trail of smoke curling upwards. The truck sidled along, its tires crunching to rest about ten feet from the cabin, crooked and made of rotting wood.

The man cut the ignition and stepped out of the truck, making sure to breathe through his mouth. The muffled slam of the door echoed through the forest. He reached over the side of the truck and grabbed the metal cage, flinching as the chicken clucked in protest. At once, a vicious noise echoed from somewhere in the forest, a sound both shrill and thunderous. In response came a series of screeches in imitation of the chicken, bellowed in a wicked, disparaging tone.

The man shivered and put the cage down next to the cabin, to the right of a door that had become soggy and misshapen, as though made of strips of meat. The chicken grew quiet but wore, as always, an expression of panic.

He stepped to the front door, his shoes sucked into mud. He knocked on the door and felt liquescent wood give way, his knuckles stained with mud and the remains of dead insects. The door swung open, creaking inward. The room was somehow hot and noisome despite the cold weather outside.

He lifted a leg into the cabin and stepped onto the floor, which squirmed and squished beneath him. He scanned the cabin, eyes narrow, closing the door behind him. It seemed empty, but he knew well enough by now that she liked to hide.

Finally, after moments of searching while his eyes adjusted, something appeared: a slight movement of black fabric and two eyes glinting in the light. As though she knew at once that he had spotted her, she said from a distant corner: "Food."

He swallowed. This moment, maybe, was one that he had not yet gotten used to. "Yeah…I have food for you. I'll bring it in." She said nothing in the darkness, merely shifted from one foot to the other, an aching movement.

He turned, his hand reaching for the decrepit doorway; then stopped abruptly, remembering something. He turned back to the woman. There was no inflection in his voice. "There'll be a girl tonight."

This, at least, provoked a raspy moan from the shape in the cabin. She moved forward, leaning into the light, a skeleton dwarfed in a large black dress.

The man turned back to the door and nudged it aside, emerging into the autumn air. He brought in three bags of groceries and helped get a fire going; and he brought in the four plants, marked with sloppy labels reading Mandrake and Balmony, and set them on a table for her to chop; and he helped scrub at a butcher's knife that had a coating of dried blood caked onto the blade. Like he had done countless times before.

*****

211

Somewhere in Grange, a witch sauntered blissfully down a sidewalk. She had blond hair that tumbled beneath a tall, black hat, an angular fake nose marked with oversized warts, and temporary tattoos of jack-o-lanterns vivid on her cheeks (though partially concealed by her glasses). She uttered a loud, resounding laugh that was carried by the wind. Her friend Katie, a pirate (because that's what her brother was last year and her parents didn't want to buy a new costume), laughed in response, one of those private schoolyard jokes to which no one else has access.

Amy Dorian was happy. She had a horde of chocolate ready at hand. She enjoyed ridiculing the other costumes with her friend, carried on by an unfettered energy that floated in the air. She loved Halloween for this reason: the October chill, the feeling of the spectacular and unknown.

Twenty feet behind them, Hannah Dorian walked, shoes clicking against the sidewalk, giving the girls their space. She had offered to accompany them. She didn't want to be home for trick-or-treating. Instead, she watched everyone else pass by, her neighbors and their jubilant children, nodding politely to some of them. *Did they know?* Hannah wondered. She had signed the contract only last night, and John had promised to be discreet. But who knows how quickly gossip travels in Grange.

She watched everyone as they passed, analyzing, trying to understand them in a way she never had before. She was, more accurately, forcing herself to think about anything other than Amy or her daughter Rebecca—as she has done, unsuccessfully, for as long as she can remember. So she tried, instead, to think about nothing at all, to let the masks and costumes wash over her in a stream of surreal imagery. But then it became too frightening—some of the costumes looked impossibly realistic, grinning demon faces and rotten zombie flesh more vivid than any Halloween store could muster—and she forced herself to think of something else.

212

None of this concerned Amy, who laughed again, feeling worriless as she and Katie approached another front door. They stepped past a scarecrow slouched on a lawn chair in someone's yard. The disheveled figure—fattened with hay, two uneven buttons for eyes—reminded Amy of the man at the funeral that morning, the man whose wife had just died. He, too, carried himself like it was too much effort to simply go on, and his face seemed constantly in danger of tearing apart at the seams. The memory of him shocked Amy even as it came to her, but a moment later her friend giggled—a gleeful, hearty laugh at their math teacher, who drooped across the street in a Captain Kirk costume—and rid Amy of any thought of Nathan Amherst.

She walked without a care into the October afternoon.

Chapter 22 — A Short Conversation About Good and Evil

661-BCT.

The six digits stared at Ben from his little red notebook. The license plate of the hatchback at the Sarona Lake Motel the night of Maria's murder—the one that reappeared, two days later, at her funeral.

Ben sat in the front seat of his Jeep, heavy with self-loathing. He had stumbled from Nathan's home in a cloud of shame, certain that Nathan was speaking to Chief Arnold at that moment. On the way out, Ben had noticed a small black lockbox on the dining room table—the kind of thing families with children often use to safely stow their weapons—and wanted to tell Nathan not to use it on himself, whatever was in that box. But the words didn't come to him.

Since then, for the last hour, Ben awaited a furious phone call from Terence Arnold—or from his own captain, the reproachful voice of Miranda Prost, demanding his return for disciplinary action. He wondered if Nathan would tell everyone, the whole town, sending a bloodthirsty posse after him; an absurd image of a rabid mob came to him, armed with torches and pitchforks like an old MGM horror movie. Or, better yet, that thing in the woods that killed Maria, their own demonic guard dog—they could sic that on him, whatever it was. At least then he'd know what Maria went through.

So far, though, there were no outraged phone calls, no violent accusations from anyone in Grange. Ben pulled into the drive-thru of a fast-food restaurant and ordered a number four without incident. He calmed considerably as he sat in the parking lot, devouring assembly-line meat and French fries, the windows covering in condensation.

661-BCT.

There were those six digits, his obvious next move.

If you were smart, maybe you'd finally take Arnold's advice and get the hell out while you can.

If you were smart, you'd have done a lot of things differently.

Ben's police credentials may not have meant much in Grange, where everyone was now aware of the outsider in their midst, but they still had their benefits. Within minutes, he had found the number for the Washburn County DMV in nearby Spooner. The voice that answered oozed with indifference, a woman asking how she could help in a tone that suggested she'd prefer to do anything but.

Ben spoke rapidly, washing down a glutinous handful of fries with Diet Coke. He gave his name and rattled off his badge number, asking for a trace on a license plate with the bluntness of someone who's done it hundreds of times before. There was the usual silence on the other end. A few transferals, minutes spent in the no man's land of bureaucratic phone calls. Finally the credentials were verified and Ben gave them the license plate number.

Ben wasn't terribly surprised by the name they gave him: Jonathan Edward Linden. The middleman, Maria said; the one who sets everything up. His address was on Main Street, Main and Second, which hovered on the edge of the so-called downtown district, only four blocks from the grade school. He jotted the information down in his notebook, unsure how to proceed. He thanked the clerk and hung up, then wolfed down half of his burger in one bite. It had just turned four o'clock; trick-or-treating was halfway over, meaning oblivious children and their anxious parents would be roaming the sidewalks for another hour. Ben had begun to regain his composure—he no longer ground his teeth until his jaw ached—but he also preferred not to watch a mob of imperiled children frolic through town, wearing anomalous smiles.

He returned to the Sarona Lake Motel, grabbed his black suitcase from beneath the bed, and tossed it into the trunk of his Jeep. He would leave before tomorrow. If necessary, he could spend the night in the backseat of his car, covered by the winter parka stowed in his suitcase.

He shuffled to the front office, where the deskman idled, reading a newspaper while talk radio sputtered in the background. The man sprang to life at first, looking up with a bright burst of expectation; but when he saw Ben standing there, his expression soured. He said unconvincingly that it was a pleasure having Ben and wished him the best of luck and do come again, but there was a tacit recognition between them, bitter and aloof, that they were both eager to see Ben gone for good.

The key was slid across the counter and Ben stepped from the motel for the last time, accompanied by the voices of sports commentators in their sweaty, statistical world.

Ben pulled onto Main Street less than ten minutes later. Approaching five o'clock, dusk had already begun to appear on the horizon, drenching everything in a cold-blue haze. Some kids continued to straggle down the sidewalks, refusing to call it a day until their plastic pumpkins overflowed with sugary bounty.

Aaron had never been trick-or-treating. On his last Halloween on Earth, when he was almost five years old, Aaron lay on a hospital bed, hooked pale and bandaged to IVs. There were the adorable costumes from Aaron's infancy, the crimson lobster outfit he wore at two years old, but no walking hand-in-hand down Milwaukee streets, no blithe indulgence in staged terror and limitless candy. Ben remembered this as he drove; he should have been reassured by his calmness, his lack of grief. But there was no reassurance to be found here.

After driving a few blocks west in an effort to kill some time, Ben came across one of Grange's seven sports bars, a one-story building with a graveled parking lot and a neon sign reading Nate's on 8th. Almost without thinking, Ben curved into the parking lot, coming slowly, diagonally to rest. He shut off the engine, glancing through the windshield, surprised by his destination.

What had brought him here? Was it simply forgotten routine? There was a time when his foremost desire every day after work, failing nothing, was a couple shots of whiskey and a few beers at the bar two blocks from home—Champions, it was called—and then the night was lost and there was no use trying to do anything else. Which, of course, was the point.

Ben shuddered in his Jeep, remembering that recent time of his life. It had been almost two months since he'd had a night like that. The foggy memory of this horrendous past, veiled by dark vaporous clouds of regret, was what finally compelled him, if at all possible, to try to be a better man. But now that he found himself in the dusty parking lot of Nate's on 8th, the amber allure of a cold beer in a shadowy bar proved irresistible. After the last several days, hadn't he earned a little something to take the edge off?

He strode across the parking lot, the ground shifting beneath him tectonically, and pulled the front door open, its surface covered with crackling paint. The interior was a wood-paneled cocoon, a dim haven of red leather couches and two or three regulars engaged in their grizzled conversation at the far end of the bar. It was the kind of place designed to vanquish time, to make its passing irrelevant.

Ben walked up to the bar. There were a few sideways looks directed at him, hostile but too dulled by alcohol to do anything about it. At last, the bartender walked over. Ben nodded and ordered a Pabst. There were a few TVs hovering over the bar, football highlights inevitably playing, but the only sound was mumbled conversation and the steady, churning hum of the heaters. Ben grabbed his beer and retreated to a corner booth, dismissing the watchful eyes of the barflies. He took a sip, then another, then gulped half the beer in a few seconds. The nearby conversation quieted, the heat seemed to throb more aggressively. His mind buzzed. A song started blaring from a jukebox in the corner, an old Link Wray tune with great stomping rhythms and a sleazy blues melody—the kind of thing that they said could start riots, once upon a time.

217

Halfway through the song, amid a nasty burst of bass and twang, the front door clanged open. A faint indigo light crept into the bar; the sun had nearly set outside. The door swung shut as someone stepped through it. Ben squinted, trying to make out the newcomer. He had scraggly gray hair, thin-framed eyeglasses, and an ugly shirt the color of overcooked spinach. The bartender spotted him a moment later, walking up with a smile. The two men leaned over the bar, trading a series of conspiratorial whispers and a few sidelong glances in Ben's direction. He watched them peevishly as they talked, feeling confrontational.

The man ordered something and the bartender stepped away. As the Link Wray song came to a close, the man at the bar stared at Ben, his lip curled in a smile. The bartender returned, sliding the man a glass of red wine. He smiled, nodded, and sipped it, savoring the taste. Then he stepped to the jukebox, his shoes echoing in the still and humid air.

The heater hummed, performing its solo.

Ben took another sip.

The man at the jukebox flicked two quarters into the slot and pushed a button. The speakers came to life with a song by Chuck Berry, sad and sexy, and Ben had to admit he was impressed by the bar's musical offerings. Having chosen the soundtrack for their meeting, the man at the jukebox turned and walked directly to Ben's booth, his footsteps silenced by Chuck's feverish howls. The man arrived at his table, his left elbow bent as he held the thin stem of the wine glass.

"Ben Dmitrovich."

Ben sat there, shifting.

"I've been wanting to talk to you. Do you mind if I sit down?"

"Who are you?"

The man gave a phony laugh. "Right. My name is John Linden. I know Nathan, and Maria." He snickered again, realizing his mistake. "Of course, I *knew* Maria."

"John Linden," Ben said. "I've heard your name."

And for a moment that was all—John stayed standing with his snifter, Ben sat stonily at the table, and Chuck Berry sang about a brown-eyed handsome man. Finally, John motioned his arm toward the booth.

"So...?"

"Oh, yeah, yeah," Ben said, apparently coming to his senses. "Sit down."

John sat across from Ben, taking another sip. The song came to a close, followed by a skin-crawling silence.

"I saw you today, at Maria's funeral," John said.

"Yeah."

"She must have meant something to you. Despite the short amount of time that you knew her."

Ben was moody, anxious, unsure if the statement was a consolation or a challenge.

"I knew she was in trouble. I wish I could have helped her," Ben said.

They both drank again.

"Nathan called you?" Ben asked.

Linden furrowed his brow. "Nathan?"

"Did he talk to you?"

Linden shook his head. "No. Why?"

Ben was puzzled; he assumed Nathan would have demanded Ben's forcible removal from Grange as soon as he'd left his house.

"Just wondering. After what happened to him at the funeral..."

John gave an icy nod. "Yep. He's been through a lot."

The sound of music rose again, a classic-rock radio station turned on by the bartender as the crowd began to grow.

"So, let me ask you, Ben," Linden said. "How long do you plan on staying here in Grange?"

Ben smiled sourly. "So that's what this is. You're telling me to get out while I still can."

"No, I'm just curious. What do you think you can achieve here?"

Ben leaned across the table, lowering his voice. "John, do you know what Maria told me before she died? She said Nathan had an arrangement with *you*, the middleman. A sort of business deal. Ryan Amherst in exchange for her."

John twitched across the booth, though he hid his discomfort with an incredulous widening of the eyes.

"Now tell me what that means, John. What kind of exchange?"

"Maria didn't know what she was talking about."

"Is that why you killed her?"

John flashed an antagonistic grin and let the silence settle. "What kind of exchange do you *think* this is?"

"Why would I tell—?"

"No, it'll be a trade," John interrupted, no longer attempting to coat his words with a diplomatic tone. "You tell me what you know and I'll tell you if you're correct."

Ben swallowed, growing tense. The sudden appearance of John Linden at a sports bar that Ben had never intended to visit—the coincidence was uncanny.

"Why did you want to talk to me, Mr. Linden?"

"What do you mean?" He shrugged his shoulders in faux-offense. "I was—"

"No, just tell me what you're supposed to tell me, deliver your message, let's get this over with and you can stop being so fucking *clever*."

"I *wanted* to meet you, Ben, honestly. I was curious. Terence Arnold told me about you, and I just wanted to talk."

"Why?"

"What kind of question is that, *why*? Because I wanted to see what kind of person you are. See if we could trust you."

220

A sudden cheer erupted from the bar. Ben glanced up to see a football game playing on the television. Wisconsin-Purdue. It seemed to be happening in a different universe.

"First, tell me if the Amhersts had a son."

The cheering continued, filling the ensuing silence.

"Yes," Linden finally answered. "They had a son named Ryan."

"And you sacrificed him to...bring Maria back. Is that what happened?"

"How would that even be possible, Officer Dmitrovich? What you're talking about, sacrifice, resurrection—do you have any kind of evidence to back up such fanciful allegations?"

Ben thought about the photographs taken in the basement of the library, the journal entries and fairy-tale cartography, but simply smiled at Linden's vainglorious tone.

"I think there's something in the woods outside of Grange that can make that happen," Ben posited. "And that's the other party, right? You're the middleman, so that thing out there, that's the third party for these *contracts* that you draw up?" He said the words with an angry hiss, emphasizing the banality of their evil.

John smiled and took a sip of wine. "You have no idea."

"You're telling me I'm wrong?"

"I mean you don't know the magnitude of it," John whispered conspiratorially. "What's out there."

Ben shook his head, suddenly more frightened than combative. John took a long moment to choose his words, then squinted at Ben with a grave and pompous air.

"Do you believe in Heaven, Officer?"

Ben merely looked at him, unable to hide his perplexity.

"Well, do you? It's either yes or no."

Ben thought and finally answered. "I believe in the existence of a soul after death."

"Okay. But you don't believe in the nine circles of Hell and a fantasy-land paradise and all that?"

"No."

"No. Of course not, it's absurd. I wouldn't believe it either. *But,* sadly—well, let me just say I'm not in a position to disbelieve it."

"Why?"

Linden sighed. "At the very least, I know Hell exists. Maybe there's no Heaven, I don't know. Probably not. But I know Hell is real, and it's close, and it's becoming harder to contain."

"What do you mean?"

At this point, a waitress shuffled up to their table, noticing Ben's empty glass, and asked if he'd like another.

"No."

"Yes, he would," John asserted.

"No. Thanks, I'm good," Ben said to the waitress. She walked away without another word.

"Mr. Dmitrovich, this town was founded more than a hundred fifty years ago. Almost all of us here, our families date back five, six generations. None of us *asked* to be here. But we are, and that means we have to keep things...under control."

"Well, that does sound noble, John, but let me remind you that you're keeping things under control by killing *children*, for Christ's sake."

"In the winter of 1901," Linden growled, "in what became known as the Second Wave of this town, the people of Grange decided to forgo the sacrifices. Ignore the elephant in the room, if you will. They went ten months without an offering. They thought they got away with it— you know, they could live normal lives again. The following August, on maybe the last hot day of summer, the beaches of Sarona Lake were packed. At the busiest hour, around two in the afternoon, I'd guess a quarter of the town was in the lake. And suddenly everyone in the water felt a fire from below. By the time they knew what was happening it was too late. The lake started boiling. A newspaper later reported that the water temperature rose to more than two hundred twenty degrees. Eighty-seven people were burned alive. They had to be identified by their skeletons. Can you imagine that? The screams…"

"Why are you telling me this?"

Linden shrugged. "You already know a great deal. More than we hoped, to be honest. Can't hurt trying to *explain* ourselves."

"Or because you're planning on killing me, the same way you did Maria."

Linden laughed—a little too avidly, Ben thought. "You have such a morbid imagination."

"So you feel good about this. Sacrificing children to maintain the status quo, you feel—"

"Do I feel *good* about it?" Linden scoffed. "Please. Give me a little credit."

"But you feel you're in the right."

"I feel we're doing the only thing we can."

"You prey on the weak and the grieving, like you did with Nathan. You convince them to kill their own children."

Linden contorted in his seat, planting his elbows against the table. "Don't ask me to feel sympathy for Nathan or any of the others. Do I feel bad for the kids?" He threw up his hands. "Of course I do, they don't deserve this. But I do *not* feel bad for the others, who put their ink and their blood on that contract. They're too weak to see beyond their own lives."

"Yeah, with a little encouragement from you."

"I put the option out there, but there are no threats, no one's *forced* to do anything. They could simply cope and move on, like people do."

Ben flicked his empty beer glass, spinning it on the table. "You don't know what it's like."

"I don't?" His shoulders tensed and he leaned forward, apparently ready to exhume the skeletons in his own past with a woeful monologue—but instead, he looked down at the table and took another sip of wine. "No, I don't need to convince you. We've all been through something."

Ben offered a dreary laugh.

"Hm?" Linden moaned.

"Nathan told me the same thing. You know, I've been blaming him for all this, I was absolutely sure he was responsible. Now I don't know…"

Linden said nothing, intrigued, waiting for Ben to continue.

"What if…there's something here, affecting him? Forcing him to do things he never would have done on his own."

"You mean, the little devil on his shoulder?"

Ben shrugged off Linden's snide remark. "I mean he was fragile. Vulnerable. Something could have taken over."

Linden shook his head and clicked his tongue. "No. Sorry, no. There is such a thing as human will. I know there are forces of evil, I've seen them, but they don't control us. There's no dark cloud that inhabits your soul when you do awful things. People make decisions and act on them. As an officer of the law, I hope you agree."

"Of course. People should be held accountable for what they do, yeah. But there's something else going on here. You said it yourself: Hell is close by and hard to contain."

"So the whole town is…what, a den of iniquity? Sinners, every one?"

"I'm saying maybe it's easier here, of all places, to make decisions like that. Things you would never do in your right mind. Doesn't it make sense that there would be *something*, an energy, affecting the way people behave?"

John snickered and sipped his wine. "Officer Dmitrovich, you surprise me. I never would have expected you to put so much stock in the supernatural."

"I can *feel* it," Ben seethed. "You're lying to yourself if you think you can't."

"And you feel qualified to make that statement after being here, what, two days?"

Ben bit his tongue. Yes, he could feel it. He felt it when he beat and bloodied Nathan Amherst on the man's living room carpet.

Linden continued. "Most of us in Grange have no blood on our hands, Ben. Most of us haven't done anything wrong. We're just normal people making the best of...peculiar circumstances." Ben let out a hateful laugh. "It's true," Linden protested.

"*Some* of you, maybe, but not you. You're not some innocent bystander. You find desperate people who can't think straight, you convince them, somehow, to make a trade for someone they've lost. It's disgusting."

Linden tried to hide an expression of genuine offense. "I give them an option, like I said. I never push. You would be surprised—no, you'd be *horrified*—at how quickly most people say yes. I barely have to pitch the idea to 'em. They sign their kids away, but *I'm* disgusting."

"You should be helping them, not exploiting their grief."

"A nice thought," Linden replied with a shrug.

They said nothing for a while. Finally, Ben leaned forward, peering at the man across from him.

"I'm curious...how did you get into this line of work? If that's what you call it."

Linden faltered, debating how much he should reveal. "It's not a very interesting story. Family business. My father had a day job, he owned a bakery, but this is what he was known for. And his father, and his grandfather, almost all the way back to the founding of Grange. They arranged the contracts that allowed this town to survive. And that was passed down to me."

Ben snorted. "Some legacy."

"In any case, Officer, I'm not looking for your ethical judgment regarding the way we do things. You don't live here; you don't know what it's like. We don't need your validation."

Ben looked back at Linden, staring him in the eye. "But you do, though. Unless you want a whole police force coming in here, performing a more *thorough* investigation."

The bar was even busier now, but none of the nearby sounds, the careening conversations and screeching classic rock, seemed to find their way to Ben and Linden. There was only muffled silence, each tonal inflection and rustling of fabric acutely audible. Linden shot Ben a seething stare before he replied.

"That would be a very bad idea. And anyway, what can the Milwaukee police do?" John challenged.

"Get all the kids out of here, for a start."

"And break up how many innocent families because the *devil* is after them? No, I don't think you'd be able to make that fly. See, Officer Dmitrovich, we don't live by the same laws that you do."

"You don't?" Ben asked dubiously.

"The laws of a police force that could never understand the nature of our existence mean little. We have a *cosmic* code of ethics." Ben raised his eyebrows in feigned admiration. "We live next door to a primal darkness and we do what we can to keep it at bay. Frankly, we don't really care if our efforts abide by the laws of American society."

"Sounds like an easy way to avoid guilt for what you've done."

Linden moved in his seat, freshly agitated. "And why are you so qualified to pass judgment? The cop who got the Milwaukee police *sued* because he beat a father in front of—what, maybe a dozen families, a few people recording everything with their cellphones, the man's own *son*, all in broad daylight. You're *supposed* to be held to a higher standard, you and your brothers and sisters in blue, and then you speak of justice every time you kill another innocent soul on the streets. Please, Officer, honor me with your moral rectitude."

226

Ben's face twisted into a scowl, the usual conjoined twins of shame and anger.

"Oh, yeah, Chief Arnold told us all about that. We did our homework. Sorry to interrupt your…mandated vacation, I guess."

Ben swallowed hard, then foolishly tried to explain himself. "I've made mistakes, but I'm a good officer. I have a solid track record, I do my best."

"I don't doubt you," Linden interrupted. "I don't doubt you. How sad it is, though, that even at your best you can't help abusing your authority. But I guess that's just an occupational hazard, isn't it?"

Ben was furious but clenched his jaw, forcing himself to remain silent. The room pulsed. Ben checked his watch. It was just after six. Through the windows, he saw that night had settled in. The sky had turned velvety black, glazed with white clouds. All at once, he felt a throbbing dread that he couldn't explain. He reached over, grabbed his sport coat, and began to throw it on.

"Leaving already?" John asked.

"Sorry to put an end to this little chat, but yeah, I'm afraid so."

"Got somewhere to be?"

Ben sighed. "Anywhere but here, actually. Terence Arnold will be happy to hear I'm finally leaving town."

"You are?" Linden practically screamed. He edged closer to the table as Ben stood to leave. "I'm almost disappointed, Ben. I'm glad I met you here, in that case. Strange coincidence."

"Yeah, guess so." They both stood now, at either end of the table, bathed in a dim glow and the edgeless energy of a bar at night. Ben glanced at Linden, unsure of his words.

"What you're doing here is wrong, John. The fact that I'm leaving doesn't mean I condone this." Linden said nothing, a long silence laid out between them. "Just want to make that clear," Ben finished.

"I'm glad you did."

227

John held out his hand, a smarmy smile etched onto his face. Ben thought twice, then proceeded past Linden without a word, avoiding contact at all costs. Almost immediately, John turned after him.

"Ben."

He stopped, somewhat annoyed, and turned to face Linden.

"I'm glad nothing happened to you. Really, I am. If we had to send that thing after you—if we had to silence you for good, well…it would have troubled me." He paused here, giving Ben time to consider the words—the sinister threat beneath them. "Good luck with everything."

Ben stood there, shaken. The barroom ambience of television ads, thrashing guitar solos, and bellowed conversations became audible again, rising to a din. He finally pivoted and walked toward the exit, that dismal feeling of dread and urgency growing heavier. He was confused, all of a sudden, how he ended up here in the first place.

Chapter 23 — Intruders

Amy Dorian hated horror movies.

It wasn't that they scared her, exactly. She could see through their air of manufactured carnage, the Karo-syrup blood and viscous monsters supplied by special effects departments. No, it was rather that they seemed too cruel, dispatching victims with cold eviscerations, victims that Amy always wanted to learn more about. Maybe it was because her mother died in childbirth and her father abandoned her and her grandfather, the only benign paternal presence in her life, succumbed to time a few years after that. She hadn't gotten used to the lonely regret of losing someone you love.

Tonight, though, was Halloween, and Amy had company: her best friend Katie, who sat behind Amy in school and whose joyous laugh had a bubbly, contagious effect. Katie still wore part of her pirate costume, the clip-on earring and gaudy eyeliner clashing with the jeans and sweatshirt she had thrown on. Amy, meanwhile, wore her black witch's cloak, mostly because it was silky, overlarge and comfortable. Her hair was thrown into a lazy ponytail, glasses perched on her face. Enlivened by massive amounts of sugar, their conversation careened from the monotony of long division to the boys in their class to the imminence of sixth grade and middle school next fall, with all its accompanying thrills and uncertainties.

They had nearly plumbed their way to the bottom of their piles of candy, discarded wrappers littering the living room floor. Even so, Hannah stood next to the microwave in the kitchen, listening to popcorn pop inside its vacuum-sealed bag. When the sounds came to rest at length, Hannah peeled the bag open and poured the steaming mass into a large glass bowl.

She glanced at the clock. She would have to leave soon, vacating the house so that Linden's associates could do their work. Each crack of wallpaper and blotted carpet stain jumped out at her, the house's flaws unforgivable. She avoided her reflection wherever she turned. She had the sudden urge to hold her granddaughter and shut her eyes until it felt like Rebecca was in her arms. But it was too late now.

Hannah grabbed the bowl of popcorn and trudged into the living room, where Amy and Katie lay on the carpet in a waning oasis of candy.

"All set?" Hannah asked as she placed the bowl in front of them. Katie scooped a handful of popcorn, her appetite inexhaustible, but Amy merely yawned. Her sugar rush had started to dissolve into exhaustion.

"Yup, thank you!" Katie exclaimed between bites. Amy merely nodded.

Hannah stepped over to the television, where a videotape of *Gremlins* sat—about as close as Amy and Katie wanted to get to horror tonight. (Hannah vaguely remembered the movie's depiction of suburbia descending into Id-unleashed hell and shuddered at the thought.) Katie, meanwhile, spoke at hyperspeed, jolted by sugar, laughing as she talked about "how cute Gizmo is. I want one, whatever they're called—Moglis? He's so cute, it's worth the threat of gremlins, you know? But my parents won't even get me a *dog*, even though I ask every day, so I guess there's not much chance of *that* happening…"

Hannah pushed the tape in, greeted by the vintage sound of spindles whirring in analog glory. She stepped over to two lamps and flicked them off, bathing the room in the incandescent glow of the TV.

"Thanks, Grandma," Amy said, tossing a Blow-Pop into her mouth, lips turned instantly purple.

Hannah stood at the front window, fingers drifting along the curtains. Their street was visible through the widescreen frame, displaying the heavy tranquility of an empty road at night. There was a truck parked across the street, a rusty blue pickup waiting in the dark. Hannah squinted and saw three figures in the front seat, crammed close together, hulking silhouettes biding their time. She swallowed and stepped away.

The movie had started by this point, the grand studio logo illuminated by spotlights, sound blaring. Hannah walked behind the couch, passing the piano—which formed, as always, a pointed symbol of Amy's boundless future.

"Okay, well, guys...I might have some tea upstairs. Do some reading. Just come find me if you need anything."

They said nothing, enraptured by the TV.

The tea was boiled, shrieking through the house; a large mug was carried upstairs, along with a massive tome rented from the Grange Public Library, whatever the non-fiction bestseller list told her to read. Hannah walked to her bedroom, sitting distracted on the bed, the canned noises of the videotape drifting upstairs. She didn't read a word, much less a page. Her mind, tonight, was filled to capacity. She could do nothing but wait, fingernails jaggedly bitten, until it was time.

*****

The closed eyelids of Amy Dorian, pressed together in slumber, bathed in blue.

The thick silence of an empty household, or almost empty—a not-quite-silence that hummed with tension.

They fluttered open, Amy's eyelids, blinking in disorientation.

Where was she? When was it? Was she still dreaming?

The TV was a pulsing, infinite blue, the kind of radiant color that can only be created electrically. The movie had ended, apparently, had crawled its way through the end credits only to shut off and rewind automatically.

She glanced to her left. Katie had vanished.

"Katie?" Amy mumbled, shrugging off sleep.

231

She was gone, there was no answer, but Katie apparently had scooped up the rest of her candy and cleared her wrappers from the living room floor. The bowl of popcorn sat there, half-eaten, looking cadaverous in the light of the television.

Amy reached out to the couch for support and stood, glancing in confusion as she tousled her hair. She realized she was still wearing her Halloween costume, the black witch's cloak. In a daze, she pulled it off and threw it on the couch, revealing a white T-shirt and pair of black jeans.

"Katie?" she asked again, louder. There was no answer.

Amy walked to the end of the couch and flicked on a lamp. A new ensemble of shadows snuck into the corner of the room. There was a noise upstairs—a muffled thud, like someone falling onto carpet. Amy thought she felt the entire house rumble.

"Grandma?" she called. She expected a cry of reassurance from upstairs, a curt apology from her grandmother. But, again, nothing. Amy shivered, feeling the encroaching fear of abandonment. She stepped over the carpet, her movements slow and faltering. At the foot of the stairs she reached out to the banister, clutching its smooth wood.

"Grandma?"

Where could they have gone? Was it some cruel joke? She peered down the hallway into the kitchen at the clock glowing on the microwave. It was almost ten.

One step on the staircase, then a second and third. The upper level of the house seemed miles away.

Another sound. Not a thud this time, but a screeching whisper, like metal dragged against glass. It came, Amy thought, from Hannah's bedroom. She stood on the staircase, paralyzed. She felt the urge to turn around, run from the house, slam the door behind her—but what if something had happened to her grandmother? What if, while she slept, something horrible had entered?

She kept walking, legs trembling as they moved. Halfway up the stairs, and further, almost to the top. From behind each doorway she expected something to swarm out at her, some shape to swallow her up.

She reached the landing and called again.

"Grandma?"

Another thud—a stomp, a violent clatter. Amy thought she saw the walls shiver. It came from Hannah's bedroom, no doubt this time.

"Grandma…," she whispered, pleading for help.

The open doorway beckoned. She stepped through it, onto thick blue carpet. A lamp on the bedside table cast a dim glow. The curtains waved, pushed aside by the wind, whistling through a crack in the window.

Amy walked to the table next to the bed. There was an open book here, placed spine-up, and a heavy mug swimming with tepid tea, brown at the bottom of the cup. She looked around, searching for answers in the walls and the floor.

From across the room, Hannah's closet door creaked open, yawning into the shadowy corner. It came to rest when it was half-ajar, the blackness inside luring Amy closer.

She had never felt so small, so unsafe. But she stepped toward the closet, inching around Hannah's bed, her eyes wide and glazed as she squinted into the doorway. She saw only the shadows of hanging shirtsleeves, waving almost imperceptibly.

She arrived at the closet door. A howl of wind outside. She reached for the gleaming doorknob, her fingers shivering as they made contact. She gripped it and pulled it toward her. The door swung open, hitting the wall. Amy cowered in front of the blackness, peering into it, fear and curiosity waging war.

But of course there was nothing there. Jackets hovering, sweaters neatly folded and shelved, rows of shoes lining the carpet like murky shipwrecks on the ocean floor.

The wind stopped. It was silent now. Or almost silent. Amy heard something else. Low, hoarse breathing, a raspy sound from somewhere inside the closet.

Amy reached out, pushed aside a few of her grandmother's shirts. The hangers screeched, the fabric wavered.

The shadows became thinner now as her eyes adjusted, and it was then that she saw it: a white face, unnaturally pale, two black voids for eyes, floating there unattached to a body.

Amy blinked, squinted again, distrusting her vision—it was only an illusion, surely.

But the shape, the *thing*, suddenly lunged at her, two black arms reaching out from the dark. Amy screamed, a sharp animal scream, and stumbled backwards. But it was too late. The figure, whatever it was, grabbed hold of her left shoulder, digging into flesh with what felt like talons. Now that it had stepped from the closet the figure looked less phantasmal, dressed in black with a bent white mask for a face; but its human shape, its tangible presence, only made it more disturbing.

Amy had never had reason to fight for her life before (unlike some of the other children in Grange), but now she had occasion. Her body responded almost on its own, swatting the shape away as she scrambled to her knees, crawled from the room, and used the doorjamb to pull herself upright, sprinting into the hallway.

In a flash, she had turned the corner and reached the top of the stairs, spinning as she held the banister for balance. She leapt down the stairs, two at a time, too terrified to question what was happening, what that thing was in her grandmother's closet, waiting for the right time to strike.

The figure bounded behind her, cutting through the shadows. As Amy made it halfway down the staircase, she felt it shudder under the weight of the two of them, felt the figure's footsteps land behind her with hurricane force.

She made it to the bottom of the stairs, landing on the hallway rug and feeling it slide beneath her feet. She tripped there, losing balance on the fabric, but planted her hands against the hardwood floor and thrust herself upright. The thing, though, descended the staircase just then, immense in the dim contours of the entryway. The front door was just a few feet away, but Amy's path was blocked.

With a desperate squeal and a flurry of scratching hands, Amy swatted at the figure. She made contact at the only point where its skin was exposed: her nails dug into a human forearm, clawing at its flesh, and ripped her hand away, bringing blood and pieces of skin with it. She rose and her feet slid over the hallway floor; the house seemed at once cramped and never-ending. The back door was there, straight ahead of her, only a few yards through the kitchen to freedom.

She had almost reached the kitchen when she saw it there—the second figure, lurking outside the back door, hideous through the window. This one wore a mask, too, though it was covered with red fleshy rubber and deep gashes and a row of daggered fangs looming over a black maw for a mouth. It was the kind of Halloween mask that could be bought for ten dollars at a convenience store, but as it hovered there now, lit from above by a harsh floodlight, Amy could swear that she had never seen anything so grotesque.

She slid across the tiled floor, scrambling to a halt. The second figure pushed open the back door. Amy remembered, in a moment of clarity, that Hannah had locked it earlier. Before she could turn around and sprint for another exit, she felt a pair of arms around her, locking her in a vice grip. Her terror, so far suppressed, now erupted inside her. She screamed, deathly screams that tore her throat on the way out.

The second figure by now had joined them, wielding a length of coarse rope. The man restraining Amy shifted, reaching for Amy's hands and jerking them behind her with a violent tug. The other figure spun the rope around Amy's frail wrists and tied it into a constrictor knot, fibers digging into skin. She screamed, screamed, kicking wildly at nothing, but the rope was unbreakable and she soon gave up.

One of the assailants stepped back through the hallway, a surreal vision of costumed villainy moving through the tasteful hush of the house. He returned a moment later with a red-and-black quilt, plucked from the Dorians' couch. He threw it over Amy's screeching, wriggling body, enveloping her in blackness. Still Amy kicked and protested, even as one of them—the one with the gruesome zombie mask—grabbed her ankles and lifted her into the air and the other carried her by the arms.

And so, past the soft-blue living room scattered with candy wrappers, two men carried Amy's body out the front door, across a neatly trimmed lawn, and over the pavement of a wide, placid street, sitting meek and useless in the night. From her black cocoon Amy heard the creak of a pickup's front door, then felt herself shuttled from one man to the next until she was shoved onto the seat. The two men scrambled around the truck and got in after her, four of them now stuffed into the narrow cab. Amy's screams weakened but never stopped, she scraped and clawed beneath the quilt, but it didn't matter. Before the door was even shut behind the men, the driver turned the key in the ignition and pulled away.

Elsewhere on Wellington Drive, prying eyes peered through drawn blinds, bearing witness to the twelve-year-old girl abducted from her home by three shadowy men. The police were not called. There were no outraged protests. There was, at most, a dreary acknowledgement that the Devil was at play again in Grange.

Chapter 24 — The Banality of Evil

As Ben Dmitrovich glowered in the front seat of his Jeep, pulling up to 204 Main Street with a sullen expression, there was only one thought on his mind: he would leave Grange by the end of the night, but his efforts had been utterly pointless. What did he think would happen when he first chased after Maria in the woods, offering his help? There were the usual clichéd answers: redemption, distraction, a need to believe in his own heroism. And now? He admitted to himself, with inward animosity, that he had failed to protect the one person he had vowed to and attacked a grieving man simply because he lost control.

Truly heroic. A knight in shining fucking armor.

Before he left town, though, there was 204 Main Street—the home of John Linden. A last chance to find damning evidence, to bring something concrete back to his superiors in Milwaukee. Something beyond cellphone images of archaic journals and cryptic cartography.

He pulled up to the curb and shut off the engine, cutting his lights. Did John Linden believe his claim that he was on his way out of Grange, never to return again? Ben doubted it. Linden had a barbed, distrustful personality, which was only understandable considering its hellish breeding ground.

In any case, Linden's red hatchback was nowhere in sight, and the day's trick-or-treaters had long since been steered inside by their parents. Ben took a quick glance around, nervous. He reached over to the glove compartment and pulled it open. There was a narrow black box there, about the size of an eyeglass case. He picked it up and tossed it in his coat pocket, then swung open the door and stepped onto pavement. Though the day had begun with ominous storm clouds, it had

237

brightened into something crisp and cool, a brilliant fall evening clashing with Ben's misery.

John Linden's house was an elegant two-story sided with dark cedar, a few black shutters embedded in the house like lancets. It towered over most of the homes on the block, a show of superiority that hardly surprised Ben, given his brief impression of Linden. He stomped up the sidewalk, which flanked a steep hill. A dog barked in the distance, adamant. When he reached the narrow driveway he turned to his right, casting another anxious glance around the block. There was a subtle garden lining a chain-link fence, a few iceberg roses brilliant before a pink anemone that had begun to wither. He passed the house and spun to his left, where a small patio with rustic cobblestones was laid into the ground. Among Linden's many interests, apparently, was the careful manicuring of a home and its garden.

On the back doorstep, Ben pulled the black case from his coat pocket. He hadn't learned to pick locks at the police academy in Milwaukee; nor was it part of his military training, as Ben had never excelled beyond Private First Class of the 38th Infantry Division, a position that offered little specialized development. It was, in fact, as a sophomore in high school that Ben had learned this skill, from a friend who envisioned petty crime as his future vocation. From the black case, he pulled a small Allen wrench and a hooked pick. He wiggled the wrench into the bottom of the keyhole and rotated it clockwise, feeling resistance. Then he eased the pick into the cylinder, feeling the pins retreat upward. There was a jostling of instruments, a soft click and an easing of the tension inside. Ben teased the wrench to the right. Finally, he felt it unlock. He scanned the nearby houses for a third and final time, then nudged the door open and stepped inside.

There was something there, a gentle shriek and blur of movement to his left. Then a black-and-white cat jumped from its perch on the kitchen counter, landing in front of Ben on the floor. He suppressed a gasp then laughed at himself, amused by the predictability of it all.

The animal mewed again and brushed against his legs, hungry; then, realizing this wasn't his owner, the cat pattered away, confused. Ben looked around, squinting in the dark. The room was as elegantly designed as the home's exterior: a polished table sitting beneath a grandiose clock; a geometric spice rack, lined with neatly labeled, color-coordinated jars; a wicker basket on the counter holding a quaint red apple and assortment of bananas.

Ben moved through the kitchen, feeling his way through the shadows until his eyes adjusted. He stepped through an archway into a posh living room, where a tan leather couch sat beneath a reprint of a Mondrian painting—minimal and stylish, if out-of-place. There was a wall of bookshelves across the room, the spines of the books coordinated, again, by color; and a mahogany rug (Persian, Ben guessed) that offset the color of the couch. It was the home of a supercilious bachelor who filled his empty hours with the satisfaction of specific tastes.

There was nothing here, however, to suggest some kind of revelation, so he set off down a hallway lined with more classic-art reprints. A bathroom to the right, white and gleaming, burgundy towels hanging on a glass shower door.

Then, to his left, Ben came across a study slathered in smoky brown. There was a black file cabinet in the far corner of the room, behind the desk. Ben stepped to it, pulling the top drawer open. He held his phone aloft, illuminating the contents in a harsh digital glow. Manila folders labeled according to year, overstuffed with students' papers, attendance reports, and quarterly assessments. The next two drawers were equally mundane: tax documents, financial information, even a secretive file in the very back containing Linden's childhood drawings (unnervingly morbid) and a novella written by one Jonathan E. Linden titled *Children of the Midnight Sun*.

Ben slammed the drawer shut, peering around the room. On the far side of the study against the wall, there was a row of bookshelves lined with what appeared to be the prizes of Linden's collection—ornate leather-bound spines, heavy tomes with gilded writing on the sides. Ben walked to it, pulling out a few volumes and flipping through them, increasingly certain that his intrusion, this last-ditch effort before he left Grange, was simply another failure to add to the list.

Glancing to his right at the lowermost row of books, he noticed something off about it. While the rest of the books jutted unevenly, this row in the corner was perfectly aligned, coated with a smooth veneer. Ben knelt in front of it, phone clutched in his hand. His fingers flew over the edge of the books, running along the surface. Finally, desperately, he pushed against the bookshelf with a swift movement. The shelf gave way with a soft click, then sprang back open. It was another file cabinet, a single row that stretched several feet into a recess in the wall. The labels here were arranged alphabetically, A B C D scrawled onto the folders in vivid red marker. He pulled out the first one, then retreated to the desk and opened the folder. *Aberman, Kyle*, read the thick, bold letters. It appeared to be a contract of some kind, smeared with the tedious nomenclature of bureaucratic paperwork.

It read:

It is mutually agreed between these two Parties that the Licensee, JERRY ABERMAN, *shall provide his/her property,* KYLE ABERMAN, *to the Licenser,* JOHN LINDEN, *on or before* MAY 2, 2002, *in exchange for goods, namely* LOIS ABERMAN, *being provided by a Third Party. The Licensee hereby confirms that recoupment for this exchange will take place within a window from* MAY 3 – MAY 17, 2002, *and also acknowledges that these terms are subject to agreement from a Third Party to be contacted by the Licenser. The Licensee also confirms that, should the terms agreed herein be violated by the Licensee in any way, the Licensee may experience retribution of a...*

And so it read, heartless, shameless, detailing the unthinkable in callous legalese. On the last page, alongside a pair of scrawled signatures and tiny red splotches, there was an ominous seal that was burned into the paper, a charred black pentagram marked with unknown symbols, characters from an alien language. Ben's eyes widened, the horror of his discovery commingling with the thrill of tactile proof. He kept the file on the desk, returning to the secret row of drawers beneath the bookshelf. Broderick, Buttinger, Caplan, Danton—a parade of damnation, sacrifices written in no uncertain terms. There were thirty-five contracts dating back at least to 2001, an even greater array of evil than Ben had initially suspected.

But it was the next file that Ben plucked from its hiding spot that concerned him most: the one that referred to a girl named Amy Dorian, who would be supplied by her "Licensee" on or before November 1.

On or before, Ben read—on or before.

There were few specific details given in the contract, and a timeframe that was unfortunately vague. Who was she, Amy Dorian—had he seen her before? And her Licensee, Hannah Dorian—was there anything excusable in her ploy to sacrifice her "property"?

This was proof, in any case, and Ben searched breathlessly for a copier in Linden's study. There was a squat black printer sitting in the corner, on top of the file cabinet. Ben grabbed an armful of contracts and flung them on top of the printer. It was one of those do-it-all machines that eliminated any semblance of human effort. In a split-second, sheets of paper began inching through the printer with a calm, efficient whir, spitting out a copy in the tray on the bottom.

Before the first contract had finished printing, a flood of headlights arced over the windows of the study, casting monstrous shadows against the walls and ceiling. Ben ducked to the floor, avoiding the headlights' gaze. The muffled roar of a car engine could be heard approaching.

In a half-contained frenzy, Ben plucked the stack of contracts from the top of the printer and raced across the study, replacing them in alphabetical order, precisely stowed away in their manila folders. He heard the sound of a car door slamming, followed by the clack of expensive boots on concrete.

A few more contracts had spit out by this point, the originals churning through a tray on top of the printer. He grabbed these last few documents—he had gotten all the way to Friedrichson, at least—and returned these, too, feeling the sting of a papercut while he did so.

There was a jingle of keys outside the backdoor, faintly heard by Ben from several rooms away. Still, the printer whirred. Ben sprinted over to it, jamming his thumb against the red X button on top of the printer. The machine didn't stop, its electric song went on and on, incessant.

The creak of the back door opening, the patter of cat's claws against the kitchen floor.

Swatting at the printer's power button with the fury of a madman, Ben did the only thing he could: reaching behind the printer, he felt the thick cord of the power cable, reached down the narrow crevasse between the wall and the file cabinet, and jerked it from the outlet. He felt the cord dislodge from the wall. The machine's deafening whir stopped immediately.

From the kitchen, Linden cooed at his cat, offering a silky hello. There was a steady clatter from down the hallway, the sound of cupboards opening and dishes being placed. The last of the contracts printed out then, a white rectangle emerged into the world. Ben grabbed it and returned to the hideaway file cabinet and shoved it into a random folder, organization be damned.

Where could he hide? He scanned the room in alarm. There were no closets, no alcoves. If Linden entered, Ben would be spotted at once.

As if confirming his fears, he heard the mellow plodding of feet over carpet, the quiet sound of Linden moving closer, through the living room, down the hallway. Ben tiptoed to the corner. He moved against the wall on the other side of the door and pressed himself against it, hoping only that Linden was headed elsewhere.

But the footsteps neared, a distorted shadow slithered beneath the door, and Ben could hear Linden breathe. That's when he saw it: the stack of contracts on the lower tray of the printer, illuminated by the hallway lights. Ben had grabbed the originals but forgotten the copies. All it would take was a quick glance through the doorway to spot them.

It was too late. Linden nudged the door open, sending it wavering toward Ben. The thin wooden door jutted into his chest with a thud. Linden entered, his tweed jacket coming into sight, close enough for Ben to touch. He lingered there for a moment, surveying the room.

Then, a ring from the kitchen—the shriek of a cellphone, calling down the hallway. Ben's faith in God had diminished long ago, but now that he prayed without even realizing it, he wondered if some divine presence had finally taken pity on him.

Linden rotated and trod down the hallway. In a flash, Ben darted from behind the door and drifted over hardwood to the printer. By the time Linden had answered the phone, Ben clutched the stack of copies, folded them haphazardly, and shoved the papers into his jacket pocket.

From the kitchen, Linden's calm, stern voice could be heard.

"John Linden." A momentary pause, the sound of the cat bounding onto the kitchen floor. "Yeah, I…I know, I realize that, Brandon. I'm on my way, just had to stop off at home."

Ben lingered there, contemplating his exit. The cat reappeared, slithering down the hallway, cocking its head when it spotted Ben.

"I'll be there in half an hour, just hold tight, all right? We have until midnight, anyway."

Ben pivoted in Linden's study, turning his attention to the windows. He crept over to them and pulled the blinds aside. There was a thick pane of glass covering a screen. He rested his hand against the windowpane and heaved upward. A screeching sound erupted. It was deafening to Ben; the noise seemed to resound to the ceiling and out the hallway and halfway down the block.

But a moment later, Linden continued his conversation, his tone becoming impatient.

"Well, are you surprised? Of course she's scared… I don't really care, Brandon, to be perfectly honest, you know you need to stay. Just take a deep breath and calm down and do your job, okay?"

There was only the screen to go now, and Ben prayed (hoping some god was still listening) that it wasn't affixed to the windowsill. He pulled on two small, plastic notches, his fingers slippery from sweat, and shoved against it. It didn't budge. Sharp air trickled inside. He clawed at the plastic. The screen stayed put. Ben wanted to curse and scream at the cheap materials that trapped him there.

The distant sound of Linden's cellphone placed on the counter. An exasperated sigh and the squeak of Linden's shoes, rotating. "Good grief," he uttered from the kitchen, the expression strangely precocious.

Ben knelt to the floor. Using two hands against the stubborn latch, he finally felt it give way, his body lurching from overexertion, hand brushing against the wall and bloodying his knuckles. Linden was halfway down the hallway by this point. Ben was sure Linden heard the noise this time, but he didn't care. The screen slid open and Ben jumped through the window headfirst, plummeting four feet to a front lawn covered in woodchips.

Linden reentered his study at that moment, feeling a sudden draft as the frigid air seeped in. He furrowed his brow and scanned the room, but all he saw were the blinds wavering in front of the window. He plucked a digital camera in a leather pouch from its place on the desk, then retreated from the room as quickly as he'd entered.

From outside, there was the hurried stomping of heavy boots over pavement, echoing down the otherwise silent street. Then the breathy sound of a car door opening and closing, the escalating roar of an engine coming to life.

Linden threw on a leather jacket, gave his purring cat one final caress, then stepped outside and locked the door behind him. He approached his '97 Peugeot one second too late to see a black Jeep speeding away down the streets of Grange.

*****

Amy Dorian stopped screaming a few minutes after the pickup pulled away from her grandmother's house. Trapped between three unknown men in the front seat, jostled as the truck rounded corners and sped over potholes, her throat couldn't stand the strain and descended into a series of snivels and unwitting sobs. The men said nothing, grim and silent, and if she hadn't felt their presence next to her she might have wondered if a phantom was driving the truck.

The vehicle sped on, through empty streets and onto Highway 63, its headlights cutting through the still night air. The engine wheezed, Amy whimpered—a symphony well-suited for the last night of October.

The ever-present sounds of nature that usually go unnoticed—the quiet chirp of a nightbird, the falsetto wail of crickets—dwindled as the pickup ventured outside of Grange, heading southeast to Sarona Lake. Here, everything was quiet, as though the animals had been cowed into submission.

About six minutes south of town, a rotten smell began filtering through the windows, penetrating even the quilt draped over Amy's body. At the same time, the truck slowed and came to a stop, then veered to the left, Amy's stomach lurching in the process. She felt a ragged movement here, the wheels rumbling over strewn gravel and mud until it gained some kind of traction. Amy grew silent, feeling a change in the air, something bleak and humid.

The truck rolled on.

Soon another noise was added to the whinnying engine: the steady electric throb of a generator. It grew louder until it roared just outside the truck, bellowing its dismal cry at the vehicle. The truck then came to a stop, its wheels settling into the ground.

The engine was shut off, the lights extinguished. The twinned sound of the doors opening, men stepping out on either side. Arms reaching in and grabbing Amy from her right, jerking her from the cab. She resumed her screaming, kicking at nothing in particular, but she slid from the pickup, turning horizontal as she fell into a sea of mud. A spray of dirt and grime washed over the quilt, turning it dank and heavy.

A pair of arms grabbed her again, lifting her up from the shoulders, and she felt the brutal hands around her, guiding her ahead. She stepped unevenly, her bare feet slipping. The odor was terrible here, thick and sour. Again she became silent, too scared to create sounds.

A few more plodding steps in the mud, and then she was suddenly stopped. She felt a strange heat emanating from nearby. An arm reached out in front of her, pushing open a fleshy doorway, the smell of carrion overwhelming her. She was pushed forward again, a violent shove by the same man, and her right foot caught a revolting knot of mud and root and bone. She fell to the floor. The quilt waved around her like a death shroud. There was the crackle of a fire, the bubbling sound of something boiling.

She heard the man behind her speak.

"Here she is."

Nothing for a moment, aside from that horrid odor. Then, from a distant corner of the room, a raspy grunt, the sound of an abomination imitating human noise. A shuffling of feet dragged over the ground. A horrid presence coming closer until Amy felt a breath of hot air through the blanket.

The man leaned down and picked Amy up again, steadying her on the ground. He walked her forward, slime seeping between her toes. After a few feet, she bumped into something hard at waist level, a table made of crooked wood. There was a hand on her shoulder, shoving her to the right. Rounding the table, she was heaved onto a meek little chair by the man behind her; the sarcophogal blanket twisted as her legs bent and she caught herself.

Each noise was violent, ear-splitting: a revolting plunk as something was dipped into liquid, a clatter as a heavy stone bowl was placed on the table before her. That same raspy voice, the sound of snakes slithering, began uttering unknown words: *Et hæc summone apud eundem, festum hæc mortuus incipe. Hæc antiquos, hæc patribus innuo, veni, veni, veni…*

It was strange—unthinkable, really—a thing to add to all the others: Amy felt something inside of her, inside her head, a weight growing fuller and heavier, as though (she didn't know how to explain it) claws were digging into the gray matter of her brain. Her body grew steelier, her limbs separated from her body. She thought she could feel her skeleton dislodge, each bone separating and levitating. She felt the pain of entropy.

While the chanting continued, she felt another pair of hands pull the blanket from her. The feeling of waking from what she thought was sleep into an even deeper nightmare: something was standing in front of her, a brittle body in a gargantuan cloak, blackened and musty and reeking with death. The hood was down. It looked like a woman, impossibly old, her face engraved with wrinkles, her eyes such a pale gray they were almost translucent. It was she who chanted those sinister words, the sound oozing from lips that barely seemed to move. A patch of gray hair streamed from her scalp, falling behind her and down to her shoulders. Her taloned hands drooped from sleeves that swallowed her up; one of the hands clutched a wooden spoon that was swimming with some kind of liquid, a broth of impossible colors. She was a figure from a Bosch painting, lurking in the infernal fringes.

The man behind Amy grabbed her hair and held her in place. With the other hand, he clutched her jaw and pulled her mouth open. She tried to scream, but nothing came out. The woman thrust the spoon into Amy's mouth, dipping it toward the back of her throat. A hot and bitter liquid poured through her body and into the nebulous pit of her stomach. Her paralysis grew even stronger now, turning her muscles to stone.

The woman kept chanting with devilish fervor, a trickle of red drool falling from her lips. There was a chicken in a cage, a frantic mass of feathers pacing, silent but observing, its head cocked. There was a horrible clay figure placed on the table in front of her, something sculpted from the stones of Hell: a mob of wizened supplicants, their ribs carefully engraved, bowing to an immense lizard whose bladed

247

tongue shot upward. There was, finally, a corroded butcher's knife sitting next to the sculpture, looming in its violence.

Whether it was the chanting or the miasmatic broth, Amy grew petrified, fixed to the chair. But she could see it all vividly and her weakened mind struggled to comprehend. Over the years, some of Amy's classmates had gone missing—such was the reality of living in Grange. And although it frightened her every time, another sudden loss that couldn't quite be explained, she had never dwelled too long on their disappearance. Wasn't it natural, death and solitude, a fact of time and decay?

But now, as something rumbled and the sickly walls of the cabin shook, she thought she understood something new, something impossible and heinous, and it was with that realization that she knew all hope was lost.

Chapter 25 — Beware Devils

In 1843, a cartographer named Thomas Von Hubbel charted a small patch of land infested with death—its soil thick and rotting, trees black and viscous, the only wildlife strewn about the ground, lifeless. There had been a warning carved there by some earlier nomad, in a foreign dialect Von Hubbel later deciphered: *Beware devils.*

One hundred eighty years later, give or take, a cop from Milwaukee, in laughably over his head, was searching for the same plot of land. What did he expect to find there? A twelve-year-old named Amy Dorian, on the brink of sacrifice? Or, maybe, the woods empty and mocking—after which he would leave in a hurry, feeling invisible eyes on him, and abandon Grange with only discomfiting memories for souvenirs.

45° 31' N, 91° 58' W—the digits shone from his cellphone as he hurtled down Highway 63, his eyes darting from the screen to the windshield. They were inscribed on one of Von Hubbel's maps, pinpointing an area where he had illustrated, in lines ragged and fearful, a desiccated pit of land.

Ben glanced at the Jeep's clock. 11:19pm. *We have until midnight,* Linden had said.

In a matter of seconds, Ben entered a simple search into his phone for latitude and longitude maps. They came to him almost immediately, measurements isolated to the tenth of a mile, and Ben coughed out a grateful laugh at how easy this part was, at least. He entered the numbers into his search bar: 45° 31' N, 91° 58' W. If Von Hubbel had known that his efforts would be recreated, two centuries later, by clicking a few buttons and waiting for the response of space junk satellites, would he have been elated or utterly crushed?

Regardless, the map appeared to Ben now, bright and minuscule, indicating not only this speck of land—located a few hundred feet west of Sarona Lake at its southern tip—but also Ben's current location, a tiny blue arrow. He was two miles away. The clock switched to 11:20. Ben accelerated, pushing seventy.

Less than a minute later, something changed. Ben couldn't describe it, maybe because it was everything at once: an acidic odor, a clammy pool of hot air, a bellicose rumble, the dissipation of moonlight into a gray, scattered nothingness.

He glanced at his phone. He was a mile away now, due west from the blinking black dot on his screen. His eyes darted through the windows, searching for an offroad, a patch of withered foliage, anything to indicate the presence of evil. There was nothing visible, only black veils of unyielding trees, but it was *here*, about five hundred feet into the thick of the forest. Without warning, Ben veered to the side of the road, slamming on his brakes. He hadn't realized that a white sedan had approached him from behind; the car blared its horn as it swerved and barely missed him, headlights slicing through the air.

Ben lurched to a halt on the shoulder, whiplashed by the sudden stop. In one wild movement he extinguished the lights, cut the engine, and heaved his door open, bounding onto concrete. He sprinted across the highway without a moment's glance, his mind indifferent to such practicalities, and if a car had been passing at that point in time it would have flattened him instantaneously.

But there were no vehicles passing and Ben leapt across two wide lanes, forcing his shivering legs to obey him. It was hard to move through space. Ben felt nauseous as he waded through the air, its putrefaction sticking to his skin.

At the eastern edge of the highway, a pocket of brambles stood in his way, cowering beneath a dancing basswood. He stepped through them, feeling their serrated branches tear through his jeans and into his legs.

He kept moving, climbing through the thorny bushes. A vicious wind came at him, nearly knocking him on his back. The autumn night, so cool and mild only minutes beforehand, had grown relentless, sweltering and frigid at once. The forest floor was gnarled and muddy, roots breaking through the soil of their own mad volition. There were wild noises in the distance, savage catcalls uttered by creatures that Ben couldn't imagine. He squinted into blackness, searching for movement, a clearing, *anything*, but the rays of the moon refused to enter and a pale fog incarnated creatures that weren't really there, or so Ben hoped.

He stumbled ahead, silencing the terror inside of him. He glanced at his phone; the blue arrow inched to the east, toward that infernal patch of land. He thrust the phone into his pocket and trained his eyes ahead. He would simply keep walking, keep plodding ahead, until he reached the lake and could move no more, or until something found him.

Over mucousy hills and dales, through half-dead ferns and muddy swamps. The deathly odor intensified, the monstrous howls echoed. The way seemed endless. Ben was sure he should have reached the plot of land by now.

Then, drifting through the air, he heard something: a faint chanting, a growled chorus of words. He stopped and listened closely, but the words floated in and out and he couldn't be sure that they came from outside his own head. He moved again, stepping into a slimy pool of water and falling to his knees, an excremental spray washing over him. He picked himself up, lurching into motion, scrambling to the top of a hill. In a low, flat clearing, he saw something move, undeniable this time, and squinted in horror. It appeared to be a sapling, stick-thin with needle arms, stabbing itself into the ground, a gaunt ribcage and narrow skull formed by jagged branches. Ben was certain it was an illusion, simply a fragile tree bending in the wind—certain, at least, until it stopped and turned in his direction, then bent toward him, bowing low to the ground, and let loose a garbled scream.

251

He forced himself to look away and sprinted ahead to the right, avoiding whatever it was that lurked there in the clearing. He must be getting close. The trees shook, clouds descended. That same chanting whispered through the forest, hissed by unseen tongues.

Ben tripped down a steep hill into a glade thick with vegetation, tree limbs bent in a massive knot, dead leaves blanketing a lake of soil. Taking two steps through the mud, he heard something behind him: a sharp hissing, breathed through the trembling earth. Ben clutched a dead branch for support and looked over his shoulder. It slithered over the black ground, a thick squirming vessel, like an ancient sea monster wriggling through the waters. It outweighed most of the trees surrounding them. Ben tried to scream but his body only allowed an awkward yelp.

He flailed at the branches, feet slipping in search of traction, and that's when he saw the front end of the creature, bursting through the black ground ten feet away: a misshapen head, a lifeless gray color, emerging from the mud with a gurgle, its gaping mouth filled with a dark, sputtering liquid. Its face was human, or half-human. The eyes were there, a milky blue, and a pair of teeth hung from sanguinary gums. But there was only a pulpy divot where the nose should have been, and the top of its head came to a sharp, oblong point, gleaming in the night.

Finally, as a matter of survival, Ben lunged against semi-solid ground and his hands gripped a young tree that supported his weight. He pulled himself upward, slicing through a thicket of blade-like branches. He could feel the mud ripple and shake as the creature slithered behind him. It unleashed a sickening hiss, a noise that burrowed deep and stayed there.

As Ben rose to the summit of a small hill, a terrible sight appeared to him. Dimly visible in the shadows of the forest, a young girl dressed in a white T-shirt and black jeans stood cemented in the middle of a clearing, at the border of a small pool of black water lined with bright white stones. The clearing was surrounded by a low, semi-circular crest.

There were four figures standing at the top of the ridge, each gazing morbidly at the young girl before them, watching from a distance. One of the creatures might have been construed as human, an emaciated woman clad in a billowing black dress, barely standing in the wind. The other three beings, though, took inexplicable forms, uncanny hybrids of human and beast. There was something birdlike, its legs as thin as stripped reeds, head matted with grimy feathers, its face a pummeled mass. Next to this creature, at a precise interval, something lizard-like loomed over the ground, its skin marked with rotting scales the color of seaweed. One of its four arms was a long, pinkish growth, coming to rest with a deformed human hand that lay on the ground, flaccid. And straight ahead of Ben, towering above him at the uppermost peak of the ridge, was an enormous hybrid of human and bull, its bulbous snout spitting steam as it exhaled. Its bovine head struggled to carry the weight of two curved horns, glinting in the moonlight.

The stench was unbearable now, an oppressive odor of decay. The trees shivered, too shocked to bear witness. Worst of all, the girl stood there paralyzed, right foot hovering over a pool of water.

"Amy!" he shouted—it must have been her. He didn't expect her to respond, not really. It was in part an effort to see if his voice still worked, if his brain and body could function properly.

He stumbled, feet sinking into the ground. He had only taken two arduous steps when he saw the girl, Amy, arms sagging at her side, plummet face-first into the pit, a revolting wave of liquid heaving around her in every direction.

He didn't scream or shout her name. Pumping his legs in desperate fury, he scraped and crawled over the land. The four creatures on the ridge saw him, he knew—and the hideous shapes that trailed behind him, whose presence he could feel—but he fought his way closer, closer to the hollow.

Below the black water he saw Amy's head sink. Then her shoulders, her arms, pulled underground, stygian liquid bubbling around her.

There was no doubt in Ben's mind when he broke the border of the clearing—an unholy seal that lined the pit, impenetrable by anyone but the damned. He could feel it in one step. He'd entered a different world, a new plane of being. He could feel the aura of death. The ground seared beneath him.

He heard it, too, when a tremendous roar bellowed from deep within the earth, an ear-splitting cry that sent some of the trees shattering to the ground. Seismic waves rolled through Sarona Lake. Residents of nearby Edgewater, Wisconsin would later say that fifty-foot tidal waves crashed upon their shores around midnight, destroying some of the smaller homes nestled by the lake.

Ben kept moving. Amy was in arm's reach. He lunged for her, oozing through the soil, and clamped onto her left ankle. She stopped, for a moment. Her entire body from head to knee was submerged in oily water. Ben pulled at her, gasping, but Amy was trapped, he felt something pull at her from below, her sacrifice nearly complete.

Finally he scrambled to the edge of the pool, his right arm breaking the surface and grabbing hold of Amy's waist. The satanic symphony continued, the beings at the edge of the clearing screamed in unison. Ben, deafened for the moment, heard none of it. He prayed that he would have the strength to pull Amy to safety, prayed to nothing in particular.

His knees digging further into soil, nearing the black water, Ben had no choice: he closed his eyes, inhaled deeply, and plunged his head beneath the surface. He felt a vicious chill, the metallic feeling of blood and pain caused by severe head trauma. Then he forced himself to open his eyes.

Hell is real, and it's close, John Linden said. I didn't know what he meant at the time. Or only in a metaphoric way, maybe. It's a convenient symbol—Hell on earth, life is Hell. A common fantasy when you think you can't go on, when life is too severe. The belief that evil and hardship come

254

from some mythical place, imposed from without instead of bubbling up from somewhere inside.

People who have had near death experiences claim to see the light at the end of the tunnel, the white light, the specter of Heaven beckoning them forward. They claim to be changed, sometimes, by the experience. Their communion with the dead, with some heavenly plane, gives them knowledge of a cosmic eternity that others, the living, can only hope exists.

I know I've been changed. How could I not? I've been given knowledge of a world beyond our own. But I saw no white light at the end of some tunnel, no divine glimpse of haloed angels. I saw, instead, a dry, rocky landscape, canyons etched into red clay, an endless desert. The color of a mesa baked beneath a ruthless sun. Wrinkled and barren, no signs of life.

Except.

Except a single stream of black water, phosphorescent below a sun that isn't there. I feel Amy next to me. I can feel her, somehow, still in my arms, my bodily sensations not yet removed from me. We're both falling through skyscraper canyons toward a thick current of water, and at the same time I feel my body sinking through the earth. Like being in two places at once, though this doesn't convey the feeling—the sensation of body and soul cleaved in half, a horrible pain I never could have imagined, the full extent of your being ripped apart.

We plummet toward the river of fire, falling as one, and as we approach the surface it becomes translucent. And the rippling dark waves and the crash of the current are only surface movements. There's something deeper, too, that we both can see, the agony of damnation, drowning in eternity. I see pale bodies writhing in the water, screaming, clawing at nonexistent light. There are other bodies, too, monstrous and merciless, pulling them down to the fiery depths. And if it exists—if this sick fantasy of Hell makes itself apparent to me—why shouldn't I believe in the divine fallacy of Heaven, too? Why shouldn't I believe that Aaron is there, somewhere else, that's what is most important, somewhere that he doesn't suffer?

And this thought—the belief that Aaron is in some other, better place—reminds me of Amy. I promise myself that Amy will not end up here. This is a failure that I cannot accept.

I feel my arms closing around her even as we fall to the deathly water. There are faces screaming, contorted, deep within, but Amy will not be one of them.

Ben heaved against the mud. The inhuman screams went on as Ben wrapped himself around her. Maybe it was fate or a grimly answered prayer or just stupid, empty luck, but his legs held firm against the weakened ground and, somehow, the two bodies pulled themselves from the water. First Amy's legs, then her torso and finally her head, breaking the surface of the abyss.

Ben rose to his knees, wallowing in the fragile earth, and held Amy's body in his arms. The two of them were covered in a hellish grime, the water dripping from their bodies in great, viscid blobs. Her eyes fluttered open, battered and fatigued, and her breath came in short, shallow waves, but there were signs of life at least, signs of terror.

He had no time to bring her fully back to consciousness. Ben remembered, in a horrid flash, the demons surrounding them. The edge of the clearing still formed a border—a portal between Earth and some other plane that the creatures could not penetrate—but they gazed in fury at Ben's intrusion, looming in a bloodthirsty rage.

Ben struggled to stand upright, barely steadying himself, and grunted as he lifted Amy into his arms. Her eyes fluttered against the heavy night sky. With his arms crooked beneath Amy's legs and shoulders, Ben planted his feet and spun against the forest floor. He could feel his energy seeping from his body, fatigued almost to the point of uselessness, but he forced himself to go on, his mind demanding superhuman exertions from his body.

A sick slop of mud as Ben took another step. The trees convulsed, wind whipping against the earth. Ben stumbled forward, squinting into the murky distance. Hideous creatures lurked there, shadows in the blackness. He had no choice. He jogged ahead, moving as quickly as his buckling legs could carry him, ushering Amy over the edge of the clearing and into the unknown.

As soon as they reentered the forest, leaving the hollow behind them, Ben could hear and feel a platoon of devilish creatures lurch into action. The ground throbbed, sending ripples across pools of black mud. He forced himself not to look, training his eyes stubbornly forward, but throughout the woods he heard echoes of falling trees and shrieks that could not have come from any earthly animal.

Slanting to his left to avoid the shadows in the forest, he raced ahead, Amy jostling in his arms. He tripped over gnarled roots and decaying tree stumps, losing grasp of Amy repeatedly. Their arms and faces were whipped with sharp branches, thin streams of blood coursing through the black mud that drenched them. He was certain they wouldn't make it, he convinced himself they would be captured and damned, but then he would glance down and see Amy's half-dead horror and would drive them forward, if only because he knew he must.

They had barely made it a hundred feet through the woods when Ben heard something massive approaching, stomping into the ground with seismic force, its exhalations shaking tree limbs. He glanced around them, fear uncontainable, and was grateful to find an enormous white oak standing at the foot of a hill. Its trunk was several feet wide in diameter; for a moment, Ben's racing mind wondered how many centuries this tree had been here, what kinds of evil it had witnessed at the hands of men and monsters. In an instant, though, he refocused on the matter at hand. Shifting Amy in his arms, he crept to the base of the oak tree and pressed them against it, holding her close against his body.

Another deafening huff as the creature breathed nearby, the sound of an old locomotive chugging from the station. It was close enough now that Ben shook with each footstep, could feel the world shudder each time it moved. He peered around the massive oak, eyes straining through the layer of mud now coating his body. He saw it at the top of a ridge nearby—the creature that was something between man and bull, matted hair thick with grime and filth, its torso wider than the oak tree that currently provided them with shelter. The bull's eyes gleamed red; its head wavered beneath massive horns that must have outweighed immense stone pillars. It glared into the shadows of the forest, detecting any trace of movement, and its enormous snout twitched and throttled, seeking out a human scent. They might have been in Daedalus' labyrinth, Ben and Amy soon to become the Minotaur's next prey.

Ben forced himself and Amy to stay still while the creature stomped through the forest. He was thankful, now, for the mud and grime that covered them, hiding them in the black night and concealing their scent. Even so, as the demon approached, coming to the base of the ridge ten feet away, it suddenly veered its head in their direction, seeming to stare into the whites of Ben's eyes. It took one monstrous step closer, gargantuan hooves rattling the earth. Ben could smell it now, a rotten stench emanating from an ancient body.

The creature would round the base of the ridge with two more steps, and there would be nowhere to hide from it then. Searching frantically, Ben spotted one of many black, slurping puddles on the forest floor to their right, a few dead leaves floating on the surface. The bull took another step. The earth shook in a cataclysm.

Finding no other option, Ben stepped away from the shelter of the tree, fumbling through the mud, knees bent painfully. Amy nearly slipped from his grasp; he caught her in his arms at the last moment. He plodded into the thick, oozing puddle, sinking three feet until he found something resembling solid ground. He crouched there until the black slime came up to his waist, then lay backwards, submerging himself beneath the surface. Amy's head shook violently, struggling to comprehend where she was and where she had been. Still silent from shock, she merely stared at Ben, eyes wide, as he covered her mouth and nose with his hand, pulling her into the squirming pool of mud and balancing her on his chest. Only Ben's nose and firmly-shut eyes now broke the surface of the puddle, along with a fraction of Amy's face, allowing her to breathe in quick, shallow breaths. The black slime devoured them, a primordial ooze that brought them back to a time before humanity.

This whole descent took only a few seconds. A moment after he and Amy dipped beneath the surface, he could hear and feel the creature take another step, the liquid squelching around their bodies. Another violent puff of steam from the bull. It was mere feet away.

Then, as Ben waited in torture for the thing to approach, he felt something else—something horrible in the muddy depths of the puddle. Tiny soft bodies brushed against his naked hands, burrowing beneath his clothes, scurrying like snakes. He forced an eye open. The first thing he noticed was the head of the bull soaring in his peripheral vision, red eyes blazing. Peeking in Amy's direction, he saw a new terror: a clew of worms crawling over her, spineless bodies caked with slime, barely visible in the darkness. There were many more beneath the surface, an army of worms that moved in unison. At first their presence was merely unpleasant, but Ben began to feel a stabbing pain as the worms dug into his skin, prickling fangs that defied zoology, hundreds of them threatening to colonize Ben and Amy. They looked like simple earthworms, segmented bodies black and teeming, but they attacked with a leech's thirst for blood. A greater danger still loomed nearby, with the size and fury to crush a man with one blow; but as Ben and Amy lay there, he wondered how long he'd be able to withstand this torment, invaded by a murderous strain of annelids who burrowed their way inside his throbbing skin.

For half a minute more they waited, pain scattered through their bodies, rising. The creature stood next to them, head cocked; it must have known they were there. But even with the benefit of whatever evil power it contained, the thing couldn't detect them beneath the grime of the forest. With a final thunderous snort, it lurched into motion and stomped away, heaving against a hickory tree in its path and sending it thrashing to the ground.

Ben could only wait a few seconds more until the sucking, squirming legion of worms became too much to bear. In one wild movement he rose from the puddle, lifting Amy unsteadily. He looked down at their muddy, blackened bodies, crawling with worms that drank their blood, gleaming sickly in the moonlight. He flailed and tore at them, ripping the tiny animals from his and Amy's flesh. But there was no time to be concerned with this. Through the forest, the echoes of hideous screams could be heard, seeking out the human intruders who had robbed them of their sacrifice.

"Amy?" he whispered, looking into her frantic eyes. He was going to ask her if she could walk, or better yet sprint, just keep moving west until they reached the highway. But she was clearly in shock, breath shallow, eyes darting. As soon as they stood on solid ground again, he scooped her into his arms, offering an apologetic look. "It's okay. Almost there," he muttered, trying to convince himself as much as her. He forced his legs into motion, feet slopping into mud and finally working themselves up to a feverish pace.

When Ben and Amy finally approached the row of spiny brambles that separated the woods from Highway 63, he felt—as often happens in the wake of vicious trauma—a dreamy, ethereal calm, a sense that they hadn't yet rejoined the real world. He arched his legs over thorny bushes, feet coming to rest against solid gravel. His knees buckled and he thought he would collapse right here, so close to safety. But instead, drawing from stores of energy he didn't know he had, Ben looked both ways and finally plodded across the highway. Amy seemed more lucid now but she only stared ahead, silent and impassive, waiting to shake herself out of some grisly dream.

He couldn't find his Jeep at first, scanning the highway for a bulky silhouette perched on the shoulder. For one spine-tingling moment he thought it might have been stolen. But, realizing he had ventured much further south in their escape from the woods, he lurched down the western side of the highway, his arms growing weary from supporting Amy's weight. Finally he saw it emerge on the black horizon. He had bought the vehicle six years ago from a friend of a friend he didn't completely trust, and he had never been as grateful for its presence as he was tonight.

So, at half past midnight on November 1, Ben fumbled for the passenger door handle with his left hand, reaching beneath Amy's body, and finally pulled the door open, setting her on the seat. A foul stream of grime and blood covered the tan leather, dripping onto the floor. In another frantic motion, he pulled at the dozen or so worms still digging their fangs into Amy's skin, revealing tiny puncture wounds red with blood. With a final anxious glance in each direction, he told himself she was safe.

Ben walked to the trunk of his Jeep, opened it, and rummaged for an old white T-shirt in his suitcase. Balling the shirt in his hand, he returned to Amy and dabbed gently at her face, mopping up the revolting mixture.

"There we go," he said. "We're okay."

He was relieved when she reached out limply for the shirt, took it from his grasp, and started cleaning herself—mute, empty, terrified and in shock, but gradually reclaiming control over her own body.

"You're all right now. It's all right."

He could almost believe this was true. But as he returned to the trunk of his Jeep and grabbed another old sweatshirt for himself, scrubbing at his befouled body and tearing the last of the worms from his flesh, he was desperate to leave this place once and for all. He knew, somehow, that he and Amy were marked by the town of Grange, and that a legion of creatures spawned from Hell would hunt them for the rest of their lives.

Chapter 26 — Breach of Contract

There were two things she noticed when she returned home around eleven.

Poor Amy didn't even finish all of her candy.

What the hell happened to my mother's quilt?

Hannah then chastised herself for such mundane thoughts. Shouldn't pangs of guilt and self-loathing be foremost on her mind?

She had been told by John Linden to stay out of the house for a few hours. Visit a friend, he suggested. See a movie. Drive a half-hour west to the express casino on Big Sand Lake, where, Linden promised, you could try your hand at the slots after filling up your gas tank.

But, instead, she had gone to the cemetery. Rydberg Cemetery, where Rebecca was buried. Along with Hannah's whole family, in fact, including her husband Henry, upon whose grave the grass was vibrant green, the plot many years younger than all the others. She had snipped a bouquet of Michaelmas daisies from her backyard garden before she left. They didn't look healthy, but at least they were from their own soil, the land where Rebecca spent her youth.

Hannah had said a silent blessing for each of her buried ancestors, mostly out of tradition; her family had a proud lineage. But she'd placed the entire bouquet on Rebecca's grave, feeling her joints scream as she bent over the cold slab tombstone.

In Loving Memory of Our Wife and Daughter. Rebecca May Dorian. April 30, 1986–May 4, 2010.

That date always tormented Hannah, the date of her daughter's death: May 4th. Amy's birthday. Morbidly, Hannah had thought of the symmetry when Amy's gravestone would be placed in the plot next to

Rebecca's—a day of death and birth, as though a grim cosmic checklist were being marked off in the afterlife, one soul for another. It had taken her a moment to realize that Amy's grave was not a distant fantasy but an imminent likelihood—a shoddy piece of wood, perhaps, impaled in the ground without a corpse beneath it.

She had stayed there for twenty minutes, nearly, sitting on the frosty ground, her back leaning against the granite of Rebecca's tombstone. She had carried a conversation with her daughter's ghost the way many people speak to themselves: half-aloud and half-internal, utterances breaking the silence.

"You know that loneliness," she would say out of the blue, peering at the blanketed stars. "You said you felt that too."

As for the unspoken words that only went as far as Hannah's synapses—well, what does a mother say to a dead child whose absence, for a decade, has been suffered daily? Everything and nothing, her feelings transmitted telepathically beneath the ground. At one point, squinting into the distance, she had thought she could see her daughter's ghost drifting through the cemetery, hovering over gravestones, pale and otherworldly. Hannah had thought the sight would comfort her, but Rebecca looked angry; she'd stared at her mother with blazing, disembodied eyes, a Medusa-like gaze that bore into Hannah's soul.

Before she'd left her house around nine o'clock, Hannah had offered to drive Katie home; and although Katie had protested, her eyes glued to the television screen, she noticed that Amy was dead asleep and realized that her parents would expect her home soon anyway. So Hannah had dropped Katie off at a small but regal blue-and-white house, occupied by a family that was loving and protective.

An hour after that—around the same time that two masked men snuck into her house, concocting the most elaborate way to mortify her granddaughter—Hannah had left Rydberg Cemetery and decided to drive around, aimless and automatic. The light had become sharp and intense, bright silver moonbeams clawing through the night. The radio was off, there was no music; only the hum of the tires and the churning of Hannah's thoughts.

After hours of self-reflection and fantasies of her daughter, Hannah had returned home. She didn't know what to expect. Neither Linden nor his "contract" were very specific with the details, and Hannah had sensed, in her faint understanding of the whole system, that it was not an exact science.

So when she nudged the front door open with a creak, Hannah closed her eyes in dread, expecting—who knows?—a living room ripped to shreds or, maybe, nothing at all, her granddaughter sleeping angelically on the carpet. Or, some kind of miracle, Rebecca reading a novel on the couch, curled beneath the quilt as she always used to do.

But there was nothing. The house was silent and seemed to pulse. Hannah picked up Amy's plastic jack-o-lantern from the living room floor, then took a long bath, vaporous steam and the scent of lavender seeping into the walls. She was tired, she realized as she dried herself off and slipped on a loose-fitting nightgown—an exhaustion of her own making. She combed her silver hair at the bathroom mirror and trudged to bed, peeling off the floral-pattern bedsheet. Before midnight came around, with only a cursory thought of Amy's well-being (forced out of mind at once), Hannah fell into a deep and clouded sleep.

She hadn't been sleeping well, however—jolting awake at three or four in the morning, unsettled by some implacable dread—and tonight was no different. At only twelve-thirty this time, barely after she fell asleep, Hannah was shaken awake by some stealthy unease.

She rolled onto her right side and lifted the clock toward her. Why had sleep become so elusive? She craved nothing but its embrace. She had felt fatigue mounting in her for weeks, making her irritable and self-absorbed. She set the clock down on the nightstand and collapsed against the pillows, preparing for another restless night.

There was a faint sound, she noticed then, a breathy whisper that might have nudged her awake. It crept down the hallway, under her closed doorway and over the walls of the bedroom, dancing into Hannah's brain.

She squinted, feeling an unbearable migraine all of a sudden, and swung her legs over the side of the bed. She mustered a shred of energy and stood, plodding over the carpet in small, uncertain steps. She rubbed the heels of her hands into her eyeballs.

She pulled the bedroom door open. The quiet hallway waited, lit with spindly shadows from the wall sconces. She walked down the hall, legs brushing against the thin fabric of her nightgown. There was a large photograph to her left, a framed picture of a Midwestern cornfield basked in autumnal sun; and an ornate mirror to her right, whose gleaming reflections startled her, at times, during sleepless midnight treks down the hallway.

The sound grew louder as Hannah approached the bathroom, a persistent murmur. The door hung ajar, the room swimming in shadows. Now, finally, her lethargy started to dissipate. She realized that something, a darkness scuttling over the floors, was not quite right.

Squinting into the bathroom, she pushed the door open. The angry whisper intensified. She reached into the room and flipped on a light switch. The bathroom was conspicuously empty, mocking her. Beneath the bathroom light she found the source of the noise: the faucet was running, a stream of lukewarm water hissing into the drain.

Had she left the faucet on? Impossible; saving water was something of an obsession for her. Then again, Hannah barely trusted her mental clarity these days. She stepped to the sink, ignoring her reflection in the mirror. She reached out and twisted the faucet toward the wall. The water cut itself off.

At that exact moment, with eerie synchronicity, the lights in the house went dead. Her bedroom, the hallway, the elegant bathroom lights, they all darkened at once. Hannah's eyes darted, scanning the gloom. Was this how it all worked? Would she turn around and stumble through the shadows and come face to face with her daughter, her daughter dead twelve years, an appropriately dreamlike reunion? Or was this something else?

Her eyes shot to the mirror, against her will. It was a full and infinite black, containing only emptiness. She found this odd. Her eyes were adjusting to the dark; her off-white nightgown and freckled hands were barely visible in the unlit bathroom. So why was there nothing in that mirror?

It shouldn't have bothered her, she supposed, and she tried to step into the hallway and toward the staircase—then to the basement, where the circuit breakers awaited. But why couldn't she? Why, when she tried to move, did her legs prove mulish and indignant?

She refocused her attention on the mirror, the sheet of glass she knew was in front of her. She leaned toward it, fear mounting. She exhaled and thought she saw a burst of steam in the suddenly frigid bathroom.

Then it appeared. A body in the mirror, an apparition, beginning as a pale and minute speck, then growing larger, nearing Hannah, like one of those spectacular dolly-zooms in Hollywood movies. Hannah stood there, shivering, as the figure appeared from nothing. The body grew human-sized, emerging from the blackness, from some intangible place. Finally it settled into position, the contours of the body wavering until they solidified at last.

As it grew larger, Hannah thought she recognized this person. She shared some of her features: the long, straight hair, dark as Hannah's was once, curling only slightly as it neared the shoulders. An elegant, narrow face, a small triangular nose coming to a noblewoman point. But this was a youthful body, less than thirty years old, cheeks flushed with red, bright blue eyes batting with ambivalence. This was Rebecca, in person so to speak, more real and vivid to Hannah than the snapshot photographs and fleeting memories that had accompanied her for years.

There was a timelessness to Rebecca as she came to Hannah now. She looked, in some ways, as she did before her death at twenty-four, but livelier, fuller, more corporeal even as she stayed sequestered in the

266

mirror. She had always been healthy, active and bright featured. But she was also anemic, full of life yet lacking in red blood, and so during labor there was a tear, the doctors said, and oxytocin was given intravenously and there was finally an episiotomy—but it was all futile. Rebecca's heart stopped while her writhing daughter was taken away by the nurses, and on Rebecca's face was a look of both agony and peace. Hannah couldn't look at her daughter after that, she was physically unable; nor could she look at the parchment sheets on the hospital bed, saturated with a thick crimson color.

Rebecca—the reflection of her—loomed in the mirror, hovering over an infinite void. She stood at a distance, lips curled in an expression impossible to read. Her skin looked like white marble, draped in a silky black nightgown.

Hannah's toes curled against the bathroom tile. She shook her head as Rebecca appeared, gaping at the mirror until she was convinced that it wasn't a mirage, Rebecca wouldn't leave her again. The more Rebecca smiled and cast her cruel look, the more certain Hannah became that this *was* her daughter, returned to her now. She brought the back of her hand to her mouth, suppressing a cry of joy.

"Rebecca," Hannah said at last, shaking her head slowly.

This elicited a full and vulgar grin from Rebecca.

"Mom."

"I don't believe it." She waited, expecting Rebecca to reply. She didn't. "I should…but I don't."

Rebecca stared back at her, callous in her silence. Hannah took a step toward the mirror, reaching a hand in its direction.

"Well…Becca, sweetie, what's happening, exactly? How do I get you out of there?"

"Out of where?"

Hannah looked at her, feeling a tinge of panic.

"I don't know how to say this, darling," she said with a bitter laugh, "but you're in my mirror. Do you know what's happening? Do you know where you are?"

Only a quick look away and a glinting smile from Rebecca.

Hannah had kept herself from touching the mirror up to this point. She didn't want to disturb what she presumed to be her daughter. But, lacking any explanation from Rebecca, she leaned across the sink and held her hand out, fumbling for the pane of glass that she couldn't see. The tips of two fingers dipped into a liquid mass. Rebecca's image refracted as the touch of Hannah's hand sent eerie ripples across the scene. It was a thrilling sensation at first, hot and otherworldly on Hannah's skin. Then, after a few seconds, she jerked her hand away. It was like reaching into an oven, two hundred degrees or more. The pain mounted quickly, throbbing. Hannah cradled her fingers with her other hand and squinted in the dark bathroom. She thought she could make out a reddened, bubbling patch on her fingers where they'd been blistered from burns.

She looked back at the mirror. There was no effort to conceal her fear this time.

Rebecca laughed, black hair skittering. She relished her inexplicable joy for a moment, then quieted. Hannah stood in the bathroom, crying and confused. Her happiness had been short-lived.

When Hannah said nothing else, Rebecca decided to speak.

"Yes, I know what's happening. I've seen it all. How descriptive do you want me to be?"

A terse shake of the head from Hannah. She had shrunk all the way against the bathroom wall.

"Let's see...I get knocked up, I guess we could start with that. By a man I never had any feelings for, except maybe when I had too much to drink. But I'm pregnant, so I don't really have much of a choice, do I? Not here, anyway, where we live. We get married. Now you and I, and Dad and Tyler, are all living in your house, and we have wedding presents to contribute but nothing else, because he's not working. But I'm gonna be a mom, so things'll be okay, and Tyler will find a job.

"And the contractions start at 5:30 in the morning on a…Wednesday, right? The day I died. The day my daughter was born. They hurt like hell and I just wanted to get it over with. I was scared. They told me, like they told you, that my blood was weak and there might be some issues. But what was I supposed to do?

"So I was in labor for—what, seven hours? You were there, you know. Finally Amy was delivered and she seemed to be healthy, and for a second I thought it was all over, we made it. But the pain was worse, *so* much worse. I didn't even think that was possible. I was shaking, I remember, my entire body."

"Stop it."

"And I could not *believe* all the blood. It terrified me because I knew it was mine. It soaked into that thin hospital mattress and they went to get me another. I think the last thing I heard before I was put under—"

"Stop it."

"Was that I had a uterine tear, which—I never *really* knew fear up until that moment. And…I guess it's a good thing I was unconscious when I died, because you don't want to be awake for that. I just drifted away. I remember, though, seeing your face before everything went black. You were standing over me and you looked so scared and frantic, squeezing my hand to death. And that made me feel *so* happy, that you were scared, because I knew it was your fault."

"Damn you, stop it."

"Ohh, Mom, that's what you have to say to me after all this time?"

Hannah looked away and rubbed tears from her face.

"And what about the time we spent before that?" Hannah asked her then, refusing to believe that this was anything but her daughter. "Traveling your senior year of high school. Venice, even, you remember?—even though we didn't have the money for it. Going to

269

Minneapolis on the weekends, getting away from here, talking *honestly* about…"

"That's what you think happened? My entire life was mother-daughter bonding time?"

"I mean…" Hannah stopped herself, swallowed, and restarted. "I was closer to you, Becca, than my own husband. I was proud of you. I wanted to give you a good life, give you everything."

"No. You just wanted company because your husband was an idiot and your son-in-law was useless."

Hannah shook her head.

"But you can't take pride in your granddaughter?" Rebecca asked. "That's what I don't understand. If you take pride in *anyone*, be proud of her, *my* daughter, who actually has a brilliant future ahead of her. And you want to take that away from her?"

Another flood of tears from Hannah, who tried to stifle her sobs.

"From *me*?" Rebecca continued. "Not only do you watch me die, you sacrifice my own daughter to bring me back." There was a harsh click of the tongue. "Mom, that might be the most cowardly thing I've ever heard."

"Stop it!" Hannah shrieked, her voice finally growing above a whisper. She leaned against the wall, depleted.

"I think it's fair you'll be completely alone after all this."

Hannah squinted at the image of Rebecca through glistening eyes.

"You're not her," Hannah said. "You're not my daughter."

Rebecca grinned again. It had once been the most blissful thing that Hannah could imagine. Now it sent a chill up her spine.

"Of course not." The voice was different this time, louder and fuller, as though it came from every direction. "Your daughter's been dead for twelve years."

The face started to change. Its shape became narrow, skeletal. The skin started to droop from its edges in a red, jelly-like mass. The lips grew thin and desiccated, the mouth a smattering of rotten teeth over an empty hole. The eyes glowed, a sadistic grin contorted its face.

"We had an agreement," it intoned, the walls of the bathroom shaking.

"I don't—"

Hannah was interrupted by a flash of sound and fury, a thunderous explosion and a resounding shatter, the glass of the mirror splintering and flying in every direction. Then the feeling of jagged shards piercing her skin, burrowing deep, passing through at high velocity, wells of agony all over her body. She collapsed. If the lights had been on, they would have illuminated a sick arterial spray across the bathroom walls. One small comfort: Hannah died in little pain, relatively quickly. But her mind still teetered in those final seconds and it was fixed on a haunting image: the twin tombstones, side-by-side, of Rebecca and Amy Dorian, sharing the same date of death and birth. A third grave could be seen between them in the distance—Hannah's own. This vision, crawling with toxic vines and unseen ghosts, plagued Hannah's mind in its last waking moments.

Chapter 27 — The Life of Amy Dorian

She prodded at her vanilla ice cream with a plastic spoon. The night had grown cold but he had taken a chance on ice cream. What kid doesn't like ice cream?

She poked at it while sitting on an orange chair in a highway overpass, taking an occasional minuscule bite. She gazed into the distance at nothing while vile memories reappeared, she couldn't expel them from her thoughts. She was in shock but recuperating, Ben saw. She was covered with three sweatshirts and two more jackets and had finally stopped shivering.

But now there was ice cream and she couldn't say no. The Jeep had sidled up to the overpass in Barron, Wisconsin, about forty minutes south of Grange. It was the kind of appendage to American highways that sits there, vestigial, offering a gas station and three fast food restaurants in a strip elevated over the freeway. There was a McDonald's at this one, and it had inspired Ben to attempt yet another conversation with Amy.

"Hey, you want some food?" he had asked with a nod as they approached the overpass. "Some ice cream? Whatever you want."

He had tried to coax *something* out of her, an attempt at connection, ever since he'd plunked her down in the front seat of his Jeep. They had tried to dry the filth off themselves as he drove. She had slowly regained control over her muscles; at first they were paralyzed but eventually, warmed by the Jeep's chemical heat, they had brought Ben's old sweatshirt to her face and started scrubbing away. Ben had applied a ratty towel to himself and noticed Amy shivering in the passenger seat.

"You cold?"

No answer, of course. He had cranked up the heat and rummaged in the backseat for a blanket, a flannel, any piece of fabric he could drape over Amy. He had found a few and tossed them over her.

"Amy," Ben had said after pulling away from the shoulder. "Your name is Amy, right?"

He'd looked at her. She said and did nothing, but at least that wasn't a protest.

"Okay. I think your name is Amy Dorian. I know you've been through a lot, Amy, more than I really understand. I'm sorry, I really am. But you're safe now. I'm gonna make sure of that, okay?" He had paused. "Do you know what happened? Did you notice your mom doing or saying anything strange?"

This had provoked a reaction from her, a sideways glance and quickened breathing.

"Hannah Dorian? Is that your mom?"

She'd quieted again at this, resuming her adamant glare out the windshield. "Grandma," she had said finally. Ben was relieved simply to get a response. But Amy couldn't bring herself to say anything else, and Ben hadn't pressed her.

As they had pulled away from the patch of forest by Highway 63, he thought back to the contract in John Linden's study, particularly its chilling last words: *should the terms agreed herein be violated by the Licensee in any way, the Licensee may experience retribution of an extreme and fatal nature.* No matter what Hannah Dorian had done, Ben presumed that nobody deserved whatever punishment awaited her.

Despite his single consuming desire to get Amy out of Grange as soon as possible, he knew they needed to check on her grandmother's safety. He wouldn't have been able to live with himself otherwise. So he had asked Amy to direct him to the house in which she grew up, cared for by someone she thought had been loving, though each tender gesture had hidden a growing core of hatred and contempt. Amy had offered terse directions muttered under her breath; Ben had had to lean closer to hear them, turning the wrong way numerous times. At last, the churning Jeep had pulled up to the curb on Wellington Drive, where Amy had been abducted only a few hours earlier. Ben had cut off the lights but kept the engine running, keeping Amy warm and locking the doors before bounding up to the house. He had tried to pull open the front door, unsurprised to find it locked; then, ignoring any sense of decorum, had kicked and rammed the old front door until its lock broke loose. The house was black and dormant as he had stood in the living room, knowing even then that there was no hope of finding Hannah alive.

It didn't take long before he had ventured upstairs and, peering into each room, detected a spray of blood and a still, lifeless body slumped on the floor of the bathroom. He had felt the bleak, heavy presence of the corpse before he saw it, and while Hannah's death had barely surprised him—this was the retribution, after all, that the contract had foretold—he still shuddered at its sad finality and what it meant for Amy.

He had drifted down the stairs after finding Hannah's body and returned to the Jeep outside, his body moving of its own accord. He had breathed a sigh of relief to find Amy still safe and locked inside the vehicle; hopefully, he had thought to himself, there would be no more gruesome surprises tonight.

He hadn't been able to muster the courage to tell Amy what he'd found, and luckily she hadn't pressed him for answers, perhaps guessing them herself. And so the Jeep had peeled away from the side of the road and then from Grange itself, rocketing southward. For the first thirty minutes of their drive—or, really, then and now and everlasting—Ben had searched behind them, expecting something evil to arise and follow close behind, waiting for the time to strike.

But no, incredibly. The Jeep had sped onward. Highway 63 became 53 and, about forty minutes south of Grange, the neon allure of fast-food restaurants had beckoned from the heavily trafficked overpass.

"Hey, you want some food? Some ice cream? Whatever you want."

They had just passed the sign and roared ahead. Two miles until the overpass. She had said nothing, offering that same resolute stare, a product of shock and distrust.

"Guess it's all for me, then, huh?"

They had pulled off the exit almost two miles later and Ben's Jeep veered into a spot next to a gas pump. He'd filled it with unleaded, peering in at Amy as he pumped the gasoline. But she didn't return his stare.

He had made two phone calls while standing outside of his Jeep. The first of them was to Captain Miranda Prost, her non-emergency line, a voicemail that the captain would receive the following morning. The second call was to another police superior, Chief Terence Arnold, asking him to meet at a highway overpass near Barron as soon as he could.

Ben had pulled open the driver-side door and leaned toward Amy, smiling. His energy had been exhausted long ago, *days* ago, but still he tried to brighten Amy's spirits.

"Okay, Amy Dorian, I'm gonna get one of everything. You're gonna help me finish it, okay?"

He had waited there, dizzy, giving her time to respond, but only silence. He had started to slam the door shut.

"I'm coming in."

She had stepped out a moment later, draping one of Ben's sweatshirts around her small frame.

The McDonald's was open until two in the morning, and even if its employees looked like they had checked out hours ago, at least the soft-serve dispensers continued to churn. Ben had ordered a cone for himself, suddenly in the mood. When it was Amy's turn to order, he had let her do the talking. He had smiled at the cashier, wondering if they fit the appearance of a father and daughter going out for casual late-night dessert. Given the trails of mud and slime etched onto their bodies, he doubted it.

275

So now they prodded at their ice cream on a bench in the overpass, glancing at the traffic whirring beneath the windows. Each vehicle that passed was comforting in its ignorance, knowing nothing of the horror that Ben and Amy had witnessed. Ben loved overpasses like these. He remembered being young and stopping at them with his father, after driving for what seemed like days but was only hours, feeling like you were monitoring the flow of traffic, a twenty-first century American Poseidon. He realized now, sitting here with Amy, that it was a cherished childhood memory he had never recreated with Aaron.

He licked his chocolate ice cream, absentminded; Amy dipped her spoon into hers.

"Where are you taking me?"

He watched another pair of headlights arc down the highway, then returned Amy's glare. It was the kind of look you could never hope to lie to.

"Where do you want to go?"

"Home."

"Yeah," Ben muttered. "I know."

"Is my grandma dead?" Amy asked before Ben could continue.

He swallowed hard. What was the point of lying? He'd never had much diplomatic tact but he believed that Amy, grown beyond her years, would prefer an unvarnished truth.

"Yes," he answered. "Amy, I'm sorry. I'm so sorry, but she is."

Amy sniveled in the bench across from him, curling her legs up under her knees.

"What killed her?" she asked.

Ben let out a sigh. "I wish I knew, Amy. Wish I could answer that question."

"What was going to kill me?"

Words were insufficient this time. He looked into Amy's eyes and shook his head tenderly.

"Did your grandma say anything to you, Amy?" Ben asked. "Anything that scared you?"

She stared out the window. "No. I think I knew she was sad. She's been so different."

They finished their ice cream. People in their cars shuttled down the freeway, thoughts carried down the nervous system of the country.

"Do you have any family, Amy? Anyone live nearby?"

Amy shook her head no.

"I don't have anyone."

*****

Ten minutes later, Amy sat in the passenger seat of Ben's Jeep. She held her empty dish of ice cream in her hands, a sticky vanilla residue coating her fingers.

Ben leaned against the hood, hands shoved into his pockets.

The restaurant had shut down by now. Blood-orange chairs were hooked over tables, floors had been mopped and dumpsters filled to capacity.

Over the hush of traffic passing below, Ben heard a car approach. He looked over his shoulder as a car emerged from the offramp, tires crunching. As it came closer, Ben could see the golden POLICE inscription on the side of the white sedan.

Terence Arnold parked the vehicle two rows away. Ben watched him as the car came to a stop; then the six-foot-three police chief stepped into the night, pivoted in Ben's direction, and strode across the parking lot. There was an uncertain gleam in his eye, a look of rage and begrudging respect.

He came to rest in front of Ben's Jeep, arms cocked. There were patches of filth caked onto Ben's skin, lit by the harsh and glaring lights of the overpass.

Arnold had planned on beginning with a fierce invective, asking how Ben could be so stupid and why the hell couldn't he leave them alone, and didn't he know he had just signed their death sentence? But before he could spout these words, he saw Amy sleeping in the front seat of the Jeep. Arnold's expression softened.

"How is she?"

Ben was surprised by the question. He turned to look at Amy, then back at Arnold.

"Okay. All things considered."

Arnold took two steps closer.

"Hannah Dorian is dead. Amy's grandmother."

Ben nodded, looking at his feet.

"But you already knew that," Arnold added.

"Yeah."

"You know, I have to say I'm impressed. Furious, too, and concerned for the safety of my town—but impressed."

"Is there a posse out for my blood?" Ben asked, half-serious.

Arnold sighed. "Yes, as a matter of fact. Good thing you left when you did. John Linden, I've never seen him like this—like a rabid dog. Armed with a shotgun and 'following your scent,' he says. Wants to kill you himself."

"And I'm guessing you didn't try very hard to discourage him, right?"

"The others wanted to get rid of you through more…indirect means. But that takes time. It's unpredictable."

Ben shifted on his feet. "Listen, I'm not gonna apologize for taking that girl away. Screwing with this evil little system you got here, I don't care about that. Whatever happens to me, I'll know she's safe."

Arnold shook his head somberly. "You can't be so sure of that."

Ben replied with a severe glare, eyes glinting. Arnold exhaled and walked to Ben's side, leaning against the Jeep's fender.

"You think there's nothing but killers and devil-worshipers in Grange. Fine, I get that. But some of us are good people, living in terrible circumstances. Doing what we can."

"Why don't you all just leave? Make it a ghost town. Get as far away as possible."

Arnold shrugged. "Maybe we think we're doing something good by staying there, keeping this thing contained. Relatively speaking." There was a long pause. "Or maybe the allure of what it offers is too great to ignore."

"Resurrection," Ben said, putting a name to Arnold's equivocation. "The cost is too high. I'm sure you know that."

Arnold said nothing for a while, feeling the icy chill of the November night. "It's home," he said finally, as though that explained everything. He turned to look at Amy once more. Her eyes were closed and fluttering.

"So you're leaving Grange for good?"

Ben nodded.

"Well, I'm glad you're leaving. For your sake." There was a touch of gratefulness when he added: "I'm glad you found us, too. For hers."

Ben was disarmed by such sympathetic words, but he merely scoffed in response.

"In this case, I'd say the pleasure was all yours."

"So why did you call me, Ben? You already left town. You should've kept driving."

Ben nodded and moved to his left, facing Arnold.

"True. The way I see it, though, we have some loose ends to tie up. Namely, the fact that I don't want you to put out some satanic fucking contract on my life. I know what killed Maria, I saw it. I know it can kill me, too. Probably wants to, now."

"Probably does. We have our own concerns, though, Officer Dmitrovich. For example, what happens if you decide to dig around some more? Return to Grange with the County Sheriff and half of the

MPD searching through those woods. Do you have any idea what kind of bloodbath there would be?"

"Well," Ben rasped, "I guess we find ourselves at an impasse, don't we?"

"You could say that."

"So that's why I called you. I want to propose a compromise. I bring Amy with me. Get her to safety. You put a leash on that thing you have in the woods and guarantee my protection."

"You know I can't do that."

Ben considered this. "Sure. Yeah. But if something, God forbid, *tragic* happens to me, I want you to know I left a message for my captain. Told her I was still looking into a possible incident here. Probably nothing, I said, but there were signs of distress and I decided to investigate. Now, if and when I return to Milwaukee in a few days, I'm going to tell her that it was a misunderstanding. No criminal activity. And everything goes on like normal, if you want to call it that. On the other hand, if I *don't* make a safe return home…well, you might have a couple detectives and some guys from IAD making their way up here."

"I get it." Arnold stood, springing from the Jeep, and turned to face Ben. "And if we do have any kind of uninvited guests come our way…just remember we can take that leash off at any time."

Ben scowled and nodded.

"Not a good situation," Arnold continued.

"Obviously not," Ben growled. "What did you call it, though— 'making the best of terrible circumstances'?"

They stood there in silence, weighing the gravity of their arrangement. Finally, Ben continued.

"Guess we're just gonna have to trust each other."

Arnold huffed. "That's a scary thought."

But he was right, of course, and there was nothing left to be said. After a moment both of them glanced at Amy. The wind had grown calm but a soft breeze waved against them. The blare of a semi's horn erupted from the freeway, soothing in its plainness.

At last, Arnold took a step toward Ben. With a steely look, he held out his hand. Ben was taken aback but returned the gesture, shaking Arnold's hand with a firm grip.

"Gentleman's agreement," the chief said.

"Something like that."

They stood there, eyeing each other with a tense, unspoken understanding.

"Take care, son."

Before Ben could respond, Chief Arnold spun on his feet and walked away, his boots thudding on black concrete. A late-night traveler filled up his tank in the distance, looking monstrous in the gas-station glow.

When Chief Arnold had made it halfway to his vehicle, Ben called after him.

"Hey, how's Nathan doing?"

Arnold stopped, surprised by the question, and turned back to Ben. He shrugged. "I don't know. Haven't talked to him since the funeral."

Ben squinted into the night sky. He didn't know if he should be alarmed or reassured.

"Don't worry," Chief Arnold added. "We'll get him through this."

With that, he pivoted and walked to the police cruiser, slipping into it without a word. The lights flashed to life, the engine churned, and Chief Arnold veered away from Ben Dmitrovich, the car swooping through the parking lot and inching onto the freeway onramp. Ben watched the vehicle roll into the distance, simply another pair of lights blending into the unknown stories throttling down the road.

He stepped into the Jeep, which had grown warm as it idled there in the parking lot. He glanced at Amy. She was still asleep, eyes darting beneath her lids. *Good or bad dreams?* Ben wondered. He lifted the soggy ice cream from her hand and placed it in the cupholder. Then he pulled up one of the blankets covering Amy, bringing it to her shoulders.

The lights sparked to life and the Jeep pulled away. Ben, nearly comatose from fatigue, stared through the windshield and pushed eighty. They had a long drive ahead of them.

*****

The Department of Children and Families in Madison, Wisconsin was nestled on the second floor of an immense stone structure—flat, crude, and rectangular, the kind of drab bureaucratic building that seemed to belong to a former Soviet republic circa 1970. But as Ben pulled up to it at half past nine the next morning, the building's limestone walls were a beacon of hope, something resembling a final destination.

They had found a cheap motel halfway between Grange and Madison, the kind of place with two twin beds to a room and a general haze of indifference. He had slept just under two hours, but it felt restorative. Amy had said little, eyes glazed, every waking moment a struggle to comprehend. Her greatest burst of activity had come as the Jeep pulled into Madison: the radio, scanning automatically, came across a Satie piece on a classical station—something with a French title that started with a G, though Amy couldn't remember what it was— and she had flicked out her hand and stopped it there, closing her eyes. Ben had cast a surprised look in her direction but listened along, the stratospheric fullness of the music in the air. He was indescribably moved.

The Jeep inched to the curb in front of the boxy government building, panting as it came to a stop. Amy was awake, barely, still casting that heavy look at the passing scenery.

He turned to her as he shut off the engine.

"Amy." People walked down the sidewalk outside the car, pulling their jackets close and clutching large cups of coffee. "You've been so strong. It's not fair what you've been through, and I'm sorry for that. I wish I could make it better."

Her eyes burrowed into his, her armor against the world still raised and fortified.

"The hard part's over. Really, I promise. We're gonna find you somewhere safe. You can go to school, make friends. Be yourself."

"Music lessons?"

"Music?"

"Piano?"

"Yeah," Ben nodded. "Yeah, you can take piano lessons, of course. There's still one thing we have to do, though. Can you be strong for me, just a while longer?"

She said nothing. The ambient sounds of a city sidewalk early in the morning.

"Can you come inside with me?"

She glanced away as tears welled. It tortured him to see them, but he was reassured, at least, to find emotion pass through her stoic features.

"Where am I gonna live?"

"Somewhere safe. You'll be happy."

He nodded, warm and pleading, inviting her to trust him. She did in a guarded, world-weary way, clinging to her dwindling faith in humanity. There was something pained about him, even she could see that, something trying to heal itself.

She nodded.

They walked through the glass front doors, hand in hand, and they hobbled together up the brown-speckled staircase. He stooped down to hold her hand in his, reminding him of Aaron, his first waddling steps.

The office of Child Protective Services was soft-lit and cubicled; they might have been selling office supplies. It was early on the weekend, but even so there was a puffy-eyed secretary manning the front desk and a few case workers looking ragged in their offices, either working too early or too late.

Jane Haskell was the name of the woman who came out to meet them, a tall, red-haired woman wearing a glum smile. She shook Ben's hand and knelt in front of Amy, complimenting her glasses and offering her orange juice or a donut ("I'm a bad influence," she apologized).

Amy said nothing.

She sat on a blue padded chair as Ben and Ms. Haskell talked inside her office. Amy watched their lips move through the window, pretending she could read them and decipher the conversation. Then, when her mind wandered, she scanned the pockmarks on the ceiling tiles and felt the buzzing throb of the lights. Everywhere she looked now seemed transient and unreal, another place, another *thing* to take from her, soon to be relegated to memory.

Seated around a low desk in Jane Haskell's office, an oblique conversation was taking place. How much did she need to know? What could Ben hide from her? Amy Dorian was a bright, well-adjusted fifth-grader with a fondness for piano, Ben said, who was criminally abused by her grandmother, now deceased. Her parents were gone, too. No extended family that he knew of. Given the trauma she had experienced at home so recently, a change of scenery might help her best, Ben said. She should be somewhere active, bustling, where the greatest threat was that of anonymity. Somewhere far away from Grange.

"She's a good kid. Strong, smart. She deserves better."

"Don't they all?" Jane asked in a brusque voice, her line of work making her somewhat immune to idealistic clichés.

She scattered some papers around her desk, finding a blank form to fill out. Ben showed her his badge and scrawled his ID number on the form, wondering when Ms. Haskell might discover his tarnished reputation with the Milwaukee PD.

She'll be placed in foster care, Jane told him at last, and made available for adoption; girls her age with a strong performance in school, she said, have a high percentage of home placement. Unfortunately, though, she continued, Amy's education and health care would be limited in the coming months until she was adopted, since public funding had been slashed to nothing, but what do you expect (she finished with a hiss) when eighty percent of your taxes go to the police?

Ben snickered at this, avoiding confrontation.

A naïve thought had come to him, idyllic and impossible. He didn't want to leave Amy behind, not when he had finally brought her to such tenuous safety. Maybe he didn't have to. But then the thought of filling out adoption paperwork and preparing his duplex for a twelve-year-old roommate coalesced; and the certainty that his application would be laughed at—what was he thinking, a divorced cop whose son just died and who has, let's just say, public relations issues?—chased the fantasy from his mind.

They stepped out of her office after twenty minutes of conversation. They both wore looks of calculated normalcy, as though they'd been talking about nothing but the weather. Amy, by now, had brought her legs beneath her on the chair; she was sitting on her feet, clad in small black sneakers. She peered at Ben as he left the office—at Jane, too, for a split-second, but mostly at Ben. She sought answers in his expression. He smirked back simply.

Ben and Jane walked over, stepping around gray desks, gray tables, gray cubicle walls. Ben kneeled in front of her, wiping a smudge of dirt from her face—that grime wouldn't *really* come off for weeks, months.

His smile broadened as he rested his arm on his knee. Amy frowned. Haskell spoke from behind Ben:

"I'll give you two a second. Amy, can I get you anything?"

She shook her head no. Haskell stepped away.

Ben cleared his throat. "How ya feelin'?"

She shook her head again, tears coming with it this time. She buried her head against her knees. Ben rose and took the seat next to her, wrapping his arm around her shoulders uncertainly.

"Hey…hey." He didn't know what else to say. He held her closer. She shifted toward him, burying her head against his shoulder.

"It's okay."

"Everyone leaves. My whole family left me. Now you. I don't trust anyone."

Ben nodded, wincing. "I know. I don't blame you."

She sniffled and grew quiet. She pulled away from Ben, leaning against the coarse fabric wall. He removed his arm from her shoulder.

"I know things are going to be okay, though. Do you know why?" She didn't answer him. "You don't know?" A sad smile as she shook her head again. "I have this skill, I don't think I've told you. I don't tell anyone, actually, 'cause it's a secret. But my skill is I can read the future. Precognition, they call it, I've been diagnosed."

She laughed in disbelief, looking away.

"It's true! It comes in waves. I can't even control it, I just meet someone new and I have a flash of their entire future before my eyes. Do you believe me?"

"No."

"Ahh, you're so skeptical Amy. Where's your sense of wonder?" As the question came out, he remembered everything that had happened the previous night and his words suddenly sounded callous. So he kept on. "I think it's when we were driving to the motel that I first saw it. You, sometime soon, maybe less than a year from now. You're at a friend's house, watching TV or something, I don't know, talking about homework and summer and all of that. The usual. And everything about you seems happy." He was gazing into the distance, enjoying the role. "And later on, sometime in the summer, I see you running through a sprinkler—did you ever used to do that? It's bright and sunny. You're laughing. Everything seems like it's in slow-motion and it's like you're made of the sun."

Amy laughed again but the tears returned, more ambivalent.

"And then everything skips forward a little bit, like fast-forwarding a movie or something. You're older—in your twenties, I think. You're at college somewhere, a huge performance hall, it's all red brick and, you know, centuries of tradition. You're onstage in a white dress and you're at the...piano, right? There's a deep silence in the hall until you start playing. The first note is like a single, infinite string that stretches out the ceiling into the sky. And you keep playing, your hands move over the piano with *impossible* grace, and even after you're done no one applauds for a second because they're too stunned to move." Amy snickered again. "I can't wait to hear you play, by the way. Really.

"So I'm sitting there driving and the images keep coming, I can't stop 'em now. Like I'm flipping through your photo album years before it exists. You meet someone you can trust, and they make you laugh. You can be yourself. And even if you fight, because everybody does, they stay with you, Amy, they never leave you. You feel a strange thrill every morning when you wake up, because you look around and see that you're where you want to be.

"So you get older and..." He stopped, smirked, and looked at her. "Well, I'm not gonna tell you *everything*. You don't want me to ruin it for you, do you?" Amy laughed and shook her head, wiping away the last remaining tears. "Some of it has to be a surprise."

There was a steady hum of silence, welcome this time. A phone rang in the background; a floating voice answered it.

"What I'm trying to tell you, Amy, is that I see you live a good life. Maybe that seems impossible right now, but...just wait and see."

She raised her eyes in his direction. They swam and sparkled, a flood of swirling thoughts, loneliness, doubt, gratitude. Ben beamed and glanced down the hallway, where Jane Haskell waited at a respectful distance, eyeing Ben and Amy, sipping coffee from a comically large mug. She began treading toward them.

Ben stood, leaned over Amy, and kissed the top of her head. Then he tousled her hair with a shake of his hand—this seemed a more appropriate gesture.

"I'll be back soon. I'm gonna hear you play next time, right?"

She nodded, a bittersweet motion. Ben memorized her face, its contours and quirks, this face he felt like he'd known forever, because he needed to remember this exact moment for years, for the rest of his life.

The world hummed as he walked out the door, skipping down the staircase and into the November sun.

Epilogue — An Old Friend

Casa de Kissick—as Ben's father had always called it since he bought the cabin in 1984—was named after the nearby Kissick Swamp Wildlife Area, nestled into northern Wisconsin about eighty miles from Lake Superior. He liked the exotic flavor of the nickname, Ben's father always said, the tasteful hint of sexuality—it conjured cat-eyed salseras and young cabana boys, wintry climate notwithstanding.

He had purchased the cabin when Ben was two years old, after his auto-supply shop found unexpected success; he had opened a second location, which brought some financial cushion to the Dmitroviches, when such things still happened in the American middle class. Sure, it was five-and-a-half-hours from Milwaukee and summer only lasted thirteen weeks—as Ben's mother was happy to remind her husband—but wasn't the point of getting away from it all to actually *get away from it all*, he would counter in response.

Some of Ben's happiest childhood memories had taken place here. He and his brother on one of the bunk beds, reading comic books and later porno mags with a stealthy flashlight. Bonfires on chilly nights when his father would drink too much beer and pass out, drooling, in the backyard. Fourth of July fireworks. The time when his aunt slammed on the windows at two in the morning, nearly making him wet the bed. Bringing a high school date up north many years later, losing his virginity then screaming during a canoe ride because he found a massive spider on his arm. The only photograph that Ben knew of in which his entire extended family—grandparents, aunts, uncles, cousins from both sides—was gathered together at once, was taken here. It was, itself, an archive in a way, the history of Ben's irretrievable youth.

He tried to tell himself that it was just a place, an empty structure, but as he pulled open the heavy pinewood door seven hours later, stepping into Casa de Kissick for the first time in six years, he was awed by its power. A sharp, swirling odor came out in a fiery wave—a musty smell, but also warm and comforting, gingerbread mixed with burning leaves. In the shadows, familiar furniture leapt out at him. He thought he could hear the murmured voices of his family retreat to the corners, startled by an unexpected guest.

Behind him, Chippanazie Lake sparkled, drifting with thin sheets of ice. A meadowlark sang in the distance, its call carried by a frigid wind.

Ben stepped inside, his boots creaking on the floor. He dropped his suitcase, which landed with a soft thud. He leaned into the room and reached with his left hand, fumbling in the dark until a lamp flickered on. As he stepped inside and closed the door, he found things that comforted him, the little tangible trinkets that carry with them profound nostalgia. The fishing poles hanging on hooks by the door. The black-and-gold quilt in a natty checkered pattern, beautiful in the way that only incredibly ugly things can be. The years of life and feeling seeped into these objects by osmosis could still be sensed.

Ben took a nap that lasted much of the afternoon, twitching on the couch, a violent montage passing through his dreams, known only to him. Then he walked around the lake, bundled up in a dark-blue jacket that was too large for him and too small for his father. He thought about the last few days, of course, time compressed and elongated, the memories taking on a hazy fog. As though they were lived in a past life, seen through someone else's eyes.

He returned to the cabin after nearly an hour—the lake wasn't large, but the wind was blowing and Ben was still exhausted. Casa de Kissick was well stocked by his parents, but he noticed next to the fireplace that no wood had been chopped.

And so, welcoming the distraction, Ben found the key to the shed outside, a red-and-white padlocked structure, and went to it. He took an axe from a peg on the walls, then pulled an armful of logs from the woodpile. This was the image he'd envisioned before he ventured north, him chopping wood with a sweaty grunt in the autumn air as the lake trickled behind him. The vacation might have been mandatory, but the solitude it offered him was welcome.

Even so, the order to retreat north while MPD attorneys took care of the lawsuit seemed, now, cowardly and shameful. He swung the axe, and as it landed he remembered the brittle fragility of the man's ribs—*what was his name? Richard Twozinski?*—as Ben's boots made contact. Then, by extension, the breakable body of Nathan Amherst. By now he knew shame in the fullness of its power, from the building storm of self-reproach to the mushroom-cloud anger of its inward horror. True, stinging shame. Now able to perceive things with no self-delusion, he saw himself as a cog in a police state, shielded from his own accountability. He had pretended to ascribe to higher ideals of justice, but he was nothing more than a man—a frail, corruptible man, twisted by the cruel and senseless forces that surrounded him.

The fire was lit half an hour later. It danced in the living room, blanketed in shadows. Ben felt comfortable here. He watched the blaze-orange fingertips of fire waving at him, curling over the walls.

For a while he just stared, stared and thought. There were some old records drooping on the bookshelf—his parents' collection—and he thumbed through them, finding something there that brought back a hundred dead-eyed memories. King Crimson—the one with the Edvard Munch face screaming from the record cover. He slipped it from the sleeve and placed it on the record player, lowering the needle with a satisfying crackle.

The walls on which the prophets wrote are cracking at the seams.

Ben had played this song every time he dragged friends this far north, three bottles of whiskey and an ounce of weed in hand, and they listened to the lyrics endlessly, finding a cosmic meaning in the bubbling cloud of cannabis smoke, a spiritual truth exposed to them.

It grew dark by five-thirty now, dusk creeping earlier and earlier, and at this point in the night the skies were already a luscious black. He lurched to his feet, feeling a pleasant surge of restlessness, and wandered to his father's study, the late-sixties psych-rock bellowing behind him. He wondered what his father had ever done in here, what kind of *work*, if any.

There was a bottle of scotch on the uppermost shelf, inscribed with the word Glenmorangie. Unopened, Ben noticed, though he'd bought it for his father three years ago. Shrugging, Ben plucked it from the shelf and wrestled the cork from the bottleneck. A burning, peaty smell drifted upwards. Ben grabbed a lowball glass from the shelf and poured in a shot's worth. Holding the glass out to some phantasmal guest, he toasted his father, sharing an imagined heart-to-heart they might not actually have for years. He took an eager swig, downing half the glass in one gulp, and cringed from its severity.

There were some larger volumes on the lowermost shelf, tucked in the right-hand corner. The dark-green leather faced outwards, unmarked. Ben remembered these photo albums, remembered poring over them with Sarah and his parents, pretending to hate the embarrassment while he secretly relished Sarah's enamored reaction.

He pulled out the photo album and heaved it onto the desk. There was nothing on the cover, only a leather sheen that had been worn from too much use. There were photos of his parents in their infancy, their first prom date as high school sweethearts, their wedding, their parents' funerals, a photo from a party in 1982 in which his mother looked absolutely hammered, the first home they bought together, Ben and his brother blowing bubbles in a bathtub at four years old, middle school, high school, Ben in his golden basketball shorts, his last day before basic training, his first return home with crew-cut hair, a photo of Sarah on the night they announced their engagement, a picture of eight-months-pregnant Sarah cradling her belly, a photo of newborn Aaron, eyes shut to the world, passed from one set of arms to another, and photos from the first four years of Aaron's life.

Existence in still images. It passed so quickly.

He took another sip from the glass, pleasantly burning his lips. The first side of the record had ended, causing the needle to skip back and forth in thunderous scratches, as though it marked the stuttering passage of the Earth's orbit.

As he flipped through the photo album, reliving the past with a vow to remake his own future, a sensation came to him. Dark and familiar, somehow coming from without and within. Like a black cloud hovering, he knew it was there before it even entered his line of sight.

How had it been so quiet? Had it materialized from nothing?

Ben glanced toward the hallway. Between the stabbing flames of the fireplace and the lamplight from the study, there was something standing there, tall and silhouetted, its serrated scalp nearly reaching the ceiling. Ben thought he could make out its red, dripping skin in the shadows. Whatever he thought he saw, there was no mistaking those crimson eyes glowing in the dark, relishing the sight of the weary man sitting at his father's desk.

There was terror, of course, a rising surge of panic, a tightening in Ben's chest as he stared down his predator, waiting for the figure to dissolve. But it didn't fade into nothingness. It neared the study door, floating over the carpet, propelled by an unseen force.

Then, to Ben's surprise, the terror subsided. What could he do? What was the point? He thought of Aaron, and Amy, and Sarah, he thought of everything. He felt calmer than he ever had, snapshots from his past splayed out on the desk before him.

With a cathartic breath and a crooked parody of a grin, he reached behind him, spinning in his chair, and grabbed another glass with his thumb and forefinger. He brought it to the desk and slid it across the polished wood surface. Then he palmed the bottle of scotch, lifted it, and angled it toward the empty glass. The golden liquid spilled out and filled half the glass, a healthy pour.

Ben recorked the bottle and placed it on the desk. He nudged the second glass across the wood with his knuckles, in the direction of the gaunt shape lurking by the door. Its knees were bent backwards, a look of imminent fury in its eyes. It stood in contrast to the placid, blue-and-white wallpaper, and Ben wondered if he had seen this very image when he was only five or six years old—not as a nightmare, but a vision of things to come.

He finished his scotch and raised the empty glass in its direction.

"So there you are."

The thing in the hallway opened its mouth in a jagged, greedy smile.

Outside, a cold mad wind whistled over Chippanazie Lake.

About the Author

Matthew Cole Levine is an author, film critic, and screenwriter based in St. Paul, Minnesota. He was born in Cedar Rapids, Iowa and grew up near Milwaukee, making him well-versed in a particular brand of Midwestern horror. He has written for the British Film Institute, Walker Art Center, and other publications, and continues to serve as Assistant Editor and Contributing Writer for the Barcelona-based *Found Footage Magazine*. *Hollow* is his first novel.

CPSIA information can be obtained
at www.ICGtesting.com
Printed in the USA
BVHW041526010622
638576BV00007B/44